*The Hoplite Journals*

Also by Martin Anderson:

*The Kneeling Room* *
*The Ash Circle* *
*Heard Lanes*
*Dried Flowers*
*Swamp Fever*
*The Stillness of Gardens*
*Black Confetti*
*The Hoplite Journals I–XXIX* *
*Belonging* *
*The Hoplite Journals XXX–LIX* *
*Snow. Selected Poems 1981–2011* *
*Interlocutors of Paradise*
*The Hoplite Journals LX–LXXXIX* *


*An asterisk denotes a Shearsman title.*

# Martin Anderson

# The Hoplite Journals

*(Complete in one volume)*

Shearsman Books

Published in the United Kingdom in 2013 by
Shearsman Books Ltd
58 Velwell Road
Exeter
EX4 4LD

ISBN 978-1-84861-291-4
First Edition

### Acknowledgements

*The Hoplite Journals* originally appeared in three volumes from Shearsman Books:
*The Hoplite Journals* (2006), *The Hoplite Journals XXX–LIX* (2010) and
*The Hoplite Journals LX–LXXXIX* (2013), which appears
simultaneously with this volume.

Some parts of this work previously appeared in
*High Chair, Oasis, Poetry Salzburg Review, Shearsman* and *Tremblestone*.

The author wishes to express his indebtedness to Francisco Ignacio Alcina's *Historia
de las islas e indios de Bisayas* (1668) for the details of fabulous beasts on page 51.

The editorial on pages 123–124, in unabridged form and with
different names of persons and places, appeared in 2003
in the now-defunct newspaper *Today*.

# Contents

"They make delightful the forests where other people could not dwell. Because they have not the burden of desires, they have that joy which others find not."

*The Dhammapada*

"Behold the driver has risen and made ready the file of camels,
And begged us to acquit him of blame: why, O travellers, are you asleep?"

Jalal'ud-Din Rumi

# I

In our own country everything takes place without us. Diverse rivers mount the plateau of our days only to overcome them, and whole villages and counties, with a dark mud in which we find the evidence of fossils. The glistening arabesques of dried-up seas, glazed shards of cobalt, petrified teeth and post holes. We look in vain for the treatise preserved in its jar of posthumous air, for the exordium we have been waiting a whole lifetime to read. The disquisition by Flebenius on the plant of immortal longing. The tireless aperture of the sky opens, instead, upon these roads upon which we are caught each day, impelled to repeat the same journey, through the suffocating heat of drawing rooms in summer, across the carpeted floors of which something has left a damp spoor as if it was leaving.

.

The tattered Royal Doulton blue of a scalloped awning draping dry red rivulets vertically down itself from the rusted iron frame on which it was stretched. In damp shadows at the end of a tunnel of flapping tarpaulin walls, in something like a vestibule, two armed security guards slouching, waiting to frisk anyone from the street who should wander in, drawn by the allure of the name *Adonis*. To come so far to seek what was so much, evidently, nearer home. Or, simply, that the signs are reinterpreted here, in this different place in this different time. And what lies, then, behind the facade of Penhurst two doors down, what mansion amid bucolic acres, festering in the fat of a wild boar, transposed to these endless sizzling margins of lechon. And what is it, anyway, that we are after?

.

We are only, all of us, an adjunct of, an interdict to the immense and inglorious history of longing. *You must be tired after your long and difficult journey across the seas. Let me take you to your rooms so that you may bathe and rest. Afterwards, you may eat and we will arrange entertainments for you in this, your city, which we have merely been looking after for you, while you were gone.* It comes round, again and again, in a full circle. Without a memory, let the stones guide you into a dark corner; and listen. You should regret nothing, apologize for nothing. It is not your own heartbeat that you hear echoing, but the jostling of all the continents through time, the voices of the oceans and the forests, and, in the air above them, the small droplet of blood that pre-dates and post-dates you, that is divided up into a million sacrifices, unnecessary, and all at once.

.

The fusillade toward the barricades at the entrance of the campus enveloped them in a slow and densely moving cloud of gas that drifted among the desks and chairs and upturned vehicles. Eyes blinked back the liquid of lacrimations. Nearby, in the botanical gardens, light, as sumptuous and fine as the beaten gold leaf on the pages of an old book, burnished the embankments. The libraries were ransacked. The ministries sandbagged. In the streets only abandoned dogs where we tread, now, lost in our illusions in shadows at noon as if we were among noctambulant ghosts in stairwells, by quays where foetid holds disgorged their cargoes to the padding of bare feet on springy planks. Warehouses of reveries. Fragrant, but impotent, lucubrations circumnavigating the brain. On the thigh of a young girl, like a mouth gaping for air, a wound you could put a whole walnut into, exuded a staunchless, red tear.

.

They have ploughed up a cemetery for a plot of land to build on. Who issued the order? Who did not issue the one to countermand it? Bones dust in the hot entelechy of air. To the gates of the white walls of certain affluent subdivisions no tax demands are ever issued, and no beggars ever intrude in that *cordon sanitaire* that is purchased by them. The votes are all counted the wrong way. The committee on overseeing elections is easily distracted. The telephones ring all day but the circuits are always busy. Talk. Talk. Talk. And in the government offices it is merienda at every hour of the day. And newspapers brandished above desk tops. And the files, in multiple copies, of official forms, waiting to be processed or "expedited", impede the corridors and every square inch of space, curling and softening in the humid air that only a few dispirited fans make tremble once in a while. And everyone smiles.

.

Having arrived at the precise point of the present, where does that leave us to go? We lack nothing, scorning sequence, scorning duration, even the "person" and its percipient whole. Good deeds come easily to us, and we are not immune to misanthropy too. They have removed the great lidless eye behind the creepers on the wall of the hotel where we used to stay. The advertisement for an opticians. Box-ads for enticing lotions to improve a man's amorous performance by enlarging what he is already endowed with fill the *For Sale* columns of the local newspapers. The *Good Ship Venus* glides, now, over the rooftops filling the terminals with a dissolute and unshaven crowd. We talk to one another in a language that lacks any form of protocol. In the equality of our desires, enshrined in the sign of the *Duty Free* store, everything is possible. At the exit, by the money-changers, the official foliage bends in the air conditioned draught, extending a greeting that carries not even the faintest trace of remorse.

.

The abysmal flotsam of our days persists. Vocalic husks. The strimmed modalities of airwaves that have nothing to offer but the aromatics of love. The sonorous perorations of our rulers, back home, elude us. Horse croakings—a seminary of herons. Here, in a charmed half-circle of mushrooms someone lays his head, and asks to be anointed. On a roadside, banged out on old typewriters, on paper so thin you can hold it up and see whatever is behind it, a decree with an official stamp with the name of whomsoever you want—dignitary, Minister of State—on it. Behind the Bureau of Immigration a corpse floated in the river for five days, snagged in the chains of an anchor, before it was apprehended and, for "landing without a permit", detained.

.

It is someone, and somewhere, else. It always was—*another*. So let us say goodbye to all those *despedidas* in dingy basements and in rooms of institutions where the drinks carbonate endlessly in orderly array under the predictability of the conversations. It is all a lie, it always has been. Only the naïf tourist believes that he will return to this same place and people at some time in the future, to these exact rudiments of smile and house front, of physical comportment and gesture. And yet what else does he have but memory with which to establish again where he has been and would wish to come back to. Under the deep blue shade of the jacaranda tree, in the courtyard, the air wanders from one appearance to another. And in the hallways and corridors of each official building the duplicity of affirmations and ardours, and of rebuttals, reverberates in the fabric of the walls and floors. Perhaps someone should write a guide not to the places we see and that we leave but to the indefinable and contiguous images that they press up from themselves; these brilliant and elusive refractions of what it is we are (at morning, midday and at evening) in the sunlit plaza or in our room staring up at the alabaster cornice, as we wait (in autumn, winter, spring or summer) to enrol ourselves in the catalogue of our deceptions, and the mystery of how we lose what was in the first place not our own, and never will be, deepens.

.

The idolatry of meaning. Through the streets of the living, apparitions and portents of happiness and despair pursue us. A hand raised in anguish, pointing to some irreversible act. A face like a neophyte's—imploring and rapt. And the fear of nothing—waiting, around the corner. The sky a bleached and endless indictment of what we cannot have. What is it? That point at which all that has gone before it is redefined. Up until that point, then, nothing is determined and can just as easily turn out to be the opposite of what it appeared to be. So, in this city that we have come to, it is always the *Day of Lamentation and Remembrance* at which the inhabitants are reminded of how we are caught in the cruel and remorseless cycles of time. Shards of the infinite are drenched in the sweet scent of the dying. Sails break upon reefs. Always more than we are, and less than that to which we aspire to belong. The earthly community so richly divided—priests, writers, whores, entertainers, vendors and artisans— on the same sidewalk. And for all of them the price of deliverance from doubt, is what? Fragrant utopias proliferate on each street corner. Democratic and undemocratic. Near and far off. The leper rings his bell and everyone runs into the arms of another.

.

In the bamboo palace that sits alongside the river—no architecture of permanent forms would be appropriate in this land of instability of reference—the dirty square umbers on walls where the artworks were looted, the life support equipment in the basement, a virtual miniature hospital, and the shadows that have eaten everything that was not fastened down, and some of those that were. Origin of edicts and imperial encyclicals. Now the cockroach and the termite digest it. The liveried orchestra. The prestidigitators—gone. And in their place the fake title deed to a property someone had spent their life's savings on acquiring. The bogus film production crew, full of blandishments and cameras, entering a house to relieve it of its possessions. A carnival of whores and politicians singing the national anthem. While in the plantations pubescents cut sugar cane faster than adults from dawn to evening for a few racattos a day. And, in the capital, a "city" of slums visible to visiting foreign dignitaries on the road from the airport, is encircled by a white wall, air brushed out of existence. *Quelle triste vie!*

.

Our little angst, in a polis of sad peregrinations towards bed and night, our ablutions almost over. Pay the leaves to entertain us, they are almost as bored as we are; open a new leisure centre; invent a new drug that will save us from tomorrow—and from all the days that will come after. The guilt at having left when we were away and the guilt, when we return, at having not stayed, are different. Where do we belong? Not to ourselves that is sure, for we don't know where that particular item can be located. And the other stands at a distance from us, waiting for us to approach. Only, as we walk through the mirrors into ourselves can we find it. And it is then that we realize that distance and time are so many false trajectories out of the mind of the inattentive. And that all objective categories are superfluous. Without landfall, without a horizon, we lack nothing, but the confidence to explore this land, and its cities, drenched with the scent of unripe fruits—including the endeavour of all its darkness and horrors. Priests, flinging the heart into the fire, should not dissuade us. Even its government's declaration of *A State of Rebellion* should be interpreted not as a disincentive, but as an incentive for us to begin the journey.

II

On that faint exiguous line (contract, horizon, point of rest) of the future someone has signed their name more deeply that the rest, as if they had been there before. The pattern of our lives is circular. The same route that takes us forward also takes us back. We wave to ourselves in passing, knowing that no one else waves back. Out of the shadows our own ghosts move amongst us. Until, finally, they sit down with us and listen to us as we talk amongst ourselves, while the afternoon monsoon rain falls raising a bright spume, a fine mist, on the roads and rooftops that surround us.

.

We remember the piles of dromedary dung freezing at night on the outskirts of town under cold stars. At the railway station it was so cold all the thermometer casings cracked. But in the morning the smell of coal dust in the streets, the gleam of fish ponds and canals, the sound of dried grass crackling under brick ovens, woke us. We had dreamed we had left for another land and woke, instead, to find ourselves twisting under mosquito nets again, perspiring in rooms sheathed in a fine mesh that shone. That normally invisible skein of our senses, sifting and mediating the world, seemed, suddenly, to have appeared before us. Behind it, time sobbed in the branches of the acacia trees outside the window.

.

To be in a place, without memory, in absolute time. To know that one has, finally, come *home*. In this city of eternal longing, this body in which we feel we are in exile, the penumbras and pandemonium of appearances unfold before us the true nature of our being. We move backwards and forwards through time in a motion that is continually intersecting itself, until we are lost amid the calated, the unsublated and the circumfused. On the long grey curb that we stepped off many years ago to get here, the same space, opening onto that moment, remains. The breath of a distance that no one has measured, or counted, runs through it. Undescribed, unmapped, it burns inside us, like a virus—a tenderly nursed prospect that has become, we know, the sad fulcrum of our fate.

.

The many voices of the living and the dead that we are assailed by, on going to sleep and on waking. Stitched into that silence that underlies every discourse. A fragment of a phrase, rhythm, tilt of the head, characteristic pause. Listening, and looking, for them we get drawn into the maze of the body's back streets and alleyways. Disoriented—without a street map or compass. The midday sun obliterates the names in the window of a bookstore where we stop. Across the road a wave drags into the harbour another fragment of that silence that seems, minute by minute, to be breathing inside us. And somewhere else, too, on a small shelving parabola of beach, it is setting down—on a light washed horizon. In that liquid, far off, ripple, we hear our bones speak in the amalgamate of an anonymous discourse above the traffic.

.

Behind the dark tree of winter—a glimmer. From the dark roots—a sigh. That distance could be disentangled from what is present. Everything bends with the weight of what it is not. A silvery thin air glides over the water beneath iron bridges. The mind has carried off what it cannot live among and cannot leave. A caravanserai of objects. Calendars and ledgers, encyclopaedias and atlases, ride on the backs of angels. We tap the glass fronts of barometers and constellations rot above airless plains where signs we cannot decipher are carved into the rocks. And then, soon, it will be summer again, and we will discover the white cadaver, left under the sheet from another year. And red fruit bending the branches, dropping, unpicked; because we have not excised these apparitions from our lives.

.

From around the edges of door frames, the serrated perimeters of palm fronds, light; from across anonymous distances, consuming the wainscots and the eaves, issuing through the windows of the library where we sit, reading, looking up at the slow luminous diffusion from the burned out xerox machine invading bodies and wall, listening to its paper feed crunch then halt. Light, omniscient, emanating out of all those porous and immense spaces, out of old forsaken imperial domains, demarcations of land and interconnecting seas, flickering, here, upon spines with such gilded titles as *Administrative Officers of the Empire 1800-1900; A Flora and Fauna Of The Province Of Medinora*. Alas, all out limited lexicons and taxonomies, all our frail genera and classes. They thrash, unillumining, within it. Leaving only the dust of a silence, a white dying gasp, like a sea drying up, that robs us of our voice.

.

We walk each day through the cluttered bazaars that run all the way along the foreshore and back up the narrow precipitous streets that ascend into hills of jungle where light filters slowly down in dappled pools and bright dust-wreathed columns. Textiles and tapestries laid on the ground and hung from bamboo frames throb with an energy derived from the same profligacy of line and colour exhibited by the flora of these hills. Beside the roads, counterfeiters and copyists, scribes and illustrators, in this land of continuous reproduction in which we spent so many years of our lives trying, unsuccessfully, to find what it is we left for. An antidote, perhaps, in the confident and fecund ways its objects assert themselves, to an overwhelming sense of absence. And, in the long, hot, uninterrupted stream of this illusion another illusion emerges—a forlorn wailing of tugs on a grey river moving through the treacherous sediments at Ggov, Horste and Ordfleur, seeping into an emptiness difficult to bear ... A loss. An acquisition ... Both part of the same ineluctable dream that does not attenuate the older we get; to represent what is and has always been irritably adumbrating, at the back of our consciousness, a self that can't be spanned—ghost ship gliding silently in and out of a harbour, whose hawsers turn hauling us slowly, again, in: to a dark hold crammed with lapping water, with invisible shores, unidentifiable and rich scents ..

.

The huge swell of the sea running up the almost vertical embankment. Perspiring brokers scurrying, this way and that, scouring the pier heads for business. In the customs sheds the interminable wrangling with officials. Bargains struck, and then unravelled. Our passports cursorily inspected. For who would suspect that as we cross this border we are anything other than we appear to be or describe ourselves as being—vague spirits, traders in the ineffable wares of an interior where, frequently, we lose ourselves amidst an array of false turnings and washed out tracks and end up at night at an inn in a dark room with the lamp extinguished, the only sound the sound of our own voices—and, in some other part of the building, a child crying. We leave before dawn our trunks lashed to our backs muttering our own names in a ritual of emancipation, going over and over the same road littered with torn inventories and bills of lading, and do not return. Inaudible cantors, the dust on our tongues of an endlessly perishing moment, we are to be found at midday crouched at some food vendor's street stall, impervious to the din of people and traffic around us, thinking.

# III

It is no use regretting this self that will not lie down. Arm, phantom grey finger of land that aches in a sea of continuous depositings and withdrawings—coast, which it keeps on, even in sleep, circumnavigating. Terminus of unacknowledged destinations. Alienated consumer of the unconsumable. In the cremation pits, exposed after excavating for gravel, it lies bleating like a chastised fool, for all the world to hear and see. The sound of dogs barking and the inventories enunciated from emptying rooms, in the quiet of depopulating villages, kept it awake for years.

.

Perpetually leaking space, like a vent in the wall of the future. Called, in one place, *Lanashka*, and in another *Kurninikustra*. Not identical everywhere simultaneously. And through it, all the cities of this world compress themselves, as if they were real, as if they were so many facial variations upon the expression of the loved one—palpable, yet elusive. And the names that issue so compulsively off the tongue of their weather—its disguises. Names that we repeat, sitting on benches in the dusk settling upon municipal parks, listening to the accents of foreign residents, the diverse phenomena arraigned before us, knowing that it is only the specific that disappoints, the transitory, that cuts into the flesh of our ultimate being.

.

The fullness and weight of a fragrance that lasted. Through arid, stoney grey soil, through centuries. What, heard of, the mind held and furnished against the drought of many lives. First, a homesickness; preyed upon, in concubinage, by the memory of those fruitful slopes of (her name never recorded) her birth-place. Till, under the king's fond tillage, the desert around her foliated, and ran with the "streams of paradise". Then, later, another longing; returning home to hard Greek soils from service as mercenaries in the court of Darius (land of her memory), for those soft slopes too. Whence the image, engraved, passed into the store of our own cultural obsessions. That we may dream, of a landscape within a landscape. The stars unable to tell us where it was. The maps inaccurate, or corrupt. The documents that refer to it rife with the obelus, or missing. So, instead, we hoed in the infertile soils of our own lives, with whatever came to hand, and washed up here, dreaming of somewhere else.

.

This sudden seeming confirmation, in a name and an address, of an identity free flowing, in space, in time; this sudden consummation of a journey. In the great humid, and haunted, sorting office behind the Spice Exchange and the Law Courts they are segregating our mails. Envelopes strewn into an ether of unknown hands, of wasted and derelict spaces, of uncertain itineraries. Through the scribbled ink of each address, standing over against, talking to, us, all that negates and overwhelms us—distance, the immense spaces, the other. All that we wish to take flight from, and yet return to, as if to a self that is coevaled with a particular place. All the complex psychology, the intricate circuitry, of our opposed yearnings, signified and authenticated in the vellum of these innocuous deliveries upon which, for months, as the slow boat rolls through indifferent waves, we hang.

.

It is the same distance from morning to evening, wherever we are, whatever obstacles are laid in our way. Now, in the past and in the future. Leaving each house, taking each different road and arriving at a new place, only the location and the persona change. Evening and morning appear—like a geometry of lost angles, fleetingly inscribed on doorsills and in stairwells, a fluctuant grid—and disappear. All that is left, the faded scent of pomade upon the hands of a passionate embrace. The body a ruined, illegible script, where the air of the hot tropical night enters and macerates. Where we wander, circling, worried by how we are measured by what is extraneous to ourselves, by how our mind dilates upon an edge of an infinitely receding object

.

From a local antiquarian we obtain, for a few racattos only, an old map of the city and its environs, replete with the names of original streets and the yellowing parchment of space provisionally divided into subdivisions and plots, boundaries defining waste. Indicated in faded red ink, the Mariners' Mission on the old praya, subsequently moved inland by a sudden rash of reclamation, and the old Officer's Quarters later dismantled, brick by brick, and deposited, intact with ghosts, in crates in a mouldering godown. And so, we too, draw round this emptiness, that we locate at the heart of ourselves, the conspectus of a divided space. In which, talking or wandering or just thinking, we are always trying to locate, in a specific place and time, ourselves—at some precise point: and yet, because of this, are always losing ourselves. And, from this precise point which we occupy, in that illusory unfolding of our own duration, that movement that annuls us, we repeat the names by which we pronounce ourselves, like a charm, as if they could arrest this endless proliferation of moments which constitutes, sustains and undoes us. We move outward, the pale flowers of the talahib rocking in the wind, of the kakawati, only to return to this infinitesimal point of ourselves that is nothing, and that is nowhere, but which we have anchored with all the particularities of a name and a locus as in this map spread out, here, before us.

.

We lost one of our number, amidst the weavers of baskets and the sellers of native made curios and mementoes, in some immense haberdashery that had grown up on the side of the road, as we were passing; the sun on his head like on the side of a cuirass, his dented pate gleaming. Habitue of the bars and bordellos of this fragrant city we gave him up almost at once to all the decadence and carnality that we knew, finally, he would surrender himself to after a life of ascesis, trusting to providence that he would succeed in finding on these far shores more than a token of what it was he sought by leaving us, and that look of a stale ambrosia in our eyes, behind. Before he left he deposited an envelope with us—a procedure common to all of us at that time—and instructed us to open it in the event of his demise. It turned out that its contents amounted to a list of items, not only severely incomplete but many of which were seemingly insignificant, and which contained no instructions as to how to dispose of them—of those which had not vanished, that is, or which were not simply the products or creations of his own imagination. They were, in the order in which he had indicated them:

*1 copy of 'Epistles To An Exemplary'*
*1 pocket compass*
*2 Andalusian Songbooks*
*1 frangible pine chair (sic)*
*1 "lock" of hair from a dog(?)*
*2 silver Mexican dollars*
*1 mortar and pestle (with his engraved name)*
*1 handbell (for ringing at angelus)*
*1 obsidian lozenge ("for placing under the tongue after dark")*
*2 newspapers dated February 24ᵗʰ 1848*
*1 Permit To Work*

*1 Handbook Of Topics For Polite Conversation*
*1 thimble full of fingernail cuttings (of his mother)*
*1 cabinet of tinctures for all ills*
*1 collection of sundry pieces of cork for plugging holes.*

.

This coastline, exuding a light of hyperborean intensity, where the entropy of the observer, faced with the stark space of his own disappearance, manifests itself; the space of his own body and its image of itself giving way to a space of a completely different order. Garlands of sampaguita thrown around our necks on our arrival. The dusty tautening of frayed ropes round capstans, odour of hot oil and steam filtering over the iron plates of an engine room, and the acrid assault of the smell from bails of salted fish winched through the air above us, all seem to confirm the dream of the empirical and proximate that we are only ever partly successful in breaking free from. "Partly"; at least, unless, then, we should not even be aware it is a dream, and would be held fast in the dense warp and woof of the percept ... Observing the slow route of our valediction amidst the grammar of size, and order and number, and all the interrupted patterns of our desire, the shadow of the fruit of the tamarind tree distils an essence; neither the word, nor the object, but an unoccupied systole and diastole in which things vanish and emerge, a deliquescent edge, like this horizon, upon which we listen for our own lives, ungarlanded and uncelebrated, as they arrive and leave without us.

# IV

Standing under a rotten timber trellis of dense fronds, in the shade of a jacaranda tree, we hear the trilling of an unseen bird. And each of us, standing alone in his own personal domain of reminiscence, tries to imagine where it was that he had previously heard that song, so clearly and longingly did it punctuate the air. Wrung from the ochre streaks of an evening sky, as if from some pre-lapsarian garden, it comes to us with all the assurance of a song that we have heard before. And yet the exact location from which it originates evades us. Issuing, it seems, out of those cool temperate mists from which we have come (but through what unknown lands did those bloodlines we inherited themselves wander?) we reach back for it into a wooded silence, all the time with the feeling, the strange intimation, that it is not the song of a particular bird, nor a composite of many, but, instead, an inward assuagement, beyond time and space and memory, of some profound and inerasable loss; and that by trying to endow it with the features of a name and a place we are pursuing only a personal nostalgia for an outward manifestation of something that has not yet come into our lives, something that ranges far beyond the identity and the song of any particular bird, or species of birds, and which lies, like an unvitiated text, behind a door we have yet to open.

.

A long, fluid blue shadow slowly envelops the hull of the Anan Bhun, a schooner of the Ephesus line, anchored in the channel. We stop and look. Tide pulled, eddied and whorled, rising and falling to the rhythm of the water lapping the steps at our feet, the ship, in its shadow, gradually and inevitably becomes a submerged outline, a datum of memory, point of transit only within the flickeringness of our being. Standing, in the rippled gloom of the channel, lost in reflection, peering, through the vapours that coil and weave off the warm sea's surface, at a ship we can no longer see, we realize suddenly how all the moments and memories of our own lives are, thus, inescapably inhabited by phantoms. Reassembled fragments of percepts, inherently fragile, untranscendental. Like the sound of our names that break down into incomprehensible parts, these infinite atoms of the acoustic and the visual, constructed against the nameless, though they attempt to enwrap and lure us, do not dissuade us from the conviction that they are, finally, constituted of anything more substantial than air itself.

.

In a capital suffused with syphilis and soot, alerted by the sound of continual alarms, lines of leafless winter trees scribble, as the wind moves them, a stubble of animated charcoal, upon pale unlit skies. *The distance between the ideal and that which confronts one, is not so great as the distance between the shadow and the one who casts it.* Somewhere it is evening, and someone sitting outside at a restaurant table looks into the eyes of the one sitting opposite and cannot hear the commotion in the street nearby, or the surf moving across the beach towards them … There are no different countries. And those distances we set off into have all come back to haunt us, draining their dust into our pores, their marvellous mosaics purloined, piece by glittering piece. A curse on all museums, and collectors. Only the light knows, having secreted itself into the most secret places of the night, what is in us, and what, in our haste to depart, we have left behind. In our catafalques on the outskirts of our suburbs, lodged behind green lawns and the stillness of stone angels, the cut up catalogues of our lives persist. And what did we bring back with us, out of those vast emporia that clogged the crossroads and highways with millions of travellers? And those we left behind standing there beside them in freezing puddles at night, what were they listening for, the thin impartite music of advertising coiling round their hearts—catchphrases and slogans; a debased language, in which we have fashioned the epicene and the self's indulgence. A language that cannot measure time, and that has cancelled all the debts that mortality fastens upon us, whose syrups we slurp with ease, the noise of our farting occluded, along with the fractious debates about that profound imbalance in our lives between giving and taking.

.

That perpetual elsewhere unfolding within us. That panoply of diverse vistas, voices. Where are you, unable to sit still, taking off to now? Into a new style. A new place. A new day … The frayed white grass of the square where he fell, without a blindfold, facing their carbines. A "where" that persists through all the dimensions of love and hate—indifference, only, excluded. At the breast of yourself you find that unappeased appetite for the other. In time you will come to see through it, through the facture of all such distinctions. Meanwhile, at the side of the road, her eyes like coals in the cooling swathe of her skin, a young girl sells mudfish. In the bay beyond, invisible to her, fine flocculent spray of the *balenas* drifts on the sea wind. We are drawn beyond each edge of where we think we should be by a space that seems to annul all the others. But what we thought we were looking for did not, in fact, move on so much as merely grow much larger and, therefore, farther away from where we thought we stood listening to a voice that we took to be our own. But nothing owns itself. The objects, in which we have so often put our trust, are not self-sufficient. And that precise point, in space and time, that eventually unbearable stasis we think we inhabit, who advocated it? Some becalmed mariner, no doubt, adrift and seeing no horizon for months, rapidly induced within himself the seeds of his own madness, mumbling for a chart wherein were marked all channels, tides and currents; all sandbanks, submerged rocks, reefs and shallows; all safe harbours and landfalls. We believe that, as a stationary object, all distances radiate away from us. But the truth is that, not having the unity of such an object, they, instead, devolve inside us: so that, in moving, we become never any nearer to that point of rest that we associate with our selves than what distance and space themselves, arriving at and meeting the bourne that defines their own extent—which, of course is boundless—allow.

.

As if there was, in the first place, anything at all to "escape" from. One simply arrives at a mode of being less inauthentic than that in which one existed before. To "escape" one would have to know what exactly it was one was leaving. So, month after month, we peregrinate up and down this coast upon the ostensible purpose of buying as many piculs of rattan and gutta-percha as we can lay hands on. Criss-crossing the track by the harbour sand banks where boatmen from a shrimp beam trawler spread out the coarse breadth of a sail and set to work to patch it, the slow stipple and glitter of water on the sweep of a Hoklo sampan as it gently lifts out and is, for one moment, magically suspended—the eye and mind waiting as if for an act of mysterious alchemy to be completed—arrests us. The action, both fluid and dynamic, yet static, seems to mime some elementary principle that one feels at work and embodied in the very structure and design of the houses here, where one feels one enters a mental, as much as a physical, space. Amid the joggled *voussoirs* the light vibrates, through carefully placed grills, against water, reflecting upon tremulous walls; the interplay of light and shadow negating the reality of weight, as if the visible structure floated rather than rested upon supports. Visiting such buildings one questions not only the validity of "where", physically, one is—it being apparent that it fluctuates as adroitly as the air and light move—but the viability of talking also, therefore, about "where" one is going to. Under the scrutiny of such a reflection the fiery architecture of the mind melts, within a light that seems to seine it. Motes, like molten ground down husks of the souls of the departed from all of time, drift on an invisible wave about us, an immense river in which we breathe all the icons and outlines of a visible and invisible world and yet still feel that further and further on within it is the source, the lambent furnace, from which, like a spooring reef, all the forms caught between light and darkness are cast and exhaled. Or, as local mythology would have it, excreted in a noiseless ink cloud by a cuttlefish pursuing its own shape upon the surface before it plunges back again into the deep, without it.

.

The heat drew him. The benign *spiritus* he heard roaming these fields, fringed with a loss he couldn't explain. No one, or thing, ever held him, he said, so closely to what he was and what he was not, without imposing the falseness of an obligation upon him to choose. The fragrant miasma of the ink in its small roadside pot, as the old man wrote his horoscope for him, overcame him with almost a childlike sense of conviction so that he felt he would, if he had to—and did he, perhaps, not?—follow it "to the ends of the earth." A musky red scent, that penetrated him like a dream and which he claimed to be able to hear, as he inhaled it, coursing through his blood. Where did it—more ravaging than the grief itself that ensued when it was withheld—come from? Like a dispersed sediment out of the stars, the grains from an immense desert scoured by winds so dry they lit the rocks they ran against. A scent in which the half deciphered characters of a world he had been able only partially to read conjoined, evoking anagrams wherein the inscrutability of familiar shapes enticed and fascinated him, and where, in the fading gold of arcades a young boy laid his hand upon his arm, and, in the dying light of an afternoon, led him through alleys and passageways too numerous to recall, slowing and turning, every so often, to smile; a smile full not only of kindness but of guile and betrayal and which, in turn, led to a premonition of that unfathomable dark script of our own final solitude which awaits us all. That a single scent could contain so much! And then he realized that it carried, in fact, the olfactory memory of a dream that had taken root in him when he was young; that had taken root in those same insatiable soils in which his own society had sown its rejection of him. And he had fed it, voluptuously, ever since on the most arcane of diets—books, people and places that were sequestered and inaccessible except to a few. And he wondered, then, if, as he suspected, it was at last taking its revenge, whether we are, indeed, led by ourselves. For at the heart of all our actions and thoughts we inhale the subtle odours of a land without borders, traversing a non-ontological space, a dimly lit imperium where shadows we are not conscious we are a part of collide with us and send us, as if through an "orderly vicissitude" of desires, into our way.

It was, he felt, from such unvisaed and unvisitable regions, from within the depths of their soundless transformations, rather than from the clamorous and loud empirical domain of our senses, that our lives are ruled.

.

Over the flooded creek that winds into the dense forest and swamps of the interior we looked out, a faint gleam of light reflecting from the water barely illuminated the opposite shore of plantains where, after a while, we were able to identify the decorated pirogues of a slow fluvial funeral. The sound of lugubrious gongs reached us as if from across an immense distance, and the dark wave, pressed out from under the soundless bows of the procession, ramming and sluicing the shingles under the small wooden jetty, broke into the deep cast of thought the scene had plunged us into with a force of such surprise—the wind then, too, coming up, warm and strong, seemingly from nowhere, and adding to our sense of inexplicable unease—that it appeared to register the signature of some profound riddle, which we were able only to embroider and annotate, hastily abandoning our words and resorting to gestures, with the most banal and trivial of sentiments and asides, before the night closed round us and we lapsed, again, into our respective silences.

# V

This vanishing and evanescent city, seat of multifarious depredations and visitations, always returning, amid reports that it was lost for good, to confront us. In the nocturnal boulevards of its immense and heterogeneous sections and suburbs our impotent reveries pursue us. Backlit figures from late afternoons on the long unlit horizons of winter, we stumble through it. All its spaces are public or private but empty. Its name is pronounced as if with the faintest asperity of syllables. Built on a foundation of aereations, it seems to move as we move through it. The scrawled graffiti on its labyrinthine walls might even, at first, mislead one into thinking that one was inside a populist scriptorium— dedicated to the diffusion of the most secular of meanings. Embroiled in the untidy array of its human and non-human traffic one finds oneself pushed and pulled by a play of forces, looking for an axis that does not exist, for an invisible centre of coherence from which are controlled all of its activities. Instead, what one hears, in its food stalls and municipal offices, what one reads, on its news-stands and in the cordite of its radical street bulletins, is only the sad plethora of the false histories of which it is composed.

.

Within the generous apportionments of the trunk of a banyan tree a painter and dresser of religious effigies sets up shop attracting, amongst others, some itinerant vendors of votive candles to temporarily lay out their wares. Nearby, in the thin highly pitched accents of an archipelagic dialect, an old woman embeds, within the torque and sailing of her tongue, fabulous genealogies, narrating from memory the congress of those long gone under the cogon topped tumuli fringing the city. The sounds of bargains being struck rise incessantly from the Zinabuando Traders Flea Market, as if the negotiators are afflicted by a *horror vacui*. Over everything the smell of woodsmoke and rice cakes descends, appearing to unite a diversity of events and voices; and, for a moment, we almost forget how, amorous, intransigent and predatory, we glide through each others' lives as if they were not there.

.

We recognise only that which we have already seen. Yet, in that precise instant of re-cognition, all sense of prior acquaintance with it is annihilated by the sheer force of its closing upon us again. In the perpetual motions of matter, through which we walk as if through a garden of concealed harmonies, the real movement of our minds presents itself, obscurely, to us. Caught between a remembering and a forgetting we greet what we really do not know, what we do not any longer clearly see, so inexplicably does it come to us, strained through the carious traffic, the interstices, of time. So that suddenly even the simplest, the most commonplace, of things can become that elusive object that floats on the borders between our appearing and our disappearing lives, filling us with a feeling of loneliness as if we were in exile, making us believe, fools that we are, that if we could, somehow, "possess" it we would possess the thin peripatetic shadow of our own fleeting and inconsequential self, and that we could bring it and hold it, here, before us, where we stand in the dust of the street, or in our homes.

.

Inserted between the mildew mottled boards of an old accounts book that had fallen behind the bureau in his room we found this short, detached entry dated just prior to his disappearance: *What remembers itself? In this dry season I stand, my eyes scanning the horizon, narrating a past to myself. On bleached white ground I loiter by walls of old courtyards. They remember nothing; no rustle of furbelow and gusset in the shadows that they cast. These arid spaces I dwell in. Hot interregnums of dust and silence. The still roads—that go nowhere. Ruminations strewn across time and space, choking the air I breathe. My own air, slowing to a still, unrecuperable place inside me. Until it seems to make little sense whether I do or do not distinguish, except for practical purposes, what is inside from what is outside me. So, at the end of the day I look into my eyes in a mirror and it's the same light that scorches the porch and cloister that's crouched there, in the packed cells of the umbra. On a burning road of motes I travelled down to get here the relic of some ultimate silence lodged in my ear. Now, exhausted by the presence and thought of it, I cannot sleep.*

.

History builds walls, tamping down red willows and reeds with a thin sandy gravel, in the most difficult of terrains. In its yearning for that stability and coherence that our lives do not have, it, in effect, preserves them but also erects a barrier to them. History that is always only one minute old, expires on the ground of its making. In the very fabric of its sounds—that iridescent cacophony of our senses—we detect a profound nostalgia for being, that can never be quenched. A pain for which there is no analgesic. The opulence of our perception, the fragrant entrepôts of our bodies, are looted by those thin altitudes in which it breathes the final delimitation of all longing. When it corrects, what it corrects is only itself. And the odour of charcoal and grilled squid, of the blooms in the flower markets, and the secret dialogues that are written down afterwards upon the dusty backs of envelopes and ledgers, fade. And, our lives punctuated by an endless succession of lost moments, we become, again, that young girl, sad profligate, drowning in a city of birds beside the decomposing odours of a river where the names of the dead drift in vaporous roilings across the surface, and are quickly—if known at all—forgotten.

.

We wonder, sometimes, wandering round the streets and coming upon the sun cracked and mildewing sarcophagi of the Company's old graveyard, whether it is where we, too, shall deposit our aching bones one day, a considerable distance from where all of us set out and were, eventually, bound for. Tilting headstones propped up against a wall where the gecko mysteriously manifests and unmanifests itself, in masonry breaking down under the heat and loosening wind and rain of endless typhoons. Lives carved into letters, in various degrees of indecipherability, that the lichen invades. A young cabin boy who toppled onto a deck from aloft during a stormy voyage to an elsewhere he was never to see, laid out here with a short and touching encomium of verse to commemorate him. Or a well liked midshipman who never made it back on deck, brought fatally low by the *anopholese* mosquito, inhaling, as it was mistakenly thought, too much of the foetid miasma that percolated through the foreshores of this coast. Under the great limpid green leaves of ferns these shadowy lives merge with the inarticulateness of the earth itself. On our way, all of us, to somewhere else. Figures in the vast emporia of the lost. Our possessions mouldering beside us. In the long fungible reaches of our discourse we return to them stumbling, through the white gaze of an insomnia, towards what we cannot keep. Then, as if there was birdsong in the thick detritus of air filling the streets, suddenly, we look up. And there, in the hollow of a marsh embankment, in a small gorse bush inched by delicate fingers apart, so symmetrical, sculpted seamlessly onto the fork of a branch, a diminutive tightly woven oval of mosses, grasses, leaves and feathers. The nest of a green linnet.

.

Like the blind spores of the kapok tree swarming here in the wind our words unroll before us down the crowded passageways of our breath, seeding the dusk with a sound of our selves. And no matter how many times we open our mouths they return, as if there was something still to be said, some place still to be visited, that we have not articulated or seen. But since where they return to is never quite the same place so the destination they set out for always shifts slightly and we never quite come at it directly. Wandering through these streets, through these markets of fetishes and shopfronts of crumbling reliquaries, we embrace, in the despoiling dusk, the light from an unknown geography in which we engrave our names, a transcendent ground of syllables in which nothing moves. And the only sound we hear is our own breath, a shadow pinned behind our ear, and the street names that are called out as we pass so that we may reconnoitre our way back safely to a place we have not left.

# VI

We are born with the fragments of obliterated spaces within us. A celestial sensorium. A wind of luminous, driven particles. The sun shod storm of our being that will not stop with us—that, indeed, does not, in all its fitful accretions and re-accretions, recognise a person—that did not begin with us. The immense music of its coming and going deprives us of any rest, and within it we are swept up on the joy and down on the sadness of its passing; its seeding, a dusting of breath deposited in our voices. Whenever, in the litany of the vestibule or of the street, we hear it, we know that it has come to demand of us again some token of supplication and of deference. A packed bag. A cleared desk. Or simply a slow peregrination down towards the rickety quays that vibrate in the wind, and a quiet reorientation of our bodies towards that great liquid horizon that portends before us, that gusts through all the precarious and leaking hulls of all the alphabets through which this world is journeying.

.

The elation of arrival on their tired faces, having moved from country to country, living often out of no more than a suitcase, learning the new language of each new place they put their feet down in. The aroma of journeying; stale sweat clogged pores, debris of high altitude air saturating their clothes. Habitues of departure. After the luggage rotating and rotating on the imbricated belts of carousels, the clatter of electronic flight boards and the profferings of boarding passes, now, on their intent faces, as they are about to meet those waiting for them at the barrier, family and friends they have not seen for a multitude of years, the quick, sudden and unfamiliar joy of the emotion of arrival, and the quickly identified and inhaled odour of pancit from a food stall that seems to assuage all the ruptures of distances over all the years they have been away. And then, quickly forgotten, the ache and anguish of that vision of a far country that they had so often glimpsed and imagined and that had seemed at times to lie just beyond the immediate perimeter of their seeing and hearing and touching, but which, in each new place, had finally turned out to be just as foreign as the place before. Now, as they are swept out into the heat and humidity of a new night, into the city's flow and baleful worship of signs, and its squalid augury of appearances, the neon of its votive lights burns for unknown destinies, and a silent and fleeting embrasure opens quite unexpectedly deep within their being, an unavoidable premonition, unsettling intimation, that they have come back to somewhere they do not know, that cannot, ever again, be "home".

.

On a short, recently completed length of praya fronting the eastern entrance to the bay the Coconut Planters Cooperative has erected a bank. Next to it is a half ruined mosque, and surrounding the mosque a clustering of marshed and tin huts where people live amidst tall toddy-palms and banana plants. Walking at midday through the ambient glow of light and heat, through which the shadow of one's body seems to pass like some unidentifiable desire, one is struck by just how much the bank's design derives from a mind not indigenous to these parts. Heavily chiselled stone steps. Huge plinth. Fluted columns. Thick monumental walls. An architectural embolism. Built to "outlast time" and endure the degradations of a hostile climate. Beyond this preoccupation with time and change there is a preoccupation, though, with space, too. Space, which is to the visible as silence is to the audible. So aggressively do the stones announce their own presence that they seem inescapably poised against its very opposite, an unarticulated void or absence. Upon such a feral space, that has not, unlike time, been tamed and bound upon our wrists, the building seems to launch its full weight. In its very foundations, then, while the nothingness of light and air threads round and through the columns, and a footloose universe breathes and scarves the stone it is gently warming, the collective unconsciousness of another race seems to locate and bear down upon another fearful colossus—that of non-being.

.

The whistle from the mailboat, a weatherbeaten and begrimed pinnace, announces its arrival. Letters from home. And our minds go back to another coast and to other apparent objects of our cognition. The longed for and familiar tilt of the script of a loved one's handwriting. As the fragrant yellow gum on the envelope is unsealed the very heart of the chimera is released, like a genie out of a bottle. A tangible apperception fills the room and, at the sight of one's own name, the name of another floats before one like an icon. In the strong afternoon light that wreathes the hand with gold, one hesitates before one reads. Thinking of the distance the letter has travelled and the time it has taken to get here, one feels that although, like envelopes, our bodies move through space, it is not the same space as that which they move through, but a psychophysical space, and that, unlike Archimedes, we cannot, from within this space, ever displace ourselves, or calculate or find in it an exact measurement of ourselves. For it is an element in which we are diffused, which is an exudate from us, and from which we can never be subtracted or added to except by ceasing. We are, agencies as such, condemned always to move through and within it, as through the thickness of our own flesh, continually trying to trace the marks we leave upon it, the scars of a lifetime spent travelling through its dark calligraphy, its breath.

.

At funerals, held usually at dawn, salt is thrown—for the repose of all named things. No one is allowed to utter a word, and the ceremony proceeds with a long undulating intoning, the breath and the sound slowly released until they expire. At which point they are revived again. During no part of the ceremony are words spoken. It is believed that at the centre of the world there is a lake called *Empyrethma*, which means the emptiness of despair, and that the condition from which all earthly existences fomented resides there and that it is there where they all return. Although it is described as a lake it often sounds more like a vast pan, or dried up bed of marsh. Into it, it is said, all the salt from the tears of the living ascends filling the air with a continuous evaporation. A snow like refulgence refracts through the laminae of all the crystal. And a continual, almost inaudible, vibration as of lattices opening, which, it is said, is what those who are about to depart for it can hear, though all those around them are deaf to it. Like, as someone has said, sustaining the image, the sound of a capiz window opening on a morning of clear frost. Or, to paraphrase another, a music of glass abraded against an ether.

## VII

Here, in the evening, along roads lined with coconut palms moist with evaporation from the mangroves, we meet ourselves coming back, trying to reconstruct, in a world that is restless and anxious, something we are only half conscious, vaguely aware of. Noiseless shadows, navigating the endless displacement of ourselves, the thought comes to us that through most of our lives it is for nothing more, perhaps, than a thing like a small complete tune that we have been walking and listening, having carried some of the diverse notes from it around with us in our heads all the while. And sometimes when passing a field of pilay that bends in the wind, the fragrance of flesh wafting over the alleyways from a roadside lechon where men in dark corners raise their heads and sniff, we wonder whether it is from the same dream, too, that they are waking: to see, at their feet, only a convoy of ants dragging a locted carapace and wings.

.

Tucked away in a small side street down a slope that is in the shade all year of huge banyan trees is the lunatic asylum where inmates, in suits of coarse white cloth, stand under the pines in the courtyard staring into nothing, or at, and through, those who stop to look. Mostly catatonic, one has the impression that their gaze is, though, far from mindless; so far, in fact, that whenever they look at an object their gaze seems to filter an infinite number of possibilities and proposals as to what it might be. Objects to which our own gaze had long since become accustomed. Not for them the anaemia of instant recognition, or of similitude and likeness; but, instead, perched on a deep verandah before red brick walls the desperate energy of a condition reflecting their own and characterised by exclusion. Whenever anything meets their gaze it is as if it is being compared with all the things that it is not; launching, in the inmates, a lonely and weary sieving through entire catalogues of substances. What, for example, is a frangipani, or the object which goes by such a name? It is not an orchid, a peony, a fern, a weed etc ... They appear to be possessed by a seemingly endless need to complete the labour of such a process before their gaze can come back to rest on what the object is, before finally granting to it its own being, and, in return, granting to themselves their own. In the distance they travel how far, we wonder, have they not, poor souls, outstripped us, who have not budged from the given, here, before us; this undespised home of the unqualified in which, unlike them, we do not hear those relentless inquisitions by a universal, sifting through a fragrant bouquet of names it does not share.

.

From the white heat of the pavement, in an effort to cool off, we step into a large emporium where the air, wafted by fans in a draught that oscillates across the moist faces of both assistants and shoppers, is mildly warm only. On shelf after shelf, stand after stand, rail after rail, a prodigality of products, a densely packed miscegenation of wares, some put together in a multiple of countries, others assembled singly, here or elsewhere. The materiality of our lives, or a large portion of it, controlled by a fluid capital that recognises no borders, into which and out of which, like a monsoon rain through porous walls, it flows. We think of all those white walled haciendas, transplanted from the Old World, where what began as a trickle of money returning home, later turned, in the form of foreign corporations, into a flood. With such thoughts, accompanying us as we wander between the aisles, we walk into a section to which the Latin suffix *iana* has been added to the country whose name, surprisingly, designates it. Surprisingly, because the country signified is no other than that very country in which we are standing, whose very air we are breathing. It is as if space has suddenly become inverted. As if the "self" has suddenly become "other", in a vertigo of self-exoticisation and, momentarily, we seriously wonder where we are; in this brilliant archipelago bathed by warm tropic seas, or in the northern hemisphere of some temperate country. As the familiar geography of all our borders crumbles not only do we begin to "consume" ourselves, but to parody ourselves. But should these selves, constructed from such frangible material as they are, put together by others as much as "ourselves", concern us, perhaps, so much. Or this "where", for it has a capability of being any where, a ubiquitous locus?

.

Only the brunt of the headland, where scrub shorn slopes grow sheerly down to exposed layers of granite and basalt at the edge of the water, seems solid. The rest of the bay appears to float through a filter of memory and dream where fragments, washed up on that thin peripatetic border between the past and the future, hover. At this deceptively still point of the present you stand, in a land of lacunae and shadows rifted by the silence of the deep. You know that what the tide brings in and what the tide takes out, in its varied scintillae of ablution, the mind cannot account for. Grave plinths on a broken hillside, dust and desiccated vegetation swirled in an ossuary of stone; somewhere, give back a sense of a leaking terrain where, on a hot afternoon, you lingered beneath trees and at corners, listening. You felt that, within that listening, you were both summoned and annihilated: so much so that you gave yourself up, in the heat, to a ripple, to the merest weave of contiguities—birdsong, wind rustle, wave slap—which would elide and, finally, settle down within you to become, with no pure chronology to punctuate them, part of those ambiguated landscapes that experience invests you with. Tokens, that is, of a continual passage, a motion, in which each thing that had appeared to be so self possessed and enclosed is left rummaging, amid the fluid and inexorable providence of memory and duration, for its name. And on that wordless broken hillside, in that hot air of an afternoon—the residues of how many other afternoons, of how many other headlands, or high places by the sea, aggregated within it—it was as if something was trying to draw you back in to a world without tenses, before the names; to a world that had no use for them at all.

.

You observe the rusting locomotive beneath tattered plantains engulfed, like a dark insignia, in steam. As it pulls trailers of logged teak towards the open holds of dhows lined up at the quay, your mind returns to those small stone stations of the branch lines of your childhood where you waited on countless mornings for the train to arrive. Finally, above a low green relief of hills, long before it could be heard, a thin white streamer of vapour announced it was approaching. And then, in a great flurry and hiss of steam through the cutting, it stood, having brought with it the pungency of soot, beside one. Seated at last in the carriage, listening to the slow and coaxing hypnosis which the rhythm, emanating through all the ties and sleepers and metalled ligatures into the very core of your being, produced, you began to wonder, after a while, as you drifted in and out of a reverie of bisected views of the landscape through which you were passing, whether you were not falling, after all, under the deep persuasion of a spell. Birdsong and voices were fading from every siding and platform along the line. And even when the train stopped, no one got on or got off. All there was, was the silence of stone and light on deserted platforms, a silence that was deep; the gleam of light on thick canopied trees, warm smell of grass, and the scent of flowers in station borders. You did not even hear the whistle of a guard as you lurched off again between the endless horizons of fields where there was no sign to tell you where you were, or where you were going. Your mind tripped into a trance. For all children are brought up in a land that is foreign, and are, therefore, natural and curious travellers. It is only later in their lives that they remember, if they remember at all, that far country in which they were young, and how it was sustained by a profound longing for a limitlessness that had not then yet fallen under the custodianship of a system of belief, or frittered itself away in the easy gratifications of some consumerist utopia, or just simply disappeared.

.

A senior clerk, by the name of Hadfield, casually wandered in off the harbour front the other day, pushing his travel scarred trunks into a corner of the office ... And so one more rootless soul found its way back here to these shores of the blossoming almond tree. One day they just suddenly turn up again and, under the lugubrious sweep of the fans, an old face resumes its place, as if it had never been away. No explanations are asked or needed, and none are given. Where they come back from, that grey capital of fogs and stewed cabbage, all the economic migrants of the world, they say, seem to pour into, filling mundane positions the locals quickly leave to go off in search of more elevated employment. It is into areas where these newcomers congregate that the returnee almost inevitably finds his way, soon taking his meals there, wandering amidst the unusual aromas of their streets. He finds himself bereft, in a culture he no longer identifies with, where a strain of vulgarity and coarseness that had in the past found expression almost exclusively in working men's clubs and places of entertainment, now, he notices, pervades the whole of society. Indeed, on the streets of the capital, it is palpably clear to everyone, even those who have not been mugged, that the qualities of courtesy and manners are to be found only within a museum of antique behaviours. Posters warning against violent and abusive behaviour proliferate on buses and in railway stations, and in surgeries of doctors and dentists ... So the returnee finds himself at noon each day in the small equivalent of a souq under the shining edifices of that delinquent city, in a culture within a culture, listening to a language he barely comprehends, longing to distance himself in it from the encroaching barbarism around him, finding in those sounds of an unfamiliar tongue some solace, as if he hears there the seeds of an incipient decency being preserved. At the same time he also hears what he perceives to be a dirge; the long funereal plaint of *patria*.

# VIII

Walking back through the city at the end of day along a street that you walked along so many times before with someone who has since died, images return, and sadness. Each year a greater effort has to be made, again, to conjure up that face that is irretrievably fading. Like the inner chain of feelings, perceptions and attitudes, that we keep reforging each hour and day of our lives to establish a sense of our individual being, it grows slack, eventually, and brittle. So much so, that we wonder whether the sadness we feel at the passing of one close to us is not just a sadness for the ending of the passage of a life, but for something else; for the mysterious entity, itself, of the *person*, that ghostly substance of what we infer we are, for that wisp of a vapour which drifts and clings to our thoughts and clothes all these years, force and substrate which holds together the disparate elements of our experience. It is, that is, as if the failure of memory to retain the image of the dead one casts doubts upon the very validity itself of all its structures but, especially, upon that one seemingly enshrined as its apogee, its supreme achievement. For all the time we are, with the aid of an abetting memory, conducting our lives, we are, consciously and unconsciously, looking and listening for echoes, similarities, for recurrence, that will have as its centre and location this "here" which, in space and time, we occupy. Which is why walking down a particular street in time is walking down all other streets in all other places in all other moments in time, listening for what repeats itself, for that determinate ground of our history. And thinking that we hear, in that repetition, the sound of something of substance, rather than what it is: the sound of the iron rimmed wheels of a hand-cart on the street, the bark of a dog, the clatter of broken jalouses in the wind … which is to say, in effect, the mythos, in potentia, of a life.

.

Under the steady light of the oil lamp and the sound of leaves of huge palms outside thrashing the air in monsoon rain, the memory of a particular evening returns. He was reading to us from a book just recently arrived on the mailboat, and which later he placed on the shelves under the window of the office in our small library. We had taken it out many times afterwards to re-read that particular passage so that it had committed itself, almost involuntarily, to our memories: "The sunlit sweep of green field with its hayricks and grazing sheep was a wholesome sight. She was aware of a sound—a sound associated with her early memories. It was the sound of running water. Unchanged where all else had changed, the stream still ran through the field between its margins of willow and willowherb. And so it remained, and would remain." Afterwards he had launched into a deeply sententious monologue, describing what he had read to us as a "dark eclogue". Asked to explain what this implied, he continued, somewhat in the manner of: "On such running waters the shadow of a romantic illusion strives to stay afloat, whilst through vast feudal swathes of land the tenancies of a nation leach, nourishing the bank accounts of a privileged minority which sits at night with hassocks under its arse, and plump red wines in its cellars. Green fields: borders, boundaries, rights of way; lines of power!—no matter how much that idealised and early eye may have roamed adoringly across them. In times of national emergency, of course, that tolerant land of green fields and staunch oak woods (most of which were, in fact, felled before it became a modern nation) was coaxed to yield up icons—giddy antique idylls and fantasies of harmony and commonality—at the expense of its populace's liberty of thought. All taken in by it. A manipulation of innocents. Singing the anthems. Turning out to wave flags at a parade of degenerate monarchy. Kowtowing to bewigged imbeciles. Deferential to sawbones, justices and schoolmasters. Footsloggers, canon-fodder, in the baggage-train of history that is highjacked, perpetually, by those who are, by general consent, felt to be indissolubly wedded to their own self interest." His voice had trailed, and his hands, gripping the air, had shuddered in a hopeless gesture of fatuity. And the wind, outside, had gone on wrecking the palm trees, bending them in wilder and wilder arcs and declivities, until it had seemed that they had become the very impresario of the storm itself, directing its tumult.

.

Old men, alms gatherers from the Cult of the Abandoned, shuffling down tracks from the earthen floors of their temples, chipped enamel bowls in their hands, empty. Another kind of emptiness, walking beside them. Chanting, to deter that ghost of a grammar, through whose dark flickerings the sounds constitute themselves. Detecting in them a crucible for souls, for persona, for objects which, like a piece of faded calico when held up to the light, reveal, woven upon nothing but air, the warp and woof of disparate strands which, if loosened, would disintegrate. Singly, or in pairs, in a cantillation of dust, through an inconstancy of colours, the alms gatherers move. Into their bowls a tinkling of tiny warm droplets of rain begins. They stand still, to allow a gathering of them. Then, silently, lift up their bowls and drink.

.

Silvery white barks of poplars in the brick-dust of an autumnal light. Long shadows over the crinkled skin of an old land; tumuli; root cracked boulders; detritus, a fine residue sifted by the wind, rolling over the plains, through the passes where one sets out on one's long journey into blowing sand and sun dazzle, with a last word to the gate keeper, who asks one's name, and the sadness of an intimation that one might not come back to be reunited, in the ground, with one's "home". The smell of dried grass and charcoal cooking fires. In the stoves and the drinking vessels, in the roads and in the walls, an overwhelming sense of the red earth, Terra Mater, from which they come. A dry exhalation, the breath of a body too worn down by war and famine and the passage of the seasons, to notice one has gone. Its graves, in the shape of upturned boats, breasting the hillsides. For who would go, journeying back through the dark waves of such a landscape, and burrowing through all its rooms and courtyards, all the repositories of its infinite miseries and joys, without a sail. And when the camel trains finally, years later, bed down beneath the city's walls, will they not pay back the hard tithe of its exile, with an exile of another kind. The soft word, the smile, of those who have seen too much, been too far and too much alone; of those, above all, who, the sweet smell of dung around the fire at night in their nostrils, have eradicated hope.

.

Pallid, and perspiring. Priests, whose language we recognise as our own. The unlovely, and unyielding, condiments of their speech. A meal we have forsaken—to bask and to indemnify ourselves within these sounds of another. To wander down the rich auditory passageways of a house we can never own; yet, we never 'owned' the one we came from, and are still posited in, either. Were always grubbers, squatters in it, always exhibiting ourselves within an accent which attracted only opprobrium and exclusion, our proprietorial rights all but denied to the air inside our bodies, the thin column of fluted warmth that rises into our mouths. Estranged from the very contours that we had tended all our lives, breath hills and valleys, from shaping and ordering them in the way we felt best. What is it, to be a part of nothing? Better to be a Mennonite perspiring amidst these fugitive forms of sounds that one will never claim as one's own and which will always be "foreign", and to be greeted as they issue from one's mouth, not with scorn, but a general and unreserved air of welcome.

.

In the yellow tallowy light of whale bone lamps soot is filtered into, and darkens, the lacerations whilst the old woman performing the act, croons. A spirit map deeply incised for days under the skin, the representation of a world removed from the senses, a continual periplus of loss: no land for compradors, for merchants. That corresponds to no known geography. Finally the bearer stands up, covers the configurations on his body, and walks over to the other side of the room and squats. The iron stylus still sings in the air of the little nipa hut where we linger at the door. Inside, she begins to enumerate a list of names, of places no one has ever, we are told, heard of, of trials and ordeals over bone hungry seas and high mountain passes where words freeze on the tongue; and she begins to narrate a cosmography of all those topoi that he will, alone, find himself amongst in times to come when, like the stranger, the guest at the door, he will seek to be invited to cross the threshold. She repeats the verbal talismans whose utterance will ensure his safe arrival and put him at ease in such unknown and untraversed places. An odour of rotting vegetation stirs in the breeze around us. The sound of the slow, rhythmic fluxion of water in the swamp. As an undulant note from a swan bone flute hangs in the doorway, and the interior of the little hut begins to grow opaque with the vapours from pots of fermented betel nut leaves smouldering on the floor, we quietly leave.

.

From the Studio of Indigenous Instruments the long hypnotic harmonies of an afternoon weave in and out of our consciousnesses as we recline, in a lassitude of iced teas and tiffin, upon the verandah. Voluted, supple movements of air that, like the heat itself, seem to issue from the borders of some profound amnesia, so that they seem to be, at the same time, strange and yet familiar. An almost inaudible vibration ripples in the shutters on the windows behind us. A ripple that departs, and then returns, and repeats itself—like a wave pushing forward upon the ever receding crest of a present, moving within both space and time but to no pre-ordained tempo or destination. The mind follows it, through all its intense diminuendos and silences; silences so sustained, it is as if the orchestra had packed up and gone home. In those vicissitudes of hesitation and emptiness to which the silences give birth, one loses one's way, drifting like a somnambulist, wondering if one will ever get back. And, if so, to where. And then, suddenly, in an almost imperceptible agitation of the air, the sound (deeply bowed) returns again carrying with it, a rhythm which one does not recognise at first and, yet, which one is convinced, somehow, one knows, and which belongs to all the long borne absences, all the anguish of the endless siestas in empty rooms, and to the multitudinous sighs of all the tired twilights that have dominated one's life. Although there are no flowerbeds nearby in this part of the city, an unusual fragrance, like that of frangipani, but it is not frangipani, something infinitely evasive and evocative, maybe not a flower at all, fills the air of one's whole being. From where or from whom it comes, from when, whether it is real or simply imagined, one does not know.

# IX

We have made love to the world in a language which is foreign to us, in a language of echoes, spectres, apparitions; and now it comes back to torment us, and the world seems even stranger. Intent on embracing its otherness, we have strayed too far. Like the young rag-picker, scavenging the mud banks beneath flags of foreign commercial houses beside the harbour, we should have been content with rummaging amidst the discarded objects of a world we did not covet. Instead, we let our pasts whisper to us; the sound of leaves in suburban gardens, the terrifying gaze of the heads of potted dahlias and of rhododendrons sighing in borders against a fence. It is now clear to us that love, also, and that language of an ecstatic communion with which it suborned us, articulated only our desire for some form of redress. And that the feeling of boredom, at the thought of yet another encounter with the self, drove it away and has left us here, the stale sweat of words under our tongues, breathing the dripping fern grottoes, the mucilage of snail tracked gardens on wet evenings, of a city we never grieved or grew old in, and the sounds of whose streets we have yet to hear.

.

The titles and deeds to the land where one lived, buried with one. To take and to present with upturned hands to the Registrar of Celestial Allotments and Apportionments in the life hereafter. The capacious vermilion sleeves flicked almost into one's face. "You will come back, won't you, to drink tea?" In the ever present dust of loess that drifts across the plain a pattern emerges, from the rhythmic waves of light, expressive of an entire range of tonalities. Inaudible, like the music of lost conversations. The earth, tethered in fine gradations. It is said that Turghick Ngawong once, in a divine moment of inspiration, managed to capture and put down in an arcane mathematical formula the very frequencies, the constants and the variants, of this landscape's complexion, and that it was lost when marauding invaders from the north pillaged and burned the library in the pumice villa in which it was housed. Onto what kind of a subliminal scale must all the duns of its autumns and dusks have been transposed, so that even in summer the sun's burnishings merely ornamented with flowers and scents a sombreness of such varied and infinitely subtle hues that, with its smoking tabours, it reached into the very depths of the invisible. Such is the reason why, surely, upon appearing before that illustrious personage of Allotments and Apportionments in the life hereafter, a denizen of these earthly parts would bring with him, in his hands and mind and heart, strains of some of these most cherished modalities, in the hope and anticipation that he would not be forever separated, even in death, from them.

.

There is an old story that frequently goes the rounds here, at soirees and even less elevated social gatherings, of an old painter who, aware of the utterly unpredictable and whimsical nature of the imperial patronage he enjoyed, in order to escape in a moment of perceived peril whilst executing a composition before his Lord at court, painted himself a boat and sculled off in it with the lord powerless to follow. Of course it was always the custom, amongst poets in particular in this country, to threaten to abandon the monotony and intrigue of official life by "untying the knot" and going off to fish. But is it, perhaps, not too far fetched to say that all our departures are, in varying degrees, associated with disappearance into such ideal spaces. What we carry within us when we depart is not only the shadow of a former street, locale or precinct, but the conviction that these entities exist independently of our behest. Many of us, therefore, when we leave them for good, describe such a leaving as "unreal", and, conversely, if we return to them feel it is like walking back into a "dream". How accurate such terms of depiction are. Protected, buffered against the chaos of the non-eternal/durational by a mind always engaged in some form of home-coming, the world, when we depart, floats on a bed of its unmaking, a moving and turbulent praxis from which we remove ourselves but which, in travelling, we temporarily insert ourselves into again. It is a world insistent with that rhythm of the primordial, which the old painter heard so unerringly and which, finally, in the form of the sea, offered him means of preservation. That same padding of our feet off into inchoate shapes of earth, air and sea fills us, always, with a feeling of foreboding. What we leave behind us, as we approach the borders of the ideal space, is the poorly illumined edifice of our own echoes, rife with whisperings and intimacies which we mistook for intimations of an absolute habitation. The sadness of farewells is always tinged, therefore, with the stale aura of this impercipience.

.

In the Temple of the Eunuchs, awkwardly disposed on the terracotta flagstone floor, late afternoon sun enhancing its hue to a deep ember-like burn, some of those recently initiated pine in the shadows of their old desires. Others, for whom the pain of an infection is slowly drawing away their life, unable now to move, cast frequent and long glances through the open doorway towards the garden where the green canopy of bamboo creaks and shakes in a light breeze, with a rustle like the tinkling of pendants, so delicate the air itself seems to anticipate an odour of perfume. Phantasms drift through the grills of the rosewood screens, brushing the tall red lacquer pillars. The silence is broken only by the whooshing shadow of a swift returning to the eaves, and by the crack and dull ping of phlegm into a spittoon. The rice bell rings in an adjacent corridor. Low incantatory tones are decanted through courtyard after courtyard. Those who can elevate themselves onto their feet to fetch for themselves, and for those who can't, do. Shapes waver from within the garden. Above the shrine the gold calligraphy of a single character, meaning *SACRIFICE*, gathers the last of the light to itself. Outside a bee in the crepuscular pavilion greedily and noisily embowers its whole body within the nectarious cavity of a bloom; and then, engorged, executes a delirious blundering flight upwards over the glazed tiles of the roof.

.

Just as without that continuous but impalpable tremor of the retina there would not be a clearly defined image but only a grey blur, so the image of everything we perceive is inherently unstable and simply the resting point in a process where past and present and future intercalate. What presents itself before us, whether a face, a room or tree, is only superficially specific; behind it the outlines of all other versions of its kind that we have encountered exist— for how else should we be able, even generally, to identify it. Imperceptibly, and instantaneously, they rush within our gaze upon the object, until, like a wave, they come to pivot and rest upon what rides, for that still moment of a present, on the edge of our attention. This reconstituted image is never, as it might appear, whole or complete, but is cut through by sequence, by duration and parts. Sometimes, however, when, for example, we look at the face of a person we have not seen before, we are granted that rare but brief insight into its true nature. For, though we know we have not seen it before, such a face mysteriously compels our attention. Compels it because within such a face are the elements of other faces we have known. They stare out at us with such forcefulness that the longer we gaze the less sure we are that we do not in fact know this "new" face. We look longer and the face dehisces, until it seems to become a mask superimposed upon some generative energeia momentarily detained within these particular contours before us ... Our acts of perception carry within them the shadow of a restless, unconfinable energy. It is only when we have had the opportunity to glimpse such an energy that we realize (for our acts of perception are inscrutable serpents devouring their own tails) that we no longer really know exactly where one thing ends and another begins.

.

The criss-crossing of innumerable dilapidated wooden pedestrian bridges, crowded with stalls and merchandise, over which hangs a continuous smog, a pall of charring flesh from roadside food vendors, mixed with the fumes from the highways crammed with vehicles that run beneath them and the noise of people waiting and pushing for pedicabs, tricycles and buses, convinces us that we have indeed arrived at some outer Dantesque ring of Hell. The heat simmers the puddles of freshly fallen rain on the rooftops from which a lurid sheen of evaporation rises, a dusty vapour that darkens, grows heavy and hovers, adding, with the fumes, to the toxicity of the atmosphere in which the sun sinks and from which there seems to issue a perpetual sigh as if the earth breathed only with a great effort. Through the throng of pimps and pickpockets roaming the terminals, men with ungaffed fighting cocks on their forearms, and pigs jammed into long conical rattan baskets, we make our way, breathing the odours of an infernal imbroglio which are so powerful we believe we have strayed into a place wherein is inscribed all the misery and disillusion of continually recurring desire, and where, walking through the obfuscated light, we breathe not so much the polluted remains of the present as that vast and supramundane darkness of a past whose lands know no borders and from which we hear the voices of trapped denizens. The more deeply we step into and are in turn penetrated by this gloom, the more we feel, too, the sad traces of our own unexemplary acts and all the ills that they have led to. At such a moment we look up at the slats of the criss-crossing bridges where people walk and it seems as if, through the tenebrous fumes, they inscribe and re-inscribe in the air the pathways not only of their own shrouded lives but of those to come and those that went before them; and within these lives, of an infinity of acts and reprisals, of confessions, betrayals and deceptions. They appear like those possessors of a forged passport, hope smiling nervously upon their lips, who walk confidently towards the border of the present, the past weighing heavily upon them, to cross into the uncertain zone of the future.

# X

In the calzada a profusion of ilang-ilang, their blooms filling the air with fragrance. Acacia, kapok and coconut palms shade the road off it. From amongst a group of visitors one clearly hears: "An Eden .. Matchless fertility .. Misery seems unknown here .. The people free and happy." Then later: "Work would moralize the population by removing it from the evil influence of idleness .. Compulsory labour .. This unique location would make them the leading commercial centre .." By their own admittance an "Eden", and yet they would replace a condition of utmost contentment, where each person grows, on a little piece of land which surrounds his house, all that is necessary for his existence in fairly large quantity, but also to yield a little income; would replace this with a condition where everyone strives in an effort to increase their individual wealth, and competes with everyone else in an endless round of acquisition, the market producing one new product after another, a condition which results finally in no one being satisfied any longer with what they have. The arrogance with which one culture sweeps down upon another and asserts its right to make it unhappy, to send it off on that ineluctably sad road of prosperity—and of spiritual ruin. One stands beneath the nipa shingles of a small hut shielded from the road by betel-nut palms, mango and tamarind trees and a garden, listening to the sound of rice hulled in a mortar and to the squeak of sagging slats on a bamboo floor as someone walks across it. To nothing. To that uncluttered sensory space of all our attentions. And one does not think how to exploit it. At night the iguana, audible on the trussings of the roof, moves slowly through it. Yet, he does not disturb it. Spread out the petate on the floor for your bed. Draw up the bamboo ladder. And let that long miasmic river, hemmed by the gnarled wash of pathogens, drain out of your dreams' shadows.

.

In the dusty shadows of the evening he draws down the words from the mouth of the solitary figure perched on a stool beside him. Words of gentleness, words of wrath, words of longing; words out of the silence that gathers at the edge of the forest, and in the heart of the distance that cannot be traversed. In the whispering glide of the hairs of his brush a silence is eradicated, a muteness circumvented. Long after the churr of the cicada has been swallowed up by the dense tropical night other silences mass their weight to march upon the still opaque dawn. Sighs of anguish rise again down in dust filled rooms the day has not yet entered. Behind shutters, a thin plume of ink hovers over the tablet as it is ground. The sun rises. The verandah in the small side street creaks with an almost articulate sound, the smell of salted dried fish in stores filling the air, as someone approaches looking for the old letter writer on his spot beneath the staircase, his papers and brushes neatly laid upon a tattered little bamboo desk. Words rise again, and settle, in the dust at his feet, and in shadows filled with a desiccated smell of the sea. They rise, too, in distances unnavigated by anything except the sound of a page being turned, and in the slow deliberate motion of an unknown hand upon blankness.

.

His longing to journey to places he had never been to was the same as his longing to return to the places he had left. It was not the objects of such a longing which his longing identified as much as the longing itself. Because he could not escape from this longing he was condemned to perpetually recreate the same journey. A seeker of substances amidst the shrines of ancestors, amidst artefacts and chants, collector of signs and portents, of potent concoctions and draughts, he was remembered in all the cities and towns of the archipelago. At crossroads messages were left for him to deliver to those who were far away, and his shadow was observed on the wayside verges by many long after he had left. At the roadsides, sellers of poultices and lineaments and spells shout out his name in an attempt to draw blessings down upon their products. Sometimes, in small towns on the plain, after he had passed through, children gathered round a foot's damp impress on the road, claiming it was his own, and hoping for a reward. Poor widows proffered their daughters to him. It was as if, moving through the shadows of the one journey he recognised no other journeys than this. In it, all the shapes of his former selves passed by him, yet he did not recognise any. And someone, coming up to him in the street would as likely be addressed as a stranger rather than as the intimate they were. Attempts to detain him for more than a short night's rest were all but in vain, futile. He moved off as if on some inexorable drift that would take him to the furthest reaches of himself, and then back again, without his even recognising himself on the return. Even his name, he said, seemed strange to him. Yet it was whispered and repeated, wherever he went, like a charm.

.

Here, no importance is attached by people to the date of their birth. Not only is it unimportant to them to know the exact hour and day on which they were born, but the year also. If asked they merely shrug their shoulders and smile in a way they might use in mollifying a too inquisitive child. For them the past engenders a space greater than any apprehensible in one lifetime, and it is through the portals of a thin green distillate (obtained from a particular root in the forests whose identity is a carefully guarded secret) fermented in large bamboo vats in every village and quaffed in ritualistic libations, that they come to enter and re-enter this continuum of their deaths, and births. Here, they believe, originate all the wanderings of their imagination. It is a region that, they believe, through their visitations, continually enriches them. In such lands where they sojourn, time and distance, not being ultimate, have no reality. In such a place, having no clearly discernible beginning and end, their lives and their deaths, just as the sea falls back and reveals the land and then rushes up again and conceals it, continually move in and out of each other. The word they use to describe this action, kolos, plays no part in their everyday discourse, being reserved for less profane occasions than what they call their "travelling". After such journeys they often retire to their hammocks or porches to gaze, seemingly, at nothing; or they retire to their small gardens in forest clearings where they spend whole afternoons and mornings shuffling between, and contemplating, the dark earth of their seed beds.

.

Trying to remember your way down streets in search of a particular street, and within it, of a particular building you have not been to in years, or have only received verbal directions to, is always a journey through the topography of memory to that place where the deep source of a collective anxiety resides; a place where the fragments of everyone's histories drift, collide and whirl repeatedly, where memory fails to locate what it is looking for and finally, in a darkness of epistemic doubt, fails to locate itself—for finally it believes that what it has "lost" is that figment it has learned to call "itself". At such moments the fear of an expulsion grips you; a fear that is not just to do with being unable to locate yourself in space, but in the history of your own body— which is not your body. Standing, in the room of a dream, on the outskirts of an unknown town, an implacable wind carries through the dense and intricate grid of its streets the sound of a whistle announcing a train's departure. At that moment, not knowing the way to the station nor where the train you are expected to catch leaves from, you are paralysed by the realisation that it is, in fact, that precise train for which the whistle is blowing that you should be on. You stand in the darkness, the wet streets, waiting. The deeper dark of childhood nights crowds round you. Of an eternal expulsion. From history, from that body you wake, walk and go to sleep in. And from the very act of memory itself, which binds you to the community of meanings in which your consciousness is grounded.

.

In the hill regions, which lie immediately to the north of this small port town, it is rumoured that there are certain trees which it is worth more than your life to accidentally wander too closely to. So seriously did some colleagues take these rumours that they would resort to taking their meals in one of the small matshed inns by the shore where the elder members of the community council would gather and to waylay them with their new found curiosity for the local flora and fauna—albeit its more eccentric variety. Along with the usual array of poisonous shrubs and fruits, some of them more than well known to the apothecaries of our own country, they were told of the ipo tree in the arboreal gloom and heat of the jungle canopy through whose shade, so venomous is it, you have merely to pass to depart this world. The only clue to the unwary traveller unaware of the distinguishing characteristics to look for in such a tree is the glimmering circle of bone fragments lying at its foot. So potent is the poisonous miasma, however, that emanates from it that even approaching too closely to it down wind can turn out to be fatal. In addition to the host of predictably predatory and dangerous animals and reptiles they also learned of more fabulous creatures such as the mago, a tarsier which lives on charcoal and which is rumoured sometimes to start fires to satisfy its peculiar appetite. The sikop, a hawk in whose nest a root or herb could be found which contained the secret of their fishing skills: this was in great demand and could be sold at a high price to fishermen or even to weavers whose arms it made light and tireless as they shuttled backwards and forwards all day at their looms. Finally the burang itaw, a species of small crocodile which is friendly to humans and draws close to listen to what they have to say to each other. It will even allow them to step on its back to cross narrow bodies of water.

## XI

Insolent scriveners surround us, impersonators, dissemblers. Quills dipped in the ink of many men's minds, citing none. Cronies. Bootleggers. Idle philanderers, with an insatiable appetite for honours. Notaries on street corners, their chops rising and falling in all weathers on a flurry of forged and unforged documents. Interminable lines of refugees from one country after another, with nothing in their pockets but apple seeds from ruined orchards. And what will ripen here, in the mind, except an affliction of putative objects. We imagine no enduring nature but this. A proliferation of egos and appetencies. The satisfied groanings of ourselves in harness. Like a dark salt this name you travel the world in, blown across a waste lot. And those who are there, wait for us, embracing a precipice of shadows and dishonoured cheques. A migrant's ticket—one way—in the pocket bound for the kitchens and restaurants of some far land. Ejected, evicted, we always return. To the small town band at the end of the pier, or the dusty square—to a tirade of wrong notes, or a sulking resentment of voices. To the incubus in our own faces—to our own lies and hypocrisies. Nothing changes. A motley parade of others beckons us across the road. The silent flowers ripen on their stalks again in the public spaces we thought we had left for good. In a broad swathe the phantasms of the avenues and the boulevards press past us. The signage of a lost place glints in the last light of evening. The past we had buried here comes back to reclaim us. Contending schools of thought, schisms, in the local university and the institutes of learning, and in the church. The pale chasuble of words over everything.

.

It was because the image of the place had formed itself so strongly in his mind that, slowly, he came to conform, himself, to that very same image that the place carried, so strongly within itself, of him—until, finally, he had difficulty distinguishing between these images that had evolved separately and that, eventually, had coalesced. Walking along the small mud back roads of the settlement early in the morning you came upon his figure moving, at a slight distance from you, as if, perhaps, it was considering evading the meeting; and it appeared, as it shuffled off sideways to linger at the gate of some small nipa hut, to blend in with the rampant vegetation which surrounded it. For one moment, in the overpowering heat and assailing odour of decay that seeped up out of the accumulated leaf cover beneath the trees, his crumpled and bedraggled form lost the integrity of its outline and he, literally, disappeared. At the end of the road you turned round and looked back; for the untidy hobbling figure, dead leaves snagged in his battered old hat, whom it had been in your mind one minute before you were about to pass, but didn't. Light still fell in brightly varnished pigments through the foliage overhead, but now, as you turned out of the little mud road, it fell upon the mottled pediments of cement pummelled and puddled by monsoon storms and on crumbling masonry, where, as you walked beneath the dark mildew streaks of plaster and ascended the broken steps, his figure seemed to walk beside you over the deep gloss of unevenly worn stone floors, and on ahead, into the penumbral corridors where you, eventually, lost sight of him. The shadow of the escutcheoned blades of a slowly revolving fan languidly stirring the air, toiled above you. A sudden hiss, then the increasing clatter and crescendo of rain falling upon outstretched foliage. It stopped, as abruptly as it had begun. Then, in the silence that reasserted itself, the breath of that musty odour of leaf mould again, and a forlorn figure moving toward you. In it, you felt, the place had encountered an image of itself, and he, vaguely sensing this, it having been intimated to him through a plethora of sightings, soundings and inhalings, stayed on to oblige it.

.

Amidst the sound of cicadas, the smell of deep fried squid and sampaguita, they committed one of their best loved writers, called simply Joaquin, to the earth the other day, following a touching round of necrological services for him in the little jasmine scented compound overlooking the open ground of the cogon fields he so loved to wander in. The frail figure of his widow, a woman who had graduated with the highest honours at the university on the mainland, but who had lived a life eclipsed by the greater renown of her husband, seemed to visibly relish the opportunity to, at last, be in the spotlight with only a lifeless vestige of the deceased beside her in his casket. As if, perhaps, sensing that she was indeed exploiting such an opportunity she unexpectedly asked at the end of the service for a round of applause for her dead husband, who would soon, as befitting such a person, be hauled in a state funeral through the streets on a gun carriage to his final resting place. Later, as his remains lurched down the Avenue de la Consuela, under the gently swishing sound of the giant leaves of the coconut palms that line its whole length and bathe it in a green gloom, you remembered that fiercely gentle music his love poems made, how palatal and velar fricatives of consonants, cracking and hissing like wood in fire, were absorbed within languorous shoals of vowels without completely

53

relinquishing the sense of conflict they embodied. And so it was with Joaquin the man. Conflating love and life with art he excelled, through the sheer lyric pressure of his genius, in harnessing that sexual prowess, which would, he admitted later in life, become his downfall, in a way which did not tear apart the fabric of the poem but held a wayward and promiscuous energy in place. In that small space of words the compulsion to compete with other poets, and to triumph over his own desire by transforming it into an aesthetic object of formal contemplation, was like a supreme kind of love making. As the flag draped cortege rolled by, your mind went back to the image of the frail widow standing by the corpse. For her was there, you wondered, consolation, in that ecstatic progress from self-advertisement to self-conquest, any deeper and any more inconsequential than this?

.

Some mornings, a blackbird singing on the lawn outside, you wake in no place at all so much as in the body of a memory that has, somehow, thrown off all the constraints of time and place and arrived to hold you in its familiar furniture, doors and walls, a room different to the one in which you lie. It is only after prolonged minutes in this intruded reality, though, that there seeps into your consciousness, arresting drift, the sounds and surroundings of somewhere else. And you had been about to call, through the gently creaking jalouses that spilled the light onto the floor, for Epistola, the laundry boy. You had almost called; had felt the word shape and begin its ascent into your mouth, and had imagined you had smelled that intense floral scent—and had imagined you had heard, also, the wringing out of suds. To wake within a memory is to wake in many places at once and, therefore, in none. Where, then, we locate ourselves at each second must, by every means, persist long enough to exceed the time of our forgetting. For in that forgetting we encounter the ghosts of the morning again, sifting through the mists of the mind, testing the door to it, wary of the spaces that elide behind it. Once opened, we should enter that continuum of space and time where all objects fall out of the sky, and where our hand, placed upon the table beside us, still holding the warm fragment of a dream, would grasp what is to come, what is gone, and what is going.

.

We sit in the little steam filled tea-house by the canal, kettles simmering upon brick ovens, rattan screens let down against the sun, propped open just enough to afford us a wide view of a watery demesne as it wanders through a horizon of tall green sugar cane. The sound of washing being pounded and slapped upon the stone steps down at the water's edge reaches us. Through the doorway dark leaf shadows in brilliant light dance upon a wall. The pure subjectivity of a moment, cut out in space and time, falls before us like some arbitrary declaration of which it is not the author. And of which, neither, are we. Outline flutters behind, and within, outline; and that predilection for narrative which reality appears indifferent to, quite dissolves. Time and space recede into a background where our voices are barely heard. What ply the air are the bright fragments, the dust or chaff-like dance of continua, not wholes; the fire of their invisible concatenation, to which no one is listening and which addresses no one, burns, is extinguished, and then reignited again in the fluttering leaf shadows on the wall. Outside, a stand of bamboo creaks in the wind, like the sound of the timbers of a boat that is already under way. Light gleams on water. You should use only water of the purest of departures, they say here, to quench your thirst, to purify your soul.

.

A sense of, maybe, a "homecoming". Before the chimerical shadows of language have driven their roads into the interior of our being. The undeclared destination that we pass through day after day, unaware it is here, it is that, at which we are looking. A place of forgetting. Lodged in the broken walls of the overrun city. In the calloused hand of the archer upon the thigh of the young girl. Its awl of letters in the soft clay tablet of the inventory. In the colossal cargoes of rotting fruit at the quay. Without a word of how it has got here, of where it is going. Opaque to us. The fluid boundaries of its beginning and ending glimpsed in the offal and the foetid smell of markets, in the spartan air of chapels. We wake before dawn in a strange room, and already the funerary odours are entering the shutters, the guests arriving at the inn downstairs. It is time to go. A thought, unsupported by sight, sound, taste and touch, or mind. We are the ghost of a sign we do not remember. Knowing nothing of our past, except the tired inflections of its departure. Poaching upon this man's generosity, avoiding that man's thrift. A word riding over every geography. A look, subduing love. We have dreamed, in this savage twilight, corpora of selves we can never own. The voice crying out, over the deserted station. The wind moving through the columns of a ruined coliseum and flooded foundries. Interrogating the lodger with our eyes on the stairs as we pass. The rain has washed out before evening the footprints of our coming and going, and left us only with the unwrapped pennant of a tear, which we would take into the marketplace and trade with the eyeless stall holder for that single pure syllable he plucks from the obscurity within him, for that droplet of clear laughter we would launch into our lives, for that sound of a homecoming which we cannot, still, hear.

# XII

He removed his hat and, one thought, in face of the unlikelihood of one's meeting such a person in such an out of the way place, and the odds being against such a person existing anywhere these days anyway, a "gentleman". Something in the even tenor of the voice, the bodily deportment, gave off the all but indefinable air not only of gravity and gentleness, but of an abiding forthrightness and courtesy. And one could not help but contrast it with the manners of those in these sun gilded islands who, in their noisy frivolity and laughter, seem to display a fear of or antipathy to any self directed energy, or any sense of a self to direct it to—for them the surface not the depths beckons—and whose energies are directed almost exclusively outwards upon displays of etiquette whose breaking they react to with a child's astonished sense of rebuke, and who seem to revere solitude no more than they do an open book. He raised his hand, and under the pale linen shadow of the rim of his hat there was, one thought, in his eyes the faintest hint of a recognition as they sought one's own. And then he was gone, long limbed and striding off into the calcining heat of the light that scorched the awnings and wooden frontages of the little stores down to their very weave and grain, off into the crowded concourse of the steamer pier, and onto the shifting tide that bore him away and that would, perhaps, return him to this very same pier head one day and, perhaps, to a less fleeting kind of encounter.

.

He sits under the dull light of a single 60 watt bulb, the Thesis Writer, exuding more the aspect of a police interrogator than of the minor fabricator that he is of undistinguished collations of ideas. In the half light the clacking of what sounds like a typewriter alerts us to the presence of someone behind a screen at the end of the room, perhaps his assistant, abetting him in the shadows. We walk down from his office with an unmistakable after-scent in our nostrils of, we think, snuff and wonder whether it is this which keeps his senses aroused in that profound gloom of a windowless space which he inhabits. We found our way to it through a maze of back streets as crowded as the columns we scoured in the local newspapers which finally yielded up his existence and his name—if it was, indeed, truly his name. More than three months later, descending those steep and tilting steps once again, with a monograph upon The Ontology Of Substance in a bag, we are amused by the irony of how in the declared author's name, as in the very fabric of the argument itself, is embedded that unknown person's voice, rather than one of our own, a name, therewithal, without an essence. And we are set to wondering still further as we leave that densely packed heart of the city and reach the outskirts, where the spherical seeds of the kapok trees drift in a cloudy diaspora over the roads and fields of rice, whether anything at all in our lives does, with any certainty, inherently possess what we call an identity. And whether, perhaps, we have not, in this land of philosophers where the concept of forgery seems not to exist, for how can one copy that which finally does not create or possess the kernel of its own being, whether we have not become, in the eyes of those back home, in our own country, morally and intellectually "corrupted".

.

We live in a metropolis of vendors. Even on its outskirts where we reside, far from its centre, to these once densely wooded foothills of acacia beside the rain forest they make their way through a twilight of ruined roads. One lies on one's bed late at night or reclines upon the verandah, the shadows of bats sweeping across tall moonlit trunks of dancalan trees in silent aerial acrobatics, and one hears, faintly at first, a far off plaint, an echo. As it works its way closer in a slow methodical vibration of air, like a lone goose honking down a wilderness of sky, one recognises the human origin of the sound, inching incrementally, road by road, towards one up the long hill, past the little Methodist chapel with its thatched roof topping the crest, to the white plaster walls of the midwife's lying in rooms at its base. It is a voice which, as it comes out of that sublunary dark, seems to suddenly measure the immense distance and space that surrounds one and in which one lives. Like a small beam of light from a torch sweeping a large room, it locates one, and then quickly passes on. The fading of it, its slow diminution, returns one to that state of isolatedness that had prefigured its approach, and which one had not until then noticed. After the sound approached and found one, one experienced an undeniable feeling of comfort. As the voice reached its loudest pitch in the street outside, through each stage of its approach one's mind silently calling out the soundings, one felt that one's being had become an invisible plumb-line and, at that moment, touched bottom, measuring the entire depth of that expanse upon which it floated. Made buoyant by the sound of that singular chant which the night seemed to have vended and conjured up out of nothing and nowhere, it rode upon it.

.

In the dark clouds of a northern city, where there is no light and the ice knocks against the quays at evening, and under an old iron bridge a black swan arcs its neck whilst all around it the ashes from factories fall on the heads of passers-by and rooftops, one wanders. Gulls wheel above sweating abutments of rock. The far off clank of freight yards echoes. The air of decompressed ethers lingers in courtyards and on the banks of its river. A Mausoleum of Martyrs celebrating the People's Struggle stands where they burned down all the wooden mosques. Architects fleeing persecution, crossing the border with the gilt of icons under their arms, redesigned and rebuilt the city. Then they came and tore it down again. In the summer hoards of ravenous blackfly. In the winter a freezing smog. Left over samovars. The relics of art deco. One's footsteps become the footsteps of another—another place, and time, across another river. A child's voice, fearful, stepping above a rushing torrent clearly visible between the planks. Beside a workshop of prosthetic limbs one finds oneself in the rain rehearsing the sadness of a name whose face has faded. The days are dismantling us, one by one. Upon their dull edges are the fields and plains of a forgetting that is more real than where one stands, than the person one is engaging in conversation. The strange air of its silence beckons. Exiled from all that one is. All that one was. Only the blackfly know one. And the dark clouds moving over the ice of a meeting one has not arranged and will not remember. Pale shadows of themselves, too, they float upon the inordinate air of the uncharted.

.

How do we, sifting the odour of this air of sweet flowers, know what a thought is? So immediately does the sound of the wind rushing through the leaves and the branches of the trees announce it to us that we are deaf to anything but it. We never question the form of the mental image in which it is arriving. Like things irredeemably dead and discarded, thoughts crowd round us, the worn out husks of our days. When we wake to them in the morning, their light in the shadows is already there, dreaming—about what, but ourselves? To measure, weigh and to establish the precise nature of their being, would be like disentangling the finest threads of a discourse upon shadows, only to find in the end, that there was nothing there but shadows, that had cast shadows. What's on the tongue, in the mind, is the mist from indefinable entities that fade further and further from us the more we attempt to bring them into focus. Ultimately elusive, is this why when inhaling the odour of a flower we breathe, in that green hollow at the heart of its being, and of our own, the scent of a sour drizzle, of a posthumous act, and can only stare longingly back to those long tree lined streets in which we had just walked, and seen, and heard, too, seemingly, nothing, except the passage of our thought.

.

Over the public address system the voice of the dictator hoarse with desire, begging his foreign mistress to fellate him; speakers crackling above a road where, later, the seller of duck eggs rested his basket, smoking. The great haciendas crumbling under a tropical sun. Fortunes of jewellery, precious stones and coins, buried at night in the fields, without any servants present. Endless dusks of knife sharpeners grinding out metallic shards, confused fireflies mating and dying. The departing Consul took his pet iguana for a long last walk around the grounds and, unable to bear the separation, shot himself. To the water treatment station they took, each day, their store of bottles containing molotov cocktails. Already the leaves back home would be shedding their leaves he thought, already the stream behind the house would be frozen. A rhythm asserts itself, and then it is interrupted. A roadblock of truck tyres and wire. The sound of ankle bracelets tinkling through a room mingled with the odour of sandalwood, and all the time a bird was singing. Across the flooded causeways they stumbled and drowned, weighed down by all their loot. "In one or two years time you will have already forgotten you ever lived here". Gleaming white atriums of marble, skyscrapers of steel and glass, eight lane highways now cover the temples and public squares. Years later they went back into the fields at night, but could not find them.

# XIII

Those exonerated from the heresy in the small mountain villages, after allowing a respectable amount of time to elapse subsequent to the hearings, quietly slipped out of the little cobbled lanes where they lived and walked, one night of deep frost and cloud draped moon, onto the track that wound from the lights of their houses down through the snow fields onto the plain. Escutcheoned saints in shrines punctuated their descent. Screes of accusation toppled behind them. Yet from what was it that they were fleeing? The blossoms of the alder tree continued to appear and disappear each summer, year after year, long after they were gone. The water in its thin pebbly course through their orchards did not stop running. At the end of their lives, they thought, they would come back and go to those secret small spaces above the door, behind the cupboard, beneath the loose floorboard, where they had carved their names, as if they held some special kind of power. Most, of course, would never return, saddled with debt, loaded down by illness and work and families. Yet all would wake, at one time or another, at night in the close air of that room where they happened to lie, and reach out for something that was not there … Nothing to leave, nothing to return to. Except the drift of dust down empty lanes, the cry of the hawk caught in its high sun shod spiral above a land the colour of belief, except a thought.

.

Permeated by a sense of its own absence. An impress, a hollowed-outness, in the very depths of space and time. A where-it-was. A being confused, by a non-being masquerading as itself. Phantom grey, an echo that crossed like a blip on a screen recording the heart. This body, which now occupies the fullness of an accommodation with time. That cannot be in two places at once. That cannot be beyond this precise moment of its own awareness. That cannot be, without this intuition of its own absence. Where is it, precisely, from one moment to the next, so re-inscribed are its journeyings and trajectories, which we have forgotten, that lie within it like a faded archaeology of lines visible in fields only from a great height? This moment that intersects itself, that we can know only by its ceasing to be. Who measures this, measures nothing, and is measured by it.

.

Ink filled days. Thumbprint. Chop. Signature and counter signature. A running script of serifs, like a snivelling nose. Entries and departures recorded and endorsed. The smudged light through a window. A paperweight of doors. Cancellations, reinvokings, break behind us. In the box, on the dotted line, a hand moves through our own; that complex, shadowy solidarity into which we are slowly inducted. The innocent appraisals of ancient typewriters, their clogged letters filling with a dark fibrous ooze, a tarred tail or eye preserving the shape of our names that have long since faded from files and the tramped floors of corridors. We hear them still, their clack like the sound of pebbles on a beach the sea long since walked away from and left to despair. An arpeggio of exculpated fingers poised above them. A wind blowing free through the unsecured sheets of a morning no force can secure, lurks in the doorways of a thousand rooms and courtyards. The absent ones whom we embrace daily in a gesture of love look on out of their grief of distances. We are running away from not only the staleness of all replicated hours but from the running away itself which takes us, finally, not closer to but farther away from what we are.

.

A list of "laudatory occupations", posted the other day on the door of an eccentric Datu's lodging, caught the eye. Included in it were:

Spayers of deformed mares and of three legged dogs
Contrivers of all earthly cornucopias
Lens grinders
Racers of dung beetles
Washer women
Milkers of the venom of serpents
Carriers of ice
Night soil gatherers
Provisioners of joss to the temple
Offal sorters and eviscerators of swine
Side street teeth pullers and ear cleaners
Invokers of rain
Wound binders

.

There they go again, off into the depth of a tumulus, digging, brooding upon the shadow and all its manifestations. At night from bar to bar chasing it to perdition. From daemon to daemon the archaic anxiety of loss accumulates. Simmering behind the earth blocked entrance. The flesh merely, perhaps, a garment. As always, there are more questions than answers. Middens. Middens. At the heart of the inscrutable there is a song that they are always trying to overhear—does it own them? And have those who sung it entered into a pact with those who listen for it, but cannot hear it? Was this corpse in the floor buried so that it could be chanted? Beeswax and abaca: tuba and camote. Where will they come upon it. Between high rock dwellings, in a valley bisected by a wash, or here, surrounded by smoke trees in a moist fluvial plain where all the evidence has evaporated? A few footprints only in a dark tuff. And what does that prove? A ritualised laughter, born out of despair. Do they hear it, now? It comes toward them, they who are not comfortable in the present, who spend all their days lifting empty amphorae from wrecks, and prints its ashy spoor upon their foreheads ... Wipe the dust off your boots. Your eye's still shaped to the outline of a trowel. Come in out of the wind; accept this offering of silence.

.

The leaves fall. Our lives return to what they were before we claimed them. A reality that is nothing. Through the strange air of rooms we have never been in, they commingle with what they are not; then hesitate, and linger, taking our arms and leading us out onto a balcony, or to a window, to whisper to us those words from which we cannot derive any sense of ourselves at all, or any understanding of where we have been or have come from. And, at some later point, they leave us, standing there, alone in the evening, talking to ourselves, leaning out above the great ruined blossoms of the cherry trees in the garden, unsure of whether to go, or to stay; listening, as quiet as a pressed stem between the pages of a book, to the sounds of some far off afternoon through which we are passing as if through a deep sleep, and against which someone—who, we do not know—has pulled heavy curtains and goes on talking. And they do not come back for us.

XIV

Another year ends. Our thoughts return again to that whiteness descending upon roads, fields and housetops; a whiteness those who live round us under these bright equatorial skies have never seen and marvel at descriptions of. How many times have we not tried to recapture for ourselves, amidst the seething jostle and scurry of our lives here, that perfect stillness which comes with the absence of the heterogeneity our senses thrive on. Slowly, as the flakes of minute frozen crystals fall and fall and accumulate upon everything, sounds are muffled, colours reduced to a sombre monotone and we taste, touch and inhale a frigidness that, for once, we do not recoil from. It is as if we are witnessing in this homogeneous world a sudden withdrawal from the principle of differentiation which, up until this moment, had driven it. Those amongst us endowed with a more introspective disposition ponder upon how it invokes a stillness where, in the infrangible drift of whiteness and shadow at evening, one seems to move towards a calm in which the very act of consciousness itself prepares to be eclipsed. Under the dark brow of thought, the hushed white hedgerows and the luminous pallor of the fields stretches on and on. Where it intends to take us, though, or where we, willingly casting ourselves adrift upon it, wish or believe we are venturing to, we do not know.

.

This city, buried beneath us. At night its dark streets forge a music composed of whisperings and silence seeping up through iron gratings. In its shadowy windows the faces of harlequins seem to be laughing. Beneath its scum stained monuments nothing is erased, the face of Odysseus, the shape of a sail against a broken mast, gliding through its back streets where harsh words and loving expostulations are exchanged. The fragrant exfoliations of the living light its lamps, while the dead congregate at outlets for surplus supplies and try on everything over and over again. Meeting one of them in the street one would not know at first whether they were from the living or the dead. A supplier of dreams turns in a mews of remote presences and engages each passer-by in a conversation resembling the subtlest of melodies, till they walk off unable to distinguish, in their own tears and their smiles, sadness from joy, loathing from admiration. The sound of dice dancing, narrowing the odds on smoke filled roulette tables, penetrates everywhere. A sea of empty syringes washes up on its beach. In its landscaped foothills, shunned by cinema audiences like a disease, celebrities announce their own deaths. There are in its skies the strangest machines for flying. As they drift above the roads one senses that they are in fact one's own desires, conveying nothing other than that sweet ignorance which keeps afloat all the opacities of the heart. One listens, and what one hears is not the rumble and tear of thunder across this city but the groan, the wounded laugh and the scream of a collective nightmare, from those under siege by an enemy they cannot identify but who, they suspect is none other than themselves.

.

The ancient nara trees exude an odour like that of ovulating women. The air brims with their fructifying breath. In the humid tropical gloom it closes round us. The great roots working under our feet all that darkness into a limpidity of green, a year round buoyancy of leaf. So, after the rains have abated, dry curled leaves forming a cerement of earth, and we think we detect, in those few brief weeks before the sun burns away the drying residue of clouds, in the faint golden glow the glow of an autumn gently suffusing the fields of the countries we have left, we remember the nara trees. In the fecundity which they so strongly aspirate we discover the corrective to a nostalgia that is so quick to reprise a certain light, a certain season. Such a season merely gleams like the dusty tesserae of a window we have long since ceased to look through.

.

Those grey hinterlands through which the navigator guided us by indeterminable routes, through such tardy heat infested days, through such narrow rock strewn gorges, often without water, without hope, so that we lost sight of our destination and could not even remember where we had set out from—from what chancrous port or soot escutcheoned station, waving an athletic arm. Due to the fact that we had endured, we wondered whether we had ever left at all, or simply stayed where we were; amidst lavender and thistledown, before an imperishable door, a step, our shadow beside us: and what else—looking at us, as if it knew through what circuitous routes we were to be taken, how far away from the dust and stillness of that quiet spot, before we would relinquish all thought of travelling further, and turn to go back? For turn we did; but on turning, realizing that the places we had journeyed through did not exist, found ourselves stranded. Just as a dream sometimes holds one for a long time in its power until one struggles to wake up, so we tried to set off, finding in the features of the landscape nothing familiar or unfamiliar to guide us but a combination of both, unsure whether we were heading back from where we had come or forward to that line of a new horizon, turbid with the journeyings of many others. Therefore we stopped, and did not go on.

.

The cortege that started out from the small village of Ecjevita in the mountains at an appropriately sedate pace, the black horses with dark plumed head pieces that pulled the casket in its glass coach sweating slightly in bright afternoon light, began to slow after a while. A pall of grey mist swept into the high valleys and hollows enmeshing the vegetation and sky in one vaporous veil through which it became difficult to make out anything but the most amorphous of shapes. At one point so thick did it become a member of the procession had to walk by the side of one of the horses guiding it step by step along the road. Finally, after moving for hours at a snail's pace, even the outlines disappeared and the sun began to drop behind the mountain. Inching its way along the road, of which there were a number on the mountain, to the sound only of the iron shoes of the horses and the coach's wheel rims on loosened earth, the mourners of the cortege began to become uncertain as to whether they were in fact going up or down the mountain, or whether they had gone off at a tangent in another direction. In the little chapel at its foot the other mourners waited. Then, as the evening began to bear in upon them, realizing that something untoward must have happened to delay the cortege, they sent a small group with lamps off up the mountain to look for it. Only many hours later, at past midnight, did they find it, the black horses standing idle beside the small hut of a hillside terrace farmer, the lamp that had drawn the procession there, they had thought that it must be the chapel, still diffusing light in a soft aureole around itself. Thoroughly disoriented, lost, before they had reached there a few amongst them had claimed that they could clearly hear bells ringing, and others that they could hear the sound of the congregation singing on the wind.

.

It is always the periphery, rather than the centre, that draws one. A periphery of slow, or non-existent, mails, of indefinitely deferred arrivals, that enhances the growing sense of one's own obscurity. Each day, contemplating the appearances around one, one feels oneself becoming simply another appearance amongst them, like the pattern in a carpet that, with the wear of the years, fades, and becomes, finally, diffuse. So we walk, amongst those who do not know us and do not make any demands of us, at ease. They, in their turn, sense, perhaps, in that shyness that makes one tilt and bow slightly one's head beneath the broad rim of one's hat, a resoluteness to be left alone, a preference for, by and large, one's own thoughts and perceptions rather than the regular company of others. One, likewise, makes no demands upon them either. But across one's mind, occasionally, drifts the thought that this obscurity one so courts might be a way of evading confronting and resolving stresses and injuries embedded deeply within one's own private and social history, rather than the choice of a voyageur for whom otherness has assumed the shape and the destiny of a final country.

## XV

A clearer of pathways, shoveller of deep snows, knowledgeable about destinations and vistas, yet adulterated frontiers besiege him. In a tent of reindeer furs within a tent of skins, preparing to cross the rooftop of the world, his confidence deserts him. Stored in the waters of his body all these centuries, the memory of a migrating, a story, recounted in the stillness of the night. The lamp sucking air. The wind died down. Where did he disappear to? Into that flickering soot of an interior from which there was no exit, where space consumed the mind that manufactured it. In a landscape borrowed, perhaps, to assuage the craving of that ancient impulse, he now languishes, made miserable by the metaphysic of its reification.

.

She was observed standing each night on the small iron grilled terrace of her house in all weather. Some roots of the old banyan tree that grew outside it, mistaking, perhaps, the grill for ground or wall, had infiltrated and twined round it giving the terrace and the tree the appearance of being one long intricate extension of each other. Within that thickly entwined covert her shadow hardly moved all night, until dawn when she would slowly take herself off into the darkened interior of the house to sleep. Her husband's body lay all the while in the Wah Tung hospital's mortuary. After the funeral and the interment of the coffin in the little horseshoe shaped grave in a clearing of scrub on the hill behind the house, she disappeared. The note she left gave no indication as to whether it was a suicide note—her body was never discovered, nor was she ever heard of or seen again—or a note of some subtler form of farewell, pertaining to herself, or to the deceased. It read: The spirit is peripatetic. It goes where it wants, and cannot be shackled. Since it has been everywhere already its sense of anticipation at where it wishes to go next is not so much because it is a "new" place—why should somewhere it has not been to be *so* compelling—but a place it has been to before and wishes to revisit.

.

They lie beyond us as if in a kind of uninterrupted sleep, the lives of the unnarrated, waiting only to be awakened. And yet so, also, do those vast expanses of our own lives, which we have yet to walk into and to discover. Annotations at the edges of events, details of something said, an action remembered, something as literal as a street name, yet we have never gone beyond them, moved out of the shadow and into the level lit tract of a land our language and our reason can, without any ambiguity, comprehend the significance of their place in, an order to which they can be assigned. We delve deeply into mysteries, looking for clues, or listen attentively to the divulgences of friends, the disquisitions of strangers. Through them all the same archetypal quarry flees, always, ahead of us, glancing sideways, veering off, peering back and taunting us with its distance. So our own lives are lived in a land of betweenness. The more they remember, the less they seem to comprehend. Time and the spaces we move between, the sleepy but ever changing borders of our selves, pack their portmanteaus of pain and ease upon our backs and walk off without us, leaving no tracks for us to follow, no address.

.

If what we look at and what passes by us each hour and day of our lives was, each time, an exact replica of itself how our boredom would deplete us. And yet it is in precisely that similarity of things (this body from one day to the next) to themselves, rather than sameness, that we go looking for what we cannot name. And why a name, applied again and again to the same object, does not wear out. Standing, after rain, beneath the deep bruise of a slate blue sky, blueness evades us. In the wind is the smell of damp roads and verdures fragrant with the scent of unnamed flowers … We remember only that which can be forgotten.

.

Falmouth Eugenides, half Greek half Irish, sat, at the end of his life, slouched at a table outside a small pension in the centre of town complaining of how he had failed, how his children had grown up and did not love him or write to him any more, how he had no wealth, no fame, and no real reason to be glad. All the spectacular success of Eugenides' first paintings, when they were exhibited in the Fusotu gallery in Kabrinsk, could not have prepared him for the sudden reversal of his fortunes that took place soon after he had accustomed himself to languishing in the warm glow of the public's and critics' acclaim. He reacted to such fickleness of taste ("Not so much an original as a fashionable painter who gives his viewers what they want") by taking himself off to this corner of the world where his days were spent, in increasing penury, wandering around the edges of rice fields and jungle clearings, or bodies of water, sketching the scaffoldings of what became an endless series of water colours, a panorama, as it were, placed end to end, of a particular place or a particular mind free falling in time. For it seemed when looking at his compositions that they were painted in a medium peculiarly unsuited to and incompatible with their subject. The colossal energy and fecundity of the tropical landscape seeped away from the pale washes and gauzy philtres of Eugenides' compositions. The predictable response such compositions drew from critics back home, always eager to repay a haughty deserter in kind, only seemed to confirm for him his justification in roundly denigrating them. It was as if his exile, and his choice of painting in water colours, was a wilful attempt to preserve an animosity to the cultured world that had rejected and largely forgotten him. And it allowed Eugenides, here, in this out of the way region, to indulge and nurse his profound resentment at those back home, his feeling of having been short-changed, which was, perhaps, more important and sustaining to his soul—to which had been added the complication of miscegenation—than ever praise or recognition, no matter how much they flattered him, could have been.

.

This moment we now have, this thin rain sliding across the river, because it repeats, ceaselessly, our past, neither moves toward us, nor moves away from us. Like part of an inner landscape, a music of lost hours, it is the destiny of one evening trying to fulfil itself amidst an inchoate cartography of streets and objects arranged behind shop windows. For one instant, sensing the silent vibration of loss through our body, it seems to identify a pattern; then hesitates, and shifts its stance. As it does, someone in a room leans back their head and inhales the dank odour of mould stirred by a fan, and then walks over to a window and lays their hands upon its sill. An almost imperceptible rhythm runs through them. Ammonite of memory, recording in faraway time, the Word's silence, to which, arm plunged nakedly in shadow, we listen, in the hope that we might hear what is to come. Not for us, as for Dionysos in *De Devinis Nominibus*, that divine insufflation, but a cellar of discarded sounds, a music that **is** the perforations of time itself; the disorganized stream in which these avenues compose not just themselves but us, and which we, and the thin rain sliding across this river, keep coming back to, convinced that it is here, now, on this narrow sidewalk, that we are going to meet our destiny dressed, just like us, in a hat and a coat, and speak to it in the same language that we have been speaking for years.

.

Two tall dispirited looking eucalyptus trees stand by the dusty road that leads up from the old parade ground beside the harbour, where it is rumoured the shadows of colonial soldiers still march before dawn beneath a ghostly flagstaff, and across the hills. They seem to wave in the warm breeze to one as one makes one's way along the former battery path and through the long narrow defile. As one takes one's leave, the tall masts of the ships falling away behind them, one thinks one hears in the sound of their bright leaves gently clashing against each other, the sound of music and laughter. On numerous days each year when one ventures along this road, it is the same. Music and laughter, but of no remembered place or time, as if the fragment of a past one has no precise recollection of has suddenly entered the present, or as if the present has suddenly and momentarily been fetched back by a past it cannot identify but which it is made dimly aware of by some chance collaboration of light, landscape and weather. In this "movable" landscape into which one unknowingly blunders, nothing is as it appears to be; everything, even the smallest object, resonates briefly with the energy of an inscrutable sign. If it is, perhaps, only in such a brief moment that the past of a former self that in one's ordinary acts of attention and cognizance one is unaware of, obtrudes, a moment when the mind is unengaged by its own powers of formulation, then why does this not occur more often? Or if it does then why are we so unaware of it? Or is it because we assign such rigid parameters of space and time to the act of seeing, to the mind, itself, that sees, that those fluid, protean shapes of a past which we wander amidst and which can cross and re-cross the parameters of our everyday mind with such impunity, so seldom appear?

# XVI

Malls of conciliatory noise. These voices proliferate round us. The difficult silences banished. In the glass enclosed air and light that is filtered into these spaces, the inescapable discernment of a collusion with eternity. At which boutique shall we, today, worship; at which brasserie or doorway filled with the latest products of high technology? The beverages, and choices of our desires, are endless. *Cognito eoram, quae sunt ea, quae sunt, est.* We have become what we contemplate. And in these last stages of that long journey back to our God, the promiscuity of our dawdling at these shrines unadmonished, what are we chanting from but the extracts from our endless supply of users' manuals, and the small print of our warranties, our eyes slurred by the screens of flickering pornographies, our mouths full of a debased coinage, fingering our mail order catalogues for a holiday to an endangered rain forest, for an exotic bride, for the purchase of a piece of a disappearing reef.

.

The trees move through the long delirium of the afternoon, bend and sway within the shuttered room, walking on their roots. The sound of the overhead fan, a laboured scuff over all the surfaces. One perceives one's shadow on a wall that one thinks is a horizon and that one thinks one must have, therefore, just arrived back from on a long journey from a far off country, so saturated is one's body with the stale odour of perspiration. And who is this, reflected in the window, lying beside one, this person with short cropped greying hair who looks so like oneself, or like someone else one knows quite well? Two broken pitchers, that one is always overturning, stand by the bed. For one moment that, at least, is clear. Then a curtain bends inward again, and it begins, and one wonders where one is. Later they would say it was "swamp fever", a paludal miasma, an effluvium, that one had inhaled, and offer one a glass of sherry. But as the old vegetable cart clatters down the rutted path by the ice house and before it disappears, as it seems, for ever, one feels the trees begin to move across the verandah and one breaks out into a sweat. Tremulously, and with a feeling almost akin to anticipation, one approaches that reunion again, that dark evaporation, that fire, where one's body becomes a theatre upon whose hollow boards the great Chimera struts and weaves his spell. Over the astonished and hypnotised audience of one's senses, he closes one's eyes, and auscultates one's being; until one is merely a fine sediment stirred by his hand.

.

Especially at weekends on the long asphalt and concrete highways of that coastline hundreds would take off leaving the city of gleaming steel and glass superstructures, crossing the river on a bridge suspended between deep cliffs, and drive up through the foothills of the three mountain ranges until they entered a landscape where the city was forgotten. Here amidst the rural environs of economic stagnation, rundown and faded white clapboard hotels whose heyday had long since passed, and their acreages, were being revitalised and turned into ashrams for these migratory weekend pilgrims on wheels. They arrived with their Gucci overnight bags and specially designed prayer mats, to listen to the latest homilies of the latest swami and to sit amidst the clean air and noiselessness, chanting mantras well into the night. Sitting there, listening to the calls of coyote packs moving through the woods and dogs barking at deer on lonely nearby farmsteads, did they, perhaps, hear the sound, too, of that small ethereal space within the heart that contains everything, that other city, that city of Brahma, to which all their highways and all their bridges could not bring them? Or did they, after they had packed their bags to return in the morning to that corporeal city of steel and glass and noise, think they caught a glimpse of a passing shadow, in their rear view mirror as they went down the highway, of it. Before they entered those suburbs, again, of incompleteness?

.

We idle at the table of a streetside cafe with our confreres, sipping cold cordials and listening to the latest news and gossip, whilst all the time a predatory oligarchy struts upon the bones of the living. Nearby, at the university campus a student pens, in sun dappled shade, another sombre indictment not far from where they recently murdered a labour organiser. The grass on the verge where he fell is still red. All the ducks have disappeared from the ponds and lagoons of the capital—into the stomachs, no doubt, of the impoverished populace. We stand in line at pharmacies behind those who have enough money for a single tablet only of a course of antibiotics, while in the boardrooms of our own countries the salaries of directors of pharmaceutical transnationals rise and rise. Garbage festers unfetched in the streets, and on the highways, for weeks. The foreign debt grows and grows. Those in government departments, asleep at their desks fifteen years ago, are still there. From the street opposite the faltering notes of a blind accordion player, slumped against an adobe wall under a sprawling pongama tree, float across to drift in amongst the sounds of our conversations, the clinking of our cups and glasses and cutlery and are, like all the voices—of despair, outrage, fear, joy, tenderness, pain...—of which this sun dazed megalopolis is composed, effortlessly accommodated.

Even as a child he had been a collector of rock specimens and fossils, and had kept them in a cardboard shoebox under his bed. When he had assumed the curatorship of the provincial museum in Orsedd he had donated this collection, which had grown to be quite sizeable, to it. Ammonites and trilobites still encased within their dusty sepulchres of rock gleamed behind glass cases on the wooden tables of the little museum, beyond whose barred windows could be seen the fragrant clusters of frangipani blossom weighing down the boughs. Whenever he got the opportunity he would padlock the doors leaving a note saying that he, the curator, had been called away on urgent business—there was no assistant—and take himself off to a deserted spot a few miles up the coast where great overhanging cliffs revealed exposed strata of schist and basalt and where, he knew, if he was patient he would, sooner or later, come upon a piece of rock which, when split open, would reveal that for which he was looking. In truth, he liked nothing as much as this. It was an obsession so consuming that he never found time to really shape his life around anything else. And though he was not a man who shunned, or could not be at ease and enjoy, company what took hold of his imagination was far too potent for him ever to accede to an ordinary existence. He was a man unhappy and dissatisfied with surfaces. Something drove him constantly to peer beneath them. Surfaces that were as much to do with the terrain of the mind as with any physical terrain. Just as most people will lovingly excavate their own lives by exhuming memories, so he pursued the ancient relics of extinguished entities that he had never, in his own life, known. Putative, uncompromising creatures. Their outlines blurred in front of him when he found them like some shadowy presence, as overwhelming as love. That search for carbonised bones, petrified bodies, the mould or trace of them, some would have regarded as no more than a morbid hobby designed to acquaint one with death. But for him it was more; it was the reassertion of a kind of gloomy teleology, and not a salve or surrogate for anything. It involved a laying of hands and eyes upon the rhythm of some primordial mystery. Like Persephone going into and coming out of the dark vault of earth, like our childhood games of hide-and-seek, like the magician's now you see it, now you don't. When he stood in failing light on that glittering shore beneath the cliff, he heard, in the wracking and wash of pebbles in surf, the simultaneous sounds of violence and tenderness from which are drawn both life and death, existence and non-existence, roll up and down the tilt of the beach, unable to stop or to be prised apart, inseparable. And he heard within them, also, the irresistible dark undertow and drift of all the forms, including that of the mind itself, which of them all is the most intractable and cannot be exhumed, rush by on the wind.

.

A porcelain vase belonging to a former place and time, unpacked from a tea chest long after it left, sits uncomfortably before one. The present seems unwilling to absorb it, or it to accommodate a time and place to which memory does not attach it. Like a relique it carries with it the shadow of exile, an aroma of absence. And what, indeed, did it mean to say "belonging to"? A vase goes where it is taken. The black stench of a putrefying nostalgia corrupts all that we touch. The unreality of being here, is matched only by the unreality of there. This is not a vase, so much as a thought of it—of a room, a city, a country, where it is snowing and not snowing, darkening and not darkening, where a figure sits on a couch struggling to invoke the image of a vase that is not there, where, in a room beside her, is a dead lover, a dried up lake, a music that cannot be quieted. Place, time and object, yearn for that ideal solitude that will reunite them. But, "All day long the floating clouds drift by, and still the wanderer has not arrived".

XVII

An agony of deranged twilights. Signwriters labouring under fluorescent light in warehouses. The wind spelling our names backwards and forwards until we no longer know what they look like. In empty moonlit emporia the smell of effluent and oil from a river. Tall skeletal towers of bridge girders above roof-tops. Fragments, as if torn from a gallery of dark neurotica. And the music of loss that all of us hear at various times each day. The poem, lost in time, unwilling to give up its secrets. The grey faced patient leaning against the wall of a hospital exit. And that music, again, that wells up inside us, that yearning for something we miss and have never seen. The translator at his desk burning the midnight oil, looking far off, the garden the people outside forgotten, does he see it? The numerist sifting his integers? Before the dawn arrives the indifferent melody will have departed. Petals of the mimosa and hibiscus will still blaze, though, in the night flower markets. Odours of offal washed from meat stalls the evening before still cling to the gutters. And out of an exhausted idiom, out of stale words, perhaps, the poem will have arrived at last on the desk of the translator. Lost in time. Like an imperishable meaning. Our footsteps will echo on the road that will take us back to where we came from.

.

All night, in a dream, you wander through your existence according to a pattern you do not recognise, in a slow somnambular repetition, crossing backwards and forwards between the past and the present. Waking, you wonder; where does memory lie? In the thing recollected? In the mind that remembers it? Or in some intercalated place, one that is neither in the thing itself nor in the mind that reifies it? Perhaps it is, indeed, in such a place between places that memory resides, across whose turbid river the forms of your life, rising like grey ghosts from the warm ashes of the morning, drift, and where the imprint and trace of everything actual and imagined you have ever encountered, and of things you have no clear recollection of at all, linger. A place you enter not so much through an act of volition as of destiny; as if it is the memories there which claim you, rather than the other way round, so subtle their overture of tinctures and sounds, the potency of their air that penetrates and pervades you. Wandering the back alleys and small side streets, suddenly you recognise, in the gaze of one who passes, in the stranger with trembling hands, the look of one who has recently just been there and, turning upon his heels, shaken for a moment, rushes back to look again at those same streets he thought he had passed along, now strangely changed, and who longs for those less dubious properties of a present to which his mind had been attuned, in which the occlusions of time did not assail him.

.

Walking down San Hing Street past the offices of what are now real estate companies it was easy to remember the days when there were only rice and rice importing stores there, interspersed with the offices of some small shipping companies whose vessels plied the local waters. At a sun dazzled desk of Neptune Orient Lines one afternoon where he translated, fitfully, the company's correspondence into English for his uncle, Ho Kam Sing sat copying one of his own verses, 'To The Lovely Cow Dung Flower': "You are not the Rose of Sharon/Neither are you the Lily of the Valley/But you are no less lovely than either./For you have brought me back to my happy childhood/The childhood when I and my brother roamed the fields of Kamshin", and translating poems into English by a poet he held in the highest esteem. Being, himself, the son of an ex-minor official who was banished to an offshore island by the forces of a disgruntled and rebellious general, and having, too, failed the official-degree-examination, only sharpened his sympathy and understanding for the poet. Forced by the death of his patron to leave his lowly official position, and later by the rebellion to wander over almost the entire country separated from his family, this poet, dearly loved by Ho, died with a scant literary reputation, alone on a small boat on one of his many solitary journeys. Ho, in countless phrases and lines of his, as he translated them, experienced, as well, his own precise emotion of displacement: "Travelling is difficult through the desolate frontier passes .. The letters I write never seem to reach their destination .. My way is south, but my gaze turns northwards .." Is there, thought Ho, as he contemplated his own double banishment, once from the land of his birth, and then from his childhood, not to forget the periods spent in an asylum to which the darkness of his manic depressive moods removed him, is there, he wondered, something infantilising in our culture and history, with its centuries of insistence upon absolute obedience to the father figure of the ruler and now to the ruling centre, which makes us especially susceptible to this sense of exile? Outside, labourers in the street haulked huge sacks of rice on their backs up the hill. The nib of his pen squeaked as he copied another of his verses. 'Younger Brother Talks with the Moon': "Eldest Sister is writing her diary, and/She hears Younger Brother conversing/With the moon./'Moonie, Moonie are you hungry? Come down/let me feed you with my conji.'" Suddenly, the fields of Kamshin seemed, to him, farther away than ever.

.

Bright fragments, from dried grass stacked for cooking fuel in the courtyard, picked up by the wind, tossed. An ebullient dance of chaff like midges or gold dust in the autumnal sun, where, because of the sun's eye-level height, the texture of each surface possesses a clarity rendered, from even far off, of such exactitude and tactility of detail, it seems to bear the intaglio of the ideal (if, that is, the ideal is that on which "no deceitful divinity has traced the signs of hope or redemption"). Strong sunlight stirring, too, a crop of glozed hair into a bouffant of smoke, a dark oleaginous cloud of ink secreting a nimbus. As one looks there is that slight, almost indefinable, pain at one's eye having been thrown into the midst of something it is too much a part of, something which, because it is partly a creation of oneself, it cannot apprehend as an independent object, and which it cannot, for that very same reason, possess. Elusive and mysterious object—and its longing for itself!

.

And this is the way, perhaps, that it must always have been, from that moment, for him. Only it took him many years, and adventures, to realize it. That long white road of dust and traffic that had so intimidated him in his youth, that he had, on his first excursion, ran almost weeping back down towards his village, feeling every inch of it taking him further away from his home, had then become that wide avenue of air and light that passed every village and town and city, winding on towards a horizon that was always before him but which he never managed to attain. Made miserable by continuously staying in the one place, lured on by the shards of an unidentifiable destination, he set out, the paper thin leaves of the plane trees rustling above his head. Over seas, over mountains, over plains where the stubble of sugar plantations smouldered and by the grey wastes of mangroves, he went, through the charred forests of uplands, through the fungal libraries and the dense discourses of cities, listening to the spectral hiss of oxygen in the emergency rooms of hospitals, waking beneath monoxide dawns under flyovers, breathing the sickly air of abattoirs, confronted by the upturned eyes of blind buskers beside mildewed possessions in underpasses and by whores beckoning to him from doorways where they were whitening their faces. Lingering on the outskirts of a last city, the image of squid in its back street markets, alabaster of the deep, turning slowly their great murdered heads into the damp shadows of the future, haunted him. With no more than a whispered, brief solicitation to the city to take itself back into itself, he turned to leave, and as he did, a face, torn from despair, from a road on a map of a country through whose obscure coordinates he'd passed many years ago, its eyes closed—he knew she'd walked through many unverifiable geographies to get there—appeared before him. Remembering the lines of a charm by a poet in his own country composed to ward off despair, he repeated them aloud, hesitantly at first, over and over, and then with growing assurance, in an attempt to make the apparition vanish. When, after a long while, he saw that the figure had gone, he walked on across the bridge. It was evening. Far up the hillsides the illicit furnaces of stills burned brightly, distilling their vapours of quixotic dreams.

.

An afternoon, trapped in its own obliquity; grey slant of light across tarmac, the roof of a greenhouse, a patch of garden beneath a washing line. Amidst thousands of discreet images, from a train or car, a plane, sitting in front of a television, a cinema screen, turning the pages of a magazine: from looking, listening, reading, where, exactly, is it, does it derive its idios from? Sitting, looking at you, you sense, in its silence, the grey deracination of time. It is, compound ghost, part of a vast *musée imaginaire* that floats before you, moving like dense herds of caribou through winter snow, like smoke, drawn off from where you do not quite know, but which engulfs you—wherever you are. Unsettled, at times, by it, resigned to its presence, you realize that you are deeply implicated in it. Like a spectral figure, too, you wander through a landscape that it has never, exactly, constituted, nor, perhaps, ever will, but which it constantly alludes to, and which, you imagine, you must, on a certain day, at a certain hour, have passed through on your way to somewhere else.

# XVIII

When only the silence of those far off noons—of which your earliest memories are almost entirely constituted—remains, and nothing else. Composed neither of light, air, water, fire or wind; not, indeed, of any thing at all. That move towards the farthest point of your hearing, and then beyond. Leaving only a voice, anonymous, that called to you from the garden, a voice in which sounds, like birds returning to their nests, had been substituted for your name. In those prolonged silences, while the air was heavy with the heat and scent of blossoming hedgerows, and your shadow was prostrate beside you, the future gave up its importunings, and left without you. When only the silence of those far off noons remains, and the front door with its flickering yellow lamp in the porch's alcove greets you at evening as you turn in off the street, and the smell of lavender and mint rises up from unseen borders, again, to enwrap you. Then you will know, as the deceased voices grow more distinct, that it is not so much that you had forgotten, or that you had some difficulty after all those years in recalling, as that when the future got up and left without you it removed, unbeknown to you because you had not left, the possibility of anything, afterwards, ever remaining for you to recall.

.

An interesting letter appeared yesterday by a certain Jan Hendrik Nijhoff in reply to an article in *The South Inferiganga Coast Times* by the Catholic Bishop Wu ... "I really cannot let Bishop Wu's sweeping statements about the corruption of Christian values in the West (SICT, July 21ˢᵗ) pass without comment. He attributes all of the problems in that part of the globe to an irruption many hundreds of years ago into the West of what he describes as the 'heresy of passion' and erotic love which have their origins, he claims, in Manichaeanism in Persia which flowed (along with the symbolism and formal and thematic literary conventions of the Sufis) through Asia Minor and the Balkans into Arabic Spain and hence to the Troubadours of Southern France. This 'heresy' and the problems in the West which he asserts it has led to, the weakening of the institution of marriage and the family etc, would not, he claims, have taken place if those regions from which it had originated had been fully evangelized by Christianity. Presumably at the point of a sword since that seems to be how Christianity usually spread its word. In Bishop Wu's vaunting of the values of Agape, charitable and cultivated desire, over the destructive deification of desire in Eastern societies and cultures that he characterizes as 'abolishing diversity', and the exploration of 'the distinct person', he over elevates, however, his own cultural patrimony by claiming that Chinese culture has survived so long precisely because it has never sanctioned such expressions of 'deified desire'. I should like to very much remind Bishop Wu of the famous 'Li sao' poem from his own culture written sometime around 300 B.C. by Qu Yuan—the 'father' of Chinese poetry—which transformed an ancient shamanistic oral convention into a new kind of written mode of lyric. In the 'Li sao' the poet searches throughout the world for a beautiful woman, his 'fair lady', a goddess. The poem is an account of the poet's passionate quest and sufferings in pursuing such perfection. The female figure is a symbol of China itself, and the poem partly a banished courtier's complaint (its author drowned himself out of despondency at his removal from the court), but its intense tone of lachrymose despair at the unattainability of the lover and its eventual sadness and, what one critic called 'post coitum tristitia', make it strikingly similar in tenor to the poetry of a French troubadour poet like Arnaut Daniel who, no doubt, the Bishop would most definitely not approve of. Not being, I am sure, as knowledgeable as the Bishop about the civilization of China I cannot claim that the passionate love, or the form of its literary manifestation, he so derides derived not from Persia but his own country, but, given the very ancient contacts between China and Persia, one cannot, perhaps, exclude the possibility that such an influence might have taken place. At least it is interesting to speculate that it might. A Manichaean church, in fact, existed in China as long ago as 730 AD. Manichaeans, like the poet of the 'Li sao,' renounce the corrupt world for the pursuit of man's spiritual element, his angel, which they regard as trapped in the prison of the body. This 'angel' manifests itself at death in the form of light when the kiss of love is bestowed upon the believer by the one he alone chooses to venerate, his feminine saviour. Perhaps the good Bishop might also wish to consider that the violence with which Pope Innocent III put down, in the year 1200, the Manichaean 'heresy' of the Cathars who had established the Church of Love in the troubadour domain of Provence, was motivated not solely by the noble sentiment of strengthening and preserving the institution of the family but was, just as much, motivated by the desire of the fathers of a male dominated religious hierarchy to keep it that way, and to repress women, as well as to control and channel the libidos of their congregations into ways amenable to the Catholic church."

.

Looking up into the as yet unfleshed boughs of a tree, its dark network of interlockings, the small green shoots and buds like nodes or stars dotting the firmament of a deep azure blue sky into which it is thrust, alive and breathing. And, in the middle of it, its beak raised to let forth an iridescence of sound, a black bird. Divine particle and animus out of the old year, undying. Scoria. Passage. Yearning. "He has tuned the tones of his flute to your name." The flowering hibiscus. Flame, of a being that includes and denies us. Pushpavati.[1] Thighs embracing the trunk. Out of what, what grows? Looking neither into the eyes of another, nor one's own. Since each is both, and both are neither.

.

In the silence of dawn all that we can hear is the wind scuffing the pediments of buildings, their occupants having fallen silent. The enduring strain of an infuscation has drifted over our lives. The days are inserted within them, like markers in books we have left open at pages we cannot be bothered any longer to read or understand. Where should we go and what should we do at the beginning of such a day? Linger by the dried up fountain in the courtyard, buy postcards from the small store on the corner, or go in search of some tawdry memorabilia in town? We do nothing. The present is not, as we had believed, confined to itself but, at the same time, points towards both a past and a future, which are folded over on themselves, which are recursant. Our attention is dissipated, our energies dispersed by a day that, each second, each minute and hour, is nostalgic for itself. Its bright retinue of epiphenomena, that it arranged and paraded before us all these years, has slunk off into the shadows, its artifice exposed—not to ridicule, or outrage, but merely to sadness, and to a mourning for those selves that we had erected upon it. Where it is now they are too; continually tending toward and wavering upon a present that is disequilibriated and not really fully available to us, that is not, in fact, a "present" at all.

.

The star-clerks have all absconded. The ministries are looted and in ruins. The Imperial Board of Astronomy has barred its doors and all its members scattered to the countryside. So no one knows what day it is, or when the New Year is supposed to begin. Useless calendars, all with different days and dates, proliferate. Cries and heart-rending shouts from the penitentiaries, the asylums and orphanages whose directors have fled taking with them the keys,

---

[1] from Sanskrit: a word whose denotations include a flowering tree and menses.

float across the streets. A handful of copra husks will buy a dish of locusts or bees, or a safe passage out of the city. All the valuable antiquities from the palaces have disappeared. Codices, hymn scrolls, catechetical texts. Soon, no doubt, they will appear in the cities far south, along with valuable treatises on governance and on the stars, sold for a small fortune in back street booksellers by unscrupulous merchants. Even the ice cutters who make their living beside the frozen river at this time of year have departed. No more pink sorbets on the terraces of the lords. And the flower sellers, and the itinerant players—where are they? On a wall littered with faded edicts a young girl scratches some words for someone who, perhaps, failed to turn up for a liaison, put off now until who knows when, or for good. In the shadows of alleyways, disguised as beggars, with purposefully disfigured faces, ministers of state sift through baskets of refuse, looking for a meal.

# XIX

All that has been promised to us and that has turned out to be unobtainable, or impossible to hold on to. Since the moment when, as children, we became aware of our self, and of others. Immense and unwieldy ledger of disappointment and of loss. Who accounts for and keeps a tally of the deficit? Not least in the way that it disenchants us with our self—tiny frail engine of aggrandizement, indefatigable imperium, from which we are always attributing the cause of our raised voice to someone, or something, else. All these dreams, these expectations—thwarted! What use are they? Pale idols of an ego that manufactures and supports them. Sacrarium of a faith whose deity is the future, that dilates each day to a subliminal afflatus. To wordy posturings. To frustration. To that which, if imbibed from too long, renders impotent even the imagination.

.

A song rises over the housetops and then falls silent, in an expiring autumn twilight. Though not audible any longer to us it is, though, present to us as a form of absence. How else would we know what had vanished, and what had stayed. The air, the light and sound, sustain every kind of cohesion, and as we move through them we note that what at first we see as a form of muteness and deafness at the heart of the world, that expresses itself as a relentless evisceration of its own substance, is really a holding back. Everywhere and at once, in all places and times, the world **is**, in accordance with its perspective and in order to be independent of us, in order for it to restore everything to us.

.

Standing upon the bridge beside the sodden mud flats, where she watched the vapours rise and fall, she heard the clamour and noise of the day and the night and of their incumbents. Gongs, cymbals and flutes of solemn processions. The wild and joyous nocturnal excursions of intoxicated celebrants. The slow contemplative progress of devotees, of mendicant monks and their apprentices, at daylight. On the wharves, and in the railway stations, she heard, too, the tumult and noise of those arriving and departing. On the antiseptic air floating from hospital wards she heard the cry of those newly entering this life from somewhere far off and, in the mournful voices from mortuaries and the clanking of steel gurneys, the sound of those leaving and returning to that same unknown destination. Odour of sampaguita and diesel fumes, of shower stalls and kitchens, of tamarind and ordure. Messages, opportunities and disappointments, visits; a vast moiling across indeterminate spaces for the purposes of love and friendship, pleasure and solace, of crime and work. Such are the impressions of a passive mind delved in the dark depths of matter, she heard herself say, her reference half mocking what she regarded, finally, as that fatuous Aristotelian association of form and the active male principle … She remembered a road that led through a bright clutter of khrishnachura and sheuli blossoms, a road she had walked down each evening with another. All roads, tracks, paths and ways trace acts of memory, she thought, and all are different even for those walking along them at the same moment together; all change and no one walks completely to the end of any of them, or can really say where they do, indeed, properly start out from. Shadows shifted on the water under the bridge. Stars above appeared in the ink dark night sky, caught for a moment like shards of the far off in the bridge's taut net of cables and girders. We are all passing, she thought, migrating through this immense terminus of time and space.

.

Looking out from the top of the seven-storeyed Golden Goose Pagoda the city's walls stretched away in all directions around one. People stood, at evening, loitering in the spring air and conversing on street corners. The odours of sandalwood, jasmine and rose-bay flared, and mingled. On the Avenue of the Pepper Flower Trees the Embassy of Eternal Sorrows padlocked its gates. In the Columbine Close behind it those petitioners for entry as migrants to the land of perpetual outlines and shadows settled down for the night. Wood smoke drifted up from their small fires. Down the fragrant thoroughfares the bells of unseen vendors selling ginger roots and blossom tinkled. To those falling asleep in the close it was as if they were already adrift and setting out on that far river they intended to cross, which when they cupped their hands into it did not quench their thirst, through which elephants bearing no loads wandered, and on whose distant shores they could just make out the music of what is to be, has been, is, and of what is fading away. For, in the morning, they knew that the iron hasp of the lock on the compound gate would, like dust, fall away under the merest impact of the weight of their fingers, and that they would at last cross the gardens of the spacious forecourt and enter into a house whose rooms were immense and empty and full of silence.

.

Draw this line around your life, here, where it does not exist; locate yourself at this particular point in space and time, and then eradicate it. At the border between the field and the edge of the village which rode up to it your life did not happen. And the bright yellow contour of the mango which you pulled from the tree, nestling in your hand, did not contain it. It was always behind or between what your attention focused upon, implicated, or even demanded, but it never dwelt in these things themselves that you described. Never imitating exactly anything itself that the senses became aware of, it lingered, instead, in the high embankments overgrown with cogon grass and thorn bushes where you never looked for it, and heard itself in the soft crunch of the earth as you were passing. Because like you it was destined to rise and pass away it named you, only to acquire a temporary sighting of itself. As you lift the latch on the gate at night to return home it shuffles off into the shadows, reasserting the presence of a whole past which it supplants and anticipates within you. An unlatched window creaks from somewhere deep inside the house into which no one notices you enter.

.

The memory of her haunted him, subconsciously, through the years. Long after he had left her. His conscious mind she occupied no more than would a distant acquaintance. But whenever he journeyed far away from where he had begun to feel at home, or whenever he was overwhelmed by some stress of circumstance—he would dream of her. At first he attributed it to a long simmering sense of guilt at having been the active principle in their separation, but as the years went on and the dreams did not subside—he dreamed more of her than of any other person—he began to suspect it had less to do with her than with some sense of his own transgression of those primordial proprieties attached to people and place. He had simply, one day, failed to return, after a long overseas visit, to her, and he had never seen a member of her family— whom he had been on terms of considerable intimacy with and in whose company he had enjoyed himself many days of the week all the years they were married—again. All that intimate assemblage of their histories—suspended in time. All their joys, their sufferings, melted each year slowly off the edge of his horizon. While, silently, they were amassing thereafter, without him, new ones. With his own parents recently dead in a far off country, and no family of his own, he soon moved on again to another country. Where the dreams – always of a touching reunion, though waking he had no desire at all to resume that original state with her, or of a wrenching parting—continued. All lives are lived in a defining grid, a nexus, of time and place, which is determinate. One repudiates it only at the risk, later, of some form of retribution. Bleeding its borders leaves a ghost land of pale visages sucking the stalks of a failed harvest. This, he thought, was where that memory of her returned from, repeatedly, as if from some unforgiving region deep within the communality of the human psyche, to, ungrateful wretch that he was, haunt him.

.

On the window of the over illuminated hairdressers store in the rusting arcade on which a local politician had draped a streamer announcing free circumcisions, had been placed, beneath a faded photograph of the deceased, a framed neatly hand-written announcement of the chapel where, and the dates when, his remains would be "lying in state", presumably for those of his long standing customers who might wish to pay him their last respects. One passed, moved by that small and sincere gesture for a life timed to the falling of hair and clicking of scissors. Above the floor indented by the weight of bodies one, whimsically, imagined this face of the barber who had shifted there over all the years, hovering, the dark dimple in his chin gleaming in the hot moist air.

# XX

She had returned, and had been walking around amidst us, and we did not know. All the time, carrying that image of her death with us, we were blind to her as she appeared and wended her way before us in the markets and the streets. Even her voice, that still rang clear in our ears, we did not notice. Like a past subsumed within a present it does not any longer recognise, she floated amongst us. Replete with all the paraphernalia of the familiar, of gardens and benches and of cool well trodden places, she defined herself more by what she was than by what she was not. And, thereby, again she evaded us. As in the nature of things, if they are not momentary they would go on existing for ever, she moved from one point in time and space to another with such frequency that it appeared as if she did not possess any motion or rest. She became, in effect, wherever she was—with such fidelity that she attracted no more attention than the casual passer-by would bestow upon the familiar shop-front or government building on their way home. The past can have meaning only in relation to the present; deprived of it for whatever reason—fear, longing or indifference—it wanders amongst us, and within us, with the transparency of a gaze that it is impossible to locate.

.

A nude dusk in which, amidst the trees and fields, the obsequy of light throbs. Why is it that at such a time of day, when all around one the outlines of familiar objects are fading, one senses that one sees not less but more clearly. As if, through the dim interstices of space and time, there was drawn at such a moment towards one the profile of an absence one would never embrace, not even in sleep—where the dream-object lingers. But as if, trembling at the edge of one's vision, and slowly falling apart, a memory-object stepped out of the river of shadows in which it had been perpetually submerged and, one by one, divested itself of those layers of its raiment woven by every act of one's cognition until, finally, it stood exposed on that opposite bank with, between the nature it had abdicated and what it had become, no ground of transcendence left, not an "it" at all. Beyond thought, beyond words. And that "I", upon which it had depended all the time for its very being, too, fled.

.

After the foreign ensign of a far country had been furled and the flagstaff fluttered with the pennant of a newly independent nation they had no one to confront but themselves. Freshly renovated and painted ambassadorial residences sprouted all along the waterfront. An atmosphere of bustle and strenuousness infected the capital. At last they were free to fashion their own destinies. In the countryside they set about dismantling the vast estates of the indigenous families who, with a natural reluctance, resisted their redistribution. Gradually it became clear that, whether due to their own cultural traditions or to the imported mores of an alien culture, they wore their post-colorial skins thinly upon their shoulders. An eruption of widespread malfeasance and plundering drove the economy downwards. Gradually law and order began to dissolve, which led to the ambassador of one neighbouring country declaring that he never got a sound night's sleep any longer for worrying about his safety. In any other country this would have been greeted with a good deal of realism, wry amusement perhaps, or self-reflection. But in this young newly independent nation it elicited a virtual furore and outcry, leading the Foreign Undersecretary to announce a possible designation of *persona non grata* of the offending ambassador. On the acacia tree lined avenues of the capital the sweetest breeze blew from the orange groves on the nearby plantations. On the flagstaff at the presidential palace, though, the lanyard clacked with an irritating insistence.

.

In the back streets of that large coastal city, in which at one time various overseas powers had at gunpoint forced the government to cede to them concessions, they arrived after a day of travelling, one humid August night, at a small dilapidated guesthouse with a flickering neon sign that was about to expire. On the wide river bisecting the city and which flowed on into the interior of that vast country, all night the wail of tugboats drifted. The balustrades and terraces of rotting colonial tenements, once banks and solicitors' offices, bulged, in a recent experiment with communalism, with the volume of many families. A ceiling fan, fluttering and creaking, rippled the still air of their room. The song of a street vendor—always, he thought, how he would love to record and collect such diurnal sonorities before they vanished—rose, and he heard within it the immemorial intonations of an ancient culture upon whose broad wave the present rested. Gently, he undressed her. As if entering The Palace of Sweet Years again, after thirteen years of marriage with someone else that had gone unconsummated, he moved within her, sometimes turbulently like a flood, sometimes calmly, hour after hour after hour, without pausing. As the light broke through the soot of dingy blinds he heard the slap of water on the embankment as the high tide subsided, the thud of flat bottomed ferries from far upstream nudging the wooden jetties and pontoons and the muted chatter of the sleepy eyed crossing gang planks. She dozed. Far upstream. Islanded. Pavilioned. Or like driftwood, something broken loose, he thought. A thin reed, bending in the current.

.

When did this night begin? Not in the same place and at the same time as that which it supposedly occurs. Already too late! It can't always have begun in the past, or be yet to begin, and no time exists in the present for it to go anywhere but where it is. It must, amidst the list of the putatively moving and eternal entities, have begun somewhere. The caress of a whisper across lips, too faded now to remember more than that, precipitate of hours into which we have decanted so much of our lives; and waited, and suffered, and waited. Astringent blooms feed on our blood, and will not appease us. Running our fingers over this thin edge of a movement that is not "ours", that does not exist apart from what it would consent to be, yet we insist on confirming that it has existence. This night, this fantasy of fear and longing, this long drawn out obeisance to them. So that, in the end, there is registered, at the heart of this surfeit, the breath of a lacuna, of many lacunas, and of a body that moves through them, in which they lie extinct.

.

One travels alone or one does not travel at all. Over the empty tract of this page voices are calling, at the edge of the farthest reaches of light. You are following blindly your own footprints into a country you have not been before. Over dried up riverbeds the sound of unfamiliar accents floats towards you. You are deciphering the script of a present you do not recognise but of which the handwriting is familiar, in a place where the spaces round things you could not bring with you have arrived before you—though, here, there are notices declaring that all space has been consumed. Instead there are echoes, and the proliferation of echoes. In the trees for miles upriver are shreds of scorched silk and the charred pages of books from when the mulberry factories and the libraries were burned, after they had attempted to restore the Dictatorship of Objects. Everyone here goes in search of that infinitely regressive "uncorrupt margin". The ordered diagramming of cartographers is despised. Instead the devious ways of cashiered midshipmen wandering by scrofulous isles are preferred, the protracted divagations, through doors, over bridges, round hills and walls, of itinerant soothsayers. In derelict churches the altars to OUSIA have not been restored. Instead, wandering beneath the shade of abundant palm trees where the sound of carpenters and joiners hammering and sawing confronts one and through the warm workshops of tailors, one realises that no activities exhibiting the mind's temporary plotting and piecing together of materials the beginnings of which it cannot find, are held in higher esteem than these.

## XXI

"I will wait for you, but you will not come," the note had said, as if she had possessed a prescience not just about that appointment, but all appointments. And come he did not, neither on that day nor any other. The note, like a dusty heirloom, vanished too. No one on the spray lashed promenade waited. Things drift together and apart not at their own beckoning. Nothing arises simultaneously with itself but, on the outskirts of a city or a town or a village, waits and listens amidst incomplete echoes for a name to summon it. Some wait all their lives and never hear it, others rush off too soon, some catch it in the nick of time only, eventually, to discard or dispute it. History awaits us, across the cloudy grey sediments of this same harbour, with its lists of appointments, with its records of dates and persons. Down its long arcades enrolled in the shadows of evening, beside quays where light glazes white hulls of luxury liners, torques of gold, polished facets of crystal, gleam. Like a premise forever in need of confirmation, our reflection, in the window of each storefront, hovers, drifts and wavers.

.

A memory of light on sandstone walls of houses. The fine depth of it, as if exhuming an ancient warmth. North. Where the air is crisp, and for much of the year there is snow on a distant mountain. Pale sweep of cloud shadow over hills. A man on a bridge above a railway terminus looking at the receding perspective of lines, and trains disappearing into the distance, dreaming of far off places. Who would, one day, die in one. An air like one through which had been sieved the edges of a thousand horizons, a lightness and buoyancy honed on itself. The icy forelock of a fir tree, swept up in sudden sun, slowly dripping stain on stone. Latinate fossil name of a village—left by legionnaires?—stranded between two hills whose names point at its throat like a threat. The opposed pull of north and south. Ice song scored in a cantata for breath, for soiled buckskins, burst pipes and blackened burns. "The way up is also the way down." Under his roof of plantain leaves he expired. Light, like a grieving watermark upon his arm dissolving the frozen current of his youth gave it back to him in a torrent of words he could not refuse. He died listening to himself talking about somewhere far away he had spent so much time and so much of his considerable energy escaping.

.

Deva nagari—city of the gods: so ancient Sanskrit grammarians described their alphabet. A labyrinth of noise, of sounds and visual symbols, in which one could so easily lose one's way. And then, suddenly, come upon it again—unannounced! The gates swinging open onto a lost pastoral, or region of infernal doubt; blood soaked cobblestones, the tenderness of caressing hands. Down its long colonnades of shadow, across hushed courtyards where the only sound is the sound of the water of a fountain mounting and toppling back upon itself, through trellis shaded walkways, the low murmur of voices in rooms deeply insinuated within walls issues, whispering that there are no propositions. If by chance people stumble upon such *sotto voce* they pause briefly but do not linger, then pass on. Like the motion of water and air on a ship already under way it does not detain their attention. Indeed to them, since it can be designated within the architecture of such a city of sounds and symbols, that, in itself, disarms it. On, then, into the immensely variegated nature of such a city's arrangement they wander unaware, for most of the time, that it is this, rather than themselves, that directs them moving them around within the portals of an edifice of unsurpassed vastness. Only sometimes, when they stop, for instance, in a strange street where the name spells backwards their own, do they glimpse the light leaking through the walls of such an impervious discourse, and hear that profound silence that underlies all thought, undenotable, into which it cannot venture without dismantling completely its own walls, those very walls of which it is, itself, composed.

.

He dreamed of a poetry/prose that would have at its heart, as the people of this country have, that graceful movement of a liquid, gradually resolving itself into many identities, where nothing would be as it appeared to be but, as in the infinite negotiability that characterizes their social lives, would incessantly cross and re-cross the border between itself and the other in an un-mapping of the heart and mind. A writing in which the quiddity of all appearances would vanish. In which there would stand in its place, agile and quick as a feather, the fragrance of forgetting and discovering, a motion of concealment and surprise. As in the deep seas that surround this bone white archipelago there abound the shapes and shadows of a profligacy of submerged forms of life, so through such prose/poetry, he conjectured, there would move, neither the medium nor the matter which it conveyed being aware of themselves as separate, words so light they would quit the heavier domains of language to ride perpetually here upon the breaking surface of a meaning whose provisionality constitutes the very nature of being itself—weightless, a breath closing over a breath, erasing each trace that it leaves behind.

.

Telephone contact, or correspondence by letter, seemed to mean nothing to them. Once one was out of their physical presence it was as if one had fallen off the edge of the earth. They neither wrote or attempted any other kind of contact with one. One became, one felt, a ghost to them, a person made porous by space and time who could be reconstituted only by appearing again in front of them. Such behaviour has been explained in numerous unsatisfactory ways by observers. One, it is not a scriptural culture but an oral one that places most importance upon vocalisation. Two, they are lazy; for surely nowadays one can pick up a receiver and talk. Three, they are too poor to do the latter. As one ventures, however, under a hot sun out onto their plains and riverways and into their valleys, one notices how predominant living structures are constructed of nothing more than bamboo and sulirap, containing no nails, but tied together by tight knots of dried kawayan or cogon grass and rising around packed earth floors covered with rattan matting. Structures not designed to last, which, in the event of the huge storms which roam this region, will not come down around their ears and injure them. Whether such an architecture is exclusively the result of utility and cheapness is debatable. It does, though, in its acknowledgement of the temporary nature of things bear evidence of a diminished sense of durability, a sense of durability that applies, also, to persons, affecting all of us who live in and then leave these islands for any period. Tenuous and fragile like memory, their habitations float upon the unstable currents of a present upon which, like memory, they are assembled and reassembled many times. Like the structures of such habitations in which they are born, live and die, their reality, too, seems to evolve around an attenuated sense of that continuity that allows it, especially in the case of the presence of absent persons, to transcend prolonged temporal and spatial interruptions. Absence seems to activate an anxiety within them about the very authenticity of things themselves, which only the persistence of a physical, perhaps tactile, presence can assuage. An anxiety that creates a sense of persons as attenuated phenomena extended through space and time.

.

Finally, he had felt at home only in that small hotel by the creek shaded with banana plants where, for hours, as a relief from the monotony of his room, he lingered in the capiz windowed restaurant in the basement, the cool flagstone of the floors easing the ache of his feet and where the waiters, mostly refugees from the war torn lands of the south, generally left him in peace to ponder the faded lace table covers and the slowly yellowing rice grains in the salt sellers absorbing moisture from the air. His grey head nodding in the diffused glare of oyster light, as he corrected the papers of some pupils he tutored in English, he, for some reason, became unusually aware of the comments he was writing in the margin: "Nouns are independent. They are powerful words. They depend on nothing but themselves". Content to be alone, living with no one, sitting there at a table in the still afternoon light he felt the irony and wryness of the implications of what he was writing in this hotel of shadows, of passing bodies and shifting liaisons, where he had chosen to spend his remaining days. For, turning the key in the lock of each noumen of his life, he walked out onto a ledge to find nothing but the sounds of the things that he had, in his earlier days, been half in love with, all those solid objects of his attentions and desires, but which now lay husked in the thin air of this late ontology which he breathed. Looking out the half open door, the leaves of the jackfruit and the breadfruit trees stationary in air, he heard, in the back of his head, the rustle of the sound of that noun "motion", thought he felt it, spelling itself out upon the landscape, as he believed he caught sight of some movement in the air. Looking out again at the trees, and the complete absence of any sign of motion at all, he realized, as if he should have needed to remind himself, that no such object of perception—to see motion when nothing is, or even when it is, moving—is possible, and turned his attention back again to his comments in the margin, and to the hotel of shadows.

## XXII

All the past lingers here you think—all the recent past. You are writing your death even as you sit here moving your pen over paper trying to recover those faded images that fade even more as each day goes by. A familiar face thrusts itself out of space and time and you know you will address it again as you have so many times before, and that it will end as it always does, with the recognition that it is a dialogue you are never destined to have. The unarticulated thoughts and impressions of a lifetime crowd round us. Every minute adds and adds to them. The conspectus, the fluid lineaments, of a further-receded past moves about you and there where a new centre for culture stands, the old train station, its stanchions escutcheoned with coal dust, its wooden floors and single platform pointing far north though loess and snow to a distant destination, appears. All the frissons of its history with it. And beyond, the high ravines and mountains, of the continent that sweeps down to it. All the images of your own life here, and of those that have been recorded and passed on to you, press round you. On the bright waterfront the inexhaustible array of the distant past, its objects and events that carried the seeds of their own death within them, that possessed no inherent or intrinsic properties of their own, swirl within and mix with those of the recent present. Through them, you conclude, we are walking most of the time, not so much through real and actual phenomena but phenomena which have ceased to be immediately registerable on our senses. Alone, each of us, amidst the floating debris of all lived moments known, and unknown, to us.

.

Lingering in damp corners. Between latitudes 14+35 degrees north, longitudes 121+00 degrees east. Of no generally recognisable appearance. Low pressure area slowly advancing onshore. Someone sings from the doldrums of yesterday a low and long tune—in a voice not to be recalled for the grace of its delivery. Precipitation high. Stale shadows stealing towards stairwells. This is how it glowers on the days of our graduation and birth. Sliding silently against an opportunity arising. An absence deciphered in the blossoms of rain. Thick hands turning the page of a book that will not whiten. Chance. O chance, opening a door. Off through the formless streets and hours intertwining. The umbrella thief. With a ragged coat and an incapacitated hand.

.

Extracted from a letter, a kind of unofficial obituary of one of us, which attempts to redress the excessive praise of the official version and which found its way into all our mailboxes in the office the other day. Its biting and unrelieved frankness and accuracy are a rare commodity in the confines of our small community. Perhaps just as well: ... "His anger frequently overwhelmed him, welling up from a source he seemed unaware of. Those close to him, and even complete strangers, were not immune to his furious outbursts. Whether they originated from some deeply abiding source of frustration whose roots stretched back into his earliest days, or whether they were merely the expression of a petulant spoiled nature which no effort had been exerted to control, no one knew. Certainly he was unusually sensitive to being crossed in his endeavours and so his outbursts had more than a little in common with the tantrums children exhibit when they fail to receive what they want. He was not, for example, above resorting to the pathetically obvious, such as simulating defecation after violent gustatory exertions had managed to produce only a paltry amount of transparent viscous fluid, simply to avoid continuing a journey in a vehicle whose motion he claimed was causing him to be nauseous. In fact all he wished to avoid was going to a particular destination. Wary of being thought selfish he resorted to a devious ploy to get his way. Though married a rampant promiscuousness absorbed him, leading him to confuse, or to pretend for the sake of self justification, concupiscence with passion. For, in the end, he had no interest in the objects of his sexual conquest other than as objects of his own sexual gratification. It is likely also that, along with the naivety of one who prioritises the indulgence of his senses into advanced middle age, he had imbibed that ubiquitous sentimentality, a copulatory fantasy, which attributes to sexual intimacy the power of meaningfully bringing people who are complete strangers together. His enthusings for each potential new conquest became tedious, finally, to his friends who increasingly observed behind them not only an unattractive male bravura but, more menacingly, a moral callousness about himself and others" ... Then, one bright blue day of wind and light, he was gone, taken by a cerebral aneurysm whilst in bed with his wife. Sitting, the following day, in the club where he used to drink, the wind fragrant with the scent of green mangoes, some of us wondered whether he had put an end to his philandering, because for the past year or more, tiring of his company, none of us had conversed earnestly with him, aside from the normal courtesies when we met of a greeting and exchange of pleasantries and shop talk, and it was noticeable that he had begun to display the look of an ageing and tired Lothario, as if his body had at last begun to reject all the demands he had made upon it. Was some timely insight into his actual behaviour, finally, we wondered vouchsafed to him?

·

Down the road, escaped from a circus, through the toil and fumes of traffic comes an elephant. Give it a ticket—for going against the flow of traffic. Ticket that verb, too, for being used in violation of what it should denote. Everything moves to a rhythm and a tune not its own. Unassuaged resentment lingers in the sweat of each pore. Give that man a promissory note to pay him on appearance at our office with a purchased copy of the issue in which his writing appeared— no matter that we didn't inform him which one. Give that man a state pension, medical care for life and a state funeral. He has written only one really first-rate short story all his life, but our leader, who reads little, liked it. Newspaper sellers, pushers of ramshackle carts of junk, girls in starched school linens, sweepers of roads, are all texting their personal messages. The air is full of a new language
✳✳✳✳✳✳✳✳✳✳✳✳✳✳✳✳✳✳✳✳✳✳✳✳✳✳✳✳✳✳✳✳✳✳✳✳✳✳✳✳✳✳✳✳✳✳✳✳✳✳✳✳✳✳✳✳✳✳✳✳✳✳✳✳✳✳✳✳✳✳✳✳
(translation): "I am here on the corner of Ambrolio Street. My toe hurts. What are you doing?" An almost naked street corner urchin lolls in the road, oblivious of vehicles, peeling the skin from a fruit off a santol tree. Give him a cell phone. Give him a plan. THIS IS THE PLAN. No signature necessary. Just the print of the thumb : if he still has one. Connect, only connect—to something—to nothing—someone—no one—a circuit, where our voices all drown in a fatuous static.


·


Twilight deepens under the long line of acacia trees. Across the wide plashy fields a vendor, two bright pails of tofu tilting on a beam across his shoulders, makes his way. Beside the road, mothers rest with children. Bats feed on an air suddenly alive with insects. The uncontemplated—a man, life expectancy 75, now 50—contemplates himself. Then ceases. A rivulet gleams as if from a tableau in which for a long time it has been hidden. A breeze rustles the thick impasto of shadows. The seat on which they sat, stays empty. Who is there to observe the sleepy sullen night that comes looking for itself?


·

## OFFICIAL RECEIPT

One brown complexioned woman of indigenous kayumanggi tones, of compact harmonious features, suckling a child through a malong.

One sky of glass shards and splinters.

Multiple appropriated discourses.

One turned over restaurant table: exhibit for the prosecution in a case for injurious loss of self control.

One lyric of endemic loss—from a "culture of feelings" that goes in fear of an intelligence intent upon dismantling the tumescence of ego.

One dead cult of beauty. A beauty which was merely part of a search for a sense of a larger perfection in our lives.

One treatise on the lightness of signs.

One manual on how to invoke illusions.

One copy of "Let Them Go Up As Dust In The Chimneys For We Are Not Coming: Altruism as Antithetical to the Foreign Policies of States."

One tear stained log of voyages never undertaken.

One object, without a subject.

One sculpture exhibiting the sad expression of one who has lived too long away from home.

One quotation from a poem in black maghribi script, its first word in an illuminated sura heading: "Abundant choice that is driving us all crazy."

One anonymous chiaroscuro sketch entitled: 'The Impotence of Nocturnal Reveries.'

One copy of the Onerokritika.

Multiple semen stained rubbings and retablos by disdainers of windows.

16 Balance Due:


**THANK YOU**
**PLEASE COME AGAIN**

# XXIII

According to all the annals and accounts of the history of that far off overseas country that had been the master of its destiny for so many years, it was a country that did not exist. Scavenging the tables of contents for its name became no more than an exercise in otiosity. Only occasionally would it fleetingly appear, under the name of an admiral, in a short footnote that would refer to a naval skirmish with the fleet of another powerful foreign nation, in some remote tropical bay, after which all resistance was quelled and the land taken possession of. For the possessor it was a place where lives were lived within the margin, which did not, in fact, "exist", moving as those lives did, far off under immense green shadows of plantations of pineapples and banana plants. There, behind surf-white littorals, they had never really made any systematic effort to conflate the myths and oral accounts of their own histories—being islanders at heart, not federalists or nationalists. In this land that did not exist, nothing happened, and no one went anywhere at all. When some happened to do so, though, especially at the borders of foreign countries, once they crossed they became invisible again, merged in, and never returned. Down the alleyways of foreign cities all you would hear would be a low brown paean, a song, for somewhere far off. Then that too ceased—along with the memory of the blood of the million invisible people who perished, too, in vainly resisting the wresting of their land from them.

.

The last that we heard of Scarious was that, after washing up safely on the shores of his homeland and resuming his normal routine of leaning at the bar of the local public house all evening, after a day spent fishing or shouting " "owzat!" on the village green, he died, at a relatively young age, of an excess of his favourite poison—whiskey. Reports of how he regarded and characterised us here, in this far flung outpost of a decayed empire, varied—some flattering, some not. If the latter one wondered, being as well qualified as he was, why he bothered to stay all those years. If the former, why he left. We are all a bit of a puzzle not only to each other but to ourselves, neither knowing which way, sometimes, to go nor whether to leave or to stay. Being single, like Scarious, would have only accentuated the demands of such a nature. Often one lingers on too long in the same place, at the same time, when all around one everyone else and everything else is changing. Caught, as perhaps Scarious was, between two opposed identities of place and time, desiring both and, therefore, desiring neither, he settled for the easiest kind of consolation most readily at hand. And perhaps the resulting fumes of that poison, so subtly undermining one's sense of where and when one is, erasing memory and patterns of meaning, only added to his confusion.

.

The same tune takes a different route to search us out and to find us, even though we have not left the place where we first heard it except, perhaps, to travel back towards it through time. And we never think to ask of it where it has been, rather than asking of ourselves that question. Perhaps if we did it would be able to tell us of how, in those squat houses the architect designed to stand under the wind's insouciance, it listened for years to nothing but the lengthening and dissolving of icicles against walls, and learned how to identify, in that distension and breaking of water, the sound of its own fate. And, perhaps, it would describe to us how, afterwards, with oboe, tambourine, flute and viol, it wandered through the courts of many despots and warlords, trying to trade places with the silence of its own memories—for sound, like water, remembers—but no one would listen to its plea. And describe to us how, worn out at last on the roads of an interminable journeying and performing, it eventually stopped and refused to go on remembering and recollecting, for those who played it and listened to it, parts of their own lives. And of how, instead, homesick for that silence from which it had come, it set off out to travel back to it, and meeting with us, again, on the way begged us not to detain it. For, it is said, we have many tunes in our head and the only one we cannot remember is the one which we, because of our inattention, have not heard.

.

One returns like Ulysses, that wanderer of the high seas, and it is as if one is dead, unknown, no one recognises one, to a shore one barely recognises oneself, but which seems to know one. And one has to decide whether to stay or to leave again. And surely there is never really any choice. For this is the archetypal dream in which our pre-conscious minds are always, like flotsam through deserted isles, intimidating yet enticing, moving. The light in the shutters, the smell of brine, are part of the unpunctuated drift, the continua, that Plato would later petrify, but which saturated the air round the ports of that old Ionian coast, where to stand still was to move into those deepest yet clearest of waters. All shorelines recede, converge and break up in them. Even as we are writing on them, as in a log, the date of our entry and our departure, some record of the flora and fauna observed and of the local customs, attire and etiquette, a wave is already lifting us up onto the next ridge of our appointment. One returns to this, and to nothing more. Element of the archetypal, and the unpredictable, on whose pages the sea writes as if it is trying to open a door onto nothing other than ourselves.

.

She died of grief at the passing of nothing but her own illusions, which had become more precious to her than the air she breathed. Used up, she had no further use for anything, not even her children. Asked what those illusions were she would probably have had great difficulty in saying, if, indeed, she was able to understand the question at all. All that she could pin her malaise down to was a vague feeling, a sense that, as she would tell those close to her, the objects around her were no longer capable of holding her attention. Taking vacations, visiting other countries, made no difference; indeed made her only more aware that what she was feeling was not in any sense local. Something seemed to be invisibly drawing a circle through her life, and through everything in it. The seasons broke upon her with the same relentless insistence that everything else in her life broke upon her, neither beginning nor ending, but shading off into many kinds of indeterminate conditions and relations, so that she no longer had any definite sense of where she stood amongst them. When will October come she wondered, one night, walking out onto her balcony. And it was already there. The scent of ripe jackfruit, mangoes and moist soil filling the air, confused her. It was raining across all the events in her life. And where was that exactly? It seemed impossible any longer to establish any precise position with regard to it. She walked back into the middle of the floor of the house and, standing there, considered the possibility that there was not even such a place as a middle to walk back into. In which case where at that moment was she, and where was she going? The warm and fecund air from the balcony, the door of which she had not closed behind her, drifted in and settled about her.

# XXIV

Having spent so many years of her life reporting from places of conflict and unrest was, perhaps, why she was always to be seen attired in the military cut and khaki shades of safari suites. Standing on the curbside, most probably on her way to the Foreign Correspondents Club, which was like a second home to her, she peered out from behind the thick lenses of her glasses waiting for a taxi and waving at almost everything on wheels that approached her. The sounds of battles rang in her ears as easily as the sounds of traffic. As the doyen of foreign correspondents who first covered the conflicts in this region she had stayed on, comfortable in her unassailed position, breathing the tobacco and whiskey laden air of that exclusive club of men and women who courted danger in far off countries to file their story, and who were as familiar with the dark and grimy back streets of eastern capitals as with the palatial residences of their countries' despots and elected leaders. She frequently recalled, in her conversation, the names and the dates of regimes and their personas, of their wars and hostilities, of their scandals and purges and ultimate demise or overthrow. Recalled, also, who covered what in which year, where she was, at a particular time, and what had transpired. She was an archive, virtually, of the continuous folly of being human. Noting the unchanging nature of her attire worn day in day out in spite of seasonal subtropical changes and the absence of any necessity to employ it as the unofficial "uniform" of a war correspondent, for she never, being advanced in years, went on assignment, eking out a lucrative living instead by lecturing, one wondered whether her continued wearing of it satisfied some psychological need of which she was unaware. A need embodied in its semi military camouflage tones and style, perhaps, for a simulacrum of anonymity with which to deflect the effects of her exposure to all that experience of human folly. After most of her life spent reporting from the front lines of human power, mendacity, greed, ambition and aggression, and on their destructive effects, it would not be unreasonable to infer a profound need in her for a feeling of immunity from them, but from, also, a sense of responsibility for their prosecution, for some measure of exculpation in fact. For surely she must have felt that, by for so long voluntarily and profitably putting herself at their centre, she was unavoidably making herself a part of them, making them part of herself; was, that is, in contrast to that anonymity her appearance contrived and which contrasted with that of a combatant for whom it signified the trained suppression of individual responsibility, colluding with them.

.

Lying in hospital with a mortal condition, sheets adhering to perspiring limbs, the hot wind blew through iron window grilles smells and sounds of a country he was not born or grew up in. Sing-song dulcet accents not from the metropolis but some up country northern province. Gradually he felt, after lying there for months on the long and slowly inevitable gradient of decline in a state bordering upon reverie and sleep, the onset of what seemed like moksha where all the differences between yesterday, today and tomorrow, between here and there, melted away. In the throes of what felt almost like the languor of such a vision, he wondered: "why doesn't everyone keep the same time?" But then the pain returned and he realized again that, just as the sounds and smells coming through the window belonged to a borrowed place and time, so the pain too had a borrowed tongue and habitation into which he had wandered and in which he was not at home. "Take me home. You must take me home" the ex-general said to his surviving daughter in the telegram dictated to the nurse at his bedside, the needle of the blood-compass swinging wildly within him. Later, as the pain subsided and a warm stillness again embraced him on the bed where he lay, he cancelled it. He had entered what, he felt, was like a final place he had never been before, a place that was all places and yet was nowhere, that seemed to obliterate all distinct divisions of every place and time he had known.

.

All the newsreels and documentary footage, all the books and all personal accounts of that momentous year, are freighted with similar images. An unusually warm summer through which high banked flotillas of white cloud drifted above a landscape of sleepy villages and lanes, with men and women in the fields contentedly toiling beside hayricks. It is as if posterity wished to suddenly draw a line between a dream time and a waking time, a space in which to let us linger and wander a while, not drawing our attention to those other images that exist, of the decaying slums, of the shadowy corridors of ministries where those who machinated toiled at an activity that no less defines our nature than does that of those in the fields. And so the line was drawn. Looking back, from this side of it, is it any different to those numerous lines we ourselves draw through our own pasts and which then assume the status of an "official history"? In some ways we are no more a part of our own pasts than we are of these collective representations which we subscribe to. We no more own our pasts than they own us. We are deeply implicated in, and yet in a way, not a part of them. They drift, as if in some halcyon or infernal zone of their own making, neither elucidating nor obscuring a present from whose structure they are constituted, and which they, in their turn, reconstitute. We are, rather, located within the intervals of such pasts—outside which the ghostly copula clanks—not in that continuum which they name and allude to and which we allow ourselves to be deluded into believing they have, inherently, forged between themselves and our present.

.

They knew that it would not last. But even then, while it lasted, they knew that it would go on too long. And both, in their silences, wished that the other would not think too harshly of them after they were gone. When the rains came she had sung songs to them, with the same beat that she heard her heart making as he came towards her. A light the colour of bile, and a tincture of phosphorous, lingered on the puddles round her feet when that day arrived. So long postponed! And then, when it was finally there, too soon arrived! And as the thought occurred to her she heard the wet cold wind, heavy with the dolour of everything that breathes and dies, circulating through the trees.

## XXV

Walking for years up and down the avenues and boulevards of this city of memory, it occurs to you, out of the blue, in a way that makes you wonder why you had never before thought of it, that you have been wandering to and fro within a symbolist poem of mortar and bricks, of asphalt and cobbles, all these years. Into the gray bloom of fog in its alleyways and on its quays you have hurried, not so much anxious to evade something as to forge ahead into a place without boundaries, a primordial place, perhaps, where everything begins again, and the slate of the present is wiped clean. Into the enigma of the being of such a place the streets of this city have led you through meandering ways which exhibit, like music, the structure of our remembering and of our forgetting. Surrounded by a profusion of signs and hurrying forward, but in no hurry to name anything, in fact quite the opposite, driven forward, it seems, by a need, personally, to disappear, to be taken along a route which leads you only to a destination perpetually deferred, you have wandered here for years within this enigma. The steps of your progress effortlessly effaced, you sit at the table of a small side street café, listening to the phrase "last orders" announced over and over in a voice whose tone seems to you, in the wry finality of its assertion, to hold the unlikely key to unlocking the enigma of these streets.

.

White ashes from heaven. Snow on the jungle. Never seen, here, before. Snow on the deepest conspiracies of our lives. These cold white crystals of an inerasable indifference. Hell borne. Hell nurtured. From behind a stiff and unbending back, from behind an absence; from behind thick walls and ice-ferned windows, we have come to cultivate the ephemeral outlines of orchids in these damp hot shadows. In the transient pools and tears of our eyes, they bloom. At last, once, a perfection to which we can be witness. And we shall leave, behind us, in these deep jungle clearings, for a little while only, their effigies in stone; bizarre, and unfinished structures, sculpted around a pain, and dedicated—O the cold meal of a misery you cannot know—to all those equally deprived and unfortunate, for whom the snow sows, silently in its wreckage, only the ruined blossoms of a life.

.

Through the high stone strewn fields surrounding the abandoned mining towns, the dust riven ravines and sand saturated air, they come each year, on foot, on their long migration from the heat of their malarial lowlands to gather, in a twilight of thin dews, the pale vented cap and stalk of what grows close to the ground, steeping and cleaning it in clear streams on their way back. But the place they go back to bears no resemblance to where they came from. For what is there, any longer, without the names to designate them, to hold them on that rugged illusory curve of their being, that pre-choreographed spatio-temporal dance of their senses? Names have no home, they wear out. Into the small iguana skin pouches tied at their waists all the names of their world have, by the priests, been ceremoniously deposited. In a prepared sacred circle, opening them, they dance, the dust from their heels rising, mingling the sound of those names with the earth and air again from which they came, until, continuing the dance, they are alone in a place where nothing, including themselves, is any longer designated, and where time and space are uninferable because the very notion of an object or thing has disappeared. Against the rusting body of an old abandoned pick up truck at evening one of them leans. In the quiet ontic air he can hear the exhausted and parched field of former references sigh, and he knows that he and his companions have brought to it in time, again, their vow to release and rest it from the interminable labour of yielding that entire array of phenomena amidst which they live. After the silence of days of not eating, drinking, sleeping and speaking—even thinking—they re-enter that circle again and, resuming the dance, rename the things, methodically and carefully, and themselves, before they depart out of the high stone strewn fields of those mountains, back to where they came from.

.

Behind the dust dimmed windows of the library the lamp threw a diffused yellow aureole over the desk where, for days, she, the local schoolteacher, had been coming to sit, opening the same book which she took down from the shelves, and crouching over it with an intense gaze. Unable to read its highly stylized script, bearing a resemblance to the liturgical markings on a hymn scroll examined once in Kirghizia, a script which, it seems, is a variant of the orthodox script of these islands, one of our colleagues, a determined amateur linguist who has mastered not only the local patois but its writing script too, became intrigued. Evidently, he discovered, this book that she so prized, had been translated, and translated, in fact, by her. Its original manuscript, in English, he failed to obtain knowledge of the whereabouts of but he had a great curiosity to see it. The book was a translation of a collection of poems in

English, a collection whose tattered manuscript had been left in the room of its author, with his few other meagre possessions, when he died. The translator, knowing him well, if not intimately, upon being informed that he was not destined longer for this world, agreed to act as a kind of literary executor for him. Being unable, upon his death, to contact any of the publishers at the addresses abroad which he had left her, they having, perhaps, no interest in the manuscript and not bothering to reply, she, out of a sense of guilt at having failed him, took upon herself the task of translating it, instead, into her own language and meeting the expense of printing it on an inexpensive rough gray paper produced here from a compound of rags and leaves, and publishing it. His verses, hardly read in his own country and language, now transposed into the writing system of an obscure hill people, wait for a barefooted reader on the shelf of the ramshackle library nestled in the shadow of a mountain where, each evening, the sulphur crested cockatoos ascend in screeching pairs to the kaimito trees to roost.

.

One wakes to the headline **NO COUP** as one would wake to a headline announcing a decision that had, after months of negotiations, deliberation and discussion, been reached by a parliamentary committee. Here coups, like rumours of rate hikes, or increases in the price of rice or oil, are common. Especially when the investigation of a top member of the government for plunder coincides with a series of power outrages and the capital is plunged, often at a time of cataclysmic tropical storms, into the unrelieved heat and darkness of a power failure, people brace themselves for a military take-over. On striated curbs are the track marks of a troop carrier left as an insignia of the last coup. But today the electrical grids are intact, and the traffic lights blink nervously at all the major intersections of the capital. The uniformed policeman is asleep at midday in his usual spot beneath the agoho tree, beside the road to the airport, where only civilian traffic moves, at a snail's pace. In the heat he breathes easily. And the troop carriers stand idly behind the walls of the army's central barracks, the sounds of shouts from their basketball court being the only indication of any sense of urgency.

## XXVI

You sit among the embers of a dying day. Soft glow of light in the west. Across the plain a cloud drifts: the ghosts of people and places you do not remember. Beneath this shroud of a landscape of forgetting, though, you ARE. If everything could be remembered and accounted for it would constitute simply a ledger of entries. In that quiet and boarded up house by the side of the road, your life began and ended—to the remote sounds of days lost in innumerable distractions and deliberations. Days which have still not, you feel, abated; whose consequences, and those of the days which followed them, have not ceased or passed out of the bourne of your existence but continue that elaboration of all that you are. Someone must have, you muse, left the door open, for you to have walked in. During gray days of music and rain you heard and saw nothing, save only dissolved whispers, rustled leaves like the footsteps of the dead leaving, as you arrived. And the soft glow, from the flames in the grate, on the wall of the bedroom; that quietness of a room in which your being first became apparent to you. To this twilight room you always return at the end of the day, drawn to this spot on the embankment under the ipil-ipil trees, as if to those "first days" years ago, and those subsequent days with their cargo of action and reflection, whose consequences, your frail rationality still insists, expired long ago.

.

She, out of the corner of her eye, noticed him as she walked by, sitting outside the brasserie under the awning, his notebook open on the table, pen poised, looking at her, her hair dark as a crow's wing and cut diagonally across her face. Disdaining to return his gaze she walked on. She was there, too, at the ruined towers of Ilium, smoke in her eyes, in the garden in Debacles, as transient as the snow itself, and moving, heavy as a shadow, through the dove gray light by the wharves of the Liffey. And, surely, she brings nothing to rest for long—she is there, now, at the moment of your reading, before you. In the changing outline of that face, the shifting dance of those mythical feet across a dark unthreshed floor, is instantiated the dance of all the incomplete objects of our perception. For perception takes place on a ground not of our own making. It provides us with images of ourselves which we can, ultimately, neither verify nor deny the authenticity of because we cannot make our own subjectivity, of which they are a part, an object. Exteriority/interiority mesh on this dark unthreshed floor of our lives where we sit, looking, "capturing within the net" of our senses and our words, a loping fritillary. Its scent, which is also our own, we inhale deeply, in a desperate attempt at a flight out of ourselves, at an "ek-stase".

.

In the gray days and nights of a northern continent they had heard the mournful strains of a musical instrument that consisted of no more than an oblong sound-box with a long neck and single string which the seated player, placing on the ground between his feet, bowed. From it, there floated a sound as solid and as ephemeral as that of the snow goose, a disembodied wheezing and groaning of air squeezed under the wings, heard, or half-heard, above the trees at evening, a flake encrusted shadow; or a sound that floated above the alleyways and spires, as ever present as that ice smog that lay like a heavy sacrament of crystal above the frozen city, lugubrious yet glistering. It was a sound whose movement had something, too, of the qualities of smoke, not least in its fluidity and flexibility, but also in the way in which smoke makes manifest the invisible currents of the air itself: so, in the sounds of this instrument, seemed to materialize emotions which the listener had only half guessed at before. Listening to it they felt themselves entering a region with their ears and their eyes half closed and their cheekbones sloped back to a question. It was, above all, a sound fecund with the sense of a distance not yet travelled. They merely set out in it, but they never arrived. And, as a consequence, they found themselves drawn, again and again, back to it. Through it they became aware of crossing frozen borders, toiling above immense plains where to have put down their foot would have been to have instantly been lost, and of entering endless forests only, finally, to find themselves stepping down, alone, at night on the black ice of a railway track, at a halt outside a town with a name they had never seen before, the crisp ground of the tundra crackling beneath their feet, the frozen handle of a carriage door in their hand, from which their fingers could never be prised.

.

You stand, for one moment, amidst the fading tenements of a final affair. The linen on the bed is still crisp, as you fold it back to reveal the inevitable farewell. The harbour glittering in the heat beyond the window. The acrid odour of salted fish and of dried squid. The city rebuilds itself around a past you had forgotten, only for a moment. The sadness of a day—its stale music. In the same place, and at the same time, another history is, with yours,

111

interwoven; and, within that, another, and another, an entire network, into which you enter and leave, and enter again. Beyond these, the rumour of a vast music, of which your own particular chord is the only one which, for you, resonates clearly. And even then, at times, the tone falters and can't be heard. Mildewed menus specify what, on a precise day, was consumed, and where. A brocaded handkerchief, left on the pillow, resigns you to the ineluctability of mementoes. Where does that leave the marriage, of which you expunged all records—the torn up photographs, the red invitation cards, and so much more? Whoever conducts the massed orchestra which plays the music from which our time is alembicated, must have a sore arm. All the transitions, the refrains and motifs, are inscribed in air—no need, at least, for a score—along with the rhythms, notes and keys. One day you will listen in to your part in all this. You will hear, between a welter of unresolved, conflicting chords, the sound of a dream, departing. And, through faded tenements, the sound of a fog, with two bells and one horn in it. That is all.

.

Out of the mists clinging to the water of the canal, in the warm languid air of that southern sugar cane country, he came, silently, as if rending a veil, like a figure from an ancient poem by a recluse, or from a scroll painting, standing, with the wooden handle of his sweep in his hands, his hair falling in a long tail behind him. Seemingly immobile, he glided, only a faint ripple of water brushing his prow. On steps by the canal, villagers, doing their washing, raised their heads to look at him as he went by. His eyes, focused ahead of him, showed no signs of being deflected. Miles away, over the level fields, a car turned in from the road. When he had gone, it was as if he had taken with him, on those few slender planks of wood with a cabin of rattan, a momentary image and left, in its wake, a permanent puzzlement, something unsettling in the eyes of those on the steps, which they seemed, even after walking back to their houses, to be struggling with. Along with the rice in their bowls that evening they still turned that disturbing fragment over in their minds. Then, silently, withdrew to their beds, without saying a word about it. A ripple of light, through banks of far cane. A tilted blade. An old injunction: "Let the river become your book. Read from it every day."

# XXVII

When time has exhausted itself, when it no longer has anywhere to travel to, as in the motion of the train taking you back to the place of your childhood, all your earlier acquaintances being either scattered elsewhere or dead, and your parents gone, a silent place, with only the sound of the trees and the lanes and river, seems to rush towards you filling you with a light full of eviscerated shadows where the wind rustles delicately over grass as if an unseen hand was about to be placed upon your shoulder and a form, your own, a former one, about to appear before you. In such a place all momentum through time and space ebbs, and, as with the tide gone out, you find yourself having entered a stillness that is neither of the past or present but which seems to breathe, in the air of a strifeless moment, that arcanum from which they both are drawn. So you sit, at the edge of a small town or village, upon a deserted platform. The breeze is turning the undersides of the leaves up in tree after tree and a thick scent of hellebore or of vetch emanates from an unseen arbour, with the scent of azaleas from the station's borders. At such a time, in that country of no arrival and departure, where timetables do not exist, the odour of creosote from warm sleepers, and the stained white glare of chips of granite, indicate a state of being that has exhausted itself with time. Between its disused tracks marigolds and dandelions grow, and the quiet flower of rust, under the metal rails, blooms with a wild abandonment, listening for the wheels that will not come, watching for the signal that is permanently down.

.

Like members of an audience in a cinema for the blind, we sit in front of a blank screen whose images remain dark to us; the sound, only, of voices and things and of silences, penetrating to us. Midwinter snow falls outside on the sidewalks and on the pedestrians who pass by. Its flakes as ephemeral as the flicker of shadows across the screen we cannot see before us. The souls of all the massacred indigenes have not risen up from beneath the malls and asphalt of the parking lots of the city to reclaim their rightful inheritance, as some predicted they would. Instead they maunder on desolate reservations or inhale the smoke of peace in casinos of their dreams. The idea of trespass should, surely, by now have become redundant, instead of being enshrined in laws. Like the sound of a sewing machine the projector catenates each image. We listen, to the sound of the flakes falling outside. Like motes in a beam of light we imagine them settling on our eyes. The cold intricate shape of a crystal forms in our mind. The voice of a person whom we know no longer exists, fills our ears. The charge of a cavalry troop destined to destruction. Like the residue of past lives. Someone sings: "Something that happened for the first time, seems to be happening again ...but I don't remember where, or when." In this great crucible of the uncorroded, we wait. Held in a beam of intense light, lips still touch lips, that are dead. The cold air from outside begins to seep in through the walls and under the doors. Someone screams out from high up in the "Gods": "Repeal all the laws of ownership and of property. Reparate us for our loss."

.

So where you come from does not exist, and where you are heading for, too, is in no topology mentioned. Victims of maps, and of the hastily drawn ontology of things, we easily lose our way. Someone gestures and points from a high window opened in the rain on a warm afternoon murmurous with bees, and we follow the direction they indicate without thinking. For a moment a new space seems to extend before us, the gilded gondolas of a ferris-wheel in late afternoon sun rising and falling above a city whose tamarind trees are mute beneath the screams. Then, as the water in the reservoirs begins to fall beneath the critical mark, the taps hiss at us, and a vacuum floats over and fills our days and ears. Like the bird in the hedgerows that is always singing as we pass, the black heart of an emptiness grows until everything that we have posited hangs, in that warm summer afternoon air—waiting. A wind wafts amid the tapestry of trees and light and we know, then, that there will always be this feeling as if everything is waiting, looking at us. At a curve in the road we halt, and listen; to that profound silence of the distance through which our lives have travelled, and through which they reach to us, here. Tyre tread marks on the road, a path of flattened wheat in a field. All the obvious signs of a presence have been removed.

.

Brushing against the branches of the calabash tree, a wind flutters the leaves and, snagged in the fork of a branch, catching the eye, is a thin piece of paper. It turns out to be what might be considered either an eccentric "philosophical fragment" by some homespun sceptic, tossed into the air to join all the other minutiae that scurry and fly into that element of dispersion, an effort, perhaps, at some momentary respite, or a wry concise comment upon its author's economic plight. It leaves off in mid-sentence. Of greyish blue tint it is a dated perforated ticket from the Palabuano Pawnbrokers of Legani Street in Tinondo, promising to redeem to the bearer, a Mr Arturo Azurin of Basilio Street in Tinondo, for the sum of one thousand racattos, plus accumulated rates of interest and storage charges, if any, the said items/effects. In the columns our, eponymous? depositor has inserted:

One footprint on the dark step where Mr Azurin went out of the store, on the above day, and stumbled.

The beginning of an unuttered phrase Mr Azurin had half formed in his head on the same morning, as he crossed the street.

The blue wash of an ocean round a coast Mr Azurin had visited in his youth with his parents and wishes to return to.

The shadow of the hand that falls across this ticket as it is

.

The old post office stands shedding its plaster skin that once used to be white but which, over the years, has yellowed, wrinkled and cracked under the fierce onslaughts of sun and monsoon rains. One passes into it through a small courtyard in the centre of which is a dust covered jackfruit tree heavy with ripe fruit, beneath which a beggar sits proffering his deformities and an open palm, uttering rapidly the opening verses of the Quran. Inside, light dwindles from a furnace intensity to a glaze within which is a profusion of shadows—inside them people, seeking refuge from the heat outside, lounge. From floor to ceiling, beneath the dank seeping spread of stains from leaking water, shelves bulge with bundles of papers and files. Unopened for the past sixty or more years their darkened twine has fused into the pulp of the contents it encircles. Containing no more than the records of registered correspondence and packages sent and received during those years since 1932, perhaps concealed within them, too, and now slowly becoming so fragile that they would disintegrate at the slightest touch, exist some of those important documents lost during the final violent and hectic days of the partition of this sad country, before its last governor left. In that rampant turmoil, lodged, perhaps, for a moment's safe keeping, the courier, seeking a temporary respite from the anarchy of the streets, determining to return and to collect the documents he was charged with delivering, either fell prey to the violence itself, or was forced to flee, along with millions of others, across the borders of the neighbouring country. So they remained here, in this damp dilapidated interior of a small and obscure post office in the east of the country, their secrets slowly softening into a pulp that would eventually, over the years, turn into a fine dust. Secrets, maybe, of a nature that might have thrown an entirely different complexion upon the official history of the version of events leading up to the division of this country.

.

Even in this far away place, during the long unbearably humid summers, when the cries of the noodle vendors from streets on the hillside above his house woke him and the sound of visitors to the temple nearby drifted up to him, he wandered out from under the deep eaves above his verandah and lingered, as if he had been at home back in his own country, pottering on a sun blessed morning among the marigolds and delphiniums, the borders festooned with pansies and lupins. Instead, though, here, the roots of the banyan trees that he trod upon came feeling, also, for his face, and in the thick clumps of bamboos the blue tailed magpies clattered and shrieked as if they were being persecuted. That extinct pastoral, which beat like a ground-note through everything he wrote, still pursued him amidst this white space of sun and heat, into which the hibiscus and the jasmine poured their rich philtre of scent. Below the timber house the narrow streets zigzagged down the mountainside, those congested with market stalls taking a straight line to the bottom, to the edge of a harbour into which, now and then, the bloated bodies of political refugees fleeing from the mainland sometimes bobbed and drifted for days. The desiccated scrub of the high hills on the opposite shore revealed the marks of tracks beaten down by grass gatherers over the years and, even longer ago, by carriers of the cuttings from fragrant trees used in the processing of incense. Here, the images of that distinct carnage that had once filled his dreams every night, and, as with every other young man involved in it, imprinted themselves indelibly upon his being, still lingered. And this garden, with its fulgurous reds, its inter-twinings, pricking, only sometimes, like the fierce entanglements of a memory unrepressed, stood like a bulwark against that harsher inner landscape, and soothed and fed the gentle blooms of the words of his imagination, and of his next collection of poems.

# XXVIII

On the wall of the classroom, on a large hand-drawn map of the world, a breeze gently lifted the thin tissue of orange and lemon wrappers pinned there. Fragrant skins, impregnated with the scent of space, distance and air. Held up to the light, of which they seemed a raiment, inhaled. Crinkled tracings of what was both within and beyond, but not you. Embossed, englobed on them, the names; Cadiz, Seville, Córdoba ... sounds, that had their jurisdiction in no place at all, in which their being was a continual shadow, an effulgence upon the wall (beneath which the hand struggled to break up the "scriptio continua" into a series of discrete sounds) of every formulated meaning. Beyond the window, light, and air, and distance. That continual lament of time. Was it here that the flavour of all those impending journeys, all those travails and circumambulations to come, in search of a loved object, of a thing without a form or name, in search of the radiance of an absolute "home", began?

.

From his room on the upper floor of the small pension he could see through the window the rim of Bayon, the old and still active volcano, home, according to locals, of the Fire God, a great swathe of blue vapour rising in the evening to the top of its cone and clinging there. On the bedside table alongside him stood a bottle of corusca, the yellow and slightly sweetish mash fermented from sugar cane, and whatever other ingredients happened to have been at the disposal of the particular distiller at the time of its brewing. He lay and watched the range of hills and mountains beyond the small triangular dusty fields of maize, obsessed by them. The division between the land and sky held for him the same fascination which as a boy, moving at the edge of a town beyond which he knew the sea lay, that sheer and palpable sense of invisible expanse, of a limitlessness unfurling itself towards a far off liquid sheen of horizon, held for him—before he could see it. He remembered too, as a boy, waking in the cold air of a morning and sensing, in the unusual depth of the silence and paler than usual light, the thin opaque skein of ice upon the panes of the window behind the curtain and, beyond that, on the wide white fields and roof-tops. Looking, now, at the smoking sides of Bayon, feeling the sharp descent of the corusca burn his throat, he realised that it was not so much the condition of boundlessness as his own boundedness which such sensations had evoked in him. Often, he surmised, under the guise of a particular condition which we think we are observing, there is, in fact, another, quite opposite condition which is observing us.

.

Compass, table and concordance sing in a twilight of rooms whose doors open into and out of each other, whose songs are a sound those crossing over that threshold at birth, and who do not seem to know any distinction between pleasure and pain, hear. A thin pool of light rain lies upon the palm there, unmeasured and unweighed. The unheard frost of a dawn. The breath of a day that does not know what to call itself. Beyond a porch and a swinging lamp a road sign points into the dark, and crickets sing with a dense music. Do they, too, hear what, in those twilit rooms, has no echo and cannot be imitated; that which, squandering itself upon the air, is endlessly, it seems, returning to where it did not set out from?

.

And in this new republic of fake healers, con-men, and politicians whose sole motive for "serving the public" was the venality of office, the old practice of reciting novenas in a time of pestilence was revived and rapidly spread. Visiting foreign celebrities interviewed by the press about their impressions of the capital, and whose observations about garbage infested streets and odoriferous canals were less than flattering, were publicly denounced and told that they'd never be allowed to return by politicians who, themselves, daily threw more dirt and ordure upon the reputation of the country than a whole host of any such visitors possibly could. Artworks, resembling those depicting the hedonistic and self-indulgent society of Berlin in the 1930s, flourished and filled the galleries. Whilst the majority slaved to make ends meet, and frequently not meet, many of those who should have been pursuing the task of forging the uncreated identity of a new nation, its poets and fictionists, instead, pampered their egos with rewards and prizes, writing poems and stories of great unoriginality derivative of the literature of their recently departed masters, the poems embroidered with token references to local mythologies. Such writing, at its worst, breathed an air of unreality or of a swooning softness indicative of the writer's inability to fully engage with the nature and experience of their surroundings. In Faculties of Letters in universities, in an ethos of personal patronage, advanced degrees were supervised, examined and awarded by colleagues who were also close friends of the awardees. In publishing, editorship withered in this atmosphere where all attempts at creating a neutral intellectual space were thwarted by the coveted rule of self-interest. So the "good times" rolled on, the fiestas multiplied on the thin top-soil of a culture that possessed no written body of indigenous work that had reflected objectively upon the nature of meaning and existence. Such a soil as there was, most of its writers manured with their devotion to themselves. And so the novenas recited in a time of pestilence continued, too.

.

They sat watching, hour after hour, the thin white oozings of sap into tin cans beneath the shade of the almaciga trees, the resin gatherers. Dark faces within the splinterings of light that broke again and ran, like water, as the wind moved the foliage. On hillsides, outside dusty villages and small towns, the sound of their tapping, mistaken sometimes for that of woodpeckers, then silence. The drift of cigarette smoke through the heat. Then a trail of scarred grey bark, by which they could be followed. Cicatrice, through the dark grove, bleeding the tenebrous fluids of the earth. Their measured tread, and tapping. A keeping time, with a rhythm they knew and did not know. Like a slow stalactite dripping in a cave of shadows.

## XXIX

A minor copyist at the Ministry of Documents, in the dark city of Hagrapolis situated in the torrid heat of a delta, he bent from early morning to evening above a scuffed wooden desk top reproducing, in a neat almost vertical hand, the tedious contents of official summonses and injunctions, a task whose dullness he found daily more and more irksome. When it became time for the mid-day repast he would take himself off out of earshot of his fellow colleagues. They gathered, with their spiced breads and pickled meats, at the end of the enormous room in which they daily toiled, and conversed energetically about ministry affairs or their girlfriends, or what went under the guise of the latest form of popular entertainment. Outside, through the thick adobe walls and stained windows, he was aware of the muffled sounds and shadows of the city, of life itself, he thought. Into that indistinct hubbub at mid-day he took himself, for as long as he thought he would not be missed, wandering the back streets and alleys, absorbed by the odours of foodstalls, the artful arrangements of poultices and potions under the glass cases of apothecaries, but especially by the small vendors of secondhand books and manuscripts at which he lingered like a wasp around a jar of molasses. Into the gloom of the ministry he returned, a barely noticed absence, to take his place at the scuffed wooden desk of his space, his head ringing with lines from the latest quasida by Merva, composed in a controversial amalgam of the speech of the cantonments and a local dialect heard more often in the market places than in respectable homes. As he repeated over and over in his head the ornate metre of its first line and its subtle rhythms, the more he felt the noose of that enormous room and its desktops tighten around him, until the air itself and his very future began to turn black—black as the river Godansku, with its dead dogs and poisonous fogs, that flowed through the centre of the city.

.

When Answar, the cabinet maker, was set the task by his friend the local barber who had lost his lower leg a while ago in an accident and who, because of his inability to stand unaided, was imminently in danger of losing, too, his means of livelihood, Answar obliged with enthusiasm, studying the drawing that his friend had been given by an old customer who owned a small workshop producing prosthetic limbs. Answar, his educated friend, he had explained to the customer, was in dire economic need having run out of orders. The customer "understood"—on condition that the drawing would be returned to him as soon as Answar had finished. In fact Answar's indigence was simply one reason. His acknowledged skills as the best carpenter in the town was another. Seeing Answar poring over the drawing night after night Answar's brother, a merchant in the provincial capital, unaware of the act of friendship which the order constituted, let forth a flow of sententious comment upon the disabled saying they should stay in their villages not go wandering and begging, that their hobbling gait was an offence to the eye that was always seeking an image of perfection. We all fall short in many ways, Answar thought, of such an ideal. Life itself almost continually fails to aspire to deliver what we wish it would deliver. He sensed that his brother's tirade was simply an expression of his bourgeois notion of visual decorum, and that it had as much to do with a merchant's not wanting the disabled loitering and begging in front of store windows as anything else. How much, though, Answar thought, is our dislike of images of imperfection fuelled by an implicit awareness of the existence of such imperfection within ourselves and our own behaviour. Are all our categories, by which we measure the world and each other, he wondered, just notions that do more harm than good because, at the end of the day, they do not possess an absolute value—in some societies, he had read, to be thin, as a woman, as if one cannot afford to buy food, was to be considered attractive. I am sure, he pondered, that the person with one leg, because there is a limit to the amount of personal baggage which they can carry, gets to go through the gates of heaven no more slowly, probably, in fact, a lot more speedily, than the person with both.

.

O the pale tropics, desuetude and languor, to which we long to return. "Pale" because, according to the common misconception in these parts, the sun does not always shine there; indeed, for a good part of the year it can be seen, through a dense spume of monsoon rains, only fitfully. But felt always, in all its varying expressions of heat. Like the ubiquitous camphor and eucalyptus of those neuralgic balms so popular here, it works its way, unseen, to the source of some deeply lodged and concealed pain. A pain that is both palpable and yet indefinable, that seems to have no precise locus within the body, but permeates one's being. A pain that is as much the result, perhaps, of a longing as of any perceived physical ill. Does some dark Pleistocene ice still grip the heart of those of us in these far northern latitudes? And yet, after a few years dwelling on warm shores, the longing returns, only this time it is that silent whiteness of the cold with its snowy drift that grips the heart. Gone is the soft sun-fringed littoral, welcomed back is that hard dry air, that iron ground that strikes through the foot. Just as the magnetic poles of the earth are supposed to reverse over long periods of time so do our own emotional poles alternate within us, our north becomes south and our south becomes north, only within a much shorter period of time.

.

On every shelf, in almost every store of every size, bars and bottles of cleanser that whiten the skin. The clean aquiline features of a pale complexion on labels. How else, being themselves "unclean", having almost exterminated the indigenous population whose lands they stole and then settled in, should they purge their own guilt but by projecting its shadow upon others? Especially since, here, in this region of equatorial light, their pigmentation obliges. Bales, on the quaysides, not of corn or other staple products but, in an old advertisement, of Pears soap; brightening the dark corners of the earth … lightening the white man's burden (sic). No burden. Just keep remitting the profits. Some things never change. In small print on the labels the names of foreign multinational companies (still). Following the surplice and sword what better weapon to truly vanquish, even after you have left, than the exclusive commercial image everyone wants to identify with, even if it does turn them against their natural shade and hue, and make them look down on themselves. What better way to "govern" a populace than, rather than exterminating it, making it economically and psychologically dependent?

.

At first, hearing her name murmured gently under the upli tree in the gardens down by the river, a light dew beginning to fall on her skin as the light faded, she murmured back the name of the one who had shaped it, its sound lingering on her breath, a wisp of gold tinder, like the muted fire at the centre of the leaves of the rain tree at mid-day. The sound of the voices of people walking along the promenade some distance away filtered back to her, like the tinkling of water. As the sound of the dry leaves beneath her, though, became an increasingly agitated rustle, and she remembered some lines from one of his poems about the sound of oarlocks and then the slap of water at the sides of a rocking rowboat momentarily tethered under shadowy willows on a lake, she was taken completely by surprise when she heard him no longer uttering her name, but passionate invocations to his "Mother"; a name which, though it transcended her, made her feel as if her flesh had become the fragrant ambrosia of a god-like devotion to an all-mothering One. Of all the rakes and profligates I have known, she thought, and I have known a goodly number, none is more mystical by nature than the one who composes verses.

# XXX

There is thunder over the plain that you are leaving. Or there is lightning, but no thunder. Either way, the rain does not come. The molave and the red gum trees sway in a breeze that might or might not betoken a storm. Clouds of exhaust fumes spill over the nearby highways and drift up to compose a yellowing, contused sky. Dust rises in the heat off beaten-earth tracks. They, too, wait amid the glare of a mid-day sun, as if for something to happen. Not to defy some point of balance is to disturb that equilibrium upon which all life rests. Disturbed, life is, though, never restored exactly to what it was. Clouds race across the far off ring of mountains. Perhaps you will return. Perhaps you will not. The smell of lunch, bitter-gourd and fat, is rising from the kitchen beneath you. Someone in the courtyard, inebriated, is bidding the caretaker goodnight.

.

O dear, where in the world can one these days park one's money? Pity the poor police officer who has amassed a small fortune after years of hard work and who is having difficulty investing it in some laundromat abroad. Numbered or alias accounts in the country are very risky these days. And even the Hordellos can only continue to enjoy their wealth at the risk of great humiliation—if that still matters to the woman enamoured with black holes. Haven't you heard how frequent her headaches are these days? So where can poor officers splurge some extra cash? Harassed they tried to burn their money in those expensive nightclubs in Brazon City until last week when remnants of the Turakong Labeleng gang tore through it going from cubicle to cubicle (O sorry, "private room" is what they are called) holding up customers. Yes, including some officers. Our advice is: stay away from clubs and any place where you could burn money. These are difficult times and the farmers and fishermen and millions of slum dwellers are watching how the elite mock them by flaunting their wealth. Laundering money is the toughest challenge these days. Stop looking for places to park your money. Maybe you might even consider returning it or finding ways to return it through civic duty. What's a community day care centre worth, or a tiny centre for the elderly? Or a donation to the city library? Try it, you'll find it's better to give than receive. Finally, stop looking for big bucks because they spell trouble. Rich people always have a problem with money; when they die their relatives often scramble to keep the death under wraps for as long as possible, in order to "fix" the bank accounts, certificates, titles and other assets or to scoop out the jewels from the deposit box. When they're still alive it's also a problem; explaining the provenance of the money is the hardest part. Ask Repella. Her eldest daughter Arleta heartily agreed when journalists attending last Saturday's Coconut Planters Bank's new headquarters opening said, "People with money are always miserable, far more miserable than ordinary people like us." Arleta waved her hand: "O my God yes, you're so right. Looking after one's money is such a headache." Amen.

*[The South Inferiganga Coast Times editorial: May 11th 2003]*

.

Out of the hot night a voice streamed into your ear. The invective of a thousand nights. And then broke off, just as abruptly, with a drunken curse. You did not know whether he was with her, or not; except that you weren't. Imperiled by your broken leg you decided, though, to stay in the house where you were, rather, than as advised, put up elsewhere. *Love for sale.* A carload of goons in the parking lot, windows open, feet poking out, smoking. An offer declined. Peremptory disappearance into the dark; where the lies accumulated, the phantom abortions, and the "emergencies." *Fresh, only slightly soiled.* O into that pitch black night you went. Why, O why, a newspaper held up before her face, a dearth of conversation, could you not see? An autopsy, so long drawn out. On the withered tree you hung your crutch. *Who's prepared to pay the price?* What dog scratched those initials in the bark to retrieve the bone at another date? A scabrous totem. A defiled bed—exorcising the stain of that need. You fled, with nothing but your naivete about you.

.

Somewhere beneath the handepara and buri trees, in the orchard that ran down to the wide silt coloured river, her grandmother, the exact location unknown by anyone but herself, had dug a hole one evening in the dark soil and placed in it, a few months after her birth, the remains of a part of her grand-daughter's placenta. Listening to her grand-daughter recount the tale, she who had wandered across many parts of the world and who had been born in a country far from the one in which that orchard grew but for whom that country had become the focus of her identity, listening to her his mind went back to the house where he himself had been born one late January morning, and, despite the fact that he had spent almost his entire adult life wandering outside that country, being temperamentally unattuned to it, to the details of that room in which he had continued to sleep until he was

124

five. Now, approaching the final quarter of his life and having become, he decided, incapable of settling anywhere for any considerable length of time, he found that her story had a particular resonance for him. The road and the house of his birth, he remembered. But who, he wondered, had been present in that room on that particular winter morning to deliver him and had, afterwards, walked, anonymous midwife in a grey skirt and jacket, out of the gate with that umbilicus, only to discard it, for all he knew, to the four corners of the wind. Recollecting the account of the scattered remnants of Osiris he entertained, for one moment, the thought that another Anubis might be found to recombine for him those parts of himself that he supposed must have, at one time, constituted an entity rather than what, now, he felt he was—a fragile aggregation of continually dispersed fragments. What buried root could take hold of him now, he wondered? What soil, except an abstract landscape unnourished by his being, could flower with a fragrance for him that he would recognise as his own? No doubt I shall, he concluded, knowing of no particular place into whose rich earth my umbilicus has been placed, have to wait like Osiris until I enter the land of the dead, for such a unification.

.

To someone coming from a land of vast prairies and plains, or even from a land of more modest proportions, the gleaming rails stretching, seemingly endlessly, into the distance summon up not a narrowing but a widening of a perspective whose bridges and viaducts span an immensity of space within them. Into this vista the lonely sound of a locomotive whistle fades and, with it, a caboose of dreams, growing smaller and smaller as they stand rooted to the spot from which it departs. So it comes as a shock to the new arrival when they step up to the tracks here to take in the anticipated long vista of the lines and they behold, between those lines, nothing but a thick sprouting of grass and weeds, in the midst of which are, sitting at tables, people. Entire families, the plywood walls of their shacks tilting just inches away from where the infrequent locomotives pass, are, as it were, at picnic. Animals, children and adults, compressed into and milling within that long avenue of obstructed air and light. To them it is home. To the unacquainted observer it is more like the desecration of space. There, amidst the clutter and the debacle of human habitation, distance and motion end. And, with them, because such qualities are at the very heart of such a visitor's culture, hope. Perhaps, however, those in the middle of the tracks have learned to latch their dreams to something other than that lonely caboose which diminishes into the distance across the unpopulated prairies of the mind of such a visitor. Perhaps, having nowhere else to latch them to, they have, instead, attached them to each other.

# XXXI

Ageing, he had wandered off, much to the dismay of his eldest daughter with whom he had for numerous years lived, and made his way into the upland villages of the province where he had been found one morning by some villagers, lying by the side of the road in a ditch where he had fallen after stumbling during the night. Unable, because of the amnesia with which he was afflicted, to tell them his name and where he came from, they searched his pockets and were able to find, written down on a piece of paper designed for just such an emergency, an address and the name of a person to contact. He had, it seems, in spite of the obfuscating clouds of that condition, moved like a shade, unaided, but inevitably, across that wide lethaean gulf between the present and the past in which he lived. Moved slowly, tentatively and circuitously. But moved, and towards a *where* that appeared to have, by some means unknown to anyone, escaped that erasure that had affected almost everything else in his life. He must have walked back, through those narrow dust filled roads that climbed the heights of a changing vegetation, into a shadow land where his senses had laid down a "road" for him dissolving the juncture between subject and object and which, mile by mile, grew more familiar to him until the solid stone houses and the cobbled streets of his birth, laid out in a regular pattern, appeared. They affirmed for him, perhaps, less a place than, as in a composition of sounds, a particular arrangement: all the landscape between where he had set out from and where he eventually stopped, unfolding before him in a subliminally registered terrain. Vibrations of line, shape, colour and smell reactivating leitmotifs and traces his conscious mind had no explicit "memory" of.

.

Setting off we depart, however temporarily, from a domain of the familiar, leaving behind a house and family, a friend or lover, or a rented room only where a valued painting hangs on the wall and where our belongings wait to greet us as we walk back through the door. We leave such things and enter what feels at once like a form of exile. Some feel this more sharply than others, almost from the moment of their earliest memories; some never feel it at all, or so slightly it hardly matters. On the road in the dark of night, or in the bright light of mid-day, it is unassuagable, for it speaks our name with an intensity which leaves us in no doubt that that is not our name at all, and that, as much as we protest, we know from henceforth we will be travelling without it. Just as there will be no room or family or loved one to go back to, so we will go on looking and waiting for that day when, in the grey drizzle of an anonymous street, a stranger will come up to us and will, uttering a name we have not heard before but which we will know intuitively is our own, disown us. Looking into that face we will, with a sudden and overwhelming astonishment, realise that it is the same face that looks back at us each morning in the bathroom mirror, and that that grief in which all our departures originate, and which underscores them, begins, as we had begun to suspect, not with our self, but with another we will never "know".

.

Everything, in a movement of indefinite expansion, is involved in a return to its origin. *Me and my companions have a disease of the heart ...* And they listened to it, day and night, through the almost vertical ascents of freezing mountain ranges and the plunges into malarial lowlands, and did not hear it, raiding all the temples they could enter, fleeing over the causeways ... *that only gold can cure.* Driving later through those cracked, flooded underpasses at night, unable to find a boy at an affordable price, your face in the rear view mirror louvered with the fleeting shadows of the city, its huge billboards proclaiming JESUS LOVES YOU, beside military camps, where they slowly torture internees, you sigh, deeply: *At the end of the day, one doesn't really need anyone ...* In this contaminated country where all the fruits refuse to ripen, and where the distances, between what one desires and what one receives, accumulate with a sly, deceiving momentum, the state of vagrancy, all points of origin abandoned, has been elevated to a principle. Under your tongue the pool of pure clear water, not for assuaging thirst but to accentuate the drought within it, lies, still; unsensed, unknown, unsipped.

.

And she had come all that distance to be with him, leaving behind the waterwheels and the dried up cisterns of her hometown. The dark mildews on the walls of the public buildings opened their veins for her. They would, for her, she knew, always be commiserating. On the frosty steps of a new country her dark shadow passed over the rent in her being—and closed it. She heard the unfamiliar waters lap against the stone bridges. And when he looked at her, she thought, as their bodies touched, that was all he could hear, the sound of that water. A water in which all those hypnotised by absences immerse themselves. Under the stone bridges it flowed and into the heart of the evening, wearing

127

away all it rolled against. Perhaps even she would become, soon, a memory to him, and nothing more. Perhaps even he was a memory of someone she was forgetting, even now at this very moment as she spoke, a memory which would release her from those endless repetitions of mistaken identities which she had, for so long, indulged in.

# XXXII

Parts of our lives are lived in secret, are withheld from us, by our fear of the consequences of facing what lies within them. When he was lying in the bare infirmary room across the road from which hymns at mass in the chapel each day could be heard, she had confided to her brother her fear that, because he'd adamantly insisted he would not be coming back home to her, he did not love her. Her brother, supposing it was his clumsy way of trying to prepare her to face up to the idea of his death, despite the doctors' prognosis that he would recover, tried to calm her by suggesting it was probably the result of all the drugs being administered to him. But her mind returned to a letter of half a century ago, and to a suppressed grief and fear. A letter found in his pocket from a woman whom she had characterised as a "prostitute"—though she demonstrated no further precise knowledge of her—and who she said had wanted to take him from her. He had met her, she said later, at a military tattoo in the north of the country where he had been stationed for a while just after they had married. She had carried this fear with her through all the years without admitting it—to anyone including, perhaps, herself. And suddenly there, again, it was, before her. A phantom eating her heart, robbing her of the power of thought and uniting her with that fundamental insecurity which lay at the core, not just of herself, but everything. A fortnight later, on the scheduled day of his discharge from hospital, as her husband had predicted, he did not go home to her.

.

What if the future and the past were indistinguishable, and the place we meet in, the present, under a cold December rain beside the river, was also? How would the dark leaves of the bitoag tree survive another cold season there? How would our eyes, glistering above the pavement, greet each other? How distant would we be, then, or how much closer, having no need to forget, or to remember, that we had met? With no histories to shroud us from ourselves how should we find each other again in that wide and indefinable avenue of light and shadows? Could we come back, making our way through scent drenched gardens, to a passion we never had, or to a cinema where they were showing the same movie over and over again, and, entering a room we had no memory of, turn on the light as if we had just walked out?

.

You have met yourself already coming down the road towards you, he whom you did not greet, but who cast a sidelong glance towards you and hurried on. In the twilight of a quiet house you had heard his footsteps already, climbing the stairs, the broken sash of an open window clacking in the wind and keeping pace with his ascent. And you moved away without a word, out of fear, unable to confront him, knowing that he, too, would leave you presently without speaking. In the garden the dry leaves clustered around the wooden table where the chairs were folded and covered for the winter. A glazier in the street outside sang into the gilt of his fading reflection. Open the gate now and leave while there is still time, pull down the cloak of mist about you and depart. From this day, this place, and these hands that will always remind you of where you have not been, and of how you got to where you did not wish to be. Bear only this in mind, though, before you close the door behind you … the farther you go the shorter the distance you will have to travel to return—to these rooms where the pale winter sunlight enters and covers the desktop at which you are writing, and across which the sounds of an unknown city, and of streets up and down which you have been continually walking, drift.

.

He had once written that to see clearly was poetry, prophecy and religion all in one. Yet observing their statues of women, whose breasts were enormous and hips more than the width of their shoulders so that they would have been so unstable they would not have been able to walk without difficulty, he, who fled from the sight of his wife's pudendum on their wedding night and to which he could not, thereafter, bear to return, had the temerity to say that they wilfully opposed themselves to all facets of nature and cut themselves off from healthy sources of knowledge and natural delight! How darkling that plain of his life must have been on which he chose to live if he could so perversely confuse such symbols of a universe perceived as animated by *desire*, with a rejection of the observance of nature. What, and whose, "nature", for heaven's sake did he mean, but his own; he who supposed himself able to see so clearly into it, and who came from a land where the experience of the erotic, being almost exclusively personal, easily shaded off into the obscene and pornographic. Such qualities their own art stood unjustly accused of by him, an art which, in its pursuit of wholeness and understanding, was entirely free, though, of such indulgence. Or perhaps he did not even take the trouble to examine their treatises on aesthetics, written when his own land was a patchwork of quarrelling fiefdoms of cattle thieves and nothing more, in which the function of art was considered to be not the imitation of features of the external world, an exact rendering of them—though at that they were more than adept—but the manipulation of such features to suggest inner states of man's conscious being and nature.

.

On a flickering TV screen left on all night day begins with the close-up of a young man in a cosmetic clinic having the hair removed from around his rectum and genitals. A frost glitters on garden-shed roofs in the stillness of the morning. Thieves and muggers lie in bed. Past deeds do not disturb them, nor those to come, walking at night with steel bars in their sleeves, ready to break a car window for anything inside, or for nothing. For the sound, maybe, of glass breaking. On buses the screamed obscenities of schoolgirls mauling each other in the aisles: a lexicon of lewdness inscribed on the ear of each citizen of this well-off polis; from surgery, to classroom, to home. The smell of latex on the breath of a conjugation without interval. The lucre of a dream whose darkness no usherette shines a beam into, but out of which millions of faces, with bleach whitened teeth, smile. Over the collective stalls of a vulgar hedonism the credits roll, while they sleep on. In the Void of the screen someone is holding up a knife and singing, amid the sound of breaking glass. No need to tell the last person to turn out the lights, for everyone has gone home—a long time ago. A programme note on the floor carries, beneath boot marks, an advertisement with a number to ring for husbands interested in exchanging with other husbands, on weekends, their wives.

# XXXIII

They called the land 'We-don't-understand-you' through a misunderstanding on arrival of what, when they had asked them its name, its inhabitants had replied to them. The name endured, like all incomprehensions of a self not intent on knowing the other but displacing it. An enshrined irony. And to it, over the seas, thousands of others would flock, not to pay homage to it, but to the opportunities it offered for power, for self advancement unavailable in the rigid hierarchy of their society back home, burning all its books and beautifully illuminated and bound codices that "contained nothing in which there was not seen superstition and lies of the devil," and by which their scholars back home were, at such "proof of high culture, wrapped in astonishment." And the land elicited from the mouths of these Vandals, again, another irony: "The world is small." But not as small as the minds of those who strapped on their cuirasses each morning. From their land of 'We-don't-want-to-understand-you' had issued enthusiastic reports, catalogues of exteriority, drum beats on the path to war, full of a language of wonder, describing the cities they had discovered as an enchanted vision, a dream, a marvel to gaze on: "Large canoes could come into the garden from the lake through a channel that had been cut, without the crews needing to disembark ... Everything was shining with lime and decorated with different kinds of stonework and paintings ... The palaces in which they lodged us were very spacious and built of magnificent stone and cedar wood, and the wood of other sweet smelling trees ... The paths were choked with roses." And aviaries, unknown in their own land, ball-courts, sweat-baths and vaulted bridges. Behind that word "superstition", though, and "devil", condemning the other and justifying themselves, (as behind so many other words similarly deployed, *civilization, democracy*, before and after) tolled the knell for a culture they were indifferent to, having eyes for that sad procession of exteriority only, for the "Many beautiful buildings which is the most remarkable thing" they could find in that remarkable country.

.

[Exit—crying]

.

Into Inferiganga had walked one day, slapping the dust off the thighs of his crumpled trousers and jacket and dragging a travel scarred valise, the diminutive person of Andrei Carpuscii a wandering musician who was, he said, travelling in search of new songs of birds. Birds were, he proclaimed with utter conviction, "choristers of the Divine." When asked where he originally came from, his background and family, he immediately brushed aside such questions with "O that is not important. The world is too preoccupied with the 'person', not enough with itself." Such cryptic responses were his trademark, always delivered with an inoffensively gentle and wise demeanour and voice, so that we went away feeling that we should, rather than being put out, ponder the response further. He stayed amongst us for a few weeks only, then, hearing that there was an unusual bird sighted and heard in a small village further north, departed. As he took leave of us to go up river he pushed into our hands, in an act of generosity typical of him, a sheet filled with the crotchets and quavers of his latest composition. We played over and over, at the piano in our rooming house, what was only very tentatively melodious. Mostly it was, it seemed, concerned with contemplating the manner of its own unfolding. For that reason, perhaps, it always seemed to give the lie to its professed title of *Sonata for a Young River-Crossing Girl's Dark Hair*, no doubt a reference to the boat-people who, for a few racattos, ferry people, here, between boat and shore. Never did sound less obviously invoke a physical object or subject. Listen as one might to it for an "it", a "who", a "you" or "they", one could not detect one. And even the "I", that one would expect to impart to it formal emotional coherence, seemed missing—instead, there was a backwards and forwards momentum which the more it moved forward the more it seemed not to progress from some deepening reservoir within itself which echoed, and, yet, which it never articulated. From that infinitely variegated surface of itself, which seemed as if it could go on for ever, nothing as crude as a thing or a subject ever violated the ear of the listener, so that without an "object" for his attention the listener's sense of himself, too, as a hearer, disappeared. "Shapeless and baggy and monotonously protracted, a music less like a piece of auditory architecture," as most local critics responded upon hearing it, "one could not imagine." To that, though, one suspects Carpuscii might have replied: "We walk round, or step inside, only what we are condemned to observe."

.

Compelled to be a ghost in his own country, he whistled up a wind, a dance, to try to re-invoke the past, to stem the tide of what his adversary claimed his destiny entitled him to—his lands, and everything within them. Ghost of a world, a word. A person without any substance, stripped naked in his own land, who owned, suddenly, nothing, including himself; a hollow syllable at the heart of the world. Treaties torn up, and, if not, not abided by. The introduction of a strange mythology of snakes, messiahs and virgins. All his victories called "massacres", all those of the adversary called "victories". Such a deep vein of hypocrisy—and then, later, to serve and die for that country that would not even bestow upon him the title of "citizen". Violent men, greedy for land and domination—where would it end; surely not at their own borders? The virus multiplies within them. And he whom they tried to obliterate, whose trails, worn so deep by the tread of his feet over centuries that they became the adversary's roads of travel, his highways; he, whom the adversary tried to render history-less, remains. Reduced to a paltry number, and scattered. And the adversary, what does he have but a present without a past, a past which is a dark cupboard he dare not open. And who is, thus, compelled to ride the wave of a future, having no morally legitimate existence in the place of his habitation. Compelled, also, to inhabit a lexicon of ghostly sounds, of prevarications and evasions, his retribution, perhaps; treaty, word breaker—to breathe that obfuscating air of a lie which runs all the way back through his actions to virtually the day of his landing.

.

In the silent foundations of a house is inscribed your fate. What, all your life, you have observed but which you have allowed to escape you, and to which you must finally surrender. In each house you have left an article, a possession, and departed. Now the sea collects the harvest of your days and deposits it at *your* door. The light of love almost extinguished. The broken lock of a suitcase. What is lost, and what is not worth retaining. The roof space emits beneath the eaves at the end of day a foul odour. Voices, animate, in the corners. The sounds of outdoors, of distant quays you set out from many times. A yellowing note left for you on a desktop half a century ago falls from the pages of a book. Did you live this life or were you, all the while, living some other?

## XXXIV

The long walls of the city, crumbling in parts, and beyond them the desert. When the camel trains set out men plucked, from this city of flowers, blooms, "ghze", from the overhanging branches of trees because, as they said, it would be a long time before they held anything similar again, except pallid dry cuttings from the margins of hell; the homophone "ghze", referring also to the long pale strips of dried pork meat and rind that would constitute the major part of their monotonous diet. Into this city of wind and sand, she came. That winter the iron-gate hinges to her courtyard froze and had to be prised loose by faggots of dried grass set alight and placed beneath them. She recognised no one and no one recognised her, so long had she been away after such a short time there. Indeed, in the local chapel where the few foreign inhabitants attended on Sundays, shortly after she had left the priest had accidentally included her name for prayers in a mass for the dead rather than for those in need of help. So she, as it were, walked back into their midst from a land none of them had ever visited, nor would care to. And she decided to keep it that way. In truth, she had no idea why, husbandless and childless, she had returned. She decided she might, gray haired now with crinkled skin, feel less alone in a country where it would be expected of her that she would, simply because of the colour of her skin and her features and accent, be an outsider, a stranger at the side of events and customs she only slightly comprehended. Something, also, drew her to the idea of living in that far off place that she had uprooted herself from many years ago, a place that had always been "foreign", and was now tinged with the sadness of a broken marriage. Somehow, her being in it alone was a confirmation, and assertion of, not so much failure, as of—being alone. It was as if that was the only condition in which she could any longer experience the feeling of being "at home". At home amidst what she had no essential attachment to, that enveloped yet excluded her, a home that denied her the familiarity she, on the one hand so coveted and, on the other, disliked. Wandering through the side streets and back alleys of the city, mingling with the crowds in which she was both conspicuous and yet anonymous, amidst the food vendors, rope-makers and haberdashers, she felt she was in some kind of elemental space where everything belonged in a state of a ceaseless continuum. It was a space that seemed to generate her drifting self; and the passage of her thoughts, closing up behind her, seeped away into what felt like a pre-incarnate whole out of which everything was blown upon the stream of her senses.

.

Cholera in the creeks. Death squads. An epidemic of malfeasance that goes unchecked. At the corner of Atalino Street one morning an unfortunate "accident". Causality—a realism that could not, any longer, be tolerated. A hosed down street, a memory erased. The same undrinkable water that's cranked from a pump each day down an alley into grateful upturned palms. Imperfect world, against which too many tardy dawns have collided and broken. In the wreckage, a film script clutched in the hands of the dying. Inchoate world in the dark rushes of a screening studio, rotated, cut and joined until it is just another image projected upon an image already existing—except, at the end of the day, no one is allowed to walk off the set of the one that is so perdurable. So at night, on the foetid kerbside where whores stand whitening their faces, "love" comes, through the mud deep compounds and the sickly air of abattoirs and wet markets where there is the smell of urine and blood, for its appointment. Like the wisp of fragrance on the air from unseen gardens. And the pale glaucoma of the eyes of the destitute busking in underpasses turns up, in response to it, as if towards some ineluctable music. Turns up to it and then down, to that dingy cubicle with a roll of tissue paper and a bottle of rubbing alcohol by the bed, and the outstretched palm. To that calculated appearance of a First Lady amongst the slums, trailing her inexorable opiate of glamour. Cunt of the cosmos. Are you breathing heavily? Good, then you are distracted. Misfit and miscreant at the edge of a changing light—but not world—turn to the camera. And the blind gum vendor at the corner of Gabini and del Minar, alerted that something is going on, turns his face, too, to the commotion. The credits roll, across the creeks and broken curbstones. For these, though, no one stands up or wishes to be acknowledged, or turns on the scratchy recording of the nation's anthem.

.

Beneath the iron struts and roof of the terminus of the Inferiganga Railway Company can be seen on wooden benches the bodies of those who have fallen asleep in the middle of their journey and who wake to realize they have forgotten where it is they are travelling to. Disoriented, like one about to step over a threshold, they simply wander off into the surrounding jungle and are not seen again, or stay to beg and wander round the innumerable streets stretching between the terminus and the harbour, as if they are not fully awake yet or apprised of the nature of their surroundings. Their faces, like those carved in ebony by the tribes that dwell deep in the forests, resemble idols. They possess that vacant, far away look of those who have engaged in protracted and arduous seances through the night, or who have arrived after a long and perilous journey through forests, and across oceans and deserts. Exemplars of the ancient paradox of motion, that a body is always at rest because it is occupying a space equivalent to its own dimensions and cannot, therefore, ever arrive at its destination, they exhibit that profound and painful expression that afflicts those who cannot renounce the actions of the devotee and yet to whom is vaguely vouchsafed that insight, attained only in full by the sage, that there is really nothing to travel, and to genuflect, towards. Resembling nothing more strongly than recusants who have consulted an oracle in which they have recently ceased to believe, they waylay us on corners or in bars with impassioned inquiries about people and places we have never seen or heard of. And yet we sense that, though they seek it, our presence to them, because it reminds them of a plan of which they have forgotten the order of events, is an ordeal. They will, sometimes, turn away muttering violently under their breaths words we do not recognize, indeed words from a language which, as they continue, we suspect does not exist.

## XXXV

The malamsampalok tree outside shakes its galaxy of white green flowers and for one, unguarded, moment you might well believe that it is snowing. And that in the heat of those over-upholstered drawing rooms crammed with rosewood chairs, Isfahan carpets and souvenirs from foreign places, once again you sit day-dreaming of lost treatises and their obscure exordiums, desperate to escape from Messire Crocodile, from the mouth of that fever and boredom brought on by the satiety of comforts. At that time of year when the malaise of a collective vulgarity asserted itself in front rooms piled with wrapping paper torn from gifts, and the green stumps of millions of coniferous trees littered the sidewalks waiting to be turned into chips, you repeated the name Amun-Re-Atum-Horakhty, and thought of the scribe Mersakhmus who wrote, praising him, that his name would be protection for all solitaries and for all those alone on the waters. Now, you know that the fertile spoor of such waters was not to be found in any such drawing rooms. Only in the dried up mouth of a devotee for whom the thought of Messire Crocodile would have tempered luxury with fear. And tempered such fear also, perhaps, with what lay in that indecipherable antiphon on the crinkled papyrus you saw, and gazed longingly at for hours as a boy, but could not read. Under the cold over-cast skies of a northern capital stuffed with spoils.

.

Just as the unobtainable < *Beatrice Helen Laura* > unguent from a male phantasmagoria is priceless—so, along with that vast array of other exhibits, it is best deposited, for good, in a muse-eum.

.

Through the grill of the open window, blossoms flutter onto the floor around her bed. In the scented breeze, to the sound of the clacking of tree-frogs and footfalls in a world of shadows, she drowses, inhaling deeply the sounds of a bereaved day. Above the road, hour after hour like an immense and unending spool of dark smoke, fruit bats cross the parched land, the echo of their inaudible click outlining tree, house, river—everything to which we give a name and from which we become, in this deepening dusk, visually separated. "So many things pass in the night and disappear. Deeper into time, I listen for other voices." And when they come, it is a voice out of the past she hears, her own, reciting in a dreamed present what could not, in all probability, be recounted in a present constituted by perception. A voice which recites, word by word, whole chapters of verse from the *Ramayana*, and the entire collection of the *Gitanjali*, over a hundred in number. And, sometimes, in these recitations the voice takes her forward by beginning from the end of the text, reversing not only the order of each part but of each word; a reversal which does not, though, make it any less immediately recognisable. Waking, the blossoms of the tree scattered about her room, she wonders whether or not, in fact, everything that she has ever read has not been inscribed within her memory, and whether those dark tablets of pages that unfold when she is asleep, for it happens often, are not parts of the larger whole of a consciousness that is given to her, but which she does not originate, nor ultimately control; a consciousness which contains within it everything she has experienced, and whose fluxion, like a dark river, abrades its messages, codes and desiderata of clues against those deep cellar walls of her being when she sleeps, playing itself back to her, monotonously sometimes in her own voice, as if in an attempt to relieve itself of an immense burden.

.

"Ah; Flapper they called him, Flapper. Varicose face, like a red lobster. Left out in the sun too long. All those years in India I suspect. Don't know his battalion. Stayed on out here though. Moved around a bit doing this and that and then joined the Jockey Club, as a steward, I think. No, haven't seen him for a long time either. Poor old blighter, maybe he's fallen off his perch." Large-eared, whence the name. An inveterate tippler stumbling, sometimes, up the steps of the club, scarlet nicks on his face from the trembling hand that shaved him each morning. To all extent and purposes a "passive deserter", whose only ambition, when young, was to escape poverty by joining up. Demobbed with only his exemplary record behind him, no trade, he settled finally into an undemanding position where he, an ex-RSM, was able to continue enforcing rules, never seeking a promotion, and to let life take him along with it. And so it did; generating along the way one child with a local girl. Weekends he visited his son where he lived with his grandmother and her own grown up son ( the daughter working most of the time in an adjacent country ) in a flat he bought for her beside a dusty path that wound up above the harbour to a white washed chapel. Hush puppies. Tweed jacket and tie. Grey cavalry twill trousers with razor crease. Shuffling, on tired feet, he would enter, at the end, with the modesty of his own expectations, into that quietness of which he was composed and which he had no desire whatsoever to offend; blending in, seemingly, so effectively with where and who he was, that no one would notice, until much later, that he was no longer there. A quietness that came from who knows where: an antidote, perhaps, to that parade ground and to all those wars that so much of his life had revolved around, and to that ever present noise of need amidst a mill-worker's family of thirteen.

# XXXVI

In the latter part of her life Roshni, the midwife of the village of Anishpura and a childless widow, took to taking long journeys on the railway. From her mud floored shack which contained only a bed she would regularly take off wandering down to the station and, with no luggage and only the clothes she set out in, and without paying a fare, join the noisy third class carriage of betel nut chewing passengers who had brought along their chickens, goats and produce for market. Weeks later she would return, from where no one knew; nor could Roshni enlighten them, for at this point in her life her memory was not as reliable as it had been when her husband had been alive. Indeed, her behaviour and her appearance had deteriorated to the point of utter eccentricity. Around the villages she would walk with sheuli and joba blossoms twined through her hair, on occasion stopping to talk with the daughter of one of her ex-customers, convinced that it was the mother instead, despite repeated statements to the contrary. Where her protracted peregrinations upon the weed choked railway tracks of her country took her no one knew. At the end of her life, though, one of the men from her village on business up in the north of the country recognized her. Amazed, he tried to get her to return to Anishpura with him but she refused. Probably going to the river each day or to a nearby pond to bathe, her home would have been the crowded platform of the station where she had alighted, and where others had decided to spend time, too, before they moved on, and where she, no doubt, managed to share some of their meagre food. But she could not recount the names of the places she returned from. Only the last one, at which she was recognized, was known. It is strange, indeed, that after all her departures Roshni should have arrived and stayed only in places she did not know she was in. She who, through her efforts and skills, had enabled so many others to successfully arrive in this world, had, finally, only the most vague of ideas about what her own destination was. Attired in everything that she possessed, and with her mind's continual divestment of its memories, she was, perhaps instinctually, preparing for that final and ineluctable journey whose destination no one, because no one returns from it, is able to pronounce the name of.

One of our colleagues, returning from Hokasaschu the other day, had attended a talk by the writer Madura Kavari. He brought back with him this short printed prolegomena to the talk on his new book *The Traveller*: "We are, all of us, born strangers to ourselves. And all our lives consist, whether we are aware of it or not, of a prolonged attempt to forget or to understand this. In traditional societies the stranger was a person who came amongst us and was valued, virtually revered, for providing us not just with news of that great world that exists outside our own boundaries and which we never get to see but, also, with news and insights into ourselves. For how could we fail not to reflect upon, or to re-evaluate, our own customs and habits with another pair of eyes and ears to guide us. These days, though, with the advent of our technologies and the kudos subsequent upon them, and our travel to 'exotic' places, the stranger seldom visits us. Instead, we have taken to visiting him, and not with news for and curiosity about him, but simply to laze on his beaches or photograph his ancient palaces, or solely to impose on him our views and values and to get him to buy our wares. Nowadays the Stranger has virtually, therefore, been eliminated from our ontology. With the embrace of an invidious homogeneity, driven largely by trade, strangeness is being driven from the world. And, consequently, we are all becoming ever more solitary and concealed from ourselves."

.

You glance, above your desk, towards the garden. The pages of the book, open before you, move in a pale glissade of light. Letter and word separate, float and rejoin again between the margins in a litter of dark print. You wonder what kind of place a book is. Beyond the window the grey brilliance of an autumn day of rain starts in the words; and you think you recognize them, having heard them in many different places and at many different times, names of things with which you deem you are familiar. Come with us, they seem to say. For a moment you are hesitant, and do not know whether the condition of autumn in the garden which you see outside is a condition of the words you silently formed, or something independent of them and which goes on existing by itself—as the autumn, there, in front of you, does. Suddenly, the ghost of an even older autumn, of past sensory stimuli, enters and inhabits your being, a copy of things long dead. In a faded place, waiting for you to revive it. Waiting, until the tongue would rot in your mouth, and even long after; until all the autumns would terminate—except the russet mantle of this one which ripens, always, upon your tongue.

.

Abu El Rhamin, small but neat rust coloured goatee and pince-nez perched upon his nose, hired by the Company to teach us the complexities of the local language for five hours every Thursday afternoon, was a very opinionated man. A demanding teacher, he would, though, stand in front of us in the library of his house and take every opportunity to go off on a discursive and tendentious digression from the lesson itself, upon whatever struck his fancy. Most of these digressions were on the subject, however, of language. In particular, he reserved an especially acerbic expression of contempt for a scholar, a "grizzled professor of linguistics" from some diminutive European principality, who he refused to name, perhaps out of consideration for our own national sensitivities. This professor had learned, at a young age, Sanskrit and read all the grammarians who had written on and in it, and he had recently propounded what was for him, our teacher claimed, and for his continent-men, the "original" idea that it is language itself which is wholly responsible for shaping our awareness of the perceived world, since the perceived world is an interpreted world, and this interpretation is almost entirely an act of language. "How many millennia ago was it," Abu El Rhamin portentously proclaimed, "that some scholar of one of our own schools of linguists put forward the proposition that our awareness is word impregnated, our awareness of *everything*, and that names are ontologically prior sources of the worlds they name. So how can such an upstart's theory, which attributes the significance of things and acts to the system of rules and relations, of values within a language, which enable them to have meaning, not acknowledge such an antecedent?" We sat, dumb in our seats, not knowing what to say, or whether to say anything. The kudos, which our teacher was attacking, seemed to be encroaching upon him too. His eyes alert, seemingly, in the glint of their fire to a conspiracy that he had himself, single-handedly, uncovered.

.

The solitary imagines he lives in a world of noise and disruption, which he shuns in an act that is willed. His condition of solitude is not a priori, therefore, a condition of isolation but one of withdrawal, and although he might choose, for even a prolonged period of time, to be alone, his aloneness is not the isolation of the true journeyer who, whilst acknowledging his preference for being alone, moves amidst noise and disruption from which he feels no need to stand apart. Such a journeyer recognizes, as the primary condition of his existence, an isolation which has been imposed upon him by fate and which he, thus, accepts. Drawn by a multitude of motifs; deserted railway platforms at night, telephones ringing in empty rooms, ships slowly rotting at quays, it is, rather than a note of desolation that haunts him, the sense of a promise of something waiting to be encountered. He moves, therefore, as a body in meditation moves, towards some subtle and invisible embrace of arrival, towards some unencountered terrain in which his own physiology has already been mapped. All journeys are, he recognizes, simply a progress towards that place—nameless and formless—from which he has always been separated. So, at the end of each day, he willingly drinks down with the liquid that moistens his lips and refreshes him, the dust that has accrued from all his internal and external wanderings; and that libation of stillness of the night through which he can hear only the silence of his own breathing, measuring the depth of the darkness that remains within and without him, and which he knows he will have to enter alone.

# XXXVII

Off the mail-boat today a letter from Europe from the former librarian of the provincial capital's public library, a majestic stone building originally constructed to provide quarters for European nursing staff of the civil hospital. On its heavily arched two storey granite verandah, many a weekend and afternoon was spent talking of books, and avoiding the shadow of the Colonial Surgeon which, it was said, day and night prowled the grounds and the building, a building which he considered far too ornate and which he had, before his death, attempted to vandalise by making its use of space more "economical": "How the warm scents of the camphor tree and Alpinia, whose leaves some of us smoked as fragrant rabbit tobacco, beckon to me some nights, drawing my mind back to the gardens around the library and the narrow bamboo fringed paths that I wandered along so repeatedly that I felt as if I had lived there even before I was born. And the old handsome lodge at the back of the library built by a Parsee merchant which, alas, in your last letter you said has cupolas supported now by wooden shoring and on which the plaster ornamentation of entablatures and pediments is disintegrating. Here, in this glittering city that all the writers and artists of the world flock to, everything is being pulled down and replaced by new constructions Whole streets disappear, almost overnight, in a cloud of dust. It is as if only the future can hold people's imaginations. I have a theory—as you know I was never short of such things. It is only the young who really possess, and live in, the future. By middle age one is already looking back. What's to come is, after all, inevitable and uninviting. Well, this is a nation obsessed by youth, by looking and staying young. 'Old' is almost opprobrious here. An entire industry flourishes by producing products to prolong youthful appearance. Insecurities are exploited profitably by the blandishments of advertisements. These people have, you see, infantilised themselves. Where does this disavowal of the old and this obsession with the new come from if not from that eternal fountainhead of pleasure, combined with an unawareness of time, which only the child truly enjoys. And since from a very early age we are all, especially boys, taught that we have a pre-ordained appointment, a destiny, with the objects of our individual egos' desires then, perhaps, as much as anything else, our heritage of Romanticism, with its Rousseauistic exalting of the innocent and uncorrupted child within, and with its Wordsworthian extolling of that child as 'father to the man,' has more than a little to do with prolonging this idyll. Gone, certainly, is the sense of noblesse oblige, and, elevated in its place, instead, is the inherent right to self-gratification. So this madness for the 'new' in advertisements here, automatically synonymous with improvement, is, essentially, for an object untarnished by time, a pandering to our fantasy of being able to renew our lives indefinitely, to live perpetually at the edge of that limitless horizon that stretched before us in our childhoods, the memory of which is revived with almost every new purchase … But I have rambled on too long, my dear friend, and taken us too far away from those delightful grounds of the library where we spent so many pleasant afternoons walking, and from that charming colonnaded lodge, with its fragrant borders of jasmine and hibiscus, which I hope, still, some day, to see again."

.

There is nothing to go back to and nothing to go forward to, and where you are now, sitting or standing or walking, only the conventions of your ontology assert. Memory remembers the act of remembering; and, so, a past comes to be—and passes away; just as, when attained, a future, too, regresses into a moment in time that you can neither see, nor hear, nor feel beyond … only to flesh out the predicate of a desire to be. Where did "it" or "I" go but into that endless succession of beginnings terminated by those almost very same conditions through which they had appeared and into which they now dissolve that temporary identity you assigned to them. So move lightly through your voice, and through its thin assertonic tone. Tomorrow, perhaps, a letter will come. Or not. With the address crossed out. And you will wonder how it reached you, bearing not even your name. Unstamped, without a postmark. Without even the year or month or day embossed on its blank vellum.

.

Beside the banks of the Araprush is an area of dense reeds and marsh that stretches for hundreds of miles down to the delta and the coast. Behind this immense flatness lies the high Shrivati range of mountains, its highest peaks continually clad with snow. In this land, where a fierce tradition of egalitarianism has been preserved over the centuries, there are many sects. It is, however, a land of tolerance and teaches in its schools the finest skills of interpretation and commentary. Theories and counter-theories are so rife that, in its places of the higher learning, the act of evaluation is looked at askance and shunned—just as, on its streets and in its homes, the voice of judgement and authority is unknown, and even punishable if discovered. Summoned by dreams, diviners, charismatics and readers of oracles flourish in such a tolerant atmosphere. Almost as soon as they can walk, children are sent to reading teachers. You see them in the streets laboriously trailing their bags of books, looking through tired eyes at a world that is beginning to fade, to be reduced to an opaque screen or sigh. All day, at the quays, ships arrive with their cargoes of texts, and through the archways of the capital's walls, from across vast deserts and mountains, merchants arrive with their trains of mules and dromedaries to deposit at the Office of Citations and Publications the obligatory copy of each book, discourse, tract or treatise that they carry with them, so that not a reference to anything that has been written and published will be lost. Motes of dust hover before the eyes of the clerks in the miles of shelves and drawers of its archives. Feet pad through the maze of its hushed corridors. And from the Office of Interpretations nearby, inspectors swarm across the country recording and collecting the opinions of citizens. Its lights burn all through the night as its copyists bend over an interminable number of printed sources and transcriptions of interviews, summarising their content, compiling the repository from which, they believe, one day they will be able to infer the nature of people's deepest needs. Not only their needs, but the meaning of the mind and life itself, which they conceive of as being nothing other than the product of this vast, and as yet un-unified, BOOK. Indeed, high in the Srhrivati mountains there exists an ultra-radical sect, violently opposed to science, math and natural science, which spends all of its time combing through every form of written material, through a list which appears to be endless—letters, diaries, menus, manuals, shopping lists, novels, newspapers, poems, advertisements, almanacs, magazines, receipts—for signs, for hidden messages, that will alert them to the presence amidst them of that transcendental wanderer who they will identify by the Sign of His Voice. Such a simple acoustic signature, or sound image, they believe will be made up from that minimal element of their language which they call the ctesiphon, and which they claim creates meaning at the most elementary level, not just within language but within the entire universe. A "voice" whose vibratory warp and woof is encoded within the heart of matter, and which is the generative matrix of consciousness itself. With bulging and clouded eyes, as if afflicted by that crystalline opacity of the lens brought on by mystical events, this sect indulges its soteriological yearnings in the high thin air of mountains where, it is reported by those living down on the plain, its members have developed a mysterious faculty which enables them to see through mists and even, some claim, to fly.

# XXXVIII

Immigrants, carriers of the seeds of loss within themselves, who seized this land from the original inhabitants by force, they named the valleys within it and the county they settled in, "hard won by dint of toil", after the same lushly verdant undulations of the land they had left behind them. To live in two places at the same time, in the same place, annihilates not only space and time inside us, but reduces, also, their equivalent outside us to the terrain of an unsustainable nostalgia. This nostalgia bears at its heart not a determinate geographical space—though, eventually, a kind of satisfaction can be obtained by holding two such contraries in the mind and fusing them—but, in its desire for possession of and by a terrain beyond the conjoining of the names, some ultimate and ontic status for the phenomena themselves. So, in the dying breath of their subjectivity these practical men, whose desire to repossess what they had dispossessed themselves of, which is nothing other than the expression of a certain innocence about the world and the mind's place within it, began to feel they were not only becoming invisible to those others who stood around their bed, watching the bedclothes rise and fall, too, on their own destiny, but, finally, and too late, to themselves.

.

He wrote all his books in a slow, hesitant rhythm and an assemblage of sounds that always seemed to strike a note that was slightly "off-key", so that they seemed to suggest an acquiescence in something they could not quite take hold of, a music obliquely and obsessively exploring some mournful prototype of itself. Always, on reading his books, you began to feel that you were listening to a voice within a voice, an echo that, sent out into the world to discover itself, came back not so much repatriated but as a voice in which reflection had perished. And in its inscrutable cadences you recognised and knew, with a profound surprise, that he had all along in his life, and in his work, not so much been drawing upon his own experience, as considering whether he was a part of it at all. This had, not surprisingly, the effect of giving his work a quality of elusiveness. Often you felt that he was translating from a language he only imperfectly understood. You watched him walk, from the window of the café where he would always appear at evening, and it seemed, under the illumination of the street lamps, that in his downward gaze as it followed the deserted path before him, in a silence to which everyone who knew him deferred, there was the look of someone who, exiting from the toils of an endless periphrasis, had finally succeeded in realizing that in the nature of his own particular existence he was a character moving within a dream, a figure, perhaps the major one, in a dream that was not his own. Whose it was, he did not know … The shrunken yellow flames of the oil lamps on the café's tables drew him in and he sat with his back to the window. With a hard, clear and intense gaze, mindless of himself, he explored, as if he had never seen it before, the menu before him. From outside above the trees heavy with dusk a moon whose light resembled the pale luminosity of a woman's thighs and breasts caressed him, as if he was a lost memory, with a long lingering gleam

.

Kelson, that inveterate consumer of fierce local intoxicants, having stumbled one night by accident into a melee and, he claimed, in self-defence, subsequently downed a man who died not long after, found himself detained in the rat's lair of the town jail for five months before, due to the sustained efforts of the Company's lawyers, he was released. Whilst detained at the "magistrate's pleasure" he amused himself by translating into prose, from the region's patois which he had well versed himself in the intricacies of many years ago, a long poem by a poet highly regarded in these parts, Juna Mustafi, who wrote over a century ago. Kelson gave us a short extract from the translation, which he said he would have printed later at his own expense. It was written on paper manufactured largely from locally hulled rice stalks. This paper, pinned to the office's main notice board, emitted a crackling sound in the breeze from the fans, and came, in the long afternoon's blaze of light across the floor, to resemble the sound of a quietly kindling fire … "What is this prison which you abjure, but the manifestation of the limitations and confinement of your own body and soul. Through its thick walls and iron bars you have, each day, discerned the beauty and the glory of the far horizons. The jailer who brings you your cup of clear water has a face that is familiar to you. In the darkness of its damp walls and its silence you hear your heart beat. Your meal is a crust of hard bread and the fatuity of all desirings. Listening for the sound of another's footfall, you always end hearing your own. Although there is little light that approaches to you, the light in your mind reaches out and illumines what lies out of reach, what your senses cannot find. All your conversations are with yourself. But in the voice that comes back, continually, to you, you hear another that is not your own. Like a freshet of pure noise it refreshes your solitariness, printing the dark wall before you with blooms. It makes birds sing within its branches all night. Your body becomes a nest of song. The iron hasp of the lock which detains you will, you know, one day fall apart. So bind not yourself with these fears and inferior imaginings which would pit you against a self which, you know, is as substantial as air."

## XXXIX

It is not the sound of the tabla that is heard, by itself the tabla is silent, but the sound of a part of the hand making contact with the taut surface of it. And even then it is not the sound of the tabla only but of the hand also, and not the sound of the contact of these two at the moment it occurs only, but later. As the sound waves strike the tympanum, the action which produced them has already ceased—a moribund event. We live in a world that is not immediately available to us. And even when we do receive it, it is mediated by our senses and is, therefore, in a way, the copy of an "original" event or object. So time intervenes in our lives at the most fundamental level, with most of us unaware of it. There is no such thing as an instant gratification. We live in a world of "copies", where the originals are not available to us, or do not independently exist, being so dependent upon our own involvement with them. Within the very fabric of our experience is a fading we cannot restore, a loss we cannot indemnify. Standing on the corner, waiting for someone to approach, it does not cross our minds that, perhaps, we live in a world where we have sought ourselves in the heart of its most impenetrable of disguises.

.

"He could never settle. Two years after he and my mother married in Inferiganga they left for Esboa. He had been born and lived all his life in this country, and it was the first time, although he was not from here, that he had visited the country where his parents had come from and of which he was a national. After a year there, when I was three, he left and never, except for a brief visit, returned to live. Something, I suppose, about this continent drew him back to it, something stronger than the pull of love and a daughter. Stronger than the lure of that imperial city where his wife and daughter lived. A white man, but there was nothing there for him but the memory of another place. Nine years later he returned. He took all of us out to a very expensive restaurant. Why he came I do not know—certainly not to just look at me. Often, in fact, I thought, and still do think, it was because of me he left. In a strange place, with a newly acquired family and responsibilities, he was not able to adjust. For six years, after he left again, I wrote letters to him every week. I never received a reply. I stopped writing. Then, a month ago, an anonymous "friend" here in Inferiganga, rang my mother to tell her that, at 49, he was dead. My mother, being white, prevailed upon the mayor of the city where he was supposed to have died to find the company he had worked for. But he said no company in the city could verify they'd had anyone of his name working for them. If they had it had been, perhaps, many years ago. So there was no confirming where he had died. Probably he had roamed around the country working, over the years, for different companies. That would have been possible, he being a white man. Jobs would have offered themselves easily to him. Restless, moving on from one place to another, perhaps that was why my letters never reached him. My mother said he was living with a local woman at the end. How she knew I do not know. When he came back that one time he was always coughing and had difficulty swallowing. A heavy smoker—five packs a day. Being a microbiologist, now, I suspect he might have had symptoms of thoracic or stomach cancer … Anyway, I am sorry that you cannot help me, and to have troubled you." She walked out of the Company's office and onto the pier. In the bright light and the bustle of passengers, stevedores and coolies, she had hardly stepped out of the door than she was engulfed, lost to our sight.

.

Abu El Rhamin the linguist who tries, every Thursday, to teach us the language of these parts describes the process of pronouncing it as setting out on a prolonged journey, a "tongue-journey". In this new country of the voice we are required to leave all our old starting-out points and destinations behind, he says. Although we will journey over the same terrain of uvula, soft/hard palate, teeth ridge and blade of the tongue etc, there the resemblance will end, and we shall find our tongue involved in negotiating an entirely different route to the one we are used to taking and to destinations where we have not been before. This, of course, did not, hypothetically, surprise us, since we had long become used to living in a place where there are six rather than four seasons, fourteen rather than twelve months, and three rather than one calendar—the initial novelty of picking up one's newspaper and, each day, reading at the top of its front page the date, which differed thrice not only in day month and year but in century, soon wore off. But the existence of two alphabets, rather than simply one, did surprise us. How the articulatory organs of our bodies would manage the feat of re-imagining the shape of their terrain in guiding the air of the mouth against the vocal chords of the larynx and in moulding the vibrations of this new music, perplexed us. As the freight of these new caravans of sounds—hisses, bangs and buzzes—set off, echoing in the bones of our faces and heads, we soon became disorientated. Diphthongs moving towards certain terminal tongue positions and destinations—the lips spread or rounded, the tongue half closed fully front, or central—became lost, or stopped dead in their tracks. "Just follow the sounds," Abu El Rhamin would calmly say, hearing the product of our confusion and distress, "do not ask them, yet, any questions. Sounds leave the deepest traces to follow. The footprints of meaning are perpetually being scattered and trampled upon by the wind. Let your ear learn what your intellect, later, will unravel. The ghostly noumena of all our earthly categories, classes and definitions, hover, after all, round a voice we cannot, yet, hear."

.

We are what we are not. We reside where we do not exclusively reside; and we leave such a place, setting out from a time, too, that is not the time we indicate only, but a time into which we have arrived already, or have yet to arrive. Everything we are not, being present within what we are, represents this break with ourselves, with what we feel, what we perceive and do. Old Cronus groans. The dark topoi sway.

H

ang a sign on the door when you leave:

## *There are no archetypal landscapes*

BAR

PERNOD

JOURNAL

The present is invisible to us. The past is incomplete. In the street the organ grinder plays a tune on a blue canvas on which someone has planted trees, and on a deep water on which the fragile little boat of our desires floats. We listen to it and, in hearing ourselves breathe, we are filled with that immense sadness which is the joy of all that we are not—which is, also, all that we are.

The cursor moved in the stillness of the night. The names of foreign places illumined momentarily by its passing. In the suffused glow of the hurricane lamp, its bulbous glass wiped free that morning of its coat of carbon, his foot's shadow loomed before him. From outside in the courtyard all you could make out was the point of light of his cigarette burning, the slow drift of tobacco smoke and, through the progress through a multitude of stations and accents of voices from different countries, an intermittent silence, sometimes inflected with static. Standing there outside you became gradually aware that what you, as the listener, were listening to was not simply the elderly figure in the room of shadows listening to a medley of voices but yourself as a child, mind moving through the lacunae of silence between each station. That disrupted signal, through the darkness of space and time, for which you had searched and listened, was it not, you thought, always less important than the silence that punctuated it; because, after the cursor had passed those shifting shapes of words what continued to exist was the silence only out of which they had been born, which could not itself, because it is implicit with noise, be erased. A silence in which, ultimately, our lives are lived and on which are inscribed, as on the face of a vast and inscrutable sea, the form all their tenuous soundings take.

.

### The Memorabilia of Drawing Rooms

The reproachful gaze of pure white anti-macassars.

Ceramics with the names of seaside resorts daubed gaudily upon them.

Nosegays, snuffboxes and assorted combs.

A set of books entitled: *The Triumph of the West and Reason: Europe from the Renaissance to the end of the Nineteenth Century.*

A creaking globe on which exist only the lands of ghosts.

Shelves filled with the hagiographies of martyrs, missionaries, scientists and explorers.

A powder puff behind a sofa.

The air of a perfect amnesia corked in a jar.

A velvet foot stool.

A black leather-bound bible.

A photograph of a trench parapet and a hand obtruding from a torn sandbag stuffed with earth and debris from no-man's-land, which troops had christened "Old Tom" and which they shook for luck going over the top.

Echoes of smoke filled levees and fantasies of harems.

Cast in bronze, a trompe-l'oeil.

.

In his late forties, after a long career as a soft spoken and bookish schoolmaster, Thrupta took his pension and an early retirement. Then, not long after, to the bemusement of everyone, except his wife, he set tongues wagging in the village by taking up with and marrying a local prostitute and setting her up in style in a house on which he lavished most of the money from his pension. For most men the extravagance and the scandal of such an aberration would have ended there. But Thrupta was not most men. Not visibly anything less than, in the conventional sense, happily married it was as if, suddenly, upon his departure from the routine of a respectable career, a desire, for a long time deeply concealed within him, which was erotic and compassionate, ("compassionate for whom?" his wife and two sons might say), erupted. Such a desire led him to marry and to squander all his readily available resources upon near destitute girls whom he met on the streets where they were begging or selling their favours to strangers. He showered these new young wives with gifts, living with them in their small rickety huts down by the river which flowed the entire length of the nearby city. The duration of these concubinages exceeded no more than six months. To behold in such a setting his tall upright figure, and the handsomeness of his features, emerging each day clad in a long white and immaculate cotton brishati, talking in a language whose lexicon and syntax were shaped by a lifetime's reading of and discoursing upon the classic texts of his culture, was to behold a phantom. One wondered whether his illiterate girl-brides ever understood a word he said. For the poise and composure of his words, spoken to anyone and to everyone, and not just on some but on all occasions, had a shape from which neither they nor his mind could depart without the painful sensation of a rupture. It was the shape of the vessel in which all the learning of his culture had been passed down. And it was, within that naïve child-man element of his personality, as incomprehensible to him that such learning, and its style of transmission, should not be valued and cherished, as it was that it should not be in the possession of, and comprehensible to, everyone. Sometimes unseen for months, sometimes a year, one monsoon night, rain lashing the tree tops, he would unexpectedly turn up at the house of one of his cousins in the hope of receiving financial assistance, walking in out of the shadows with another young girl whom he had recently married. He had ceased living with his wife who survived on the rents and crops from his extensive lands, and, for the next fifteen years, wandered over the entire country; in which time, it was said, he had married more than fifty young and destitute girls. If his cousin happened not to be there when Thrupta arrived he would decline all attempts to persuade him to avail himself of the use of the telephone to call him and would, instead, request some tea and the provision of pen and ink and writing paper and then sit down and, whilst slowly sipping tea, his young bride hovering behind him, begin to compose the first of many pages of a letter, writing in an elegantly flowing hand and employing all the resources of that refined and euphonious phrasing which characterized his conversation. His cousin, when he eventually returned, would never refuse him. Often a part of the assistance would be spent on purchasing materials to erect a small makeshift structure for him and the girl to live in, or to improve, if she already had one, her existing accommodation. It was, his cousin often concluded after such a visit, as if Thrupta could see only the nobility and thought of a great deed, saving, like a Don Quixote, vulnerable young "maidens" from squalid lives on the street. In that image of female depredation, an idea, directing itself with all the force of a universal, became an actual object of Thrupta's perception. And, his cousin thought, like that Knight of the Sad Countenance, something deep within him, resisting the parades of conventional appearances and counting them of little worth, could not but help assert itself in the name of a cause which would upset them. For there was no earthly reason why he, well brought up in such a well-off family and well educated, in order to have sex and to live with such girls should have had to encumber himself by marrying them and living under a lean-to of tin and wood, often on a muddy riverbank, or sometimes under nothing at all except the wide, and frequently merciless, sky.

.

We observe, beneath a parasol at a corner café in the early morning, three men sitting quietly, smoking and drinking coffee. And we know that, though we have not seen them before, out of the dream of indeterminate space and time they are vivid apparitions, striking their poses within an energeia which is directionless and positionless, and which reminds us that all gestures are simply temporary arrestations of its flowing. Nothing disappears. There is nothing new. We are all intimate, yet alien. We have already met and parted and met again in this inexhaustible twilight whose stale music plays over the tables. In it, concealed from us, are the melodies we have spent so many lifetimes evading, travelling to those farthest corners of ourselves that, still, we do not recognise and which, sitting down, greet us again like long lost accomplices.

# XLI

You went looking for your childhood and found it in too many places and in too many times all at once; so that, finally, you had to relinquish the search for it. Your parents' peregrinations early in your life had left you with images so forcefully pervasive you felt you never would be able to track them down. On the casual map of their encounter with the places you had been able to establish existed—for they were nothing if not cavalier about up and moving off to new places and thought nothing of not informing you, either then or later, if they in fact could remember at all, exactly where they were going or had been—there hung the dusty grey pall, churned up from the roads over which they had always seemed to be travelling, of a doubt. So deeply did such a doubt run that even now, walking down the street in which you have lived for so many years, there will suddenly come over you the sensation that it is unfamiliar to you, so insistent is the feeling that the objects of your immediate perception originated somewhere else, though where you cannot tell.

.

The question does not know itself, nor to whom, or what, it is addressed. In the rank smelling toilet beside the kitchen of a busy restaurant it is as much, if not more, at home than in the well-upholstered room of a suburban house. The phraseology, the long curriculum of its career, changing and unchanging, incised on the stone pediments of our lives, its silence drawn from a well we have poisoned over and over, takes us in diverse ways. It asks, when we are unaware of its asking, asks without us, and with a tone that is the only sign of its asking. The dream holiday, or house, the paradisal vapour. We hear it, and do not hear it. Follow it, and then lose it. On the darkest of nights. On the longest day of the year. The tongue a cinder burned through and through in the mouth. Do we not observe ourselves as we are leaving the fragrant shoreline? What we take with us in the crates of statuary and of papyrus—O Lesmosyne—will it float on the low tide, or quietly sink, too, as we ravish our own taking?

.

Disenfranchise them, legate them. So that their likes, their self-regarding tribus, will not be seen again. Walking through this inner city the wrath of their language falls upon you with the weight of a corpse. Spoiled, and spitting, with their child allowance benefits around them—*to claim which bring one child allowance benefit book and one ID with you. ID but no book—result, refusal to issue allowance. Book but no ID—result, refusal to issue allowance.* Result: a tirade of the darkest most virulent abuse, claiming he, an inconspicuous clerk whose voice in the bureaucratic labyrinth is unheard, is changing the rules to suit himself. Result: polite and friendly reiteration of the rules, not his but his government's. Eliciting, from the unstaunched sluice of her mouth, threats and parting obscenities: "F_ck your mother … You c_nt." And racial jibes: "Unlike you I was born here." All the Augean stables of a first world's pampered, who, the next day, will stroll with the sleep of reason in their eyes into a polling booth and make, after long and arduous reflection, a judicious choice of candidate x and place their mark, for it is by no means certain they will be able to read or write, against a photograph … Ah, "mox daturos progeniem vitiosiorem."

.

In a ruined topography, gouged long ago by the detritus of a slow glacier, was it not located? Between a shore-line and a gradual inclination of fen. A landscape long ago too readily abstracted in writings into a "diseased" landscape. The terrain of a desire, now, in which all we can hear is the exasperated shout, or puzzled groan, of those who did the abstracting; who woke to find a landscape, that they had observed from their cold height and which they had only tried to make sense of through a system of ideas, changed. Was it not here, in the shadow of those writings, uncomplicit with history from which they withdrew as if dirtying their hands, that you grew up, not in a place of faceless inhabitants but where the exact measurement of speech and gait, of close observation, implicated you. Leaving, did you not take with you the urgent need to make sense of why and what you'd left, not content merely with an oblique, symbolical language to represent what you'd experienced? Writing in a particular place at a particular time, what they wrote should have had no need to instruct the reader to "Look … now." Unless, as with them, it was an admonishment to do that to which they themselves might only aspire—or were not interested, really, in doing at all.

.

They had devised a portable technology that allowed individuals, men, women and children, in the seclusion of their own homes, or in public, to view at their leisure on a screen images of every kind and on every subject. Each user would receive hundreds of offerings daily from merchants, many of whom purveyed scenes of "live" sexual congress. Men, women and children in copula with each other, in pairs or groups, or with animals of all sizes. Vivid, lewd images of lubricious genitalia. Men energetically lunching on the tears of spread-eagled and held down virgins. Sodomised pubescents and infants. An insatiable lust bearing down and feeding on itself, obliterating the "other". Valorised by a language of fear and repression. Punitive and puerile, obsessed by "enlargement", espousing a language of deep misogyny. And its faecal dilute trickling down through all strata of their society, through their media and advertising: "Bigger is always better…" Politicians, absorbed by flickering images at meetings, surreptitiously watching men doing to mere girls what they would (feign?) outrage at if it was done to their own daughters—for how can the one pass ignored but not the other? And that n̲ltimate annihilation of the other, assertion of one's manhood at the expense of it, strangulation in the act of coitus. Yet it continued. A society which had the ability to send people to another planet outside its own atmosphere, and to sustain them there, could not prevent it? Connivance in high places. A doomed, corrupt patriarchy that, at the end of the day, could think of nothing more satisfying to do than watch itself ingesting its own ejaculate.

# XLII

In the glass fronted map shop on the Street of Ossuaries, the disquisition by Flebenius nowhere to be found, a copy of *Galeub's* long out of print 'The Geography of Metaphor,' with its outré thesis, awaited us. Part "thinker", part traveller and adventurer, he had made his way many times on those great camel trains that voyaged, in the time of The Seven Empires, from high northern latitudes all the way to the east. Their camels, coughing in the cold damp air, were coaxed on, so it is written, by a linctus funnelled down their throats with instruments still visible in the local ethnological museum. It is said that, falling out one day with a group of fellow travellers, he had set off on his own, knowing the caravan's route well, but never arrived at his destination, nor was seen again. Some say that he was murdered by dacoits. Others, desirous no doubt of legends, that he ascended into a cloud to escape a violent sand storm and was lifted out to sea and lost. Whatever the truth his book makes curious reading. His underlying theme is that the development of cartography, as of all activities of our mental life, is linked to "entities" which move as much through an eidetic as a perceptual space—which is why, he claims, it is so very easy for us to get lost, even in places which we know well or possess maps of. For the consciousness which imagination rests upon can never be confined to one place but inhabits everywhere and all of time. Unknown to us, then, according to *Gaeleub*, when we are exploring a particular geography we are exploring also the residues left over from other geographies, visited and unvisited, that are part of the consciousness each of us has inherited. A consciousness largely unmapped, but which bears within itself the faded imprimaturs and signs of everywhere it has travelled. And in which through time and space the cloudy outlines of all its routes, of all those loci it has manifested, wait to be re-encountered.

.

A moist wind off the sea of that far coastline, rippling the plantains; bright injiris stippled in light beneath them. Where even lawyers, with their fees, are barely able to make a living. No savings. For thirty years an annual depreciation in the currency of ten per cent. Takes the shine off all the tropical gilt in our travel agents' windows. (One can always go "elsewhere".) Forget the donated school—left over timber and tin scraped together in the yard of a multinational—a sop to those who manage to survive. A public relations stunt. Twelve wells of liquid off-shore gold. Twelve families with so much loot they don't know where to put it. Bought off, and sustained in power, year after year by a foreign corporation. A degraded political culture. What do we care? In the brooding gloom of the largest river that flows through our country, refinery tanks garner the light. And in its estuary's luminous space, welding sea and sky together, ghostly baskets hover, still, with their contents: a welter of chopped off hands.

.

Unable to control themselves, and all those unruly and confusing appetites of which they were composed, they tried, instead, to control the world outside themselves—by finding what they termed "laws"; unalterable convictions of matter which, once understood, as in persons, would allow them to anticipate its behaviour. A "rational" world. "Grant me but the one and only, poor empty certainty". And so they started out on their long journey of obeisance to that strange god they called Science, (and to its political apothecary Democracy). Those who would not bow down before them were subjugated and brought into their fold by force. Such a journey was, in effect, a slow and arduous tracing of a route that would, like the prayers of childhood, lead them, although they were unaware of it, to a metaphysics of presence—"Behold, the light of universals is amongst us!" Which was, also, a metaphysics of disengagement: from a world which they had made "other", and from those very selves of which that "other" was a part, but which they felt so threatened by.

.

In the stone courtyard off which a small garden lay with a glittering fountain and benches and paths, behind a gate that was locked, you thought you had found it. Pathways upon which, as quietly as apparitions, the shadows of grey smocked friars moved in the tropical light. That perfectly ordered arrangement of borders and shrubs, of gravel and grass, and, at its centre, a perpetually rising and falling jet of clear, uncontaminated water. Yet not far away, on the sere grass of the public square, they tied his hands behind his back and blindfolded and then shot him. Under the illusion of the stillness of such a garden there lay the entire weight of a solemn machinery and apparatus arranging the fate of millions. Coming out of, and retreating back into, the shadows you glimpsed its colossal force in an anteroom's thick and dark hardwood chests as high and long as a man, in which the chalices and appurtenances of their order were stowed; and you imagined the half naked and sweating bodies straining to heave them onto rollers, and then winch them up onto a cart where a train of yoked and sweating bullocks dragged at it for hours and days. Your eye and mind travelled back to that garden of infinite repose and you began to see, at its centre, instead of repose, an attempt, in the deceiving stillness there, to form an artefact which would give the lie to such a strenuous administration of power. Who, you wondered, amongst those grey smocked apparitions gliding, day in day out, beside that jet of water, on those hushed and gravelled walks, had ever considered that such ideal proportions and harmony as they represented, was anything more than a device to aestheticise and, therefore, imbue with an aura of legitimacy and respectability, the ultimately ruthless nature of the prosecution of a dream of control and power?

# XLIII

With no one to provide a missing context, or narrative. A forgetting—of almost everything. Phantom, above the grey mist that flows beneath a bridge through the heart of this city. Unsupported wisp, loosened knot of dreams. Yesterday a narrow pathway through a field shaded by calabash trees drew it into a landscape it recognised. Dust. Hogs covered in filth ... Memory, like a tributary from some vast sea it has never done anything more than approach the littoral of, never put its feet into. Where does it reside? In the fundament of a present, a dried up creek, drifting, into former shallows? On the other side of itself? What did it do there amidst the long canes of sugar, the factories spinning into the night their thin gossamer threads unravelled from cocoons on mulberry leaves; behind those doors of compounds full of quietness and the scent of ginger; in those streets where they took down its name and address and told it to report regularly to them? Did it not simply abscond with all their luggage about it? Forgotten. Wandering through the huge plantations of watermelons and peanuts on the other side of the river that rose to meet it. Through those afternoon solemnities where a bright retinue of dreams paraded outside its window. And on whose nocturnal steps the water forever slips, asking it to enter, for it has been too long wandering the fragrant roads where those who have never returned delude themselves they are exploring a land they call the future.

.

We write on air. In that tenuous element where all our lives are lived and where we put down no roots, the sound of our voices occupies a space through which they travel, that recognises no borders or boundaries and in which they, eventually, dissolve. There is no ministry for the issuance of titles and deeds to this air we move within, for it is an element characterised by the most "cosmopolitan sympathies", and all the spaces that we lay claim to it moves through with the utmost contempt for and indifference to their demarcations. It follows no route, coming and going, but its own. Hostage to no courts, encyclicals, codes or by-laws, it is the ultimate tenement of desire. Except that one cannot embrace it. Immobilely seeping through distances we hear in it our own fragile existences contract. In the breath of the failing light of our conversations it crosses between us, leaving no mark. And, as it presses against a window, we listen and we know that ultimately there are no exact locations, and that what we perceive as such is simply the mysterious ground of our perception, of which we do not know the source. The air which travels through all the cities and towns and back-streets of our bodies looking for a personal inscription finds only the broken tablets of a dream on which the phantasmagoria of our senses has scribbled this question: Ισ τηερε α ρεαλιτψ ινδεπενδεντ οφ οβσερωατιον?

.

Down by the rotten timbers of the wharf that had gone out of use many years ago, beside the dark cavernous ribs of hulks that had once sailed the wide seas but which now forlornly pointed in a jagged rebuke towards an overcast sky, in a little corrugated iron roofed garage attached to a junior officer's bungalow, there had been confined, for the last five years of his life, the ageing and reluctantly proclaimed emperor of one of the most cultivated, rich and powerful countries that had ever existed. Like a slippered courtier, he silently padded up and down in the dank gloom squinting out of the garage's single barred window into the fierce tropical sun, looking, perhaps, for that river which, thousands of miles away now and in another country, had greeted his eyes each morning from a sun drenched verandah of white marble upon which he had practised his calligraphy and composed intricate ghazals. Banished from his eyes were the palanquins and entourage of his peripatetic court, its saddlers and perfumiers, its fine silks and brocades, odours of musk and amber, the equipage floating upon the backs of elephants through the dust of a road straight as an arrow. Beneath the garage door the acrid smell of the brine of a mud flat entered. Out across its stagnant pools his imagination moved like a spectre. Cradling, always, the three severed heads of his young sons in its arms (delivered to him compliments of the Company), it drifted. In the blossoms of the neem tree, white outside the window, distracted, it came back and stopped. In those fragile blossoms it identified an odour of sweetness mixed with the waft of decomposing wood from the mud flats and sour residue of oil in the earthen floor of the garage. Together they gathered up, and wove into themselves, all the disparate threads of feelings of boredom, despair, loss, fear, longing and loneliness that seemed, now, to constitute it. Looking again at the tender white blossoms, however, he knew that just as none of those feelings of which it was composed had started out or would end with them, so neither had they begun, nor would they end, even, with themselves. As the evening light began to ebb over the mud flat, the artefacts of a distressed and divided country floated upon a mutilated map of arbitrary and blood filled borders. Slowly, as if from across a far floodplain, the shards of an unfinished ghazal drifted out of the waters of an unquenchable longing.

As if they had come to seek admittance at the metal doors of the garage and, finding, instead, them locked, they faltered, and did not, again, begin.

.

"These sounds find their way to us through the golpata and dhundul leaves, across the dust plain of Ahrusha and the many villages and rivers between there and here which we wander amidst. They do not belong to us, any more than the air or the grass does. They come and go, as if at their own bidding. Those who convey them want no applause. Those who hear them do not cognise them. The first sound that you listen to is the one that has no name, and that you spend the rest of your life wandering after. Like we do, mendicants, meeting up, sometimes, as here, under the ficus trees in the shade, chanting together and labouring within our breaths for what we cannot see, or touch, or feel, or smell—or hear. That which does not long for any habitation, other than these moments passing before us into a groundlessness which vibrates, a silence which cannot be excavated" … or so their slightly rambling, opium and ganja induced utterances, according to our guide, went. "Curious," Hadfield noted, "how these itinerant jongleurs, if that is the name one might in one's own language attach to them, curious," perspiration matting the thick hair of his brows, " how in everything they say and do they seem to express nothing so much as the feeling that they are utterly indifferent to those gathered around them. Our concert-goers back home would find this, and their contemptuousness of applause, puzzling, to say the least."

.

Down through these narrow cobblestone streets over the years, in a cloud of dust, the endless armies came, on foot, on horse and in motorised vehicles. Under the trembling arch of the city's wall, against which the desert throws its showers of silica every minute, we can still hear the angry shouts and jostling of their entry. Dawn breaks, still, in the grey solitude of their eyes from which we are always trying to awaken. Strangers. One morning the sign writer simply appeared, steadying himself at the top of his ladder, and erased the names of streets and shops and buildings, and painted over them new ones and in another language which no one really knew and was reluctant to learn. New laws, injunctions and regulations were promulgated, new passports issued from another country. Like the cloud of dust that came under that arch our lives tread the dark rubble, day after day, still, of the same streets, hearing in their names a ghostly avatar of no-meaning. The names stand above the corner of each street and stare at us as we are passing. At night, sometimes, when we move back from the crumbling edges of our balconies into our rooms, someone addressing us, as if anonymously, from a sofa, will say: "Perhaps it is time the sign writer got out his ladder again and invented for us a new language to dream in."

# XLIV

At the Desk of Eternal Returns you collect your keys. The impedimenta of past acts, thoughts and feelings, coil around your fingers informing you that you have some unfinished business in this city which you thought you might have left for good. In the corner the bellhop waits with his trolley to escort you to your room. It is the same room you occupied before you left. You have returned, almost unaware, to the same wine-red carpet you paced up and down for years before the same window, to the imprint you left in its slightly faded and depressed nap, and to the same threadbare spot where you used to stand and shuffle uneasily before lighting a cigarette and tracing the monotony of a circle in the air with its smoke. Under the door in the morning the newspaper arrives, with the same headlines and news. As you open your trunk the odour of a far away place invades the room and it is, you realise, only within that determinate space between two places that you have ever for a moment managed to disrupt the relentless opacities of time and place and the self. You leave. Then you return. And the key turns, too, in the dark door of your self. Following the same course, your hand moves slowly in an arc as it opens the window. So do your thoughts and feelings and perceptions arise and re-arise in a pattern they recognize and repeat without being conscious of doing so. And as you step outside, again, into the street with its familiar noises the weight of all that appanage goes with, and does not leave, you.

.

The faint odour of libraries in warm summer air. Their shelves brushed by the long cusoks of readers. The pages of their books turned by the slow ruminative gaze that reads them, that moves past the forms of those shadowy watchers at the door covered in ashes and lime, who whisper behind their hands. It leaves, having consigned the shapes of their letters to its memory, and, catching the tide at its turning, intermingles with the sound of other voices. A word, an equation, an idea, stored, like the fragrance of an arboretum, in its imagination for years, passing out, diffused, amongst us. At dawn on the solitary tongue of a coenobite, even, transported. On the warm summer air we hear it, sifting the silence within us, borne on the shoulders of opaque cataloguers and recorders, a reed singing, the afflatus of the eternal amanuensis in the faded scriptorium of the ear.

.

And he was not to be observed, descending the stairs. The odour of the hibiscus plant winding around his legs. The light standing upright to let him pass, silently, the shadows upon the grass waving to him. The heron in its high perch above the river declining its head, slowly, to look at him. The breath, sunk within all the stations of the body, did not cognise him. Though the eyes looked, the ears heard, they did not perceive him. Where were they? Out on that long grass sward beneath the agoho trees, in a space where all movement and sound and outline were as nothing, where all attention and diversity was in the ground of the inchoate, and profoundly sleeping. Oblivious, no one uttered a name when he was descending. Oblivious, the mind inhabited no locus, but, like a blind guide through a drowned metropolis, found the names of everything to be without form, invisible, unapprehended. So he was not to be observed, descending the stairs. The odour of the hibiscus plant winding around his legs. The light standing upright to let him pass, silently, the shadows upon the grass waving to him. The heron in its high perch above the river declining its head, slowly, to look at him. Where was he? In a scattering of worlds out on a perimeter where the mind was absent, was elsewhere, where it had not awoken to that breath of appearances as it was passing, to that name, your name, he uttered as he descended.

.

She looks out onto a landscape you are not familiar with and breathes the air of a strange evening where the light drains from walls. Succubus of a voice. Heard many years ago, unsufficiently attended to. Derelict, rundown hotels. Was it a fore-knowledge of where she would arrive? Only the mucoid yellow fat of a pig's knuckle is left upon her plate. The forlorn wail of a pager alerts the night to the loneliness of a stranger in a room. Petrified pulchritude. Rat's stool in a bouquet of roses. In the deserted hall of a provincial conservatory her voice echoed for years. A music summoning a life. The bruised kisses of a final farewell. Then she breaks off, in the middle of a shuffling embarrassment, or despair, careful to expunge any look of interest. As if trying to erase memory. Running down through garbage infested streets, through blind underpasses, to meet her fate. The stale sweet smell of the sweat of strangers cannot be laundered out of the towels. I am equal to it, she seems to say, the ghostly flickerings of a smile crossing her lips.

## XLV

Down the Avenue of Stars red lanterns sway in the breeze. The bones of the dead glitter. They give back no light but that which under their feet the living generate, stooping to read the names. Their sounds sway with the gold tassels in the breeze. Echoes of an empty sign we long to fill, lying on the phoenix brocaded vermilion of a pillow, listening to the night awakening our desires among the shadows. Even the sea, awash with the white of its own virulence, cannot distract us. Down in the blue houses by the river the dancing never stopped. The milky way streamed silver through the night. Dusk is an exile we peer into. The future a face in a mirror we no longer recognise. What is this music doing moving amongst us across these dark waters that are full of the silt of our lost memories? Touch me, lean on me, it seems to say. I have gathered nothing from you but the noise of these dark stars that in your flesh you are continually reigniting. One, upon hearing this, set off to gather, amidst the withered scrub and parched earth of a place of deserted and ghostly dwellings, one perfect memory. He came back, weighed down only with a basket of worthless assorted artefacts. On the Avenue of Stars the red lanterns swayed in the breeze. In the fullness of dusk the perfume of time saturated the air A young woman with an anxious expression upon her face hurried by, intoning to herself, over and over, the recipe of an ancient aphrodisiac.

.

By two rivers they stood, in separate places, at separate times. Two journeys accomplished. Each no more than a thought in the other's mind. With no one to join them. Stepping closer, they embraced their reflections. As the singer embraces the song only after it has left their mouth, has gone, in fact, out into the air. *Take a dark lamp to the ferryman at the crossing. If you can see his reflection in the water, ask him what the likely fare is. Do not look at him. Listen, though, for the sad pilgrimage on his breath of all those others that he has borne before you. The dark water lapping around his feet is both your burden and your behest which, at some point, he will scoop up and invite you to drink from.* By two rivers they stood, in separate places, at separate times. Each one embracing the frayed notes of a song, which the river bore upon itself. Each one listening, intently, for, within it, the voice of another, that was also their own.

.

The ticket is ordered and arrives. The clothes are packed One final cigarette is smoked, and a long lingering look cast over the harbour where the reflection of the Anan Bhun ripples and breaks upon the water. You lean gazing into the depths. As you walk away you feel and hear the weight of your going like the movement of an anchor being hauled up from some unfathomable depth inside you, drawing with it an endless succession of such goings. Their weight, or lightness, is reinstated in a silent ascent through the obscure layers of a past which you try to lay claim to, but which, in the sheer opacity and immensity of the number of reoccurrences within it, dissolves you. Before your hand loosens its grip upon the flaking rust of the rail beside the harbour, you realise that in such a precise instant of your going there is left to you only the unvanquished sense of that thread of a continuum in which you, and your present, count for nothing,—in which "nothing", itself, is sustained by nothing more than the act of its own dissolution.

.

Once during one of those prolonged bouts of painful separation which regularly punctuated their relationship, when a diviner in the street outside his room, recognizable by his wild shouting and ecstatic announcements, stopped before the dusty iron gate beneath the neem tree to sample its shade, he remembered how after one long night of tormented restless turning and writhing, on at last awakening and having described the tumult of all those dream landscapes that had, with their displaced persona, washed over her, she had, propped half upright against her bolster, expressed in a wistfully sustained sigh her desire for that dreamless sleep which seemed, she said, to continually elude her. Utterly alone, now, he watched the old diviner attentively weaving a garland of fallen flowers from the neem tree around his wrist, and he detected the low, almost inaudible, rhythm of a chant. Motes of dust spun in the light beyond the dark stones at his feet. Looking out from his room at the scene, absorbed by the objects of his sight and hearing, his conscious mind slowly seemed to seep away so that it could no longer see or hear them, resting, instead, within itself, as light as the dust within the air and, like the air, as formless. Only a faint sound, as of a thread being woven, was perceptible, barely; originating from, and journeying to, nowhere. He fell into a state, seemingly, neither like waking or sleeping, all external images lost to him, all impressions, including those of which she was constituted. For one second, perhaps, only, or two— but which seemed like an eternity. The gust of a sudden breeze shook the leaves of the neem tree. Outside of him everything floated, unstructured. He did not recognise what anything was. Then, as if somewhere a gate had been opened and a deep silence interrupted, he gradually noticed his toes and then his feet propped up before him and he experienced the sensation that he was dreaming, dreaming that he was conscious of being awake. Not until the leaves of the neem tree shook again in the breeze did he become aware that he was, in fact, conscious, conscious of not dreaming; not until the shadow of what he recognised as the neem tree quivered upon his skin like the shadow of the unknown person who trod behind him often in his dreams, unseen, untalking, filling him with an apprehension that lasted long after he had woken, and whose presence filled his conscious mind like that of another self that was, and yet that was not, him. At last, seeing where, and when, he was, he looked down, at the space where the canopy of the neem tree rooted in its shade, for the figure of the old diviner. He was not there. In the stillness, fine motes of dust floated on the air, borne as if upon the rhythm of some inaudible music. Maybe, he pondered, the music of a measured vibration from which the figure of the old diviner might, as it is said everything is, have been manifested, and which, because of the power of his abilities, he had caused, perhaps, out of nothing more than sheer playfulness, its simulacrum to dissolve. Such a thought, remembering the old chronicle which said that only that which we truly do not recognise does not disappear, caused him to mutter to himself half in wonderment and, because those impressions of which she was constituted were, in fact, fading daily more and more, half in despair: "The world is glass."

.

A suitcase swayed down a garden path, a bulging, scented Samarkand. A door opened. All the perfumes of Arabia. Both hands raised, an arrowhead to bowed head. The run of rippled silk through her tremulous hands, glitter of glass churis. Tall shadow cast upon the lattice, a dome of swaddled hair. History a painted dais. Its curtain pulled across our sight in public. The body exhumed later. Lingered, in that rural wilderness of fields and lanes and hedgerows. Where did it—its hawkers and peddlers banned—come from, where did it return to? That private, infinite space of longing? Sang, as it was going, a song in a language he had not heard before, shut tight the gate. Early that evening, unable to sleep, he looked out of his bedroom window. The tide was out, and on the mudflats the wreckage of doomed vessels lay exposed. Dark clouds had gathered in the offing. The shadow on the lattice, beside which his mother had stood, fragrantly, still, held its hands aloft. Should we be joyous or sad who have gone so far, and who have never travelled?

## XLVI

You find yourself at last, physically, in a place your mind has already, like your body, journeyed to. As you stand in front of the hills steeply rising above the harbour, though, the sound of hawser ropes straining and raising thin clouds of dust in the fierce light, the ratchets of iron ferry-turnstiles clattering, your memory has already moved off again, comparing what is before you to what was before, and identifying the differences. So, although you stand in the "same" spot there is always that subtle sense of a bereftness accompanying your sensation of arriving at a place you have been in before—which is, for most of us, most places, most of the time. Through that small space in your perception where memory constantly shuttles, unnoticed, back and forth, if you attend carefully to it, you hear the constant slippage, the rift, in that tangibility of a present, which as soon as you become aware of it seems only to become more magnified. As you listen to the creak of the ropes round the hawsers you realise that you are often straining, too, in this constant journeying within your percepts, between the past and present, to hold on to a point of arrival that is, perhaps, unobtainable; that there is, within our conscious lives, an area just like that between waking and sleeping, where the mind is unsure where the source of its sensory information can definitely be located. But since mind cannot travel without body and body—for whom an inner world does not exist since "all its elements are equally external towards it and towards one another"—cannot travel without mind, you have the choice either to not hold to this particular line of rumination or, if you do, to accept that you are condemned to frequently visit this "place" of bereftness which accompanies the constant and unconscious shuttling back and forth of memory within your seemingly immediate experience.

.

This smell has bedded down in the alleyways and archways of your body. On worn down earth tracks, in moist tropical air, it exudes a weathered, almost used up, breath which seems to carry the residues of something very far off, yet close, intimate yet unfamiliar, a staleness which seems to combine both the human and the non-human. Through its detrital drift the night and the voices of vendors call. And, perhaps even more strongly, vanished autumns and dusks, leaf moulds, bonfires, musty cupboards and godowns—the ghosts of elusive sensations that do not distinguish between an inner and an outer reality but which are constellations of parts of a whole which evades us, of a consciousness whose store is forever being added to and shifting, and which is not dependent on any single thing or any single cause; in this case an odour which is part of a cumulative process where object and subject, substance and quality, do not exist, only a flow of intercalating data, of involuntary antecedents to which one can give no name. The "perfumed" trace of their obscure order haunts the mind—like a prose in which the words have begun to fade but which still yields the taste of unknown origins.

.

Every moment we are on the edge of doubt. Of doubting everything. Including ourselves. Especially ourselves, which, the more we linger in this life, come to resemble the creations of a ghost writer, rather than ourselves. For, indeed, how could the fiction of what we (supposedly) behold ourselves to be, from moment to moment, be the product of anything other than a collective effort of mind? As we leave the cinema, where the inevitable script of a life is playing itself out to an audience with mouths agape, and we stumble into the heat and bright lights of a thronged street, what exactly do we leave behind us, behind the heavy iron bar of that clanking door whose echo should break the spell of such a collaboration, but doesn't, into a street where we are jostled by the ghosts of all those other selves moving through "real" space and time? For as the credits descend, and the curtain finally comes down upon all those shelled remnants and wrappers littering the floor, and the music falls silent over the empty rows of seats, the audience having departed, we see in the tired gaze of the usherette who, all her life, ushers us into our seats, a dark moth alighting and alighting. The allure of the spectacle has forsaken her. She knows that in his high loft the Projectionist is poring, frame by disjunctive frame, over an assembled image that is no more than that, an image, of someone approximating a "you", a "me", moving through a time and space that is, ultimately, no more "real".

.

In an old cardboard box up against a wall of a room which housed the "archives" of one of the many foundling hospitals scattered all over this city they found, whilst looking for the papers of one of our recent janitorial staff who had died whilst in service, a file that bore the name of one of the late employees of the Company who had some considerable time ago gone missing. Along with the documentation for his adoption of one of the hospital's foundlings a scribbled and inscrutable curio in his own handwriting was found. How it had made its way into a file full of the most innocuously institutional of information adds yet only another piece to the tenebrous mosaic of our late colleague's life. Its title: 'Will and Testament Of Losses And Encumbrances':

*In a world of expectancy expect nothing but news which is bad and in that way be disappointed by none that is, and delighted by any that is not.*

*These little vials of essences inherited from my mother I leave to all foundlings, because they, above all others, are in need of such succour.*
[missing]

*The singer leaves but not the song. In the corner of the small flag stoned café where each night she used to sing before she left for another country, the song accompanies itself; the history of "her" song, with a limited range of one octave and always behind the appropriate tempo, departs. Unlike the singer, wherever she might be, the song follows its own vagrant path and, even though it might linger there in that same spot, is never the same song, no matter how hard the singer might try to return to look for it.*

*There can be no ultimate distinction between the past and the future. The present is always beyond the measurement of time. One can purchase no ticket to it. It is a pure moment, indivisible, which few ever really manage to travel to, or, if they do, do not return from. In the stillness of all our journeys, short and long, from that Terminus where, running to no schedule, they all start from, only a ghost train leaves for the land of the living.*

# XLVII

Poor old scholarly Unsworth died the other day after a long lingering illness brought on, some of those who have lived most of their lives out here say, by the rigours of the climate. This extract is from an interesting letter he sent when he was on his last expedition up country amongst the Ferassi communities in Abdherva province ... "Lists, you see my dear fellow, are mere determinations of difference. Their nature is that variable, but invariable, object which in these days of 'defilement' rules and delights our desperate lives. Lists which plunder the boundary of conventional classes, grouping what are customarily unrelated objects, are especially sought after nowadays. Not because they, as they should, hold up to us the facticity of that notion of identity which drives our lives, but because they don't, being regarded, instead, simply as arresting diversions with which to while away the time of people whose lives, over stimulated, need constantly refreshing by something 'new'. As with inventories, catalogues, archives, tables, compendia, concordances, all those collations which shadow the immense desiderata of the mind, these people, through thousands of years of acquaintance with the wisdom of their own scriptures, find them more than a little amusing, for they perceive, quite rightly, that our belief in difference is based upon a mistaken notion of identities persisting through time, and that we have, consequently, come to see objects as no more than extensions of ourselves. Whilst they recognise and enjoy specificity and distinctness, too, they see our obsession with personal experience and the individual as the obvious source of all our anxiety. Seeing us scribbling in the Company office until late at night over our lists and inventories of stock they see us as engaged in the useless act of the enumeration of a commerce of identities which ultimately do not exist, but which contributes to the very rigidity of an ontology which is slowly and surely tormenting and driving us all mad, enveloping us in a vast communal hypnosis from which, like sleep walkers, we are unable to wake."

.

He sat beneath the dripping thatch of the hut built from nara wood and cogon grass, that had been his "home" for a number of years. Fireflies ignited in the gloom of a humid evening. The bottle of whiskey at his feet dimly gleamed under the sparse light of a moon occluded by vapours rising from the jungle canopy. Night after night he sat there communing with memories, nodding to the few others who passed by on the way to their huts on the other side of the clearing. Having finished, too, his labours for the day, each evening was spent in the same manner. A bottle of whiskey and tepid murky water and the slow descent into memories in his creaking rattan chair. He felt no sense of belonging to where he was. No loathing for it. And felt no desire, greatly, to be elsewhere. Neither a clear sense of space or time impinged on him. Only, at the edge of the dark blind of trees facing him, which the fireflies partially and spasmodically illuminated, did he remember, again, as the evening wore on, the little wooden post-station dwarfed by old nara trees. And, in a room that was the final resting place for unclaimed luggage and effects brought up river by one of the coastal steamers on its way to Analupo, one of its more eccentric objects, a shrunken Egyptian head and a crate from the East containing the remains of a retired civil servant who'd desired to be laid in his final resting place in one of those cities of the dead, a marble monstrosity on the outskirts of the imperial city. He had, inexplicably, ended up here, marooned, his bones interred in a packing case that the termites were quietly digesting. We all, eventually, come to linger, too, he thought, in a place like this, where the weather inculcates in us the perpetual sadness of farewells, at the edge of a road under the streaming tassels of a coconut tree, or on a small jetty its pilings swollen and splitting in the rising levels of a river. Or we linger on a dusty little dirt road before a library of endlessly unobtainable titles, conversing with no one, looking into the depths of an unsurveyable and unnavigable void into which the sound of our voice simply disappears and does not come back to us, and before which we can only sit, knowing the utter futility of posing any questions to it. To belong, to belong, he thought, to this absolute nothingness, to be possessed by it, taking with one into it no hand shakes of friendships, no hand clasps of loved ones…

.

We descended the worn stone steps beneath the black floral motifs of the railings leaving, as we descended, the pavement's noise and commotion behind us. At the bottom the sound of the street diminished to a distant rumble, fading, as the door which admitted us closed behind us, to no more than a barely discernible vibration. Entering the museum's under illumined basement, with its intricate maze of corridors, rooms stocked full of cabinets, drawers and shelves, was like entering the hushed catacombs of a city that had forgotten itself, for whom its bright and clamourous upper reaches were no more than a show, a cosmetic parade. It felt like, so few and far between were our encounters with any of the museum's personnel, one was entering some tenebrous region of lost souls who, in this underground expanse's quiet gloom were vainly trying to seek, walking backwards and forwards as they did, some souvenirs of their lost pasts. Above us the street of this powerful and prosperous nation throbbed with an incurable energy, its restless torrent of people moving over the earth, filling its termini and departure lounges. In the bleak architectural uniformity of its ministries and corporations men and women were carefully plotting, to the detriment of far off places and people, commercial and military campaigns designed to secure for themselves, and a tiny proportion of their own populations, untold riches and power. Down there *Hippocampus Kuda*, invisibly suspended as in the deep permafrost of a sleep, lay in a thin wafer of its own tissue, its dreams soothed by the hum of electrical compressors. Beside it, below and above it, thousands of other species, now extinct, lay, their evolutionary histories brought to an abrupt end by war, pollution, and the destruction by man of their natural habitats. A large number of the natural inhabitants of the earth reduced to an index of duplicates, of ghostly cells that at one flick of a switch, or a power outrage, would dissolve into a briny trickle. We stood there and it was as if the sound of hooves and the sight of immense herds crossing wide plains, portending, perhaps, our own fate, were nothing more than the flicker of an image, a fleeting silhouette, an apparition, pausing in the white mists of a dream.

## XLVIII

It was a journey he had made only four times, perhaps, in his life. But each time he was about to make it he had looked forward to it with a sense of anticipation that was unusually keen, especially as the train approached the border between the two countries. Here, the coastline, divesting itself of its bucolic gentleness, began to take on, with its ragged rocks high cliffs and foaming littoral, a less cordial aspect. But with the lessening of cordiality there increased the sense that he was approaching a landscape that had some preordained claim upon his imagination. It was a place perching at the edge of a river that widened out into a vast expanse of sea, which always seemed suffused with a cobalt light. Perched there precariously, the slates of its house roofs following the curve of the river through a green flatness to where it met the cold sea, its old stone wall reflecting the river's silty hues, it seemed to offer a final confirmation of calmness and warmth before the eye became embroiled in that chaotic element, its white fringe lapping menacingly. The gleam of the small estuary's puddled mud threw up a sombre light onto the town's cobbled streets. It seemed to exist, in its isolated position, within a state of some charmed intimacy between land and sea. It appeared, always, as he approached it, like a suddenly flung-open casement; onto what he was not quite sure. Looked at from the passing train it was, he thought, one of those places which almost prompted one to half rise from one's seat and to pull the emergency chord and get off, with a view to wandering and lingering for an indefinable period of time in its streets. Yet by the time the urge had registered the vision already had sped past and lay miles back down the line. There was not even a station there for one to alight at. Looked for later on his map it was as if it did not exist. Perhaps it was too small, he thought, to be included in such a survey, or perhaps the cartographer had made a mistake and omitted it. Or perhaps it was simply a random contiguity of elements from past and future excursions, that had suddenly found themselves accidentally inscribed in a now that was nothing more than a perishing moment in a traveller's dream. Elements which, interacting within the store of his memory and his imagination, had mysteriously migrated towards this particular locus in space, to congregate here for that fleeting moment, only, as he passed.

.

As Xmas approached, and a dry hot wind blew through the banyan and agoho trees, the Hacienda Lusitra was blanketed in a layer of thin dust as white as snow. The poor farmers who tilled within its sprawling sugar plantation and who had done so for generations, first under foreign masters and now under their own indigenous comprador landlords, and who were no better off now than they were then barely being able to afford to feed themselves, looked up at the immaculate white walls as if they might have suddenly sprung out of thin air. If it had not been for the fact that a few days ago those same walls had run with the blood of hundreds of their kind for daring to strike at the refusal of the owners to redistribute lands under the government's land reform programme they might have been forgiven for thinking that they were looking up at a whiteness more beneficently disposed, especially at this time of year, towards them. Beneath the glitter of a chandelier in one high ceilinged room, if the armed guards and their dogs had allowed one to approach closely enough, could be seen a white crêpe covered crib draped with imported mistletoe and holly and three white faced figures standing around it proffering gifts. Tall flames of candles flickered in the shadows. Hazardously perched upon the roof of the hacienda a carpenter had been instructed to construct a false chimney, of as much use in a tropical clime as a fur coat, into which an over stuffed, life-sized effigy of Santa Claus struggled, now, in vain, to insert its bulk.

.

Eduardo de Cruz the self styled polemicist and writer of *A Syllabus of Pretensions*, which was featured recently in the Academy's latest index of books purveying spurious opinions, begins: "Are we not tired of all these modish contemporary mantras about the "construction of subjectivity"? Most of them are merely vapid rehashings by intellectual mediocrities of what the previous one has said. Such a notion is peddled by self-satisfied mono-culturalists who have never made much effort to read anything written more than one and a half centuries ago. If they had, and from a language other than those in propinquity to their own, they might cease strutting upon their soap boxes and crowing as if they had just invented the wheel. Why, let them roam further afield if this idea really appeals to them, if they wish to comprehend the full working out of its implications, and read in that far flung culture of which I am such an avid admirer myself, whose ancient scholars first traced the genesis of such an idea and whose culture then devoted centuries to the most painstakingly minute delineation of it, in a fertile and challenging environment of ceaseless argument and counter-argument, extending it so that it illuminated the entire range of human experience. These scholars were, appropriately enough, scholars of language rather than, like in our own day, scholars of theoretical "disciplines" of a questionable and diffuse nature. I said "appropriately enough" because language is the very medium in which all our thoughts, about everything, are conceived and conveyed. It is their substrate. Whatever thoughts we might have must surely be imminent within, and conditioned by, the nature of its structure. So what better place to begin. It was such scholars who first formulated the idea of the interdependence of separate linguistic elements, or features, within time; an interdependence which constitutes the basis of our cognition. Where, to take a simple example, a letter goes in search of a syllable, a syllable goes in search of a word, and a word goes in search of a sentence. Not until the time it takes for that final sound of the last letter to be pronounced is the role of all those separate elements of letters, syllables and words, and the meaning of that statement, resolved. (Just as, only in the entirety of a person's separate sensations, acts and reflections within the duration of their experience does that person resolve all the competing features of their own identity.) Such a sentence, if reduced to a random sequence of the separate and different sounds of its letters, like the parts of a dismantled object laid out randomly upon the floor (though they might very well from one person's, or group's, reassemblage of them come to constitute an identifiable object or entity) does not, inherently, possess any identity at all—O, but this is all such old, though very, very interesting, hat…"

.

That year the snow came early. He died, as he lived, listening to a performance of that same piece of music he loved above all others without ever having listened to it, perhaps, to its end. Or without ever, perhaps, having heard it in its entirety. Either he used to fall asleep as he listened and wake to find the recording ended. Or he arrived at the end of it fully alert only to realise he had missed, because his mind had wandered, some of the intervening moments. And so he was forced to go back to the beginning and to listen to it all over again: with the consequence, of course, that the ending often, again, escaped him. Perhaps this was the reason why he found the piece so overwhelmingly compelling—it drove him, quite unlike any other piece of music he had listened to, so deeply into himself that he frequently ceased to hear it. As the snow fell silently outside the window covering the road, erasing all track and trace of moving things, there was only the sound of the stylus which, at the completion of each revolution, stuttered, trapped, back into the same groove. The static of an infinite regression filled the room. The brass bed-warmer lay cooling upon the floor beside his bed. In the adjacent drawing room, dominating an entire wall, within the black and white lithograph engraving of 'The Destruction of Jericho', as the sound of the trumpets and horns swelled, the huge walls of the city slowly began to crumble. "We shall all hear" he used to say, "before we die, the sound of such a music."

## XLIX

We stand at the window, day after day, composing what we know is an incomplete history of ourselves, going over a ground that is, at best, familiar, at worst almost unrecognisable. It changes and is modified with each revisitation and accrual, until we enter a landscape in which the names of places, as of ourselves, no longer matter, in which there are no meetings under trees on shady sidewalks; or, if there are, at which we can no longer attend to greet whoever expects us. And where they, leaving a present that is unknown to us, fail, too, to arrive. We all long, returning from the future, to greet ourselves rather than to be greeted by someone who is not us. And this obsequious imitation who struts before us, or who lounges in the shadows of auditoriums, can it be ourselves? What we remember of ourselves is of a past that is continually dissolving into a present, and then a future in which it cannot be found. Simultaneously opening onto each other they survive only at a rate equal to the rate of their disappearance. So where we are and what we say, think, feel and see do not cease, but become, simply, a part of that essential incompleteness of ourselves in time; of that ambiguity which our words strain to bring into their compass.

.

"Perhaps this is why, after all, we see so many people in so few faces, and so many places in so few locations. The only reality is the reality of resemblance, which we discover in this shifting parade of objects within our experience. They appear and then disappear—perhaps to return again, almost unrecognizable. There is no substrate but this, nothing more 'real' than this. And even this, being so unreliable an element within our experience, is perhaps not 'real' at all but only an effect of our imagination, part of our innate and potent desire to unify it by generalising. All words, names, forms, cognitions, are part of this action. I am always reminded in relation to this, of a painting, centuries old, dulled with subsequent layers of varnish, hanging on the walls of one of the oldest Christian churches here in the tropics; so still, and reverential in its stillness, it felt as much like an icon as a portrait of a cleric. In a way, an icon, now I come to think of it, of the reality of predication. It was a portrait of a certain Father Blanco in his room—how ironic a name, in retrospect, I have always felt this to be. The good father dominates the foreground of a canvas of unrelieved shadow. Except that, at his back, a profusion of clearly detailed palms, fronds and assorted vegetation, framed within the high light filled space of a narrow arched window, relieves the gloom. The good father is stooped over his desk with an array of unnamed specimens of plants spread out before him and engaged in the activity of giving to what he has recently gathered from the fields around the church a Latin nomenclature; classifying and categorising them into species, genera and classes. In the stillness that surrounds the painting, for there was always only the hushed pause of an infrequent and solitary pilgrim's sandal shod feet in that part of the church, I imagined I could almost hear the air breathe the nothingness of words and their predication. And Father Blanco so mired there in their shadows believing he was advancing to those inanimate specimens spread out before him, and to their poor relata, as indeed he believed his church did for the entire world, the light of some ultimately real entities or set of class-essences." He sighed, a long low sigh, sounding more of sympathy than of dismissiveness or impatience, as if he was, perhaps, sighing as much for himself as for the "good Father Blanco"; as if he, too, might, as it were, be in thrall, still, to the shadows of those words which drape and clothe everything, investing it with immortal "flesh".

.

It was real, before it existed, she believed. In fact it would not have existed if it had not been at first real. Even its not being there was real. A tremendous homesickness seized her, and she wanted to turn round and make her way back. Yet to whom or to where she did not know. Perhaps, she thought, to a reality to which she did not yet belong but to which she would wish to submit herself. As on a crowded street, to a complete stranger's gaze that seemed to hold within it the key to something one had so often sought; or to the first few bars of a piece of music heard for the first time, but which one knew were a part of one, of which one was a part, and of which one needed to hear no more. It was real, she repeated to herself, before it existed. In love, as in travel, the mind seldom at first moves freely yet it is always to that model of absolute freedom from contingency of any kind, that the mind and body give themselves—where did they first learn it?—as they are about to embark upon that dangerous excursion.

# L

In the cobbled streets behind the market where blossoms of the fire trees fall like splotches of fresh red blood the steam printing presses are, in vaporous rooms, reduplicating sheet after sheet of the local currency. So little are such things worth anymore they are no longer counted by stallholders but stashed in small fat bundles upon a scale and weighed. The parks are stripped bare of trees by those desperately searching for firewood. Over dilapidated terminals where buses used to depart every few minutes of the day for the provinces but only a few now leave carrying their disconsolate passengers with them, their faces pressed to the windows, the poisonous air of a twilight hangs. Down streets the faint and ruined signature of light begins to expire. It is as if in the faces of those hurrying down sidewalks one can detect the image of a forgotten dream which they have just come upon again. As if this city, like its predecessor and the predecessor of the one before it hidden under the accumulated rubble of centuries, is to them a lost city. They walk beneath the neon signs of its boulevards where the products of a surplus value still present themselves. Back streets brim with foreign missionaries and musical ethnologists scurrying from one blighted or deserted sacristy to another, or from one depleted parish library to another, trying to salvage the scores of hymns or the scores of compositions once played by fiesta ensembles late into the night. In the twilight that rapidly descends the bright red blossoms of the fire trees thicken on the roads and the streets. Not far north they fall, too, upon the pathways and tracks of upland villages in what once ominously portended that time of year in which to go "in search of heads". In the market, now lit by the light of flickering bare bulbs, a man with an intense and wild gaze suddenly lunges between the stalls, shouting incoherently into the night.

.

He felt he could no longer bear to look at any of the objects around him. Only those residing within his memory no longer wore away at him. The snow that would have melted upon the hot tropical stones in front of him did not melt. His senses, he thought, alienated from this present, were just as much alienated from that past, whose whiteness seemed recuperated before him. How could an object, if it was independent of him, and not subject to the operation of his own consciousness, whether in the past or the present, suddenly become apparent; and if it wasn't independent of him how could it exist elsewhere, elsewhen? In this ebb and flow of autonomous and non-autonomous objects he felt that his consciousness persisted with no ultimate status of its own, since upon them it also depended for its manifestation. It was as if it was continually moving through a geography which had forgotten him, moving around within its own porous temporal and spatial borders, suddenly announcing its arrival and departure. It will be the same place and the same time, he thought, today, tomorrow and in the year to come. All the things that are rendered visible and audible in it will appear and reappear, whether summoned by him or not. Like a fine snow descending upon the stones in front of him he listened to it fall, silently, across the entire landscape of his life, erasing every evidence of his existence, and leaving "the beholder" bereft of what he beheld.

.

You are under the spell of a city you will never know and that, because you may only enter it surreptitiously, will never know you. Under the spell of its language, a language like no other, whose sounds are the most fleeting dusks made audible, whose modulations are an apparition caressing the air. In the lithe bodies of its inhabitants, the gracefulness of their gaits, you hear the whispered nuances of a fate you yearned for but which always remained concealed from you behind thick walls of rooms in that country you grew up in. It is a city you will never leave, and a city which you will never be able to become, either, a true denizen of. The voices of those who come up to you and greet you in its thoroughfares do not carry within them silences of dying conversations at the ends of roads in the middle of winter, back there in that country of dankness and fogs remote to you now, which contained the forfeiture of all that you felt you were, or could become. On that country you have closed the door. And to it you can no longer, now, ever return.

.

High up in the mountainous northern regions of the country, where most people never ventured, through small settlements without electricity accessible only by tracks too narrow even for horses, over which supplies have to be manhandled from the nearest small town an eight hour walk away, the doctor proceeded. Ringed round by a river her destination was reached either by her wading knee deep through water or being floated upon a banana plant "trunk" across to the other side. If she was visiting when the river was in full spate they hoisted her across on an improvised pulley system while the water toiled beneath her. Plotting her way one night to her next place of call, under the flickering shadows of an oil lamp, her host's map spread out before her, she was intrigued at how the contours of the adjoining provinces in that remote part of the country looked, somehow, different. Returning from her room with her own map she confirmed the difference. "And have you never noticed" her host enquired amusedly "how, on your map, the recontoured boundaries strikingly resemble the profile of a very important person?" Dumbstruck, the doctor then realised that on her host's map, a yellow and crinkled thirty year old veteran of cartography, not only were the boundaries, indeed, configured slightly differently but that on her own map, in their new boundaries, she did, indeed, recognise the characteristic high pomaded roll of the Dictator's hair, cresting the familiar profile. "And he didn't even come from this part of the country" she observed. "The contours were so naturally inclined it took only a little minor readjusting here and there to achieve the likeness" her host responded. And then, laughing: "Our well-coiffured land."

## LI

Years later you return to the small hotel where he, and you both sometimes, stayed. Being in that country again and finding the date of his death coming round you decide it would be a fitting venue in which to sit down and, with his favourite drink, engage him in silent conversation. Some of the old retainers, whom you recognise, float across the lobby's faded carpet, encumbered with the luggage of the latest arrivals. You decide not to distract them. Probably, you suppose, as far as they are concerned, despite having been an annual visitor, he simply stopped coming to the country or decided he preferred a change of hotel. The décor seems even more dated, and more scuffed and worn, than the last time you were here. Although you have an overwhelming desire to march straight off into his favourite room, convinced you will find him there lolling on his bed with a book beneath a cloud of Gitanes smoke, you resist the temptation. You sit on in the coffee shop beside the lobby, fondly re-running memories of how frequently the night staff's jaws would drop as he returned and, before entering the hotel, briefly embraced one of the country's most famous cinema celebrities, actor or actress or director, goodnight. Tiring, at last, of your silent monologue, and feeling not a little inebriated by the unexpectedly large amount of alcohol you had consumed whilst reminiscing, you call for your bill. Outside, under the rain-pooled tarpaulins of their tilted shacks, the poor, of which this country is mostly constituted, gaze into the infinite burdens of the night with that seemingly inexplicable, for a foreigner, equanimity which is, in fact, the product of centuries of practice.

.

From the campus, even on an unclear day, loomed the cone of the volcano. Every so often you would wake to a fine dusting, a scattering of ash upon the rooftops and pathways. And you would look up, through the haze of heat in the direction of Amarsuno, for that small telltale plume of smoke. And, on not seeing it, you would breathe a deep sigh of relief and then lapse back into thinking about your ordinary cares and obligations. With that smile always upon his face, which, sometimes you thought, fluctuated between benevolence and condescension, slightly self-satisfied and wry, as if he knew secrets or had solved an important riddle, an ageing member of the faculty, whom they simply referred to as "the philosopher", made his slow indeterminate way beneath the rain trees across the winding bamboo filled paths and creaks of the campus. Often, at noon, he could be found under the broad leaved shade of a banana plant reading, or just thinking. Outside of the class his students steered well clear of him, intimidated by the uncompromising thrust of his dialectic which informed even his casual conversations—he had a profoundly Western, either true or false, syllogistic frame of mind. So he sat on peacefully, to all appearances, undisturbed. Evenings, one would often come across him making his way home, stumbling in the deep shadows of the track beside the Infirmary where the groans of those about to depart this world could sometimes be heard, that smile, as he raised his head into the feeble light emitted from the rooms, still discernible. Mornings found him adroitly circumnavigating the pandemonium of assemblages of students on sidewalks, in corridors, on his way to lecture room or the lull of his office. In summer the pale fluffy hemispheres of the seeding kapoc trees settled upon his desk. They matched exactly, his students thought, the colour of his hair. Later, lingering still in small groups by the squid vendor on the road side, they would greet him as he passed them on his way home. Slowly, as if he did not see or hear them, that indeterminate smile spread across his face, he would lift his head until his eyes were in perfect alignment with a distant image—Amarsuno, towering silently above the dense green tropical vegetation of far valleys and hillsides.

.

For the first time. This archetype bleeds into your whole being. Diluted, traduced, later, maybe. Not now. Transcending, within itself, differences of time and place. You go walking into a landscape that is perpetually present, that loses its shape. For this reason you, too, lose your way in it. So many horizons layered, one over the other, so many towns and cities. Their ghosts walk in your blood. You are haunted. The train leaving from platform three leaves for no particular destination, other than this. For this, the prow of the ship cleaves no other water. And these voices that you hear all the time, are not yours. They come from a place where they have never abused the injunction of No Private Property. Where that face, a blank which you fill in with your own longing, passes through a clearinghouse of broken statuary. Of small groups crossing a frozen sea calling back to you, but who you do not hear. Standing in this garden in blue borage on an afternoon of rare sunlight you stand in all places, and in all times. "Whisper my name again into my ear" you say, "before I forget it."

.

This morning, it being Xmas day, the gift of a cooked Peking duck was delivered to the house we were invited to by the butler of the next door neighbour, the Vice President of the Republic. Not being, like every other politician in this land, a devotee of the principle of public service but, rather, of private aggrandizement, one wondered, looking at the elegant livery of his employee who delivered the gift, at how the emollient of power must work to utterly inoculate its possessor against a world in which the vast majority of us live and breathe and die. Gone, for him, is the entire range of mundane cares that occupy the rest of us. For him are doors opened, cars ordered, bills paid, repairs arranged and carried out, the bath tub filled with water, and even the nails of the toes and fingers clipped. The list goes on and on. His existence rests, whether he likes it or not—and none do dislike it so much they willingly dispense with it—upon a cloud of the most potent of bromides, just as a child's does. And, perhaps, this is one of the greatest attractions of wealth and power, that it enables one to fall back into some of those deeply assuaging docilities that are available to most of us only as young children, when, in our helplessness, we inevitably form the centre of others' attentions, being totally dependent upon them for our every want and need. Not far from the quietness and neatly trimmed and well watered verges of the Vice President's subdivision suddenly erupts, at the end of the road beyond the heavily armed security guard post, like the vision of a far off sea, the noisy and anarchic flow of humanity moving under a thick stratus of vehicular fumes, scrambling hither and thither after unaffordable medicines and barely affordable rice, living and dying under the hot glare of a sun which is mercifully tempered by air conditioners in those mansions that glow behind the security guard post. Like the walls of a white mirage, an unfathomable dream, they hover in the clean undisturbed air of a paradisal, pre-natal calm.

## LII

We seek forgiveness amongst the living rather than the dead. Though they who could have offered him partial placation of his guilt—they who were always a voice (long distance) heard in the ear-piece of a handset, a signature at the end of a letter—were no longer alive, he knew that she who was, and who was dearest to him, would withhold it at the end; indeed, would finally repudiate and curse him. A way of assuaging, he thought, the weight of that need for forgiveness fortuitously presented itself to him in the form of a poor unmarried grilled pork vendor's seven year old daughter, the result of a transient liaison in a provincial seaside resort with a foreigner from his own country. Auburn haired with large brown eyes and light olive skin, a disposition of the most unaffected gaiety and gentleness permeated her smile. The graceful agility and quickness of all her movements only added to the impression of an even greater agility of intelligence of mind informing her slender frame. Who seeks forgiveness but is incapable of giving it themselves, he thought, to such a person forgiveness will not come. On this account alone he considered he had earned the right to seek it in this pale offspring of a passing moment, and with this objective in view set about establishing both her and her mother in a small room in the capital and ensuring they had, beyond the mother's meagre earnings, enough to place the child in a good school until such time as she should graduate from university and be able to support herself. Whether this would be enough, in the end, to outweigh that terrible unforgivingness, which to him would be extended by another, he doubted, though. This thought, ironically, only made him doubt, beyond the secret self-interest which motivated his act towards the daughter, those other actions in which he, instead, believed he had acted with no consideration of benefit to himself at all. In the end, then, he wondered whether it mattered, or did not matter, whether anyone knew or did not know one's motivation. For that turbid source from which all our actions spring is so often unknown, even to ourselves

.

Standing there side by side upon the bank of that wide river where, as a child he had played and swam, he felt a curious intimacy with her, she who had been born so many thousands of miles from there in a country half way round the world, an intimacy different to any other intimacy they had. It was as if all his memory of that river, which he had not seen until then for many years, had become redirected towards her, and as if it had accepted her. How, or why, he did not know. Perhaps, he thought, it was no more than an idle fancy on his part, of one too over fond of another. Yet the feeling remained. Standing there with her, looking out over the glinting mud flats revealed by the receding tide, her presence began to feel more and more like a silent collaboration, as if her mere being there confirmed for him what that river, and the past it betokened, could not, by themselves, confirm. As if her presence resolved something within that memory he was unsure of, by salvaging from it something that was not only his but also, partly, her own. Just as, in the twilight, although her face was fading, he knew that he had dreamed it before they had ever met, and that he would continue to dream it in the days to come long after she had departed. Just as she would his own. In a different place. A different time. Long after he, being so much older than herself, had passed on.

.

From the sand blocked edge of the town, where the storm wind had amassed huge dunes across the road, the gleam of the sea could still be seen, if one looked hard enough, a glitter upon the white washed walls of the taller houses. She lingered there, watching from afar a town muted—as if deep snow had fallen upon it and reduced all its activities to no more than a whisper. She listened, for nothing in particular, knowing that there was nothing to listen for, listening simply for the sake of listening, enjoying that calm which came from a lightening, almost an evacuation, of the content of all her sensations, twisting absentmindedly in her hand a long tress of her hair, her senses so dispersed, her consciousness barely of objects and almost of itself—of that activity, that is, of the nameless movement of light across a landscape of her own breathing. She stood there. Unmoved. Unmoving. In a listening from which, from moment to moment, she was excluded.

.

It was impossible for him to recall the exact nature of that moment of her departure. She had made her way down the narrow pathway from the verandah of their house, and he had never seen her again. There was a look on her face that only she could have, perhaps, deciphered. And the tilt of her head and angle of her body as she walked away from him across the room was one he had never seen before. And had never seen since. Where, and when, they originated he did not know. Perhaps through some distant night of fog and drizzle. In, undeniably, another place, another time. She had once declared that neither the past nor the present could be fully accounted for. And that, within them neither could our actions. Where she was now he did not know. The more he thought of her the more she came to resemble a shadow walking backwards and forwards, all those years, through those rooms of their life to which even he, though he had walked so many times through them, found himself, now, a stranger.

# LIII

He ambled through the decrepit city of the dead, and the dying, pushing his way down the narrow alleyways. They were overlooked by iron-grilled balconies which were festooned with airing carpets and rugs. The balconies were so close one could almost have passed from one to another above the heads of those below. As he traversed the light and shadow of these alleyways, inhaling their odours of incense, he entered a heat whose fierceness seemed to suffocate all smells, rendering sensible only its own quiet conflagration. A line from a book that he had been reading suddenly returned to him: "The present is ancient, for everything that ever existed was present." Perhaps, he thought, that is why this city seems to carry within its appearances the sense of an abiding reality. Even the middens appear incandescent, and the white heat of its walls at noon carries that very subtle sense of an oblivion in which one feels there is contained the contradictory and simultaneous affirmation of both what is about to be eclipsed and what seethes with the palpability of the fully present. Roused by the tart smell of arabica he turned, like that haunter of cafes and habitué of shadows whose observation he had just recalled, off into the low doorway of a coffee house to smoke. Looking out at the red brick fenestrations visible through the doorway and at the top of a distant stupa he pursued the observation, wondering whether there was in this city of philosophers and pilgrims anything at all waiting to reveal itself within the drift of its appearances. A blind man stumbled against his table, the echoes of the street guiding him safely to the door where he turned and, in his white tuba, dissolved within the conflagration of so much light. So, too, he thought, we enter the fiercely coruscating surface of our own perceptions only to disappear into them. Who knows, then, where we are. After he had paid and left, turning out of the alleyway and passing the drowsy hostelry where amid congregations of wet backed flies the saddles on which the pilgrims had journeyed glowed in the gloom, and the slow stink of their sweat that had seeped into them over all those miles of desert and mountain and plain reached out to him, he, the unbeliever, wondered whether what abides, only, is this: the shimmer of the manifold succession of sensations which envelop us each day. If so, it is, perhaps, he thought, enough.

.

from *The Emancipation of Birds*

They worship at the shrine of vacant memories, where no one remembers them, and where their bones lie for years before they are pounded to a white powder and drunk by select initiates in rites inducting them into the arcane properties of flight.

They ponder the invisible barrier between themselves and what, because their bodies are foreign to them, they wish to launch themselves through into the hereafter of permanent song.

They celebrate their entrapment by singing for us at dawn, songs in which are instantiated all the obscure choreographies of air.

Their flight hints at a pattern at which they never arrive, and from which they never depart.

In sleep the story of time is revealed to them, all its intricate passageways its diversions and re-tracings. On their long journeys they narrate them to each other to stop themselves falling asleep.

Where they head for at dusk has no name and no fixed location. To find it with your eyes closed is an improbability. To find it with your eyes open means that you will never find it at all.

At the top of the high mountain called Aramaphuta is, reputedly, a sky school for birds. Covered for most of the year in deep snow and ice the trail that leads up to it is littered with excuses and the blandishments of idle vows that easily broke.

[From a 6<sup>th</sup> century illustrated manual discovered amongst the remains of a tent-like structure in the sands of the Bhomati desert and containing the seal of "The Guardian of The Properties of Flight|]

.

With the cool dry wind gusting down, as it does at this time each year, from the northern steppes and deserts, everything, branch leaf and stem, is tossed, swayed, lifted up, and glows. Each object seems illumined in a fire that does not burn, in which shadow and outline persist, in contrast to that overwhelming heat of summer in which, caught in the white hypnotic intensity of its glare, they are robbed of definition. Now, though, in this kinder light, they reassert themselves. It is a light which, carrying the clippers in a white rush and frenzy of spray, gently kindles. So gently and beneficently, that one feels if one held out the tip of one's cigarette to it, it would light it! From the heart of some immense quietness, as from a crystal, comes this longed for effulgence in which everything dances beyond the confines of its own name to a shared inner rhythm.

.

Do you hear? Are you coming back from where you have never been, to loiter around your life? The sky-blue-tinged hem of your garment suggests it is so. The look in your eyes, of a remote destination. And in your voice, that curious lapse and hesitation redolent of the passage of a lacuna. Do you no longer recognise who, or where, you are? Changed irreparably? The telephone rings but when you answer it, now, it is always the wrong number. Perhaps you have moved so far beyond the point of all departures there is no coming back— except to this; obdurate, stale retinues of words; grey pall of light hanging over the streets where, from lamppost to lamppost, you walk, more like an afterthought than a person fully present, your hands, in a gesture of futility, frequently thrown out before you as if they would grasp what is not there. It is not this street you remember, but all those others that have joined the nameless platitude of the hours into which, at last, all our moments must subside, surrender. A dark niche in a wall holds the message we cannot read. Shadow serifs. The evening coils like a colophon around itself. In it we hear that voice which is our own and into which each silent emblem that it would kiss bleeds into the coolness of a distance no words can heal.

## LIV

It was rumoured in the small town of Marabhre that Telughe, the young peddler who also acted in an occasional capacity as the cleaner of the house of the town's Datu and who had often in snatches of half-heard conversations whilst he was cleaning heard the Datu talking in his inner rooms about the Golden Land of Endless Prosperity, had found upon the morning of the Datu's unexpected demise a map with no names on it but consisting of intricate and involuted arabesques of contours. Linking this with the conversation he had heard the day before about that golden land and recollecting what he thought he had heard in it as a reference to a map, he took these intricate and curling lines to be none other than the setting down of that promised location. Probably, he thought, the Datu had intended to put in the names of places later. Or, perhaps, as a safeguard, had memorised them rather than committing them to writing. So Telughe, in his desire for immediate enrichment, with the map in his pocket and a copy of a standard map against which he would attempt to match the contours of the Datu's, and little else, had taken off to discover the location of that fair country. Years later he returned, haggard and, it is said, with a pitiful look of disillusionment upon his face, to resume his life in Marabhre. One night, slightly drunk in a public place, he had unwittingly revealed his secret. The following morning, fearful that he might be arrested, he fled—never to return to discover the truth. That what he had taken to be the contours of a map had, in fact, been nothing other than the graphic reproduction of the disposition of a recently sacrificed goat's intestines which the Datu, being indisposed to the odour of offal, had consulted as an aid to studying the propitiousness, or not, of making, at his age and that time of year, a long pilgrimage. That endless prosperity which Telughe had heard the Datu refer to, of course, had, too, an inner location; and the way by which its riches could be reached was not one that could by any ordinary cartographer be represented.

.

A tattered and stained satin banner attached by two thumbtacks to the inside of a dusty oak cabinet in the crowded lumber-room of a community hall was the missing symbol of a nation's coming of age when it had first risen against powerful foreign occupiers and asserted its independence in a furious and bloody, but short lived, guerrilla war. For almost half a century the banner had disappeared, and was thought lost. Snatched from the nation's first declared

President—the official office of President would begin only half a century later—by a victorious foreign general, it had been taken back by him and his wife to their country where he was reassigned to the Presidium after the war. Donated by his wife, upon his death, to the local legion it would languish in that dim lumber-room, unnoticed, until a chance encounter brought it to light. In the middle of that far away continent, off the quiet main street of a small town whose only sound, frequently, consisted of the lament of a song from a jukebox and the tinkling of a cash register through an open door, the banner's hand painted bright sun, that had been lifted high above the balcony of that unofficial President to the rapturous gaze of huge crowds who were conscious for the first time of their identity as a nation, faded. In the unknown banana plantation where it was painted in secret at night, and on the nearby tracks imprinted by the hooves of water buffalos, such a sound had never penetrated.

.

The old quarter of Tsimale was once the haunt of the rich who built their seaside villas there and their mansions; later, it housed artists and writers and bordellos. With its fretted stone balustrades and abutments supporting an escutcheon of mosses beneath which they are slowly crumbling, the place wears an air not only of faded gentility but of a past from which, one feels, it had always been superannuated—and which it had, therefore, never left. The old Catholic church at the corner of the square, from which successive invaders directed their campaigns, still stands long after they departed. In a small café at an inn where each Sunday for years they used to meet and drink, a resident of the quarter toasts his deceased friend, filling the empty glass opposite him with wine. He knows that it is a gesture, nothing more. But a gesture performed, like a ritual, in a place where the very stones seem to be sleeping in streets so cast adrift by time, playing upon them in its many guises and impersonations, that we might almost, ourselves, believe we might be walking along them not awake, but dreaming.

# LV

Vainly we struggle to re-apprehend what we experienced in those first few years of our lives. Under what circumstances could such a length of time simply vanish? The overwhelming darkness of that time was not so much a darkness as a time of dream, when the gates of an immediate contact with our experience were, still, fully open—unlike later, when our creative imagination would, instead, be forced to seek a contact with it through words. As we walk beside that dark wood of lost years what we hear, then, is the silence of a time that never found its way into words. Possibly it is for this reason that we look so hard for it, having reinforced, through all those years of thinking, writing and talking, a belief in enshrining our experience in words. We are unable to accept that at the heart of that dark wood neither word nor concept might exist. Do we, also, fear that this is as true of our experience now as it was then and that what we so infallibly transform every minute into words has an objective validity that is ultimately without any foundation at all, apart from the conventions of the language in which it is enrolled? We are all walkers beside the dark wood of lost years, a time our minds return to at the end, brushing the dull fringes of its shade, listening to our own voices, voices that are, really, only a "threadbare whisper" in the night.

.

In the dull light of the quiet sala behind the tulle curtains, on the wooden floor that was husked twice over each day, she paced up and down or simply sat reading from one of the latest romance novels, dreaming of love. As the first rains fell through the bright light of early summer turning the grass in the plaza green she took her missal and walked over to the window where, though a gap in the caimoto trees, she could just make out, bordering the dusty square, in the windows of the farmacia the handsome face of Roman the young assistant in his white coat taking down some item for a customer from the shelf. The mostrador upon which he placed it gleamed sharply and her heart ached with the faint pain of a longing to which she was reluctant to admit the cause. Up and down before the kiosko on the opposite side of the plaza to where the farmacia stood she would often wander as if undecided whether to buy something from it, only to return empty-handed and to sit again silently behind the tulle curtains. At night, lying in bed, the wind carrying, across the endless fields of cogon grass around the house, the scent of what she thought was dried wreathes or withered garlands and the sound of a distant train heading for an unknown destination, she silently wept. And as the fine rain began to fall and rattle the galvanized iron roof of the shed behind the house she felt that it was falling upon "all the bloodstained alters of the world".

.

Walking under the shade of the molave trees he passed the small shack of coconut tree planks in the garden of a house backing onto the road and heard, as he did every day he walked down that road, the vibrating sound of what was unmistakably a washing machine, its cylinder rotating in the dark as if it would, he thought, never stop. And he thought of all the distant galaxies of the universe that were at that very moment, and had been since time "began", racing away through endless space as though they were debris fleeing from a distant cosmic explosion. Our bodies, he began to think, are not only composed of the same dust from such an event but follow a similar pattern. In them, none of our actions is ever complete or ends but leads on to an effect, which in turn begets another action, which in turn begets ... Only in this way, he concluded, in this constant rush of events, is everything, place, time and the objects and thoughts within them, kept from fusing. In this continuous expenditure of energy and motion in which our days go forward and from which we seek some momentary pause, some stay, trying to close the gap between ourselves and others and between ourselves and places, was not, he speculated, the model of that primordial dispersal imprinted in the very particles of our being—"they flee from me who sometyme did me seke"— forming the fabric of our senses and cognition?

.

Out of the deep mauve, just-before-dawn, shadows cast by the mountains over the deserted asphalt basketball court, out of the restless hot nightmares of dark hours of stifled sleepers on the floor of a shack its roof held down by two large bald truck tyres, into the clean uncrowded space of the court a young girl carried in her arms her baby brother, struggling with his weight. Behind her the mists slowly climbed the sides of the foothills dissipating what was left of night, a tenuous luminosity struggling to surface within them from the sun slowly rising behind the mountains. But still the deep mauve shadows held their ground upon the basketball court. And still the small girl with her load wandered as if out of an unruly dream within that clean uncrowded space, deserted but for themselves, whilst all around it, from the massed and tilting wooden shacks, no sound of life had emerged.

## LVI

On the rundown, in some places almost derelict, campus that was once the scene of violent and prolonged confrontations between the military and students who opposed a corrupt and foreign backed dictatorship, and beneath the quiet amplitude of shade from the acacia trees beside the little rusting shopping centre, the expensive limousine of a senator, its driver idling and smoking beside it, could often be seen. Within the damp shadows of the hairdressers the senator, who as an undergraduate had his hair cut by the same ageing hairdresser and for virtually the same insignificant amount of racattos, reclined easily, chatting and laughing as the old barber wielded around his ears the long blades of his scissors. Every now and then the barber addressed a question to the senator as if he was talking to an old and respected friend, the senator amiably replying and elaborating at length, glad, seemingly, to be able to confide some element of revelation to this trusted figure from the past. Indeed, as he sat there before the tarnished mirror it seemed to him that neither he nor Aguido had really changed very much. The image of his youth, those carefree days, wavered but never disappeared from the mirror, and from the tones of Aguido's low pitched voice, in which it seemed to be fastened. His patronage of this establishment, rather than the expensive and fashionable salons in the city, was a testament to the need to maintain a sense of continuity amidst the change and vicissitudes which characterise our brief lives. As Aguido arrived home and, as he always did, recounted to his wife his conversation with the senator, one of a number who regularly returned to him for grooming, as he recounted all those treacherous currents involving details of coups, plots, intrigues and well known personalities, she announced to him, half seriously and half jestingly, that their son, now a student at the same university, was for an end of semester project compiling a "shadow" history of the country over the past half century which was partly based upon the recounted confidences to his father of such senators. Aquido frowned, the deep furrows in his forehead deepening even more in the dim light, and became unusually silent.

.

Nose and cheek guards, javelin, shield and greaves: all paid for. Short sword, breast plate, helmet. When the wind blows we close ranks against an enemy we cannot see. Dust under our eyelids, our feet, our fingernails. Who can see into this trotting phalanx without faces, that shouts at whatever approaches

"Death to all tyrants!" See, the loping Siberian tiger does not see us. It is almost extinct and hugs the ground, keeping away from us. Stone throwing environmentalists, overbearing humanitarians steer well clear of us. Trinkets of jade and obsidian make sweet music to our ears. The oilfields of Azburkestan mean nothing to us. Liberate yourselves we say—but if you can't we will assist you. At weekends. We like our beer warm, warm as this armada of naked arms we lovingly caress. We sleep with our eyes open and dream of unimaginable wealth. All the spoils of the boudoir. We shall carry them off in their queen size beds, to a land of infinite boredom and TV, news-speak and journalese, where they will vote for whoever will supply them with what they want. We remember the smell of burgers, of vinegar and chips on the quays as they were waving us off. "Footsloggers" we heard some of them say. Bringers of enlightenment was what we thought we were, looking down into the toil of our white wake bobbing with styrofoam from a weekend picnic. "Landfall" we heard one of our number shout, not long after. Another: "Land-fill, more likely."

.

In sunlight, pale yellow-green, the spliced leaves of the coconut palm, sculpted Palaspas. Through the swirl of traffic fumes they walk forward with them, men women and children. Along the highways. Beside the rice fields. Beside the steps where the assassins waited for the labour union organiser, an extract from the elegy of Engles for Marx affixed to the wall. Beside the playing fields. The weight of an irremediable poverty upon them. The cries of newborn infants, daughters—"Rejoice daughter"—not a curse but a blessing; born, at least, into a profession. Juveniles trained to adroitly throw themselves into the paths of oncoming vehicles—for the (out of court) settlement. Penitent. Write your own obituary. Fulfil your own prophecy. Drive the nails deeply into your palms. He strides towards those who are waiting for him—the "King"—his face in the viewfinder, his smile, always playing the role of the small man who triumphs over the corrupt and powerful, the unjust. His triumph torn from him in a contested count of the votes. Waving. Around his casque hundreds of thousands from all over the country. Bless this frond. Pale yellow-green, a sprig of fire. A tall column waiting to ignite. " He was poor, and riding on a donkey."

# LVII

He had come back after being away for many years. After his long journey, the husband having helped him from the station with various items of luggage, he went straight up to the bed they had made up for him in their little spare room overlooking the garden out back. "What did he say?" the wife asked. "Very little," the husband answered, "except that he had been here and there, and in many other places the names of which I forget." "He looked tired," the wife said, "as if he was not well. And his luggage—so scuffed, tattered and patched." She wondered how long he would stay. His telegram had merely asked for a few nights' "lodging", nothing more. That night, lying in the quiet of their own room at the front of the house they discussed his appearance, and the general air of tiredness he seemed to exude that exceeded the weariness of any journey. A tiredness, the wife thought, that she had never encountered in him before. It was not until after lunch the following day that he made his appearance, leaning rather unsteadily against the banister at the top of the stairs before he descended. In crumpled khaki shirt and trousers from which most of the colour had long since faded he entertained them with accounts, wry, amusing and fantastic, of his adventures. Later he went out for a stroll to "stretch my legs" as he said "to take the air" as if he had been confined for a long time. That evening under the influence of a nightcap he unwound a little and, at the wife's puzzled expression on learning of his intention to rent a room in a small town somewhere along the coast and stay there indefinitely, tried, somewhat cryptically, to explain: "Every where that seems far away from one, and tinged with that slightly precious air of the exotic, when one has arrived at a certain point in one's experience, O call it the sudden realisation of the unfamiliarity of the familiar, rapidly loses its appeal. Perhaps only in abstention from movement do we discover that place we initially thought we had set out to look for. On finding it, though, we find, also, that it is, essentially, no different to anything we had left behind."

.

The ennui of boudoirs. *Black sunlight* behind the veil of lace in a window, face silhouetted above a cup of tea and a family photograph album. On the street corner a lugubrious young troubadour, fierce and unrepentant, shouts and whistles into the air the song of ages. The years are a dark anvil under his breath. Births, deaths and marriages. Beer, cigarette smoke and sawdust. Feet shape a pattern. Hours whirl within it. Behind the empty swimming pool in the garden, the torn and crumpled tennis net on the lawn, a voice hovers above a pile of dried up leaves swept there by wind. Wallpaper lines a frontier of receding dreams. It listens. The young girl, pregnant, with a suitcase in her hand is imitating the song of a bird. As she leaves she inhales the smell of flowering verges, warm asphalt and rain. Somewhere, the sound of a river. Running over rusted iron bedsteads, it carries within it the memory of an ocean it has never seen.

.

In her letter she had appeared beset by a crippling nostalgia: "Across the courtyard of the hotel the long drawn out call of a Peilau floats over to me. But it is not, I realise, so much from those high plane trees beside the approach road to the hotel it echoes but from a tape recording made many years ago which I sent all those thousands of miles back to my parents so they could listen to some of the sounds of this far off place to which I had come at an early age. How it comes back to me. Unheard for so many years after I left here and moved even farther east, away from where I had come to call 'home'. And I thought, all of a sudden, perhaps it is the same Peilau, for they have a reputation amongst avians for longevity, beseeching me to return those notes of its song which, unasked, I had appropriated so long ago. And I thought that if that is indeed the case, if by doing so I could free myself at last from the crushing pressure of this pain of longing for something I cannot identify, I would do so at once. But always within those remembered objects which seem to summon up within us a sense of loss there is another, greater, even more unassuagable sense of loss which evades us, for it has no object by which it can be represented. It is older than the oldest Peilau that ever lived, and yet so deeply is the very air which we breathe impregnated with it that we always hear its call. For in that call—whether it is in the sound or look of a remembered object, or in the most vague and yet most profound of yearnings, each one of us recognises the fundamentally partite nature of our being, and wishes that it were not so."

.

The past lies in wait for you, ambushes you, greeting you like a long lost friend when you least expect it. In the square by the outlying islands ferry pier the number 22 bus still runs, travelling backwards and forwards to that place where she would always be waiting. We all share a past with at least one other person. But no one else can complete—for there are always pieces to our pasts which are missing—that past for us. Stepping onto that bus again you are starting out, therefore, upon an inconclusive journey, attempting to repeat the narrative to a past that is no longer there, or that, indeed, did not exist. For even when the past was not past, but present, it was being obfuscated; vanity, fear, embarrassment or shame concealing a part of it. Or her face was looking at you out of a confusion of times and dates, intentionally involving you in a deception. The desire to return is nothing other than a metaphysical predisposition at the heart of our longing, and all its protracted actions, to believe in the existence of an original place from which we have been cast out, the scent of which, from some paradisal bloom plucked there, still imbues our being. Whereas the truth, perhaps, is that it is the present, rather, with all its dissatisfactions, and dissemblings, that has usually stood solidly against us and denied us admittance.

## LVIII

A man who tends to a garden every day of his life comes to regard it as his project. But perhaps it is more revealing to say that it is the man, rather, who is the project of the garden. For it is its heavy clay slopes, its tangled undergrowths and the rampantness of its green vagaries that outline to the man, over a substantial period of time, his own features; what he is, and what he is not, to that other which no matter how often it escapes him never lets him diminish the scope of its engagement with, and its investment in, him. Without which, he is nothing. And while as a garden, as an unnatural space, it might tend to overwhelm him he cannot deny it, as he might with the human other, or repudiate it. It exists. It is there. And it exists as a counterweight to, and a confirmation of, as he surely comes to know, his own being.

.

Miguel de Torres the archivist had, as was known in his family, always wanted to write a book. So it came as no surprise when on his death his sister, for he had never married, found in an old leather trunk beneath his bed a crinkled manuscript with his name on the title page. Handwritten, its loose pages bore like the dull yellowish glow which filtered through the skylight of his apartment at the end of day, the warmth of a well seasoned secret. Like his life, she thought, wrapped up in the mystery of a routine she considered unpalatable; the freezing archives of a ministry in the department of the provincial secretariat where, in hand knitted woollen mittens, he frequently wandered, humming his favourite piece of music Bochsa's *Célèbres études pour la harpe*, all day between his desk and the honeycomb of shelves and drawers reaching deep into the recesses of the old converted stables. An endless series of subordinate clauses was, she remembered, after one of her rare visits to his workplace and the crepuscular room where his desk stood on the threshold of that immense repository, the image she retained of it. Indeed, she wondered, now, whether even his manner of speaking, which had been characterised by an habitual qualification of statement, as if each opinion he expressed required further elaboration, might not have been due in some small way to the influence of that dim interior where so much information lay concealed and not immediately accessible. If anyone had asked her what kind of book her brother might have written she would probably have ventured the view that, if nothing else, it would be distinguished by baroque structure—like an indrawn breath only slowly and, very reluctantly, released and on which the reader would, as from a labyrinth, be expelled. About what he might have written she had no idea at all. Nor did its title *The Aborted Muse* provide her with any clue. Opening the manuscript she had been amazed to find that, apart from the title page and table of contents, all that each page contained, in addition to its number, was footnotes. It was a book, in fact, consisting entirely of footnotes. It was, she felt, disappointingly, as if all her brother's solitary hours spent in the vast edifice of that gloomy archive had infiltrated the core of his being. As if those innumerable peregrinations of thought and feet down silent corridors housing millions of dusty cards in files had eroded in him any sense of intellectual substance or body and left him, instead, with only a sense of the auxiliary action of thought carried out in indexing, annotating and citing reference. A continual deferring, to something that was not there. Or that, as was, perhaps, the case with his "book", that he would prefer the reader inferred. For, as she once remembered him enigmatically say: in a world given over to relentless proliferation of opinions masquerading as facts, it might be salutary to reflect that (and here she suddenly wondered whether he might at that moment have been thinking ironically about his project), every insight of any importance at all which we have we have by dint of inference.

.

In one of the many Plazas of Heroes, from which all the streets that ran off bore the names of those now long dead but who had in their day carried out acts of great sacrifice contributing to the country's independence, there had stood a dozen or more silver-painted wrought iron benches cast in a local foundry on the day of the country's liberation. Now, on a sandstone terrace beneath the louring grey of a cold and overcast northern sky, beneath leafless trees, they stood, and appeared to be waiting. On the raised boss in the centre of each backrest, surrounded by spokes of a giant Quetzal head-dress, a bonnet rouge sat and, beneath it, the word "Libertad". Under the word a large eagle, perched upon a cactus plant, fed on a serpent. Hardly anyone came to sit on the benches, even when the sky brightened, and a slow rust had begun to stain and grow in the curves and angles of the rich tableau of indigenous and foreign motifs which adorned them. It was, though, as if in the heart of that hot iron from which they had been cast one could hear the liquid tongue of an exclamation still smouldering. Somewhere, amidst the dust and sun of a small plaza, treading within each shadow, there moved, beneath the laurel trees like an apparition, the name of a god. And in the finely wrought façade at the end of the plaza, facing it, a statue of Our Lady of the Navigator kindly bent its head towards it, the heart of a bloody baptism beating, still, behind it in the quauhxicalli beneath the font.

A spoiled and supported (from a trust fund set up by his father) scion of the first-world who had learned nothing about life, Serge Vladimir Masturbon the II, overweight and perspiring and always obstreperous, loafed his way around many countries, occasionally, for pocket money, teaching his own tongue inexactly—for, in truth, he had mastered nothing, not even the use of his native language—and deluding himself he had a talent for writing. Such a delusion could easily have been spared him by a return to his own country. But, understandably, desperate above all else to see his name in print, he preferred to delay it by lingering in a country—an ex-colony of the nation he belonged to—that was amenable to him; not only because his allowance went such a long way there that he had no need to work, but because it allowed him to indulge his fantasy, publishing his writing in local English Language newspapers, in church parish magazines and almost any publication, including the newsletters and annual reports of various societies and organisations, that would accommodate it. Despite not being short-listed for an award in a competition with others less than half his age, writing in what was for them a second and imposed language, he sought out and found a publisher in that country who, for a generous remuneration, was willing to publish his work. Such work, derived mostly from other men's writings to whom he often felt no obligation to acknowledge the debt, was without any merit. Indeed, when he did not apishly imitate or purloin the efforts of others, his own efforts were unbelievably prolix, diffuse and sentimental. What he knew about literature was considerably less than what a well educated fifteen year old in his own country would have known—knowledge of what an iambic pentameter is would have been as foreign to him as the mathematical formulae required to calculate stress on the superstructure of a large modern aeroplane. For, again, in truth, he had not the humility or concentration necessary to impose upon himself the discipline which is indispensable for any aspiring artist if they are to acquire an understanding and control of the medium they wish to work in. And, being one for whom the existence of himself did not imply the existence of another, a non-self, he had not the minimal curiosity about the world necessary for that power of heightened observation without which all writing lies dead on the page. In a country where the aquiline nose and the fair complexion of the foreigner was designed, in all but the most upright of them, to facilitate hubris, and where there was an aversion to expressing views of an unflattering nature in any venue that was public, Serge Vladimir Masturbon the II's delusion of being a writer, therefore, flourished.

# LIX

Fondly referred to by all those who had dwelled there for any length of time as the City of Swallows it was a place upon which as we walked the shadow and the presence of another city always fell. Which city, or where, we did not quite know. Built by a succession of nomadic princes, as a kind of way-station on the route of their many transmigrations, it had flourished and, over a long period of time, grown. Saturated with the incense of temples, the odours of stables and camel dung, bad drains and the delicacies of a myriad of food vendors, into it were brought for distribution the multifarious products of plunderous expeditions, so that there seemed to breathe at its heart the very essence of a variegation into which we were absorbed. In its alleyways and streets too, as we listened, the irresistible tide of its many different accents took hold of and carried us along. The geography of a permanent un-settlement seemed to abide in the stones of its walls. And beyond them, from a landscape of sand, altering minute by minute, the wind constantly blew open its doors.

.

"Sailed from Faifa today. Arriving Galicia tomorrow." Plus the photograph of the ship S.N. Co's 'Dunera' 11,162 tons was all, on the postcard, there was. On a sea whose white plumage was legendary, he had been cast into the doldrums. After landing he began to write about what he said felt like a place that had ceased to exist, wandering through streets which crossed at what seemed to him like secret interstices of time. Where he would stand and for one moment listen to faint cymbals of a Dionysian rite and then, the next moment, to a giggling throng of white frocked schoolgirls making, up the steep slopes, their way home. Wandering over the cool flagstones of markets and mosques he was sometimes unsure whether the scenes and objects of his perception were actually the result of the immediate data of his senses or the product of what he had mistaken for dreams, lingering on long after the act of sleep had ended. Day after day solid objects of his perceptions began to take on for him the aura less of a waking than a sleeping mind. The sea lapped all night beneath the open doors on his balcony keeping him awake. In the intense heat of those long nights he mistook his ruminations upon the events and scenes of the day for dreams believing, in the morning, that he had slept when all the time he had, in fact, only fallen into a deep reverie. The fragments of such ruminations rapidly dissolved within his "waking" mind. So much so that a street he had walked down days before, that had been filled at that time with a slow procession of mourners and a small white draped casque inscribed to the memory of Felipe Hassan aged fifteen hours, was, when he found himself within it again, tinged with a feeling of sorrow which he found inexplicable and for which he could not account.

·

In General Garcia's pantry were many provisions. At any one time countless items of ordnance, vehicles, fuel, clothing, footwear and food necessary to equip an army either in barracks, on manoeuvres or in combat. A sizeable proportion of these items which he was entrusted with procuring never made its way to those for whom they were rightfully intended. So a poor nation's poorly equipped army became even more poorly equipped than before. Bank accounts with large deposits in major first-world capitals, expensive houses located all over the world. When, finally, he tried to enter the detention cell to which he was to be confined it was found that due to his immense girth it would not admit him. So the jams were taken off by the carpenters and the doorway was widened. In General Garcia's cell there was hardly any room, afterwards, for anything other than the General himself.

# LX

A sky of high cloud and spoiling shadow erases in its movement any trace of the observer. He has woken on this fair morning only to witness his "demise", the mute accomplice in the creation of a flat surface lacking any perspective. It is not what he wants, or does not want. All the cinemas are closed, the TV and radio stations deserted. All the presses, the telephone exchanges and the satellites have fallen quiet. The electricity generators fail to whirr. For a moment all conversations cease. A language without an abyss. A sky without words. The uncognised, at last, beckons. Only the "I" is lonely. Lonely amidst its Niagara of wants. Lonely for what will not acknowledge its existence.

.

Lying at a slight angle to the world, a position he claimed he had always been forced to take, in a rickety old wooden bed in the rundown port city of Entemia, he watched the boats move in and out of the harbour all day. When the wind blew in the right direction he inhaled the fragrance of *Zingiber officinale* being unloaded and could hear quite clearly, on the quays, the cries of fish vendors and the wrenching hiss of steam winches. Even the shadowy personages of his past, he claimed, came up to his room there sometimes to talk with him. "Perhaps" he said "it is because Entemia is such a convenient place to pop into on the way to somewhere else. Being mainly a refuelling station now they can easily land for an hour or two before going back on board and completing the rest of their journey". Such statements we put down to his frequent delirium; not overlooking, however, their plausibility—his room, amongst the peeling tenement blocks upon the hill, was hardly a ten-minute walk up the cobbled street ascending from the harbour. But as far as we, his acquaintances, could ascertain he had withdrawn to such a place precisely to avoid people. That day, though, the last on which we saw him, his withered foot exposed beneath the thin bed sheet upon which the fierce sun flooded through a broken shutter, all he could talk of was himself and his misfortune. We could not but help detect, we later confided to each other, a strong hint of self pity in what he said, almost as if he had come to regard his deformity as a kind of wound bestowing upon him the fate of a mythical figure. And, in fact, it is said that one of Odysseus's crew had indeed washed up there upon his oar in Entemia, not drowned as the poem would have us believe. "She … too … visited" he said "the other day. The last of them. And the most dearly loved. Dispensing, I think, not sympathy but pity. She …So selfishly betrayed. I concealed, you see, year after year, all knowledge of my deformity from her. I concealed it, too, from my self, not wanting to think about it. After she had gone I lay reflecting, and wondered how anyone could really feel sympathy for someone who had so deceived them, taken their own nakedness and given back only a simulacrum. No one likes ugliness, but I compounded an ugliness that is physical with one that is moral ... Trust ...Have slept badly since ... Whose name I can't remember, a Jesuit. Wanted to say to her, except it would, if the pity were true, have compounded with ingratitude ... His lines. Something to the effect that you grieve for something but it is, rather, yourself you grieve for ... Too strong a word though, in my case, grief. Revulsion the least I deserve ... Impelled, you see, by self-interest and love ... both." It was not a pretty story, as we all agreed afterwards.

.

The best tales that her grandmother told were, she believed, always told beneath the banyan tree beside the pond in the garden of their house in Anishpura. Whether it had something to do with the setting, for a visit to her grandparents always marked the release from the everyday routine of school and the noise and crowds of the city, or whether her tales would have exerted their magic upon her wherever they were told she did not know. For such tales she only ever heard in the house of her grandparents in Anishpura. One tale in particular she remembered with an abiding sense of enchantment. Visiting one day, many years ago, the local market with her mother, her grandmother, only a young girl then, had overheard a conversation between two ladies in which one of them had said that it was the kind of weather, bright sunlight accompanied by rain, during which the foxes got married. Intrigued, she had asked her mother whether this was true and she had said "It is said to be so" though she herself had never had the opportunity to observe such an event. That night her grandmother did not sleep, so intently did she prey to the gods for sun and rain. Waking early the following morning and seeing her prayers apparently answered she quickly finished her breakfast and then announced that she was going for a walk. Setting out on the path that ran alongside the river she crossed a number of fields ripe with rapidly swelling watermelons until she could see, stretching for miles, the tall tips of the sugar cane bending in the breeze, the fine rain and light making them glint. She pushed her way into the tilting green sea of stems towering above her convinced that it was there, where the foxes always fled to hide, that she would, if anywhere, be able to observe their ceremony. In that rustling world of thin, dilute and watery, shadows she felt as if at any moment, as she pushed the thick clusters of stems apart in her progress, she would catch a sudden glimpse of a party of foxes officiating at their solemn nuptials. For hour after hour the stems of that quiet and dappled underworld grazed her arms and legs. She had no sense of the direction in which she was going, or of the amount of time that was passing. Every new and then her mind, bodying forth its secret fantasies, arrested the fleeting wisp of a form before her, only to be disappointed when, upon approaching nearer, it turned out to be no more than a gentle rise in the ground. Sometimes, as the wind moved through that colossal expanse of cane, she heard noises that sounded like the tinkling of bells, or the sonorous and melodious barking of what she took to be inarticulate celebrants at some festive gathering. So on and on she pushed, alone and unafraid, until, suddenly stopping short, she realised that it was no longer raining and that, instead of the light of mid morning filtering down upon her it was the fading light of evening. Then a hand of what looked like a young boy, raised and proffered before her, phantom-like in the quietness with which it seemed to have stolen upon her, appeared. Hesitantly, she took it and, as she did so, she was led gradually to the edge of the sugar cane and, after a while, out into the broad space of the world again. Although she had no idea of where she was the people in the village close by to where the young boy had exited the field, and where, it turned out, he lived, knew whose parents she was the daughter of and quickly saw that she was returned to them. When questioned as to where she had been and why she had stayed away for such a long time, causing them to become worried, all her grandmother would say was that she had gone out walking and had wandered off into the sugar cane and after walking for hours had got tired and lay down to rest. When she awoke, she said, she did not know where she was and did not know in which direction to go, so she walked for a while towards where she thought she had heard the sound of voices.

.

In his short treatise "On Names" Ramash Prajna, the Abbot of the monastic university of Japoche, the great centre of Absolutist learning and teaching, dwells, in passing, upon the published accounts of foreign sojourners in his country. Journeying through the diverse cities of its plains and high plateaus, despite such cities bearing the marks of successive waves of invaders who'd settled in them over the centuries, all ventured the same observation that the identity of those individual cities had always on recollection evaded them. Instead, the details seemed to merge, they claimed, until they were not sure which details belonged to which city. "This is not because" explains the Abbot "there is some mysterious or mystical property operating in our lands, but because there are not many but only one city. Whichever names and words might be employed to evoke its various properties it is impossible to know the relation of these singular and yet, not withstanding, general verbal designations to all those properties which together constitute our cities; for these are properties which, in themselves, are incomplete and whose nature resides in the scintilla and flux, only, of that eternal city. Therefore, although one might travel to scores of different cities it is not surprising that each proper name, after a while, might begin to evoke not one particular city but all the cities one had been in, and even ones one had not. Such cities, such accretions of particular sights, sounds, smells, tastes and textures, though empirically real, are, as collections of existents, ultimately incomplete and to be differentiated from that uniform and universal Existence of which they are merely conceptual divisions. The diversity of all cities as, that is, of all names and words, is merely apparent.

# LXI

## The Builder and Assembler of Fountains

Thinks continually of that perfect coincidence between the point of arrival and departure.

Abstains from the composition of all diatribes, invectives and polemics.

Calculates, from all the levels, the flow and fall of water, and the pressure required to raise it.

Washes his hands over and over.

Hears continually the rhythms of yesterday, today and tomorrow, overlapping.

Familiarises himself with all the dry wells between his birthplace and the site of construction.

Compiles a reservoir of shadows for time to feed upon.


Watches, in the quiet courtyard, as water gathers at the rim, falls and then rises again, and begins to dream.

.

His life consisted of a past which he felt had no real borders, no boundaries. Childhood had come and then adolescence, and then his marriage and his divorce. Under the sweating papaya leaves of a humid spring he sat in his garden at the foot of the hill and there seemed to be nothing separating him from that life, from those stages of it that were now consigned to a "past", and from a self, too, that was chopped up and remorselessly defined by its progress through them. Through what, he wondered. Ghostly parameters the mind furbishes us with, a group's collusion. Nothing more? I, too, he thought, am thus. And she who I seemed to have met in dreams, she, too, was, perhaps, less substantial than she seemed. And as the Peilau sang high in the trees on the hill he knew, at last, after all that time, that she had betrayed nothing, no one—though he had not thought so then. And that her dissatisfaction at being with him, like his at her being with another, was no more than the dissatisfaction with a dream that they had both woken from many years ago, on a day of fog and fine grey autumnal drizzle in which their faces could barely be seen.

.

In the heat of the long tropical night her taxi made its urgent way down the steep back streets of the city until it arrived at the entrance to the hospital. Large round wicker baskets full of refuse and rotting debris waited on the pavement to be collected: from them emanated the sweet and acrid stench of decomposition. Married, now, she had never really, although he was her father, known him. Already living with his third wife when she was a child, what she remembered most vividly was the uncomfortable experience of being sent to his office one day to beg for some long overdue money for housekeeping. The war years of his chaotic wanderings with her mother because of outbreaks of bubonic plague and besiegings by bandits of the walled village where they lived, and their flight through the bombed coastal southern cities, happened before she was born. His life, typical she thought of his generation, one of displacement, finally came full circle when he returned home two years ago, his lineament and embrocation business in the West, as well as his last marriage, having floundered, to settle uneasily with her mother and younger brother and sister in a rundown apartment overlooking the harbour. She looked at him, now, his body foetally curled on a bed behind a screen, mouth wide open, the sheet drawn back. And she moved, very rapidly, over to his side and bent over and, tenderly, touched him on the arm, uttering quietly the word "Ba". Then turned quickly and made her way out again into the night.

.

Within the throng of shadows which hovered upon the tables of the dimly lit Czarina Café there seemed to hover, also, the air of a conspiratorial silence. Even as one sat there spooning a dark and richly seasoned borsht out of one's bowl one could sense it above the conversation and noise of the other diners. A silence on which dissimulation fed. Beyond their continual coming and going the proprietor, a tall thick set northerner with an accent that was foreign to those parts, presided aloofly. Many years ago he had been driven by civil war to these shores where all the major foreign powers, eager for intelligence, vied for a foothold. With his White Escoffian chef he had, from within a monarchical enclave, suddenly extricated himself one night and floated across the river that formed the border, and then, slowly, drifted south. The silence which seemed to inhabit the Czarina Café was, more than the silence which betokens absence of sound, a silence of unanswered questions. And since the questions were never overtly put, except in the mind of the asker, what grew in their place was a flourishing and unassuaged suspicion. Suspicion feeds energetically upon silence. Indeed in more advanced states it begins, without being either threatening or nefarious, to evince a kinship with the Unknown. Perhaps it was this which drew such a motley gathering of artists, writers, musicians and radical thinkers to the Czarina Café. Amongst such liminal figures there came, also, the purveyors of "official" papers, letters of transit and visas, and those of dubious provenance proficient in numerous languages and of mixed bloodline who, frequently, had lived in the capital cities of those far northern provinces and, attached to foreign embassies or legations or government departments, eked out a living by, so they said, translating or interpreting. Like plotting émigrés, they would sit in a corner quietly but passionately conversing in a foreign tongue, frequently looking over their shoulders. The café's owner and customers inhabited a crepuscular region where rumour, rather than fact, predominated. Drawn to it, like the members of a secret club, customers arrived and left at all hours of the day and night, many making their way down the steps, which ran almost the entire height of the island, to the unsteady pontoon at the bottom where the air off the mangroves hung, heavy and moist. There they waited for the ferry to take them over the narrow stretch of water before they disappeared into the "towns" of ramshackle squatter huts dotting the hillsides, or into the maze of concrete tenement blocks thrown up many years ago to house the flood of refugees who'd poured over the border.

.

Raised here, on the hot coast of an ancient and turbulent country, amid the dust of its crowded streets full of temples and teahouses, odours of incense and salted fish, the earliest strata of his memory contained impressions he had no difficulty, later, in relocating. Latent fires, they lay smouldering within him. In the gently rolling green hills of that land his parents took him to, and in which the remainder of his life was spent, the teeming streets of his childhood never receded. Before he died he wrote, largely at his family's behest, a book evoking them. In the wild winds and storms of our lives the earliest years are usually a harbour. By returning to them we are not escaping, nor trying to set out again to inscribe a new course, for that is so patently a delusion, but savouring those moments before any course was set: when all that came to occupy the horizon were objects we had not any memory of and which we could not, for only an object which has been sufficiently noticed to be remembered can be forgotten, forget. And which could not, as a consequence, disappoint us.

## LXII

"Don't I know you from somewhere else?" he had said. Mind being a necessary condition for the appearance of all phenomena that is not only possible but, perhaps, inevitable, he thought. The smell of ammonia drifted up in the heat; from the old stone tenement blocks without any septic tanks he suspected. Later the night-soil collectors would come towing, on bicycles, tanks of it down unlit alleys and streets, their pedals creaking under the weight. No doubt I have known you, too, in the dingy apartments without any blinds that litter the back streets of this life where we have sauntered and shuffled our days. This is not unimaginable. Even in the better and well off parts of town, closing the shutters at four o'clock in the afternoon to the fatuous entreaty of chimes. And so you have known me, too, in exactly these same environs, and in others, stepping out onto icy balconies at dawn all the fountains and the taps frozen, lingering and smoking in doorways and staring idly, as the evening enveloped the housetops, into the dull water of canals. The smell of ammonia, again, drifted up to him. Like a percept, he thought, that enters the circuit of its own dissolution and, having nowhere to go, turns back into these self same streets only to find me, or that other of which I am inextricably composed.

.

By all accounts Unsworth had not so much "gone native", with the consequent adoption of all the outer, as well as inner, accoutrements such as dress which the term implies, as "gone primitive". He had abolished in his thought and behaviour any evidence of the singularity of the moment and event, denying history, his history, and that inevitable unfolding within it of time and destiny to which we, from the West, have become so addicted and whose ideology, without being aware it is ideology, we expound. He had no fear of his life standing still. It was a life which, he felt, rather than wasting itself on an endless pilgrimage towards the future had peered into the depths and seen the structure of those infinite repetitions, oppositions and combinations that along with many other abstract patterns revealed its true nature. Having lived and travelled for so many years in that country where rather than the dynamo of the present, it was the past with its potent yet impersonal armoury of annals, legends and myths that gave shape to experience, he began to realize that in order for the present to be, it was obliged to imitate the past. In effect, therefore, there was no tomorrow, except as a prolongation of and recurrence of yesterday. So, in the jasmine scented and leafy pathways of

Inferiganga, amid its perfumed gardens above the deep blue of its harbour, Unsworth increasingly spent his days reading the signs of a present from which the meaning of the moment seeped almost as soon as it had been addressed. Instead, in place of that ever transient present, that instant upon the train of whose passing we are ineluctably bound and on which we are forever looking back, there came to him, in spite of that obligation he felt to interpret all the analogous signs of oppositions and similarities within the intelligible and sensible surrounding him, a feeling of liberation. Liberation from the corrosive insecurity and anxiety which had characterised his former self. A self that had struggled to affix upon the passing show of appearances some abiding motif. To the mobility of such a passing show he now felt himself transposed through the unconscious workings of that collective knowledge into which his being had sunk its roots; yet transposed, also, to the deeper immobility from which it derived and which was continually replenished by those formal equivalences in the outer world of that framework of ideas he had come to believe in. To many of those who met and talked with Unsworth, however, his having "gone native" had less to do with a change of ideology than a change of clothes. One can, it seems, in a small and closed community such as ours, overlook more easily the heresy in a man's thought than in his appearance. But not, certainly, in both.

.

It had been a book written, as its title *A Guide to the Underworld: the Hill City of Uzgistan and its Environs* suggests, with a certain tongue-in-cheek quality. To reach Uzgistan one has to cross, though, one of the numerous tributaries of the Erbutz River which encircle the base of the mountain on which it lies and the thick gloom of their mist wrapped waters might, indeed, be said to resemble, in this respect, an aspect of the River Styx. Once inside Uzgistan one becomes aware, also, of how much of its social life is conducted within or around its many public baths which are fed by the warm underground sulphur springs which are one of its main attractions for visitors. Its numerous limestone caves, entrances to which are spread all over the city, also reinforce the impression of a place where the population spends a great deal of its time beneath, rather than on or above, the surface. Added to this there is the generally moribund air which clings to Uzgistan, to its transport services, its hotels and cafes, and many of its buildings: its trains departing for obsolete destinations, its buses operating to out of date timetables; its reputable hotels either boarded up or demolished and many of its cafes and bookstores replaced by government offices. It is as if the swift, therefore, with its streamlined body and its dizzyingly quick aerial movements, the symbol of which embellishes the baronial pediments of Uzgistan's dowdy visitor information centres, and from whose numbers so many find a home in the walls of those deep and extensive limestone caves, is the least appropriate of symbols by which to represent such a place. Until, that is, one remembers that its name, Hadji, which is also displayed on the walls of such centres, possesses, also, the connotation "pilgrim". Whether displayed because of such a connotation one does not know; for those who are compelled to reside all their lives in such a place, settled as it is, despite its elevation, beneath the clouds of a perpetual occlusion, are not pilgrims, and for them such a connotation might only enhance a despair at living in such a place. But for the true traveller or pilgrim, such a place might well authenticate their sense of it being another stage on the road to redemption, allowing them to derive from the anarchy of its maze-like streets, its dolorous and posthumous workings, a sense that they were, indeed, navigating a way to their goal. That Uzgistan, with its mouldy pediments and worn down plinths, its meandering and sodden paths, was in fact a guide, a Baedeker of their weighed down, yet soon to be unburdened, souls.

## LXIII

Towards the end of the affair he had always wondered why when he had mentioned places they had visited and stayed in together she would deny being able to remember. He had put it down, initially, to not only the burden of her legal studies which, taking place as they did alongside her regular employment, imposed upon her formidable feats of memorisation but, also, her imminent departure with her husband and son back to her home country many thousands of miles away, and a consequent determination to try, for the sake of her emotional equanimity, to put the affair, diminished in intensity, behind her. Of the stone grottoes and temples, of the lakes and pagodas, the canals and fenestrated bridges where they had wandered and lingered for weeks on end, or the light like liquid gold on the Pond of the Eels under Mt. Misho, she professed to remember nothing. Like a self that she had "lost", or denied, she had not so much put that part of her past behind her as erased it. On her arrival back in her own country after a journey of months by steamer she had, much to his surprise, written him a letter, part of which dwelt upon the "forgetfulness" which had so troubled him. " ... the more I tried, therefore, knowing that we were soon to part and were probably never to see each other again, to hold on to the memories of those places, the more they slipped from me. It was as if that part of the past, summoned and re-summoned by such sedulous effort within me, was consequently deprived of its ability to arise spontaneously, and had atrophied and died. The names associated with those places, though familiar as names, had become empty of any personal experience that once attached to them. Recalling them, then, was rather like trying to recall the faces of those close to one who had died. All that I could summon up was—a blank." Perhaps, he speculated, if we had never begun our affair she might have, imagination nourishing itself more thoroughly upon hints and intimations than on completed actions, imagined more durable places.

.

"From this silence from which the sounds of all the different instruments are cast, it is to this silence that you must attend in your playing, and in your listening. It is what each chord, as it ends, breaks upon, and which is woven back into it. It is the inaudible crucible of sound." The Teacher let his arms rest upon his knees. The shadows of the badam leaves moved noiselessly in the breeze, stippling his bare arms. "What does not manifest itself, is as important as what does," he continued. "Just as the multiplicity of phenomena around you appear, so do they dis-appear moment by moment, only that the action of your consciousness and your senses sustains them. Where, into what, do they go you might ask. And I would answer. Into no place, or accomodation of time, that your individual mind would recognise. All sound returns to its origin: all objects of sight and taste and touch and inhalation too. Nor should we think to ask "who" or "what" produces them. This "silence" of which I speak," raising his hand to his lips as in a sign, "which eventually your senses will be trained to apprehend, also does not exist."

.

As he descended the steps into the underground station he looked a last time at her, his soon to be erstwhile wife, as she walked from him. Her face, half turned towards him, head slightly down, eyes directed upwards, forming an expression he would never forget, contained something of reproach, and of infinite sadness and farewell. It was a look, he thought, that he was, somehow, destined to be the recipient of. As if his consciousness, beyond his knowing, had once assumed such a look and exact angle and disposition of body, as if they had lain always in wait for it. Descending those steep steps from the street what he felt he took with him was not just a look but the expression of a phantasm. How powerfully it claimed his attention, then as now, suggesting to him the sheer irrelevance of the time and place in which it occurred, holding, as it did, simultaneously within it both past and present and future. So she had floated, and still did, past him, carrying, he felt, all the weight and burden not only of their own lives, but all lives—all lives that were gone, going and to come. Into the dark tunnels of the station with their dripping walls he descended, her pale visage intractable before him. On the vibrating rail a single gleam lingered. As if amidst vast halls of anthracite, he was overcome by a dank malodorousness of seams. And by, dwelling within them, the terrible impermanence of all forms.

# LXIV

Hadfield's eldest brother's services were finally dispensed with the other week. None too soon really. A strange fellow. Did a lot of drifting before he ended up here. Was always propounding ideas. Very grand ideas as well. Ideas about justice, equality, those sorts of things. In fact, he was the most self obsessed person one might ever have the misfortune to meet. Not a clue about how to participate in a discussion, always highjacking it as quickly as possible to talk about a subject by which he was currently preoccupied. People would often get up from their desk and leave when they saw him coming. Or sit on—and quietly wince. The same with conversations; the only subject he could ever countenance was himself—except, that is, when he wished to talk about what he considered the latest example of injustice or persecution in the world, and what "we" should do about it. Always going on about defending the dignity of others, about how his own was "not negotiable"—we often wondered what was so dignified about a life spent focussed solely upon oneself. He possessed, that is, no experience of imagining the other; except in the most general of senses. The closest he approached realising an other was when it appeared as an identity within a political cause. Ironic, really, how someone who could not interact effectively at the most basic level was passionate about sorting out all the injustices etc., of the world. Looking back on it, perhaps that abstract interest in others was simply a way of compensating for his lack of ability to empathise with those whom he met every day. Not much of a consolation for them though! You could be visibly sick and stressed in front of him without so much as a word of enquiry from him as to how you felt. He was always ready, though, at the drop of a hat, to seek your help when he needed it. Because of that abstract interest in the fate of others he never knew the enduring reciprocity of real friendship, let alone of an intimate relationship. But at least it served to sustain for him the illusion of being part of a group—albeit an ideologically driven one, brought together through correspondence and solely by interest in a cause involving people most of whom, however, would never meet. Membership of such groups, "guilds of the disaffected", is hardly ever revoked and is easily earned, not by deeds, but simply by the parroting of formulaic and unchallenged, but shared, sentiments. His self-obsession was such as to render him incapable of ever becoming part of an informal group, one nurtured less by proscribed self-interests than by the sympathies of people who found each others company congenial and stimulating but whose views might not always necessarily coincide. All his professed altruism, then, concerning helping others was, instead, designed to help himself ... At the end of the day we all kindle our own fires for a little of the warmth and glow of human companionship and acceptance—in whatever way we can. A poor beggar, really—Hadfield. But everyone breathed a great sigh of relief when he left.

.

When they came upon him in the city he was as naked as a fakir, and murmuring some lines of verse: "the sweet breeze from the east comes from some better world." On the embankments the linden trees were in flower. The sea shone in the distance. He neither, they said, seemed to hear a word they said, nor really saw them. Rather, they said, they appeared more like a voice in his head, a vision that he projected outward, so complete did his withdrawal into himself appear to have become. He had, he said, lost the ability to re-form the outlines of the commonest objects and events and he, therefore, could be of no possible help to them. And so they had, intent upon returning the following day, left him teetering, as it seemed he was, upon the edge of some temporary or sustained insight. The tramcars rumbled along the street in front of the ruined house where he sat waiting. Street musicians played intermittently when the fit took them. And the vendors of shoelaces and religious reliques ignored him. What use had he of them? Waiting. Waiting for what seems, he said when they asked him, to recognise us but which has not within itself the power overwhelmingly to convince us of its presence. Waiting, for what "manifests" itself to us in a way which starves our senses. As they walked away down a narrow unpaved street of instrument makers and left the old part of the city they were all struck, doubly so being practising musicians, by the haunting tune played by an old craftsman sitting in the warm evening air in front of one of the shop fronts. Later, having not thought to stop to enquire of him the name and composer of the music, but humming and intoning it over and over again amongst themselves, it suddenly occurred to them how the sequence of its succession of keys, when placed together, constituted the exact spelling of the name of he who, a few hours earlier, sitting before them in front of a ruined house in the old part of the city, had conversed with them. The following day, returning to the street where they had met him, named after a well known and loved flower, they could not find him. Nor anyone there who knew of him. Nor could they find the street of the instrument makers—though they searched high and low for it; looking, eventually, for a record of it in the city hall registers, combing through them hour after hour until it grew dark.

.

It was a narrow and smoke filled oblong room with a piano close to its entrance door. A bar ran two-thirds the length of it. A pianist was regularly in attendance; as it seemed, too, was a heavily built grey haired man with a familiar face, and a thin tall man dressed always in white. There was no resident singer and it fell to whoever was there at the time and wanted to sing to do so. In a country of widespread poverty and relentless heat where no matter how badly you sing they will always give you a round of applause, music was one way they had found, and at no expense, of assuaging misery. Through the smoke that lay heavy as a blanket on the room's bar and booths there passed the fugitive faces of a cross section of the community. Those who wanted to sing, and there were many who had good reason to, always found there way there as did those who wished merely to listen. Many, too, came in hope of hearing Ferduze the country's legendary old lady of dark song. Her voice thickening with age, alcohol and cigarettes, a voice which she had always refused to have recorded making her appearances that more poignant, some nights she would just stroll in and sit down by the piano, lift her hand for a drink and sing. At which the whole room would quieten. And the man in a white suit would lower his head still further and tap his foot, the gleaming white spat of his shoe a metronome moving silently beneath him. As the heavy entrance door momentarily swung open the bleached tableau of the street, a man caught in mid-stride, appeared. Then, held and highlighted for that brief moment as if the dark frame of the door had taken aim at him, just as quickly disappeared. Later, in the voice of the thickset grey haired man, too, cradling the microphone tenderly in both hands as if it were the face of the beloved, an old passion rose up—and then withdrew. After visiting the club with our host many times we came to understand that he was the half brother of a prominent senator, and one time presidential front-runner, from one of the country's oldest and most powerful families—hence the resemblance, and the feeling that we had seen him before. Of the dapper dark haired man also in regular attendance, dressed from head to toe almost entirely in white and always with a neatly folded handkerchief in his top pocket or a delicate scented sprig in his lapel, who, too, would frequently take the microphone to sing songs about the blighted odysseys of love, our host professed to know nothing. Until, that is, one night when, a little the worse for wear after consuming a rather larger than usual quantity of alcohol, he divulged to us his secret. He was a "hit man". "Retired, though, of course." Previously employed also, it was rumoured, by the intelligence service of the foreign power which once occupied the country. His predilection for, or rather what appeared to be his obsession with, sartorial neatness and the unvaried and immaculate whiteness of his clothes, was something we speculated upon. Until, finally, one night one of our party expressed what immediately struck us as a most plausible explanation by drawing our attention to Lady MacBeth's "Out, damned spot! Out, I say … Will these hands ne'er be clean … all the perfumes of Arabia will not sweeten them." Unsullied, he sat there. His spotless attire, upon which no evidence remained to indict him, investing him with the raiment of an absolutely clear conscience.

# LXV

Days without food, traversing a countryside laid waste by war and famine, he, who was to eventually become the founder of an illustrious dynasty but who was then still an obscure member of an aristocracy depleted by internecine strife, dismounted and wandered amidst a place of stones and rocks which had once been a well off family's garden. He sighed, having been away from his native province for years and having longed for and frequently been beset by memories of home. Amidst the devastation, the wall gone and the trees hacked down by starving soldiers for fire wood, the evidence of their presence, and of other rampaging armies crisscrossing the land, was still visible in the ashes and scorched grass of recent fires. As he wandered sombrely amidst such ruin he noticed, in the northeast corner of the few stones of wall which remained standing, a single tree. On it frost bitten persimmons hung. They were barely ripe. After consuming them he left, quietly grieving. Years later, passing that way again, having by then acquired power and having taken province after province in his military campaigns, he stopped at the ruined garden. To his delight he found the tree still standing. Describing to his entourage his previous visit he dismounted and, taking the vermilion cape off his shoulders, enshrouded the tree with it, saying "I hereby invest you with the title 'Marquis of Ice and Frost,'" saying to himself "Why should the record of a tree be more fragmentary than the records of other things."

.

From those labyrinthine galleries and their perpetual gloom deep within the earth, bent double with their faces to a wall of darkest anthracite, the only sound the sound of their axes chipping and the drip drip drop of water; from those endless dust ridden and air depleted galleries hearing nothing for hours on end of the wind rustling wheat in fields mile after mile above them they came, each evening, slowly up into the world again into a light which hurt their eyes. The vapour of an ancient dream filling their minds, the whisper, somewhere, of an afflatus in which the body dissolves all its spaces. Into the sky each weekend they released, from lofts in their back gardens, a restless weightless spiritus mobile. Stood there, looking into the air, while something they did not fully comprehend, winnowed from darkness, ascended. And then carried its image back with them again, each Monday, into that sepulchral gloom into which they would descend.

.

As we open the gate and step into the road to go to the rust streaked arcades of the shopping centre our feet are already off on another journey. Unannounced, and unknown, to us. And when we return, with our baskets loaded, the leaves of the bamboo grove streaming in the breeze like exultant pennants, it is as if we had never gone. So frequently do we set out on this excursion. And so frequently do we return empty handed. One day, we think, when the evening darkens, and it gets late, and we do not come back, they will not send anyone out to look for us. For within that emporium with its infinite number of provisions and of sections they know they would find no trace or outline of us. And, latching the gate behind us every time as we go, knowing the way but forgetting what we have set out for, we wave to them always until the final bend in the road, hoping that we will remember.

.

In the town of Aranpur, high in the Srhrivati range of mountains, reached only by a long and arduous climb through steep defiles, every spring a pigeon market is held. It is well known amongst the lowland villages that the inhabitants of this mountain stronghold as well as prizing pigeons for their aerial graces and beauty, giving them names such as Wild Duck of the Great Dipper, Falling Moon, Oblique Light of the Evening Sun, Half Water Half Sky, prize them also for their practical uses. Almost as soon as they can fly they are taken down the mountain to be familiarised with the location of the Imperial Granaries for the express purpose of plundering the grain reserves, their swollen crops on their return from such expeditions being forcefully made to yield up their contents. As well as their countless flocks of pigeons the inhabitants of Aranpur hold almost as dear the fountains which proliferate in their public spaces and in the courtyards, too, of almost every house. This fascination with, and reverence for, water has led some commentators to propose that their ancestors might originally have migrated from those arid far desert regions to the east. The fountain builders of Aranpur, fountain building being a skill acquired early in their lives, are famous in the surrounding villages and the towns of the valley. Believing, as adherents to an ancient cosmogony, that the material world is, itself, but a manifestation of variations within the range of dense sonic fields which vibrate inaudibly to the human ear but which certain creatures, such as birds, can sense, they have developed an elaborate repertoire of carefully guarded rites which they perform when they construct a fountain. In these rites the water is invoked to rise and fall to the accompaniment of a metre, each metre composed especially for each fountain since, it is claimed, no one fountain possesses exactly the same rhythmic pattern of sound as the other, and chanted, crouched by the new fountain's reservoir, softly out of earshot of any eavesdropper. These metres are recorded and stored at the Office of the Board of Lyrics. To such metres are sometimes written lyrics of great beauty which are recited at festivals. This almost mystical reverence of the people of Aranpur for fountains and water, is closely allied with their reverence, also, for birds. So that if, upon the construction of a fountain, after three days a snow white dove, of which there are a considerable number in the adjacent environs of Aranpur, does not appear and linger on or near the fountain it is considered that the constructors of it have failed to perform correctly the necessary rites. And so they have to be inaugurated all over again. Usually the dove, after feeding and drinking, and so having been seen to have bestowed its approval upon the fountain, departs after a few days.

.

Amid the sad obsequy of spittoons something looks at you. Out of an evening through which you have never loitered. A diarist gathers the scattered tesserae of the hours and then walks out of his house into the street to stare at his image in a puddle. Your own gaze is not the gaze of today or tomorrow but of a guilt, and of a past, you do not understand. It is the gaze of rain glazed roofs and empty gardens where your life has fallen asleep. Trying to count the shadows that pass along the street, the imprecations of distressed voices, you remember all the appointments you missed, the deadlines you did not keep. In a city at the edge of a desert they are making a film about a man who single-handedly challenged the entire bureaucratic machinery of the state. Poems written in bold red calligraphy and pasted on the walls are torn down. In the trains leaving every hour people crowd the corridors to take a last look. The diarist closes his diary. The shadow on your hand is the shadow of a garden into which you cannot enter. A dusk in which you cannot see, only hear, one of the many voices that interrogate and accuse you.

LXVI

Sitting alone in her living room the sounds of children in the playground of the school, like the sounds of oblivion, slowly penetrated to her. Laughter, shouting and screaming drifted across the space between her and where, out of her field of vision, they originated. Sitting there she let her consciousness be enveloped by them, rising and falling, ebbing and flowing, the air which surrounded her alive with the most intense vibrations. Those voices could have been, and in fact she felt they appealed to her precisely because they were, voices measuring, also, that distance between herself and her own childhood and its playground more than half a century ago. Within the constant and audible reverberation of air was, she knew, that distance which exists at the heart of everything, both near, and far. That distance which separates one from the most intimate objects of one's experience. Comprised of the raw data of our senses, such "objects"— in this case, she thought, an auditory configuration of air transmitted in waves by a set of vocal chords—are, contrary to what is commonly assumed, always elevated above those sensory data which constitute them and are, thus, credited with, somehow, mysteriously creating self-perpetuating identities. For this reason, she thought, the voices which she now heard were no more, or less, real than the voices she had heard and remembered more than sixty years ago. Both were traces left upon the air, whether auditory or visual, of perceptible events which had ended. The putatively external sources of such events arrive and then, almost immediately or after a while, depart leaving only an echo or after-image of themselves in the mind. We live, she concluded, within time and space much as migrating shadows do, pulled this way and that, hither and thither, by objects to which we ultimately, inherently, have no abiding connection; and through landscapes which we acquire for a limited period only and in which we try to see the face of who we think we are, and to hear the voice of someone we believe ourselves to be.

.

In the middle of the bridge she paused. She was, like so many times before, aware all of a sudden of being in the process of performing an action which she knew had already been completed. Whether by herself, or by another, was not clear. She was not sure, either, whether it was an action performed here, or in another place or country. One action amid so many, contending for attention. And now, motionless, to stand here in the centre of a bridge, reflecting—on what? Was it, she wondered, simply the activity of consciousness itself—that medium through which materialises the very fabric of our spatial/ temporal being—attempting to remind itself of some lacuna at the heart of its "continuity" in which had been misplaced one moment linking an action with a perception of it? That had come to pause here, for a second, within her own literal crossing? If only she could remember she might, she felt, prevent such a moment occurring again—and again. These continua, these details, which none of us can retract from a lifetime of repeating; through which we locate neither ourselves nor our non-selves, through which, in time, we are neither the same nor different, but through which "our" time is blended with all the other times and places which have existed, and will exist, within us and into which at such moments as these we receive a rare glimpse. A glimpse into a landscape of forgetting, and yet, at the same time, a landscape of recognition.

.

Was Hortense Aloba, who was recently imprisoned for causing bodily harm to her lover and whom the judge, in his final remarks, described as "Everywhere seeing plots designed to forestall and to quell the advance of women" not, perhaps, justified in her suspicions. Ever since, and long before, our good Viennese doctor talked about the "problem of women" men have cast a wary eye upon that figure of the opposite sex, judging her to be not only "other", but also sensing in her a threat to their sense of themselves, without realising that they could not have arrived at an understanding of, or interpretation of, what they are, without her. The subjectivity of that act of interpretation, of course, is all but lost on most men, preserving, as it does within itself, a sense of what they want themselves to be seen as being rather than what they, in fact, are. One wonders, indeed, because of this, whether men fear women half as much as they fear themselves. And into what hypocrisy such a position has led men. On the one hand they have—from the Cathars to St Valentine—refined and idealised women, and on the other hand they have subscribed to a stereotype which envisages her as the possessor of "primitive" qualities, most notably of irrationality and sensuality—is it not significant that the phrase, "dark country", used by 19thC western politics to describe that continent of Africa which it regarded as in need of civilising, was also used, by our good doctor again, to describe the unconscious mind which he regarded as possessing such a dominating sway over women. These qualities, they imply, make women inferior to men, who, they pretend, are rational, reasonable and self controlled beings—despite the chaos and the destruction of war which their lust for power and land brought, and still bring, to the world. The sexual "other" is, then, located only at extremes on the male's radar; evidence, surely, if of nothing else, than of a "set-up"—a false identity proposed by men to justify themselves to themselves. Not to that other who, unlike the male, realises the folly of the game he plays in trying to sustain such a contradiction at the heart of his identity. And who suspects that her periodical pedestal is nothing other than an attempt at atonement for the slanderous lie which he so regularly visits upon her.

.

There waits for you in this city a room prepared and adorned with the silence of many memories. Behind its layers of ancient wallpaper the masonry of many years lies undisturbed. The bones of the dead are laid down in the minds of the living. From its windows you can see, out over the park and beyond the river, the mist that clings to the outer walls where the beggars sit with open palms from dawn till evening. The balcony quivers under your weight. It is a city that you long to leave and that you long to return to. In the labyrinthine dark that lies unmapped within its streets they have set up idols for you. Images flicker on the air. You return carrying a tattered book and the withered flowers of an unknown species. For a while people do not recognise you. Only the child who stands, always, at the corner of the street looking into the river acknowledges your reflection. He turns and nods mutely towards you as you pass. In a grey hospital of fevers a doctor you do not know summons you towards him. The pipes of a leaking dream hiss in your ears. They are reciting your name in a wooden synagogue beside a crossroads of frozen ruts and you listen as a collapsed horse shapes with its last sigh the sound of a benediction for you. The smoke of too many evenings which you do not remember engulfs the bridges you walk over. "The being of a past moment of thought has lived, but does not live, nor will it live. The being of a future moment of thought will live, but has not lived, nor does it live. The being of the present moment of thought does live, but has not lived, nor will it live." All around you the bistros and the brasseries are closing on your life. You are leaving but you are returning. Neither now, nor in the future, but in a past from which you have been expelled.

## LXVII

"A word is only the adventitious mark of an object". Pursuing it. Even in silence. Pursuing, perhaps, what is less a thing than an apparition. Until we can no longer tell the pursued from the pursuer. "This present which I inherit", she thought, "is no more destined to become a past, than a future about which I know nothing is destined to—such divisions needing an object or event to mark them—become a present". Down the long leafless dark of an afternoon from a winter road there came the sound of a bird above traffic. In what felt like some pre-existing substratum of sound she heard on the air, the note suspended. In her throat, too, a thick dark note, in which were assembled all the words of which her being was constituted, struggled to free itself.

.

We never go seeking the objects of our desires but, instead, they come seeking us. And, in truth, that seeking is not for any individuality which we may possess but for a state from which, rather, it has been expunged. For desire, seeking only itself, cannot be satisfied by an other. The simplest room satisfies rather than the most elaborately furbished. For within desire, if one might venture to see to its core, there is the longing for the extinguishment of desire itself. Only, ironically, the sense-object, occupying, as it does, a kind of halting-place within the endless process of the prosecution of our desires, stands in the way of us fulfilling them. For desire is, and this is why, finally, it is always frustrated and why the quest is always renewed, never, as we believe it is, for the empirical object, but for a transcendent subject which does not exist.

.

In the songs of a particular species of bird resident in Takshasila he had identified and outlined, in a soon to be published article in an academic journal in his own country, what he believed to be a tentative "phonology" and "syntax". As he stood in the dusk of that ancient city, after a day spent carefully listening to his archive of recorded songs, he was convinced he could overhear the "conversations" of the birds. "In language there is no private property" he recollected. Whether the minimal units, which he believed he had isolated in the acoustic stream of bird-talk, and the relational system in which they occurred and which determined their meaning, would be verified by his professional peers he did not know. Of another proposition slowly formulating within his mind, of a more far-reaching and controversial nature, he would say nothing, however, for he knew they would reject it. As the light filtered through fine clouds of dust upon the shurki red brick archways of the city he wondered how many nights, full of the odour of decay and of the forest, had settled upon it—upon the silent betel gardens and senduria orchards and upon the prayer rooms and the marble floored loggias. For, amongst the extant festivals of this city there was, surely, one at least, he believed, of immense antiquity. It was a festival in which selected bird-men of Takshasila, schooled from an early age to imitate the bodily movements and postures of birds, would, attired in costumes of feathers and painted in bright avian colors, dance all day through the streets. They would fashion with their feet and hands in the dirt, as if in some shadowy mime of a linguistic creation story, the characters of that Takshasilan script whose formation was attributed to the observation of marks left on the ground by the feet of birds. His fascination with this event was inehaustable, and it was deepened by his knowing that it was the belief amongst Takshasilans that man first learned to speak and write by imitating birds. This archaic tradition, its origin existing in mythical time, appealed particularly to him because ever since he had succeeded in, he believed, determining the code of signification within a particular system of bird calls—based largely, but not solely, upon a classification of opposition and agreement—the possibility that such a myth might just be true, that the calls and spoors of birds might be the avatars of human language, had begun to haunt him. That early human understanding of avian song might have been in terms of what he identified as recursive patterning—a speculation which he regarded as plausible, since the Sky God of the Takshasilans, Aranphur, bore, as well as the written character for speech upon his tongue, the motif of the chakari bird, noted, above all else, for its extreme garrulousness—and that it might have been thought possible to realize something similar within a system of organised human sounds and that this might have been found to have occurred here in the bird-men and the mythic consciousness of the people of Takshasila, seemed to him not entirely impossible. Nowadays, he thought, language is, much to our detriment, revered more for its powers of aggrandizement, for its reification of self and all those contingent objects of the self's actions, than for the miracle of its transformation of sound into sense. Nothing could be more different, he thought, looking up at the steep and crumbling lichened steps of a temple to the Sky God Aranphur, to that belief amongst the Takshasilans in what they called a metaphysics of breath, of air.

# LXVIII

He carried around the world with him all those years as, he thought, some kind of talisman, an old black and white postcard photograph of the village where he was born. In this well travelled reproduction of a certain street, at a certain time of day of the year, a man had just crossed onto the pavement, one foot still poised behind him as he stepped up. The awnings were drawn down across shop fronts. The lower half of the photograph consisted of "empty" space where the photographer had positioned himself in the road looking toward the point where it joined another, on to where it made its way up between half a dozen Victorian villas on the one side and the same number of shops on the other. Its date he approximately gauged by the street lighting, by the conical shaped glass tops of gas lamps with their characteristic spikes, like the tops of Prussian first world war military helmets. He re-imagined all the lives of those he knew who lived there at the time he thought it was taken, and which now were ended. Including his parents'. Where was he, he whimsically wondered, on that particular day on which the shutter had opened, and what had he been doing? In the depth of that empty space, and the remainder of the photograph virtually devoid of people, was a stillness into which his mind entered. It was as if on that sunny well-lighted day the photographer had found the village asleep, fastened in a dream of quietness and immobility. Perhaps that is the way he wished it to be remembered, at a certain time on a certain day of a month of the year that would always remain unknown. But as he looked at the photograph again he noticed, as he had not before, that the sky took up as much space as the road itself, the houses and shops occupying only a thin horizontal strip of the view. Suddenly the photograph seemed to give the lie, therefore, to what he always thought had been its attraction for him: the sense of belonging to a particular place and time. For, together, the wide road and the wide sky took from that stillness all sense of an abiding habitation and, instead, imbued it with a deep sense of longing. Was it a longing for departure, though, he wondered, or arrival? Was there, in fact, a difference? For the road in leads, also, out; and the sky, too, makes no distinction. Within those quiet houses he imagined the dazzling white of anti-macassars. The light that poured through the shutter, and that had poured on all the previous generations of the village, pouring, too, on them. The whole sky, like the eye, alive and open. And he wondered whether he, too, in all those years of his wandering, carrying the photograph round with him, had ever arrived in any one place at all, or whether he had been perpetually disengaging himself from and departing for some single place which seemed to forever elude him.

The social anthropologist and poet Benitez Loeb (his great grandmother had married a visiting German missionary) had no time for the majority of his ex-colleagues—he regarded them merely as hangers-on in an academy rotted by the infusion of spurious theories from those parts of the world to which they frequently went bending their necks at conferences. He lived, with his mischievously named dog Plato, in a tumble down shack within the margins of the campus, a shack without electricity or piped water. It lay unseen from the road within the obscurity of a thicket of bamboo, and was tolerated by the authorities, as were, indeed, the hundreds of similar structures hidden between the trees, where families of the poor were born, raised and expired. But it was not for the majority of his ex-colleagues that Loeb saved his most ardent scorn—despite being an impecunious maverick his writings were widely respected—but for what he saw as the "brokerages" of foreign intellectuals (lulled into intellectual indolence by the material comfort of their lives), dealing and trading in intellectual "futures", those ideas and theories, particularly in the humanities, which almost take as their unexamined premise the belief that what is "new" is tantamount to being self-validating. Such intellectuals, Loeb felt, exhibited a profound uncomfortableness with the present, an unhealthy infatuation with the future and a corresponding devaluation of the past. One must not, they professed, at any cost, stand still; one must move forward. On the crest of that "eternal, omnipresent speed," in search of a perfect state of being or consciousness which their culture had convinced them they had once inhabited and been expelled from, one would, then, be launched into the eternity of "progress". It was because of such speed, chuckled Loeb, that they were so soon able to revere a toilet bowl as a work of art. Loeb was often amazed at how, also, in the works of some of their most revered and canonised thinkers, suddenly and inexplicably the thought would congeal around a concept without any detailed account of the process undertaken to arrive at such a concept. He considered, as an example, the concept of Geist in a highly regarded 19th century treatise on aesthetics and how such a concept, uncontested, became enshrined within its author's, and others, discourse. He compared this unfavourably with the procedures in other, much older, cultures in his part of the world. Here all philosophical positions, established as they initially were within the forum of the public debate, were inscribed in the form of a commentary upon a foundational text. Each thinker attempted to validate his position in such debates by first summarising fully, step by step, the position of rival thinkers from other schools, or from within his own. These he systematically exposed the defects and contradictions of. Only positions which were considered to have been successfully defended in such debates were thought worthy of enshrining as "commentary" and of being preserved. Such a procedure, where each thinker had to be prepared to meet criticisms for which they were not in the least prepared, ensured there could be little or no room at all for independent speculations; and, thus, of the phenomenon of the one-man-show, of "new" systems of ideas which, as one writer remarked, went up like rockets, and came down like sticks. Such a method meant that deliberations of any particular system were manifested in a way in which they were so closely argued against the premises of other systems that they could hardly be understood without them. It was difficult to suddenly overturn a system of thought erected over thousands of years on the rigorousness of a procedure such as this. "Charred fingers" for the sake of it Loeb scoffed. Only those over endowed with the facilities of libraries and museums, but shorn of respect for the items which filled them, and under endowed with the mental facility not to be able to see a childish act for what it is, can afford to talk of burning them down and flooding them. Such hooliganism frightened Loeb. And the hooliganism, too, of putting up one theory, then another one to countermand it, and watching as out of the rubble of their debacle yet another rose, sweeping those before it away. Such waste, he thought. In going forward one cannot, also, avoid, and why should one wish to, returning to where one began; for nothing is ever completely detached or removed from its point of origin. If the human body, he thought, worked upon such a principle of obsolescence, rejecting, for example, the condition of homeostasis, it would never have sustained or advanced beyond the condition of a bacillus in a paludal pool. And yet it is precisely these cultures, with their idolisation of "newness" and of the future, which stereotype older cultures whose intellectual systems are based upon centuries of rigorous and minute examination, criticism and extension of a core of formal concepts, as being steeped in mysticism. Surely, he decided, it is the other way round. These cultures have elevated the future to the status of a deity. What could be more mystical than that? The hubris of such cultures also extended to their self-styled leadership in the arts and, amongst other so called innovations, their writers' devotion to producing modern literary texts of reduced iconicity. However, writers of these older cultures were never attracted to such a practice which, they rightly knew, by so removing itself from the shared communicable world of its users, cut itself off, too, from any appreciably shared range of knowledge and experience of such a world. They, also, knew that, aesthetically, the only way to successfully remove words so radically from the matrix of linguistic convention and yet not to trivialise their nature was, not by becoming political/aesthetic puritans but by retaining the powers that lay within them, at the phonemic level, of pre-articulate communication, where vocal sound was most untrammelled, evocative and procreative, operating, as it did there, from auditory strata of the primordial human imagination As he made his way back at the end of the day to the thicket of bamboo a dog barked and lurched at him from deep within the shadows. Then, recognising him as its master, it continued forward to greet him. "Only dogs bark," he said, simulating admonishment and anger, "at those they do not recognise."

.

She wondered as she got older whether that void introduced into her grandfather's life by the death of his mother, the "unobtainable female", was not, rather, an archetypal space, and whether that smile on the face of the deity, which he had never tired of describing, had not always been there; had been, in fact, what had lured him, though he was unaware, all those years upon his quest to unearth the crepuscular city. For, she thought, man always founds, or if he does not "found" what better alternative than to "find", a city, and has done since time immemorial, upon a site that is sacred. Her grandfather had been one of the first to enter the lost city of Arrathrea when, in the fury of a prolonged and violent storm, the sands were lifted from it and the outlines of its deserted streets and houses, all of a single story, were slowly revealed. In one street called Half Moon Passage (they all bore the inscriptions of their names on them) he had found in the wall of a small temple an engraving of a female deity with a likeness so strongly resembling someone he knew that he was visibly taken aback. After the initial amazement and excitement at the discovery of the ancient city had died down, unable to identify exactly who the engraving resembled he had said that it must be someone he had met but whose identity, for whatever reason, had temporarily abandoned him but would return. For years, long after the remains of the city had been restored to something resembling their original condition, he pondered upon that inscrutable image. Not just pondered but went over the entire succession—as far as he could remember—of the females he had seen, met and known. A number not insignificant considering his prominent position in the archaeological world, and his advanced years. But, despite untold sleepless nights and afternoons when his gaze was, to those who observed him, fraught with a distracted look, it was to no avail. Until, that is, and here she was cruelly robbed of the opportunity to see for herself, at the end of a long and final illness, the city having been destroyed in one of those massive earthquakes typical of the region, he had gripped her mother's wrist and urged her to come closer, whispering into her ear, in words all those present could here: "It was

... I saw it just now in a dream ... I am convinced of it ... It was ..." and then all she heard were the gasps of those standing around him but what she later was informed was "my mother," and what sounded, they said, like a quotation: "Love ... is born of a face perceived and never really seen." Whether such an ambiguous vision was the result of nothing more than his weakened state of mind as he drifted in and out of consciousness during those last hours, she thought, was impossible to say. But since his mother, of whom no image had survived, had died only twenty months after he was brought into the world, such a revelation, at the moment that he departed from it, had seemed to her to have about it an element of, if nothing else, satisfying symmetry.

## LXIX

From a very early age he had been intent upon books and reflection. At the age of sixteen he had started his working life in employment with the post office. Behind the iron grille of a single counter he pressed the chop upon countless documents and orders. Within a dark parabola of ink he saw, after a while, the letters of his destiny begin to dry. And when, after only three years, he was transferred to the remote region of Jaradpur to take charge of the station there, away from his few friends and his family and the dusty and noisy streets where he had grown up, a cry was stifled within him. Arriving after three days strenuous journey by bus, boat and mule and, finally, on foot, he approached the station. It lay, a small hut with a thatched golpata roof, in three square metres of land cleared from the overarching jungle, positioned on the rough mountain track between two hill tribe settlements from one of which each day an old woman would bring him meals and water. After the first week the silence and isolation, broken only by the occasional customer who spoke to him in a variety of his own tongue he had difficulty in understanding and the weekly visit of the carrier to collect whatever mail had accumulated, became steadily deeper. The forest seemed to gradually close in on him. In the darkness, darker and more unfathomably deep than any he had known before, his body a mute wraith enclosed in stillness, the night came looking for him, trying to see in him what, precisely, it was. From the heavy rotting odours of the floor it walked across, beneath the dripping canopy that shut out the light of all stars, it breathed his fear. And he, lying alone, assailed by the silence and shrieks of unnameable creatures that issued from it, gave it its answer. "Not this. Not this." Slowly, in the heart of the searching silence of what seemed like an unending night, he began to wrestle a thing unlike any single emotion. Instead, it seemed to bear, deeply within itself, some incarnate principle of disguise. So that, with the sharp breathing under his ribs he began to sweat and imagine what was neither himself, nor the dark night, nor the shadow of the emotion of fear that had assailed him. The veins on his hands and arms began to throb. A bulbul sang deep within dhundal shadows. Its song a bright flame consuming itself. And suddenly, on a dark shore, he heard and felt the body of an enormous wave move under him, rushing up into him. A sensation of joy filled, then emptied him. All his muscles, that must have tightened under the invisible assault, untensed. Wearily, he stumbled out and sat down before the front of the station. He did not stir for a very long time. Indeed, to anyone passing by he might well have given the impression, angled awkwardly as his body was in a half sitting half lying position, of someone who had died. Not until the following day was well advanced did he make his way back into the station where he slept. The old woman roused him momentarily for his meal, but when she had gone he slumped again, as if from exhaustion, into a deep sleep. From that time onwards he wore a slightly altered look, she thought, but had not within her the power to question him about it, attributing it to some news he must have received from home. A year later, after he had been relieved of his tour of duty at the station, walking back into the dusty courtyard of his parents' house they beheld, immediately, apart from the dense encumbrance of beard adorning what had once been clean shaven features, the look in his eyes. From within the glimmer of such a serenity one would have thought, they said to each other afterwards, there had been cast out a million devils.

.

It is not so much that we remember the moments into which we step, most moments we forget, as that an emotion, thought or perception, becoming detached from a particular time and place, makes its way to us, here, persuading us that it is our own. Desperate, as we all are, to find what it is in this moment that must resemble ourselves, we open our arms to it in a wide gesture of embrace. And the bird sings, no matter how much we might have forgotten the song.

.

It is the complete which, always, lies in wait for us; and which, always, eludes us. What we identify as being fully in possession of its own qualities is so only because it is not in possession of others. Is it not those others which make it, when we have come into possession of it, finally unobtainable? For what it is, in itself, is impossible to ascertain without them. So we are condemned to continually trace the route of its, and our own, incompleteness, "asking the wind to stand still, not to blow away the trail." Though it is never clear, as in the old folk song, by whom, or what, we have been abandoned.

.

From apocryphal offshore glimpses and sightings of such a vast continent there had been forged in the mind, which was already predisposed to discover what the imagination demanded, and then set down as maps, the afflatus of a fantasy. From within the stinking, starved air of steerages, where men succumbed fatally, almost daily, to bilious fevers, where they feasted on wormey and brine soaked biscuit, the fragrance of the Garden of the Hesperides could almost be smelled, the Fountain of Eternal Youth almost be heard. Such knowledge of ancient civilization, acquired through re-discovered classical authors, had quickly become the staple diet of popular romances and broadsheets. Little good, though, such romances did them, in both the short term and the long term. For as they, taking on water each hour, ploughed through those sluggish and morose seas to imagined destinations peopled by freaks and curiosities, of the kind used to frighten children and to stimulate adults, and even after they had found an anchorage and taken possession of the land, but were unable to rid their eyes of the spell of an other that was created in the other's despite, phantasms of an eternal retribution were beginning to mass beyond the horizon. And, are, still, preparing to mass. For the sum of all such fantasy is its reluctance to engage not just with the true nature of the other, but ourselves. And, in the end, allowed free rein in the individual conscience, such a quality, rather than enhancing compassion, diminishes it, and easily facilitates an intolerance which it can exploit for its own end.

# LXX

He was rewarded with a high diplomatic position in the Foreign Service for his leading role in the assassination of the President of his country—not just the President but almost his entire immediate family consisting of young children and pregnant daughters-in-law gathered for a family celebration. He sat, now, on the balcony quietly smoking and looking out beyond the brown brick minaret and date palms to where the sea lay in a long thin band of blue on which the sky seemed to be becalmed. It had become his habit not long after arriving in this distant country to visit his colleague at the mission, also an ex-army officer, and his wife in their large flat overlooking the city. A habit that amounted, sometimes, to almost daily visits. Whether they were to bring over new recipes for the wife, he was something of a gastronome, or gifts for the precocious young daughter whom he would engage in conversation on the balcony, he would always seem to end up on the balcony, alone, looking out to sea, adoring the view which, being an accomplished painter, he said he would love to one day paint. His visits would, under ordinary circumstances, have seemed only natural but for the fact that after the assassination many of the close family relations of his colleague, occupying high positions in the army but belonging to a different faction, had been by various means eliminated. Despite both of them being aware of this the visits continued. Not a word was spoken about it. Sometimes the elder daughter, seeing him alone on the balcony smoking and looking out to sea as dusk came down over the olive and mastic covered hills, wondered whether he was sad. Her parents had said that unlike the members of the group of other young army officers involved in the assassination he never went back home. In the dusk, though, in which only the scent of the carob trees seemed to be clear, she could not see his face. A few days later, though, returning from school and finding him on the balcony alone whilst it was still light she looked carefully at him. It was, she thought, as if his gaze was interrogating the landscape for an answer to a question which he had not been able to formulate. Not long after the family received news of their posting to a different mission. One evening, after the packers had divested the flat of virtually every item of furniture, he called by to wish them farewell. Bringing a drink out onto the balcony, where he had almost automatically deposited himself, her mother, as she approached him, observing the weariness in his eyes as they scanned the steep streets and the turbulent dust churned into the light by the feet of crowds entering the kasbah, thought he resembled a man looking for a city without a past. Handing him the drink, and watching as he turned towards her with his usual polite and slight deference of the head and body with which to thank her, she thought one could, almost, feel sorry for him.

.

As she, the Professor, was walking down the street past the cremation ground and about to approach the Anishpura courthouse the shimmering penumbra of what seemed to her, for she had been for many nights now deprived of sleep by insomnia, like a chimera, part animal part man, confronted her. She stood and pondered. The dark insufflation of a rain cloud, dust hovering beneath its shadow, might, she thought, be the cause of what she so imperfectly observed. The stability of the external objects of our perception is, she knew, always fraught with disruption. For we are always intent upon prioritising the unity of them and the internal subject who grasps them, over the plurality of our sensations. Such sensations, she thought, constitute the ghost in the percept and always lie in wait for us. Her sleeve brushed the dark shadows of the fountain, and she heard the quiet whisper of water. The whisper of a shadow which seemed neither to be awake nor asleep but which hovered always around her. This thing, this potential word, which waited at the edge of her circle of attention, was it not, she wondered, like that elusive integer of a face or a location in sleep, whose identity was always waiting to be revealed. Content not to proceed any further but, instead, to remain in this state of uncertainty where the object remained inadequately differentiated, she seated herself upon the rim of the reservoir of the fountain. From out of the cool wash of its sheen she peered into the shimmering ground of what lay before her. The hot breath of a dried up shadow blew across her face. She bent and in the dust between her feet she drew with a finger a perfect 0, a zero; that which, having a value only in relation to something else, does not, by itself, exist.

.

He suspected his desire to return to the place of his birth was not solely a desire to satisfy a common nostalgia to which we all at one time or another are prone, but a desire to return to the place where his consciousness had first begun to recognise and name the things of his world; a naming through which we realise that we live in, and experience a world which is shared. Such a place, however distant and remote is, he believed, imbued with a profound sense of connection, because its landscape, the "first-landscape", bears our imprimatur of consciousness. A consciousness at first free of any formulated content, in which our inchoate "I" is not by ideation detached from what it observes; then, later, a consciousness characterised by our struggle to inhabit that mysterious space between words and what they refer to, a struggle culminating in a kind of article of faith, of faith in our imagination—yet, ironically, at the expense of that more direct apprehension of the world which the acquisition of language dissolves. In this "first" place, infused with the dim memory and shapes of the place that first gives back to us an objective form of our thought, we begin to differentiate our perceptual field. Perhaps this is why, he thought, some men go all the way round the world, suffering the extremities of climate and moral and physical discomfort in order to attain fortune or experience, only to return to the country and to the place where they grew up. In doing so, he thought, they are, without realising it, returning, perhaps, to what is for them not just the place of their physical birth, but the original undifferentiated "ground" of their being. For do we not all wish to taste, before we proceed upon the long and unknown journey into oblivion, that first fresh impress upon our minds once again of a world which, out of nothing more than mere syllables and imagination, we have made? As well as the simulacrum of that world prior to its vocalisation, whose memory haunts us like the fragrance of a twilit grove?

.

Amidst the fading and cockroach eaten books and papers which had accumulated for more than a century in the Company library there was found a text in Latin bound between thin boards of card. The original was attributed to an Egyptian Greek of the fourth century and had gone through many harmful redactions. The copy in the Company's library, however, was, according to its translator, judged free of these, and close to the original. A certain St.Ambrose had rendered into the Latin what purported to be an account of the colloquy between Dandamus, the Brahman, and Alexander of Macedon. Read within the context of our own day, when arrogance, rapacity and lack of self-control appear to reign, it sounds a timely warning. Affectingly eloquent, one part of the text, especially, where Dandamus speaks, struck everyone in the Company forcibly: "It is the same thing to lie and to believe the liar. A man who is told a falsehood by another and seems to believe in it does harm, as long as he believes the liar before he is able to reach the truth. A false accusation is the mother of hostilities and of fighting between men; it breeds ill-temper which again gives rise to quarrels and wars. And yet, there is nothing valorous in killing a man; it is, as we know, the way of the assassin. As for us, we call him truly valorous who, all naked, contends against the changes of the climate, checking the cravings of the lower appetites and overcoming their varied conflicts by abstinence and patience. Therefore, conquer first of all these vices, those enemies of yourself, if you would appear brave in your own eyes, and then there is no need for you to combat anybody in the world around you. For you stir up wars against those outside, only to supply food and to bring comfort to the enemy that dwells within you. But you see yourself that, while you conquer those with whom you fight abroad, you are vanquished by those whom you know to be at home."

# LXXI

Reduced to poverty by a plague that had carried off his entire family he found himself in the port city of Shinghu after wandering for days through the depopulated villages of the Zhu delta and, for want of food, growing fainter and fainter. His first meal was a mess of leftover rice from some restaurant kitchen shared with him, from a sodden piece of jute sack-cloth under an iron bridge, by a fellow vagrant who'd taken pity on his plight. He would spend most of the year in that city hovering around its dark alleyways rattling the lids of dustbins as he looked inside for something to quell the pain in his stomach. When the first summer after his arrival in the city came, he left. Looking up one day he saw, high in the sky, in their unmistakable formation of an arrow, a flock of wild geese, their necks stretched out before them. Remembering how each summer they would gather beside the village ponds under the wild mulberry trees, he felt that he could never go back. Instead, he began to work his way down the banks of the river which ran through the centre of the city, a river so long it would, he thought, take him a lifetime to get to the end of. Hovering, as he went, for weeks within the precincts of the notorious blue houses perched at its edge, a coin was always to be earned for steadying some light headed departing guest as he put his feet onto the planks of a bobbing pontoon prior to being ferried to the other side. The further south he progressed, putting, as he thought it might, a distance between him and his suffering, the less assuaged it became. Finally, contrary to his earlier decision, he began to follow the river's course north, back in the direction he had come from. And it was then that he realised that he had, from the very first day, been following not the river but, rather, the tinkling laughter of the young girls in all the blue houses along its length. It bore in the recesses of its sound, a likeness to that small thin voice of his wife which, everyone had remarked, resembled the tinkling of a jade ornament in the wind. He would, though, he knew, neither by going up river, or down river, find its source. Nor would he escape from it. For he understood that his suffering, like the river in full spate, derived its impetus and form from the invisible bed which the restless currents of his thought gouged within him. Their traces, present in every moment of his consciousness, he could not, he knew, obliterate. Unable, or unwilling, therefore, to completely step out of or into the full velocity of that body of water which was his pain, all he could do was to listen to its drowned and doomed tinkling as, each day, he followed it home.

.

It was, on a campus beleaguered by the roar and hot breath of exhausts, a place sunk within quietness. Behind the dark green shade of egg fruit trees, which almost palisaded it, the bindery stood. Upon the long wooden trestle tables which filled it beams of tropical light fell, burnishing the grain of years. At noon, the binders snoring gently through the siesta behind closed shutters of some back room, the books lay in their various stages of completion, stretched upon sewing frames awaiting the fragrant bees-wax thread to gather their signatures together, or open upon the table their page edges waiting to be trimmed or their paper boards to receive a vestment of dyed cotton cloth. End papers lingered, longing for glue. In the yard outside, a gmelina tree looked in. Did it behold, in the rough fibrous texture of those pages, the soft suffused glow of its own species' pulp which contributed to their making? The yellow gum on the spine of a book began, like a wound drawn by the weight of humid air, to shine in a thin ooze. The oleaginous odour of printers ink warmed. And the words waited as if disconsolately, perhaps, upon their pages for a reader. As one lifts, in the quietness of that room, or another, one of the finished books and discerns, under the thin end papers the tiny hardened rivulets of glue and the indentations of margins of leather covers folded tightly across boards, one senses, in that stillness of completion, the undone work of hands, the signature of intention prolonged. And one remembers the tall motionless outline of *ficus elastica* stretching one of its great angular branches above the bindery, the thick black juice running from a fig down its bark in a trail of incandescent burgundy, its sweetness brimming in the heat like an incarnate word.

.

He had spent most of his life moving from country to country and from one place to another, until that entire itinerary of his movement, of his peregrination, had come to seem to him no more than a faded map upon which he had trodden—as faded then, the first time he had trodden on it, as it was now. Sitting in the small pebble-dashed bungalow where he had been born he inhaled, in the slightly musty odour of its contents what he had come to think of as the peculiar compost, within which the savoured objects from the places of his travels had settled, of time. It was not an unpleasant sensation, he thought; indeed, it was almost comforting filled, as it was, with the debris of his past. It contained, he felt, a certain burden however. Not just of repeatedly re-visiting a place or condition he no longer occupied, and the associated effort, but of a doubt that he had somehow ever truly arrived at those destinations. For if, travelling as we always do with a memory of ourselves as we are rather than as, however imperceptibly, changed on the way, perhaps we never, in fact, arrive at where or what we set out for. And inhaling, again, amidst air drenched with the scent of fuchsia, that slightly stale odour of a present within a past which was also present, he knew that, if this was so, then there was no point in time to which we could go. For the movement which takes us to all these different points in time is ultimately, he reasoned. a movement of posthumous arrival. Of an arrival always deferred.

## LXXII

Nowhere, especially in its less developed and organised regions, is the dramatic transition from the pandemonium, the searing heat and light of day, to the stillness and gentle warmth of the air of night so forcefully manifested, perhaps, as in the tropics. As dusk descends it is as if, from the main thoroughfares and the narrow back streets running off them, an army has abruptly decamped— the jostling sweating crowds, the hectoring beggars and vendors with makeshift stalls of variegated merchandise and food are suddenly nowhere to be seen. And with them is gone that continuous hubbub of sound, of movement and smell, which so excited the senses: the stillness and quietness which envelops everything makes one almost doubt, indeed, that it existed. And in that stillness, as one stands in the dusk's shadows, a firefly suddenly evokes for one, in its spark of dying luminosity beneath the buri tree, the overwhelming muteness of the day—that which, despite the clarity with which it registered itself on one's senses, and which, yet, still remains vividly in one's memory, has so completely disappeared. Like a vanished country, whose borders one crosses and re-crosses throughout one's life, it is an entity which does not, despite our faith in it, exist. All that exists, as the firefly reminds us with its dippingly erratic and diminutive light, is a succession of moments—visual, auditory, tactile, gustatory, olfactory—which occur and expire on a ground which, lit or unlit, we walk dimly through on our way to somewhere else.

.

He had entered the Company's service on the lowest rung of the ladder and worked his way up by sheer dint of industry and natural intelligence. At first the extreme heat of the country had bothered him. But he quickly, as in all else he did, adapted himself to it. The skeleton of the lower origins of his accent he kept in a cupboard from which only the faintest rattle could, sometimes, be heard. As he mastered his tongue so did he master that elegant shapeliness of the structure within which it moved. As the mind moved through it it became, he thought, a dance. In his sentences' frequently long labyrinthine torque he struggled not to let the sense get away from him, sometimes expanding for sheer delight the radius of clauses and, to test his skill, adverting only at the last moment to their main subject. This is how "they" spoke and wrote. Sometimes to frustrate by circumlocution. Sometimes to divert attention from the subject. He wished to be like them. In the authority of their syntax, its order and control, he saw the very act of that larger appropriation and control of land

and lives upon which the Company's revenues and profits, and thus his own, would depend. In their pronouncements he sensed the power of incorporation and exclusion. And, as beneath the surface of words lay always an abyss of meaninglessness waiting to swallow them if they wavered in their sense, so within the surface of all those lives around them lay a fundamental instability which would career out of control if not continually taken in hand by those fit to administer to it. That by taking on the airs and ways of his employer he had, in fact, placed himself within their control never seemed to perturb him, since they were part of that larger whole to which, he assumed, he would submit, ultimately, his identity for confirmation—unlike the greater number of those whose land, by birthright, this was.

.

She moved away, uncertainly, from the middle of the floor, passing, as she went, the globe of the atlas which had belonged to her father. In the dim light of his study she vaguely remembered asking him, when she was a child, where she lived. His answer, filtered through the cigarette smoke of a dying day, came back to her, now, like a haunting echo: "In a country. In a province. In a street. In a house. Make your choice. Remember, though ... whichever one you choose obviates all those you do not".

# LXXIII

The grey pathos of a day that is ending. Onto the rotting wooden piles of wharves in the deserted wetlands the sky is lowering itself. All the residues of unrelieved feelings. Dark clouds dragging themselves in from the ocean. What do these seek but, in the quivering angelus of a smile or handshake, some unobtainable resolution. Lonely, he wanders down a road inventing excuses for not arriving. At her door the pink Birashilata blooms all night without her. You have heard only the specious rhetoric of dreams. A discourse of greed and fear. From a plundered dystopia they are carrying the wares of estrangement. Specifically: a batch of lottery tickets. A gross of unused condoms. A bottle of unpolluted air. Across the sunken wetlands, amidst the flies and the detritus, you imagine you hear—codicil of exploding concrete and mortar—the unresolved conflict of another war.

.

Here, where we are migrating across borders of non-absolute sense, the telephone rings all day in the office of the Inspector of Customs and Levier of Duties; but no one answers it. Under a corrugated iron roof and the deafening clatter of monsoon rains the lights sway gently in the wash of air from fans. Parcels, cases and trunks, with names scrawled on them, lie in the corner; but no one comes for them. All day and night the lantern burns above the door of the office. A seemingly quenchless fountain overflows its bowls, and porters lounge around the courtyard looking out, longingly, towards the harbour. "Journeying through life, journeying through death", they say, "is the current, carrying no face upon it. It is our fate, as it is yours, to sit here, waiting". Inside, the Inspector rustles his papers once more as if there were some persons about to be processed. Then pinches his nose, and sighs.

.

After a few days the face of the loved one, or of one close to one who is no longer there, begins to fade, and to rapidly disintegrate to the point where one can no longer effectively recover it and one has to turn to a photographic image instead. Seldom does one realise, when the person is there in front of one, however, how incomplete and momentary, even then, one's view of them really is. One never sees them in their entirety: always, a part of them, or parts, are withheld. And of the part one does see, part of it might be in light whilst another part in shadow. Even what one does see clearly of the person, changes with their movement and their expression. Situated before one, spatially and temporally, it has, therefore, no extensity. Consisting of thousands of separate images its completeness is made up by our imagination, constantly hovering around it, assembling and reassembling it bit by bit. Without the reinforcement, though, of its proximity to us in space and time the assemblage begins to lose its coherence. In its place there comes to stand a flickering image, wearing out. Like a fading reproduction of a reproduction the image becomes disjunctive, discontinuous. Each reproduction of the original dilutes the memoried object. Finally, memory, in fact, becomes, rather than a celebration of the object's recovery, an elegy for its disappearance.

.

She turned back from the balcony and the quietness of her garden at the end of the island, the channel between it and the mainland transformed into a luminous bar by late afternoon light. The heat was ebbing away, but the fierceness of light remained. She went into the bedroom and lay down upon the bed. The window was a frame of verticals and horizontals, the leaves of the wooded hillside shimmering behind the louvres of the shutter. She closed her eyes and tried to doze. Without success. Each time the darkness descended behind her lids there remained the negative of that pulsing world she had just shut them against: each louvre, reproduced exactly the way it was when she opened her eyes again, and the massive bulk of the hillside and the iron window frame. Each glowed in a forensic black and white like, she thought, the embers of some immense, but quiet, fire that was at rest within them. Rather than an after-image, she began to think of it as a pre-image: the rather raw binary "footprint" of an energy without beginning and end, which resided within everything. Perhaps it was even, she thought, the heat, the vibration of consciousness itself, of which matter is in its various forms merely the hypostatisation. With such a picture in her mind of a charged, shimmering bonfire of atoms combining and re-combining repeatedly, she fell asleep.

## LXXIV

# THE SOUTH INFERIGANGA COAST TIMES
August 1ˢᵗ., 1894.

ROUND UP OF LONDON BOOK REVIEWS by EDGAR FULTON-LEWES

In his review of Gertrude Mirs' 'The Unconditioned Moment', (Glebe House Books, Oxford) in The Sunday Times of London, Gilbert Hearn describes her collection of poems as attempting to integrate itself more by what it leaves out than by what it includes. Its mode of strenuous fragmentation, within and beyond its syntax, is, according to Hearn, excelled only by the necessarily more strenuous exertions required of the reader to "make sense" of how all its myriad parts conjoin. Perhaps such an unusual modus operandi will one day achieve a more general acceptance because it does, he believes, have its source very firmly in the *mysterium* of the romantic imagination. Mirs' goal in presenting perceptions and feelings almost exclusively within the domain of a fragmented discourse, he claims, is to invoke that absent value to which they seek to retrace their steps. It is a value which the gradual illumination afforded by all the fragments eventually allows the poet, and the reader, to gain access to. To a transcendental state, a whole, which reason, or systematic thought, alone, would not. We can see this development of the romantic *mysterium* as an anti-Enlightenment action, contends Hearns, first surfacing, perhaps, in the 18thC in an unselfconscious manner in, for example, Arthur Young's 'Night Thoughts', where Young's preoccupation with ruins incites his imagination to reconstruct from the rubble of a few pieces of ivied masonry the missing, living, whole. It reappears much later in an urban landscape with the fragmentary clues which Edgar Allan Poe's Dupin assiduously follows and in the singular sojourn of Baudelaire's *flâneur* through a city of multiple and estranged signs—a place "devoid of any *religio loci*", where that other proto-Romantic James Thomson's "dark way-faring stranger" first, perhaps, "breathless, toils". Hearns further says that although the book will come as a shock to many it should not prevent them from enjoying it, for it is, he claims, a poetry which owes its rather formidable newness of form to nothing which we, in essence, as readers of English literature, are not already acquainted with. It is, however, clear to this reviewer, at least, that no amount of special pleading can exonerate an author from departing from reason. Hearn's reference to anti-Enlightenment should put all of us on our guard against letting such a volume fall into the hands of impressionable, especially young, minds. And especially here, in this distant part of the empire, where we can, so much more clearly, see all those moral temptations and dangers which issue from a rejection of reason. But, equally, where we can see all the benefits that accrue when it is introduced. Under the benign influence of an intervening power which has as its sole aim nothing other than the eradication of an irrationalism which has for centuries plunged such parts of the world into an abject state of disorder and chaos, it can have nothing but an improving effect.

.

You stand, on the evening of your arrival, after having travelled for days, in a thickly wooded valley looking down into the eddying depths of the waters of this river and it seems neither to have come into existence at this precise moment of your arrival, nor to have ceased to be in that long duration of time since you were last here; but rather, as in a dream, to have coexisted all the time, in your absence, with what it was not. To deny the existence of anything is only to affirm its presence elsewhere, or in some other form. Arriving, and departing, therefore, one finds that one's being, and one's non-being are, both fully commensurate with what they are not.

.

She remembered holding the shuddering ship's rail as she set off back home. The sound of *Troglydites troglydites* rose from the thick shrubbery covering the hillsides around the city where she had spent so many years of her life. She wondered, again, whether there were, beyond the declared reasons for both her departures, others just as instrumental—her final justification for her return was, being an enthusiastic amateur musician, her need of a regular supply of classical Western sheet music unavailable in those parts. Sitting at her desk, at last, in that country she had first set out from, she listened to the sound of the bird again—resident on obverse sides of the planet. It seemed to her, for a moment, that she was entering the dark forest of sounds from which its song came, as if it was singing solely for the purpose of luring her toward its source. Just as it was the same species of bird she'd listened to as she'd departed from both shores so, coincidentally, it was the same species of bird which greeted her now on her return. Perhaps our lives take place, she mused, within such endless cycles of repeated song, the bourne of whose shores we are only dimly aware of, playing out our destinies according to melodies which we have not ourselves composed. Perhaps the different species of birds, with their constant reiteration and variation of motifs, are always alluding to this. And perhaps it is only we, finding it so difficult to hear and deaf to it amidst all our talk and thought, who are so confused by it when finally it confronts us.

## LXXV

You are not here, at the edge of evening as it begins to deepen into night, looking, looking out over the fields onto a darkening estuary. Nor were you there, earlier in the day, when the leaves were blown into the air in a scattering of sunlight. Longing has no place to settle, in the grass, in the orchard or on the road that divides you from where you do not stand and where you would not wish to be. Voices cling to the embankment like mist. Words attempt to enunciate a memory that is not, really, theirs, but which goes in search of a cogniser. All these years it has lain here, without you. Waiting. And you, loitering above the shoreline, oblivious to seasons, inhaling the air of a completely different location. Where were you, when the land first formed around it, as round an absence?

.

Impersonators of food were rife in the province of Scarvenger, luring old ladies, pensioners, the indigent and footsore to their sites down dim alleyways and behind the backs of buildings where, deaf to the hum of the city, they poured into their ears a tale of such blight and adversity that they soon had them weeping and thinking of their own sad lives. With such amazing dexterity in the limbs and trunks of their bodies did they present to those gathered there, aided by the articulateness of their commentary, the aspect of a cut of choicest lamb or beef, something those gathered there had not seen for months or years, that they were wholly convinced, weak from the effects of a sustained and impoverished diet of watery gruel, that what they beheld before them was truly what they wished to see. So entranced were they that, seemingly without a moment's hesitation or pause for thought, they reached deeply when so asked into the recesses of their burlap pockets to pull up the few remaining coins that had disconsolately jangled there, and proffered them to the animated carcasses before them. As they, upon receiving the money from all those still gathered there, took to their heels and rapidly sped off, that small destitute huddle of appetites simply stood on, as if dazed, looking at their hands.

.

# The Inferiganga Choral Group
Accompanied by
Ida Lo Yu Bazie - Xiao, Marcel Mallet - Clarinet

Presents
## *En le Ombre de Temps* Andrie Carpuscii
8.30. p.m. SHARP
January 10th, 1898.
### Inferiganga City Hall

## RATES OF ADMISSION
First Class (reserved) Rs 20, Second Class Chair Rs 2, Third Class Bench Rs 1

## WORDS FROM THE COMPOSER

Just as some birds have evolved their voices to the backdrop of running wa-
ter or developed pure tones which exploit the resonance of the forest rather
than open spaces, so I have found in the jungle interiors of this country a bird,
known locally as the Peilau, in whose vocal repertoire of calls I have identi-
fied all that I should wish as a composer, or as an archivist of the Absolute,
to attain in ordering sound. In the fecundity of this solitary bird's majestic
syntax the listener is absorbed into and united with an order which seems to
have at its core no order and where the absence of harmony seems, indeed,
to be the harmony. As you listen tonight, then, to this music I trust that you
will feel that it is not sound and silence idealised beyond experience, but
goes forward in a sonorous expansion of it, via a multiplicity of simultaneous
rhythms and tonal variations, so that, eventually, as you accustom yourself
to it you will feel you are not witnessing that spectacle of organised sound
which you are most used to hearing at such events. For it is my hope that it
shall not, as with the music venerated in the part of the world from which I
come and which has achieved such popularity here, lead you toward some
glorious sound palace of gorgeous melodies and harmonies, there to sus-
pend you, whilst all the time returning you to those undissolved passions
and that world to which they continually aspire. But toward a sonority which
covets no destination, which seeks only its own dissolution. A sonority the
twilight silently sifts. And, like a latch noiselessly opened, within whose space
the call of the Peilau mysteriously floats...

.

On a single-decker of the local motor bus company he looked out of the window as it turned uphill beside the parade ground and the pale yellow ticket in his fingers flared in sharp winter sunlight as if it had caught fire. As the bus gathered speed smoke from the cremation ground floated up into the window and, for a moment, he forgot his destination entirely and the purpose of his journey. The printed black box of the ticket, with its division into the names of twenty six fare stages, seemed to hover like a token before him. Above Hibiscus Inn, as the bus sped past, he thought he heard a sound in the air like that of a wild goose. Resonant and deep, a mournful and agitated honking. He could see no sign of any bird. An omen, then, he thought. In the yellow dust thrown up by the passage of the bus he briefly made out the face of a young child weeping distractedly beside a well. There is no such thing, he thought, as unified experience. Each part struggles against the next. Sand bushes passed. Then an empty garden, still white with dew. The refrain of a begging letter he had received some days ago monotonously re-announced itself to him. Along with the urge to embrace the breasts and naked shoulders of the woman sitting in front of him. Willow cotton, drifting up from the river, touched his face in the open window, the ticket flaring before him in his hand, his eyes settling back upon each finger. A man with a refined face standing beside the provincial library recited a poem in classical metres very loudly. Finally the bus horn, honking as they approached a blind corner, reminded him of the sound that he had heard above Hibiscus Inn, and it was then, the sound of a bus passing outside his bedroom window, that he awoke.

LXXVI

The empire had ceased. The imperial afflatus yielded. Across the grey channel on a humid sub-tropical day the ensign had been furled in this last substantial possession of a far off nation. From its shores had surged a wave of aggression and greed upon which its fortunes had prospered. But now the corridors of the civil service rang with the sounds of a language that was not imported. He looked out over the channel from the edge of the island where he sat on his balcony knee deep in shadow. Beyond the hills opposite him stretched northwards for thousands of miles the alluring shadows of the ancient nation which had drawn him, and still held him. Those who like him had retired and stayed on anticipated spending their remaining years here, having lived too long too far off to be able ever to retire to that place which they had left in their earlier years. On those rare occasions when they did return it felt more foreign to them than the place they visited it from. So, desperate to reinforce a foothold, they lined their bookshelves with accounts and histories of these coastal regions, and hung framed monochrome prints of early photographs of them on their walls—handsome white western style stucco buildings standing in seeming tranquillity beside the warm sheen of harbour waters—their imaginations inhabited by drained swamps, industrious compradors, mould stained godowns and malarial matshed townships, as much as by the present. These coexisted, incongruously, with valued childhood memories, valued the more as each year passed, of listening whilst lying in bed to the wheels of horse drawn carts on roads cracking the ice of ruts, of watching the fading flare at the tip of the lamplighter's taper as he disappeared down the street into the enveloping darkness and fog of a winter evening and of being mesmerised by flickering shadows on the wall at the foot of the bed from coals sputtering in a grate on a cold night. In this strange place, between the ghostly personae who moved in a wispish blur across the coastal foregrounds of old monochrome prints and their own vivid impressions of their early years, inhabited by equally apparitional figures and events, they existed. On bustling quays, sitting astride stalls in the open fronts of barbers' shops, they began to conceive of their lives as afloat upon unnavigable waters—waters such as those which, moment by moment, were shadowed in their features. Features which stared back at them when the mirror was finally brandished by the barber. From where, within the time-held mask of such features, they wondered, shaped by invisible movements of cognition, feeling and perception, did they, in fact, look out? What, from the vast storehouse of that memory, most fed and determined their present? As they gazed out upon the long liquid horizon, at its continual flux and toil within so many differing tides and currents, they knew that this was the place, no other, in which, all along, they had been destined to dwell.

.

Because the question, "Where is the way to return?" is hardly ever asserted, we return in our minds over and over again to places and times with which we have become familiar and to the actions and objects they contain. Walking, and talking in the street to someone we know, is, too, an act of remembering. Looking at a face, or the façade of a building, suddenly from an angle that is different to those we must have looked at them from before, or looking at them in a light in which they are subtly re-composed, we realise something has been added to them. We do not, in fact, know how not to return. But whether where we return to is the same as where we left from, we can never entirely be sure. And, consequently, whether where we leave from is exactly the same place as where we arrived, we will never, absolutely, know. We forget much more than we remember, and a great deal of what we look at, or listen to, we do not succeed in registering at all. Afloat upon our lives we are afloat upon, rather than the solidity of firm ground, an act of remembering from which so much is lost and left out. At the corner of a particular street, in a particular town and time, we find that we are exiles from both the past and the future. And that where we stand, in a light adrift upon doors and walls, is less a place to arrive at or depart from, than simply a place to stand.

.

Reading in the newspaper that morning the editorial on the war in which the phrase "the white man's burden", taken from a recently published poem by a well known English writer, appeared in support of her country's involvement, her feelings for her neighbour whose husband, she had been informed a few days before, had received a mortal wound in the prosecution of, were ambivalent. The leaves, she thought, moving away from the table where she had been reading and towards the window, had fallen early that autumn. As the rain came again she heard the squelch of feet on boards outside and the sound of horses shying at lightning from an approaching storm. The wind blew across the level prairie as waves do from a distant shore, without a pause; and, as she felt the temperature drop, snow fell. Like a temporary passport to nirvana, she thought, the low lachrymose lamentations of a drunk swimming in the "river of the water of death" in the outer regions of the town's dark; dreaming, no doubt to his heart's content, she supposed, knowing who it might likely be, of the procuration of virgins. She walked back from the window and sat at the table. Her eyes settled on the flickering pages of a recently published collection of poems, sent to her from the east, a collection by a poet who had died ten years before. She read aloud, savouring the sound of the lines from a section entitled *Démocratie*, which seemed attuned to her mood: *"Aux pays poivres et détrempes!—au service des plus monstrueuses exploitations industrielles ou militaires ... Nous alimenterons la plus cynique prostitution. Nous massacrerons les révoltes logiques."*

.

The forms, human and non-human, which filled the canvases he painted, especially in his later years, were of a sketchiness and incompleteness which baffled the viewer. Unlike the analyses of critics, which attribute it to a reaction to the burgeoning ideology of a Capitalist economy and to the "finished product" of its bourgeois ethos—would they have seen the young girl's steaming of the carriage window with her breath to obscure the copulating form of her sister and client from the eyes of the authorities as expressive, also, of a similar dissatisfaction?—was it not, simply, due to the realisation that nothing in this life depends solely upon itself for its existence and definition, and that the "clear bounding outline", standing apart from the rest of nature, is nothing but an expression of that artifice of eye which wishes to make us walk between these phantasms as if they were, in some way, not only permanent but independent of our act of looking at them?

# LXXVII

When the exhausted amateur archaeologists in their pith helmets and topees stood over the trenches they had made in sun-baked earth and perceived the extensive nature of the city they had uncovered they could not have realised that, rather than solving, they had merely reopened the old conundrum of whether the ancient city beneath their feet had existed, or had not existed. For since the completion of the excavation of the city of Rhaam, if that indeed was what it was, revealed no inscriptions to confirm its identity, the answer to the question remained unresolved. Led to the site only by references to the city's putative position in recently discovered texts from an adjacent culture the dubiety associated with Rhaam would simply be amplified by the excavation. In those texts it was referred to as the "city of metaphysicals". Whether this denied it a corporeal existence was not clear. Certainly its verbal descriptions were not accompanied in these recently discovered texts by its inclusion in any of the rather crude cartographic representations of the area, therefore only increasing the doubts about its actual existence. And what was said about Rhaam, at the time when it was supposed to have flourished, whether reliable or not, added only yet more weight to such doubts; especially when it was learned that it was commonly referred to as the city of "Nine Gates". Nine Gates also referred to the nine meridian points of the body associated in that region with the soma of a transcendental school of exercise and meditation. It was recounted in the texts how the Governors of Rhaam regarded it as the only true locus. For them the city state of Rhaam, only, existed; nowhere else outside it did. To live outside its walls was to live in permanent exile and unbelievable torment. They described such a landscape as consisting of untold miles of foetid and fly infested swamp, leading down to a rocky coast where the wind blew continuously over a black, icy sea of mountainous waves. Those who lived there lived in perpetual half-light and had to resort often to biting their fingers to reassure themselves they were alive. Despite making allowance for the propagandising features of such a discourse the texts also contain examples of a less unreliable form of reasoning. For evidently the scribes of Rhaam wrote that for a city or state to be located, that is, to be, anywhere there had to exist something else beyond it, something which contained it. But outside of Rhaam there was, so we are led by its Governors to believe, nothing. According to this reasoning, therefore, Rhaam was not anywhere. So whether, indeed, it did or did not exist no excavations have so far been, or would seem capable of, ultimately, proving.

.

Strange cities surfacing on the plains. Collapsed walls, choked wells. Signs saying "Go This Way", "Go That". Unfinished roads. Lines in time, in space. Silk, damascenes and nutmeg. A boleta to paradise. Lines, erased. Restored. A bogus tradition. The undeciphered script that waits behind closed doors like an incendiary. Distortions. Fear. An identity at any cost. To own, to possess, what one is owned by. A conflation to be ignored. Dried up river. Derelict wharf, pier-head. Midnight midden. Partition. The site of your house ploughed over and sown with salt. Lines: in time, in space. Silk, damascenes and nutmeg. Rubble and blood.

.

In the immaculate whiteness of the walls of the convent of the Beaterio de Santa Catalina with its alcoves of alabaster saints, and in the fierce adamantine glare of the marble vaults of the necropolis beside it which he passed each day, he sensed a presence—as of the unnamed—which was, perhaps, nothing more than what he thought of as an absence deferred. A "presence" which did not inhabit its own being but whose being, defined equally by what it was not, was derived elsewhere. He began to speculate whether there exists a declination within objects of those very qualities of which we believe them to be unequivocally constituted. In the intense mid-day heat he felt his heart beat heavily. He looked up. Surrounding and suffusing the pounded tobacco leaves of cigar makers on the Escolta and a procession of chanting prelates, there was the light. A fierce, white, ever-present light in which things burn, and fall away. He seemed to understand, then, why whenever his gaze tried to enter it his being became the ground of a longing he could not explain. Longing infused with loneliness. A loneliness at the core of which lies the doubt that anything can, as in the immaculate whiteness of the walls of the convent of the Beaterio de Santa Catalina, *in itself*, be.

# LXXVIII

With the taxi window open, its glass jammed tightly by a broken winding mechanism, there came in humid and thick with the detritus of air which hung heavily above them a breeze carrying the sounds of vendors and exhaust fumes, making her cough. In the market, sitting or lying on the ground, beggars with deformities and wounds groaned, gazing hopefully about them. There came in, also, the odour of green mangoes. As it did, the recitation by her three companions of some lines of poetry upon the subject began. Sighing, afterwards, at the mysteriously evocative power of the lines' images and sounds they settled back into their seats as if having inexplicably resolved some matter of outstanding concern. "Did you know that Abdul al Matali Yasouf, who composed the lines when he visited and lived in the Armenian quarter of the old part of the city, is supposed to have also written some marvellous prose pieces, accounts of his visions and hallucinations whilst under the influence of hashish?" one said. "He was seldom un-intoxicated" another replied "it's what finally ushered him off to the other world." Leaning slightly forward, as if to disengage herself from her companions, another said, "Yes, they are marvellous. I've read all of them." Incredulous that she had read what they had actually never seen, or even heard had been published, they looked at her expectantly. "I found a copy, when I was living for a time in his country, in a small booksellers in his home city of Ehafa. Unfortunately I no longer have it." As she said this there came in to her through the window, with the odour of green mangoes again, as if borne on a long sleep, the smell, also, of dead words. "Name has no power of its own" she heard herself silently repeat. There being no mango present only the sound-form, the sound-scent of it. It is only within a consciousness which unites them, she thought, at those times when it takes place—words usually conjuring up merely a pale echo of their object—that we find anything to assuage the immense nostalgia residing in us for the fullness of being.

.

In that lush subtropical region the rains came early one year and were heavier than many could recall. They also lasted longer than usual so that much of the crop was flattened and waterlogged by the time of its harvesting. Such occurrences were not unheard of and during such times the authorities who collected the land revenues would adjust their demands so that the farmers could earn enough money from the sale of the surplus grain saved from good years to buy enough seed to plant again. But now the revenues were collected not on behalf of the local lords but of lords from overseas who had, by sheer force of military might, supplanted them. Indifferent to the wellbeing of the farmers they made no concession and issued, instead, the demand for the full tax on the land. "Pay Before Dusk" became, therefore, after a number of years of the same adverse weather, a notice that sent a tremor of fear through the landowners' hearts: "Seven entire battalions were added to our military establishment to enforce the collections … [that] carried terror and ruin through the country." Eventually, unable to pay, the lands were forfeited, and the terrible sceptre that had begun to haunt the land fell upon it with implacable force. Famine, barely before known there, walked abroad. In a short time one third of the population of one of the wealthiest and most populous provinces of the country was slowly, men women and children, starved to death, causing even the historiographer of those foreign lords to lament: "Why should I be doomed to commemorate the ignominy of my countrymen" those "plunderers of the East." (He didn't. He stopped writing.) But as a haunting testimonial to the psychic devastation which was inflicted upon the survivors, a nursery rhyme, sometimes recited to coerce children, was passed from generation to generation:

> In the peaceful village the children slept.
> Through the night the barbarians came, looting .
> The bulbel has plucked all the fresh green stalks
> We would have traded for money.
> In the barn the rice and the betel leaf are almost gone.
> What will we use for taxes?
> Be kind to us, be patient.
> The seeds of the garlic are sown already.

.

Without failure there would be no art. With the achievements of art we turn our minds away from what makes its inception possible. Our inability to tolerate difference and to not exploit each other condemns us to its permanent production. All art is simply solace for the imperfections attendant upon being human. Of all species we have made a speciality out of the infliction of suffering upon each other. And whilst we cannot resist the temptation to crow as loudly as we can from atop the nearest dung-heap about the lofty achievements and refinements of our artists, musicians and poets etc, seldom do we perorate so profusely, and confidently in public upon what greater happiness there might be without them; without, that is, their need to provide themselves, and us, with solace.

## LXXIX

Behind the stadia and turrets of the red brick water towers of the capital the horizon was on fire. The sky, like a blotter, absorbed a deep orange glow from what burned beneath it. Hotels, libraries, airport lounges and factories continued to feed it. Soon they would crumble, like the ashes of scattered apocrypha, beside motorways and upon pavements, their charred girders inscribing the air with brutal angularity. From all over the country they came, by train, motorbike, plane and car, drawn like moths to the "lurid glare" of the city, to ransack its stores, making off with anything that would appear to have made their journey worthwhile. The ghosts of those who had once proclaimed the Future above all else hovered contentedly around the emptied cases and the cavernous halls of the museums. The past was gone! But not back to those far off lands from which its artefacts had largely been plundered. Instead, a man walked down the street bearing in his blackened hands a copy of an original treaty transferring the right to the land of a vast country from those who had no concept of ownership of the earth and air and water to those who had. Looter, saboteur and rapist skulked in the shadows. The flooded underpasses—from the last surge wave that had swept away the city's tidal defences—hissed every now and then as a sudden rain of glowing debris was deposited into them.

.

Things, she knew, get lost and then turn up again unannounced. It was, she concluded, becoming a pattern in her life. And she did not mean just things, but people as well, and memories. So much so that she had begun to feel the reason why things disappear is not so much because they are mislaid as not recognised. We always look for and expect objects to appear in the same place and the same guise and that is why frequently, she thought, we cannot in fact see them. If we could believe that nothing actually exists in a necessary relation to locus or time, then things might not stray so frequently from us. But to achieve that, she deduced, we should also have to believe it of all products of the processes of our consciousness. How, then, she wondered, should we ever hold on to our selves?

.

Here, all the old dark gods have departed. Upon that deserted alter where the shadows of killing and eating, of "death as the life of the living" linger, there can no longer be heard, above the roar of the twelve lane highway which threads through landscape turned into plots for real estate, the cry of blood in the long glade leading to the wood. [If there were just death but no reproduction. If there were reproduction but no death.] A wood, now, of leafy superannuated rites, in which the resins of a powerful non-reason wait.

> There is God (some say)
> A deep but dazzling darkness; As men here
> Say it is late and dusky, because they
>         See not all clear;
>     O for that night!

Those ghostly avatars moving through the blood. Do you hear them, noiseless, almost, through the dusk? They call out to you from the shattered wood at Delville, from the bombed-out city in the newscast. Passing, with the light tread of the abandoned, they accuse you with uplifted finger, whispering "apostate" onto the air, then flinging the curse "hypocrite" at you.

.

Our lives are lived in a net of days, weeks, months and years. Caught in that net they are unable to free themselves from it. The cherry tree blooms through the night without any thought of it. Footfalls through a room. Cloud shadows on a wall. Shall we follow? Into hours, minutes and seconds. Until the mind in extremis slows and falters. Was this not when an action was completed, a woman moving her arm up and down in response to some unseen stimulus; or was there only a certain combination of movements and shapes undergoing transformation, a series of momentary "events" marking time which because of the replicating power of the "illusion" within us sustain the impression of a continuity? Not even the absence of the flowering plant on the sill could confirm that there was a limit to her action. Its scent lingers in the hall. The whole house is a museum. We inhale second by second. Exhale. Minute by minute. In the dusk that is falling upon us. Boundaries no bird obeys or knows, flying through the close shadows in the garden, in the far field. Calling. Shall we follow?

## LXXX

In Ghetong, a city by a lake, it seems he had died—one of our number who many years ago had gone missing. Before his death he had instructed "a friend", who remained anonymous, to write to us on his behalf explaining and apologising for his sudden departure. In the course of which there were filled in many of the blank spaces in our knowledge of him. Evidently he returned, finally, to the nearby country of his birth, in what was to be a futile attempt to discover the identity of his parents. He was, unknown to us, a foundling and had been brought up in an institution for similar unfortunates. Having after a number of years grown tired of the monotonous routine of office work at the Company's headquarters, as if he had more urgent business elsewhere, he impetuously decided to take himself off to explore the vast wastes of forest and swamps which form the greater part of this country. In this he was, perhaps, inadvertently aided by a short initiatory trip into Abdherva province with our late colleague Unsworth. He had returned from there proclaiming the "wild beauty" of the terrain, and of the native settlements and towns whose names— Urofalgo, Gonbikin, Deltheora—he loved to pronounce out loud to all around him, as if by so doing he was actually summoning them into our presence. It seems, then, that soon after he set off by himself to explore the remoter parts of the country, crossing it on foot in treks which lasted for months at a time. Acquiring a command of some local dialects enabled him to more easily obtain guides for these feats of prolonged exertion and to more easily dwell among peoples along the way. Being no longer a young man, however, these journeys through humid mosquito infested forests and flood plains the size of a small country, existing on a diet frequently of no more than leaves and roots, small vermin and occasionally birds, wore him out. Beset and bedridden by fevers, concerned that he might not have much longer to live, he decided to set out for that country where he had been born. He was observed eventually, the "friend" says, at all times of day stooping amidst headstones, scraping lichen and mildewed plaster from almost illegible names, engaged in the arduous and imperative task of exploring and uncovering his parentage. Armed with nothing but the reputed family name of the young woman who had one night deposited him at the orphanage—he was, it seems, the product of an illicit liaison between a soldier and a native woman subsequently shunned and denigrated by her own kind and haughtily ignored by his—he spent his time straining his eyesight in the dimly lit recesses of public records offices of births and deaths, and turning over the yellowed pages of baptismal and marriage registers in churches and chapels. He ended up, ironically, spending more time breathing the air of the ink-pot and bureaucracy than if he had remained with the Company. All his efforts to confirm his mother's identity and burial place and the registration of his own birth were to no avail, however. His father also died, from a virulent strain of pneumonia then sweeping through Ghetong, without him learning his name. He passed away, then, unable to confirm whether his surname was really that of his mother, hastily written as it had been on a scrap of paper thrust into the bundle which contained him on his arrival at the orphanage. "Hastily", because that was how he interpreted its handwriting's reckless progress across a page with a tattered edge torn clumsily out of a writing tablet. Evidence, he consoled himself, that she had made a last minute decision fraught with reservation and doubt. He always carried the piece of paper with him in a little lizard skin pouch. "Only those without a name, or with an imputed one" he is reported to have said before he died, "can understand how a fascination with names is a fascination also with that which cannot really ever be touched or embraced".

.

And what *is* this country of the one and singular moment that you have walked into? Does it have a name? Can it be heard, felt, seen, touched or even tasted more than once? Or is it continually re-made, beyond the scope of all dialectics? From the deserted pier head where you disembark the little wooden rowboat has drifted away with a song in its bows and a rattle in its oarlocks. Abandoned landscapes move in and out of the mind. On the tide there are voices. In the voices there are notes left on tables. From the doors all the locks have been removed. All the maps have been torn up. You encounter no one, not even yourself, here. For you have walked beyond the end of all beginnings and the beginning of all ends, and neither end nor beginning has recognised you. Here nakedness is just another disguise in an endless series of disguises. And the shadow against that wall where the sea daily throws its reflection is a shadow hewn from a rock that has ceased to exist. A rock which you mistook for a road, and down which you walked, after the obliteration of all ailments and afflictions, looking for the silence at the heart of the world.

.

As he wandered down to the steps of the pool to perform his ritual ablutions prior to entering the mosque, the munshi pondered the fate of his poor country. A small but populous nation richly endowed with natural resources sitting, as it did, in a strategically important location astride the world's major sea-lanes could not help but attract the attention of powerful countries seeking to impose their authority upon that part of the world. Its possession of a large deep-sea port, ideal for stationing war ships of a modern fleet, added yet to its attractions. Yet today, he reflected, in the medieval quarter of its capital where millennia ago groups from the west who had travelled there with the armies of a land thirsty conqueror had settled, there was an audible sigh of relief. A corrupt and murderous government put into power by a supposedly free election—manipulated, in fact, partly by a foreign power which subsequently held the government up to the world as "a model of democracy"—was rapidly unravelling. With apparently no limit to its venality—politicians and their extended families and friends lining their pockets from pilfered public funds, unfairly awarded contracts and "squeeze"—finally it was the unprecedented conspicuousness and excessiveness of such venality which was bringing it down. A great many of the ruling party and their relations lived in houses in the city to which the description floating palaces might be more appropriate—to which rows of garages to accommodate their ever expanding fleet of luxury foreign cars were attached. Often they were situated on large tracts of land, classified as "non-residential", to which they had managed to have the classification changed. They had, the munshi knew, turned these into virtual deer-parks, full of exotic species of animals, reptiles and plants. Some had even incorporated into the structure of their properties miniature zoos. Spacious outhouses, built from materials which they had not even bothered to remove the markings PRIME MINISTER'S RELIEF SUPPLIES from, were full to the ceiling with of sacks of lentils and rice donated by foreign countries for the poor. From such materials were built, also, lavish holiday retreats. Today, though, he had heard, parts of the city were virtually underwater as nervous politicians, wondering anxiously when the next group of armed police and army officers might call, dismantled the moats around their residences and drained the water, along with that from their swimming pools, onto surrounding roads. In this rash of material renunciation, prompted by arrests for possessing assets grossly incommensurate with earnings, the capital suddenly found its flooded roads littered with expensive and brand new luxury foreign sports vehicles that had been abandoned. Down the avenues and streets of the city, too, liberated deer, gazelles and other animals that had been turned loose, roamed and leapt, their eyes wild with freedom and with fear. The munshi, whilst marvelling at the avarice of his fellow men, stood before the marble step level with the water. He slowly removed his sandals and moved forward and immersed his feet. At first, still pondering upon the events befalling his country, he was unaware, merely a few feet from him, of a large pair of eyes darkly observing him. Then, alerted, perhaps, by a slight tremble or quiver of the water, he raised his head and, not knowing whether it was an illusion or real, noticed, casting a long tapering shadow beneath the surface, an outline of enormous girth. As, narrowing his eyes in the bright light, it slowly began to raise its whole length he stood and, suddenly realizing "crocodile", fled, leaving his sandals behind him.

## LXXXI

She could hear, above the clatter of rain and tendrils of malamsampalok trees on tin roofs, the song of a bird. Then it faded. Across the low rooftops, in liquid riffs, it came, again, to her; a richly textured throating, a woody arpeggio. Where the song began and the silence ended she could not tell. Listening, she was no more surprised by silence than she had been by song; no more surprised by song than she had been by silence. Delighted by both. But, she pondered, if they were not different, if song and silence, so interwoven, were the same neither would be able to retain its identity, its defining characteristic. However, if different, then, being separate, how could they combine into yet another, a third, unique identity; and how, independent of song and of silence, could such an entity continue to exist, when they both were not present, by itself? But if, being different, they simply succeed each other then how could song abandon the air before the arrival of silence? For, if this is what happens, silence would arrive only to find the air already silent ... Something, within that dark door of perception, called out to her. Called out to her, in the guise of a yellow bill in black plumage deep within leaf shadow; called out to her from a moment beyond the end of the world, beyond duality, beyond reason and the senses. Called. But she could not answer.

.

On this sound stream of speech, this modification of the act of breathing, you lean, listening to the acrimonious music of the self. Listening, in a side street under the green suffused light of plane trees and dusty desideratum of air, to its small solidarities of love. Looking longingly at the particulars of the receipt from the Pension Kanumayan [room number/date/room rent/sales tax/restaurant charges/telephone bill/laundry bill/electricity bill/miscellaneous] as if it lingered there, as if what existed in a state of undifferentiation could be differentiated, cognised, only by the separate and independent sounds contained within those words as they are released upon the air. As if in that most common currency of breathing there was pronounced unknown to you the utterer, from a phonemic and semantic substratum, the prototype of all words. Invariant constant. Love. Receipt No. 29225. In partial/full payment. Whorled up into the breath, the mind. Mistaken, frequently, for a pre existing reality independent of words.

.

Beside a paddock the great blossoming hawthorn tree bending in the breeze. The rustling of its thick impasto eliciting rich music. Box hedge, weatherworn stone, mullioned windows. A countryside suddenly unaffected by the alarums of history, all its bloodlettings. Instead, in the rustling of leafage across fields, in the stillness and sunlight across road and wall, a lineage is traced, a predilection confirmed. Who, objecting that the past has been falsified, has not manipulated his or her own? History is simply a spectrum of correlatives for states of being running deeply within us, over which we have little control. The seductiveness of such states, although established within history, is that they, seemingly, take us out of history and relieve us of the burdens of its content. As we take our place within the company of all those unseen others the apparitional nature of our affections should become clear to us. Feelings, like events, do not happen in time, but flow as time. As a wave which forms within water. In them the future and the past have no destination—other than the moment. And it is in this moment, this state in which we continually arrive, that history perishes and we endure. But within a circularity whose increasing exertions we cannot escape from.

.

The faces of people we meet in dreams are hidden from us. We recognise the people they belong to not by the singularity of facial features but by a non-particularised sense of their identity. The face, that part of the body our gaze most searchingly falls upon, with its evocation of the turmoil of all our suffering and joy, the face remains hidden. For it is a dream face, decanted from the data of the senses, but insensible to the toil of perception, and immune to time and space which regulate the motility of objects and bodies. It wears the final blankness attendant upon an erasure of all which might consolidate it into what is called a "personality". Wears, that is, the final blankness of a disguise.

## LXXXII

The pandit in his white cotton dhoti sat with the foreigner in the Cold Weather. The kash rustled in the field behind the house. A bulbul sang. Only famine, and the threat of starvation brought on by the loss of his traditional patrons, had brought the pandit to the meeting, and all the others that followed, to teach the foreigner the secrets of the sacred script. Later, discovering that the earliest known roots of the cognates of his own language were to be found in such a script the foreigner published his findings, adumbrating a new group of languages from which his own, and all those related to it, with exceptions such as Semitic, were, he asserted, derived. He published, also, his translations of some major poems and plays from the language he'd been taught. To one culture, in particular, of those far off lands from which he'd journeyed, suddenly the source of its origin was revealed. It was an origin which involved also, a far greater antiquity of time and place than it had suspected. Into the thick mists of its phantasmal past would be launched not only the energy of a defining desire but the destiny of a culture which, unknown to itself at first, would stop at nothing to turn such mists and shapes into a reality. Into a reality which, starting from language and culture, would soon move to nation and race, and thence to the notion of a superior identity. Thinking upon that rich and sun-soaked land of the pandit and its culture, evoked in one foreign novelist a sense of swaying at the edge of a "vertiginous abyss". "The road" it had been claimed by another writer "to Rome lies through [it.]" The road, too, to Romanticism and its "emotional hashish." Road, also, to eventual ruin. His arm raised rigidly before him in a salute, a copy of a long ancient philosophical poem composed in the pandit's language always in his uniform pocket: it justified, he said, his detachment from the act of sending all those of inferior origin up in a column of smoke. Finally, too, as retribution for draining that land of the pandit, where the kash rustled that day in the field behind the house, of its wealth and dividing it, a nightly cascade of bombs upon capital and cities, the threat of invasion.

.

"Nor can we … deprecate the practice of taking Wheatears since the lower orders of creatures were made for the service of man." (*Our Native Songsters*, 1852, published by The Committee of General Literature and Education appointed by the Society for Promoting Christian Knowledge).

.

All of life is nothing more than a desperate attempt to persuade itself, and us, that it is something more than a fleeting impression, a shadow emerging out of and folding back into that vast and unknowable vacuity from which it has come. All of its sudden settings-forth and odysseys of return, the entire impetus of its action and thought, amounts to no more than an attempt to establish an authority for a journey which it neither initiates nor ends. Similarly, the entire ritual of reproduction rehearses, ad infinitum, the fundamental insecurity at the heart of everything about its own nature, as if the only act that can reassure what exists that it, indeed, does exist is the act of replicating itself. Down to each echoing particle, life listens for, and attracts, what it is not. And only by attracting such an antithesis, by asserting oneself at its expense, can one succeed in being what one is.

.

On that land of conjurers, jugglers, dissemblers, storytellers and street musicians, the sun never set. This was not because the country was so extensive but because it was covered from shore to shore by a canopy of dense forest. Into a nationwide network of canals, lakes and rivers the phytoplankton from the prodigal surrounding oceans fed a continual luminosity: a quality of illumination which could, at all times, be described only as crepuscular. Some nations, deducing that the reduced awareness of solar and lunar movements had adversely affected the inhabitants' sense of the difference not only between day and night but right and wrong, suggested that they should to, as it were, throw more light upon their lives, remove from their land the entire expanse of forest covering. Without it, they said, your minds would be free to generate the processes of thought which would enable you to eventually divide the things of the world into separate and distinct categories; which would enable you, for example, to draw a dividing line between day and night, and to discover and explore the world of opposites. One visiting delegation, stressing this point, drew attention to an event which it described as illustrating an inability to differentiate between seriousness and frivolity. The police department, it reported, had recently issued instructions that instead of those committing the offence of jaywalking on the cities' busy roads being fined they were, instead, to be offered the choice of executing, there on the spot of the offence, ten press-ups or of singing the national anthem. Responding to the delegation's observations, a government spokesperson admitted that to an outsider such an instruction might be thought to bring the law into disrepute and to lower its dignity. However, they said, you must not forget that in our culture the qualities of ambivalence and equivocation are not seen, as in yours, to be faults but, rather, to define what is at the heart of our being. They are, you might say, among our defining characteristics. And while you might say that such characteristics are not ones we should be happy to so readily admit to it is a fact that they are there precisely because we do not, unlike you, so readily admit rigid demarcations between things—which is a defining quality of who you are. The sun, you say, rises or it sets—well we have never seen it, except those of us who have left these shores or who live right at the water's edge, do either. But what we can say is, that being so equivocal and ambivalent about where one thing ends and one thing begins means that we can seldom be found, unlike you, to contradict ourselves. And, almost certainly, it means that we can never be found to be guilty of hypocrisy.

## LXXXIII

The eye, which has no capacity for introspection, scans the near horizon taking in as it does what it regards as the entire vista. Moving from left to right, first the harbour mouth, then the long headland with a scattering of small settlements and, away far off as far as it can see, the stubble fields moving down to the shore where flocks of noisy crows hover. All of this in virtually one fell swoop it takes in and appears to almost immediately register. Only when it comes to rest, attentive to one thing alone, does it become aware of the blurred periphery, of the margin which presses round it and into and out of which it enters and departs. A margin which constantly recedes before, and advances upon, it. For, in truth, the eye does, at each moment, have cognizance of a small, infinitesimal point of focus only. One might as well in such circumstances, then, talk of viewing a memory-scape as a land or shore-scape. Memory, as the eye moves across, up and down, each point of "contact," records a series of sections which it assembles into a terrain; a terrain in which the eye, alone, would be lost. As there is a need to continually update this ever-changing vista, that whole to which the mind always aspires and without which it is condemned to dwell in a state of fragmentation, is always out of reach—even at this rudimentary level of visual sensation. How much greater, then, must be that gap between itself and the entirety of its being. How much further away, there, the wood must be from the trees.

.

In the drawing rooms of their seances the lamps burned all night. Priest like eminences in white gowns officiated at ceremonies in towers of steel and glass approving and blessing the funding of projects to discover ways of prolonging human life. In the depths of their libraries that Whole which forbids every formulation by concept or speech and which, alone, makes sense of all the minutiae of life, was pursued. It never occurred to them that the presence of a name does not, necessarily, confer upon it the reality of the named. And, all the while, the small birds withered in their back yards. The glaciers melted. The rivers dried up. And all the forests began, along with the animals, to disappear.

.

At last his trunks, transported up the hill from the hold of the Anan Bhun, were safely deposited in the front room of his lodgings. Exuding an odour of unripe jackfruit and durian, the Anan Bhun's main inter-island cargo, they stood where they were placed for days, unopened. He sat and merely looked at them, vestiges from another time and place, as if he did not know what to make of their sudden appearance before him. Fragrantly mute, standing there, they had not the power to return that which in his intense gaze interrogated them. Festooned with faded and tattered stickers bearing the names of the ports they had over the years lingered in and the scrawled marks of customs officials—official graffiti regulating the motility of bodies and objects across waters indifferent to man-made borders—they came to seem, especially when the sun sent a swathe of light to envelop them, to be, however, interrogating him. Opened, at last, they were, he thought, with their cargo of perishables and their medley of place names, like the bearers of some eternal flotsam. To the cry of a low flying gull above the harbour, a cry similar to the one, perhaps, which had roused Aeneas from his dotage upon Dido, he realised that in this city, in which he had made his final home, his life had come full circle. He watched as, down on the quay, the customs official, in his white peaked cap and with a cigarette between his lips, scrawled on each item of arrival its mark of clearance. Across what inviolable border, he wondered, does the mind seek its final destination, a destination hidden, always, in a fog of stations and terminuses, of arrivals and departures? In the harbour mouth, above the churned up foam of the wake of the Anan Bhun, a gull dipped and hovered.

.

A rhythm of fragments, she thought. Glancing, echoing off each other. A vagabond music. Cries heard, and unheard. To walk through these spaces. Pale green spots of the leopard. A rictus, of wrenched air. Without fear. "I could, then, make an affirmation or a denial, on the basis of these things perceived or inferred. But these (separate) things do not exist for me."

## LXXXIV

Standing in your apartment at the centre of the city, watching the snow descend upon rooftops, your eyes begin to roam over the precincts spread out before you. In the smoke-smog of pavements grilled meat vendors stamp their feet to keep warm. Street lamps exhale misty nimbuses onto the air. The sound of roosting birds rises from the tree-lined avenue beneath you. Samovars hiss in cafes. The high piercing whistle of night trains about to set off over the ice bound plains for cities in the west drifts on the wind. Along a narrow dimly lit passageway you make out a man and a woman locked in a fierce embrace. From somewhere there comes the odour of tanning leather. The particular, the discrete object, alone, you think, is real—no matter how much it's contingent upon a complexity of conditions. It alone, as an object of the senses, irrefutably exists. Standing there with the freezing night air collecting round you like a fist you remember on your walk that morning through the graveyard how the sun had begun to melt the ice on the heads of stone angels. Looking up at them high on their plinths tiny drops had begun to run and collect in the sockets of their eyes as if they were tears. A last few beams of light flicker futilely across the globe of the atlas in the corner of the room. Looking out at the city and becoming aware once more that only ideation, not perception, can encompass it, you wonder whether it does, in fact, apart from all the particulars, really exist. Or, perhaps, being the city that it is, a place dominated and defined by an unparalleled variety of sensory stimuli, it refuses to sacrifice them to the unity, and the tyranny, of an idea.

.

Inmates from asylums in the East occupied the large four-floor red brick building by the side of which, each Sunday, flocks of sheep were driven to cross the High Street to the fields which lay just beyond it. Their bleating, mistaken by some of the inmates, perhaps, for the sounds of a foreign tongue, would send them hurrying off screaming into cupboards and under stairs believing they were back in those far lands in which their debilitation had begun. Masons, railway employees, constables and planters, all were diagnosed, under the terminology of tropical neurology—a terminology derived from a neuropathology of the apoplectic—to be suffering from incipient softening of cerebral tissue and senescence brought on by the climate. Some were also diagnosed as suffering from serious toxaemia and fever due to the retention of faecal matter which, because of its dangerous raising of levels of bodily heat, led to enervation and outbreaks of explosive and violent behaviour. Most of the inmates had, thankfully, been prone only to murderous outbursts in which they had vented their aggression on those around them; unlike, as with the natives of that country they had left, to the cerebral liquefaction and dementia which is the lot of all those living in the hotter regions and which inevitably leads to physiological and moral weakness and decay. Freed from the warming effects of such a climate, and returned to their temperate homelands, many of the inmates rapidly recovered. When they did, from the four-floor red brick building standing just off the High Street, they left quietly through the door at the back carrying their bundles of possessions with them. Some of the young street urchins, whose habit it was to linger near the house in the hope of scavenging left over pieces of food and who had noted the regular uproar inside that always occurred at the appearance of the sheep, on seeing the departing inmates, vigorously and enthusiastically set up a loud chorus of bleating.

.

Her husband had gone. She sat down, relishing the coolness of the earth floor. After all those years of being together it was as if his going had robbed her of the most deeply rooted tokens of familiarity with her life. Making the bed in the morning, turning down its coverlet at night before they retired, drawing and warming the water for him to wash. All the little rituals of a routine which, observed, would, and had, produced the desired effect. Its object, now gone, such a routine was powerless. Everywhere about her the silence held the sound of an absent other. A silence as after a question when the conversation pauses and one waits for a reply. It did not come. Neither that day nor the next. She watched the long shadows of the malamsampalok tree outside her room shorten as the sun reached its zenith. Performing all the paraphernalia of the ceremonies of self-sacrifice would, she knew, not bring him back, nor would uttering his name restore his form to her. She wondered, whimsically, whether, as with ceremonies performed in the presence of the gods of old, she might not have pronounced his name exactly to their liking, or whether she might have neglected some minute detail in her daily performance of the household routine—all irregularities would have rendered the rituals invalid. A small spider stumbling into the shadow upon its path, and noticing it move, began to perform a wide detour around her. She watched it from, as it were, the top of the mountain. As she sat there continuing to survey the progress of the spider and the condition of her life her mind returned to those dim figures of the gods upon whom in the past so much time had been spent by supplicants performing the right observances in an effort to secure the desired effect. Performed correctly the result was like the fulfilment of a natural law in the physical world. Performing such observances gave one limited power over the course of one's life. And that, she thought, is what we all require some share of. Without any we are plunged into the jaws of insecurity and fear, not knowing what will happen next. At this she remembered what her husband, noting the lavish entertainment, feasting and pomp paid for out of the public purse, had said when the new Governor of the province was invested. It is nothing more than unbridled greed which drives men over seas to a distant land to wrest wealth by force of arms and, by such an act, deprive its people of that very security which they themselves sought and could have obtained by staying and diligently applying themselves at home. The desire for power in moderation, he'd said, is the natural concomitant of fear, but greed is its perversion; it is an abuse of what, in sufficient measurement, is a healthy and life-preserving response to uncertainty. Her eye was on the spider. It had not left it, not for one second. Idly tempted to further delay its progress to where it wished to go by moving her body, she resisted.

## LXXXV

In cooling air the fire tree proffered the fulminous red of its blooms to him. The rampant perfumes of the day had subsided. They lingered, in the clearings and by the paths and the river, with hardly a breeze to disturb them. He inhaled deeply, as if he was inhaling the fleeting nature of all things that were transformed around him. Eyes half closed, quivering slightly beneath their lids, he felt he was teetering upon the brink of an immense cornucopia or abyss. Things are neither plural, he thought, nor are they momentary. The discovering of that inexhaustible variety which he'd considered the ultimate determinant of his pleasure was finally, he decided, a discovering of the truth that the diversity of things arises only because they are united and linked with one another. Just as, for example, we cannot know what the different parts of our experience of that which we call love are parts of—if, indeed, they are "parts" at all—without identifying the whole, so that whole, by its very nature, annuls within itself all the distinctions of those so called parts. Because without it they could not exist the reality of the non-existence of those parts must be greater than the reality of their existence. In recognising the distinctions, therefore, between things in space and time we are pointing, ultimately, only to their sameness. Through undivided space the perfect uniformity of the blooms of the fire tree moves, he knew, as with all the other objects of our senses, within the perfect uniformity of all time and all space.

.

This impulse to encompass all space and what it contains, to brook no barriers being placed between those things and themselves, was they suspected not so much an act of expansion as contraction. For in the process of attaining such a condition it was not the parameters of the self that were overcome. The self did not cease. Rather, it redrew the boundaries of itself, and became, in effect, an insufflation, an overblown weltgeist; with the result that it had the effect of, rather than making the world, and the self, large, making it, as one discoverer observed, "small." Out of such smallness, of course, came opportunities. Markets. A space made homogeneous by desire. Amidst the dismantling of all boundaries the boundary of the self was reaffirmed. A boundary around a space littered with traders' lists and inventories of auctions which never fell silent, and across which the luxury of traders' surpluses took them breathing in the fine cirrus of dust from great Pepper warehouses whose deep basins glowed with reflections of varnished prows. When they carefully listened, though, what they had heard, in the sound of the prow cleaving the wave, was something which frightened them: the death of space. Taking its place, a carnal mobile. The flesh of that ancient kinesis which brought everything into being. Where movement was Mind, and where the "fundamentalism of self", of the afflatus of individual consciousness, did not exist.

.

To a cold sleepy little town not far from the city of Horste your wanderings at last will lead you. Situated at the mouth of a wide river its once fashionable guest houses and hotels will stand with their ramshackle balconies atop an embankment, looking out imperiously over an esplanade where, a century ago, dignitaries from Horste would flock at weekends to take the sea air. And where, sometimes, during the heat of summer, a royal party would ensconce itself for a weekend on the top floors of the Vox Hotel. The sound of their merrymaking would ring out over the narrow streets of the town until dawn, gig lamps of carriages, bringing more guests, bobbing through a light sea mist to the hotel's front door. Beneath the Vox's faded gold bosses and the ghostly regalia of its rooms, most now given over to pale sky blue wallpaper with floral motifs accommodating coach-load parties of travellers and commercial salesmen, you will wander. And, at the newsstands and the billboards by the pier where the grey sea heaves behind flaking black paint of intricately filigreed iron railings, you will read each day headlines of accounts of alleged incompetence and failure of government servants, and of all the social institutions and services, and wonder how a nation once so proud of its long dominance in the world, its people raised to believe in their innate superiority, could now be so sunk into such a widespread and profound malaise of self denigration. At weekends you will observe the trajectories of fireworks spiralling and tracing their ascent over the dull gleam of the mudflats only to abort and implode with a whimper in damp air. The pyrotechnics of a katabasis. And, as you wander for the rest of the week through the salt laden air of the esplanade with its finery of manicured parks and deserted pavilions, and its handsome large houses financed centuries ago by the wealth from those now extinct far off dominions, you will, for hours, ponder upon that sad ineluctable dream, remembering how from invisible shores its rich raft of scents took hold of and sent so many hurrying off across anonymous distances and out into the light of immense and porous spaces. Many never to return. And, later, behind rain streaked window panes, in the early gloom and bitter cold of a dank evening, wonder how the spell of such an intoxication, fragile as the re-assembled fragments of percepts which make up the moments and memories of our lives, could snap, and how no one any longer could hold it together.

## LXXXVI

Larcenous acts do not detain us. Sons of petty autocrats back home always on their hands and knees scrambling for loot, grubbing in the tills of a despised populace, what could we do to offend them. Except sing our own praises. Horse traders, money changers, sellers of sudorifics and analgesics, we cross continents by day and lounge in our mistresses' laps by night listening to contraband verses. All that is for our own taking, the linden trees in full bloom, the air of a music that can't be heard. And on the roads that lead to us, the compilers of gazetteers lost in the storm. The snows of yesteryear that pile up behind us melt in the welcome of rusted axe heads and arrow flukes. Mausolea. Theodolites. Railway depots. In the counting houses we are mistaken for our servants. On the borders of our canals we plant rows on rows of forget-me-nots to remind ourselves that the nature of time cannot be reversed.

.

Desecration of public spaces. Defilement of monuments and sarcophagi. Lapidary inscribers of masonry, perspex and glass, slashers of tyres and seats, eviscerators of public urinals and telephone booths. These inhabit, like the wounders of septuagenarians on lonely canal paths, like the spikers of drinks in crowded bars, those unruly and uncivilised spaces their distant forebears colonised. In the faded scriptorium of their seed they fester like a disease in dank urban and suburban basements and drawing rooms. Harvesting, like atavistic ghosts, a psychotherapy of fears, of an insidious infection from the East, they roam through deserted shopping centres, housing estates and parking lots with guns and knives. Brute crop of bludgeoning and graffiti. Invisible on steps at night—beware!—they watch where you go, eager for another space to leave their mark on, drawing a belligerent red line through your life.

.

In that final City of the Philosophers which they had come to, built in the form of a perfect stone circle on the coast, no information was sought when they entered as to their name, trade or profession, or the purpose of their visit. Arriving there they had arrived at the end of all cities, and all lines of investigation laid down within them. They had endured untold arrays of pageantry and processions of effigies of gods and demigods swaddled in fusty layers of garments; on countless dusty tracks they had danced to the dissonant voices and music of assortments of musicians and devotees—butcher, gelder of horses, amanuensis—blowing through, and beating upon, ancient and dilapidated instruments; or they had merely sat and observed as the neck of another common criminal was stretched upon a wooden frame constructed for just such a purpose; or had turned into the Square of the Artificers at precisely that moment when the device was exploded, whilst in a side street, cross legged upon the floor and turning their eyes toward the light, a group of neophytes had intoned the sutras of a new system. They had observed all this, and much more. In that final city, a city of stone, that they had come to, however, men sat upon the ashlar quays reading all day their namastotras. Of all the cities they had been in, none had been more given over to reading aloud such "praise of names" for the gods. And none had, emblazoned above its main entrance gateway in a globe inlaid with blue onyx, the words: IN THE CIRCLE BEGINNING AND END ARE THE SAME.

.

She felt she had descended to the substrate of some infernal city. Inundations from the sewer. Through porous cochleae, a herpetic ooze. Dark polyps in the vomitoria. She shut her ears. Yet, still, the prodigality of the sewer. Upon their lips the sickly graft of what should have issued, under the press of time, in darkness. Running like a subterranean alluvium through the gut of the primordial city, its clays and marls. Not, indeed, here, above the surface where she sat in a public carriage; mouthed, not in the shadows by those overpowered by persecution and want, by those who had drawn each curse from and known the futility and weight of the detritus. But by these, the offspring of those who had never breathed "the enormous foetidness of social catastrophe" or upheaval. Words, she thought, diseased excrescence, sinister foliage—these, though, have assimilated, understood and suffered, nothing. And smell so much the ranker for it.

.

Brandishers of loot. Arsonists. In the hillside towns their feats of cruelty survive them. Blood on the thawed out scarp. Thigh bone of jackal. Trinket of a child. To appease some inveterate longing. Assuage some guilt. Justify a belief. In the river mists all their baggage carts dissolve like smoke. The warmth of their night fires barely warms cracked lips. Memory of sun on stone capstans. Pellucid isles, naked arms. The raw rich grief of a moment never to be regained. In the violent vanquishing of farewells, all they obtain—the permanence of exile.

# LXXXVII

We are born, live and die, amidst an illusion, "an ash grey essence, unperfumed." The essence of such an "illusion" is, in effect, the world. A world for which thought can, finally, establish no meaningful boundary between "inner" and "outer"; a world which has, subtly and slowly, been alembicated over the centuries in the crucible of our verbal symbols. Most of us do not recognise the product of such an alembication for what it is. Instead, we regard the reality resulting from it as originating and existing independently of us. There is nothing in this world, however, which we can verify or deny the existence of without recourse to cognition. And the consciousness associated with cognition is impregnated with words. The reality which issues from the order of such consciousness, the reality of "the sombre rose of the shadows", satisfies our need for self-justification and realisation. In its humanly created depths we lie, as

> El limonero lánguido suspende
> una pálida rama polvorienta,
> sobre el encanto de la fuente limpia

dreaming of

> los frutos de oro

Such golden fruit, being the object not only of our senses but of our mind, a mind unified by the illusion that what it grasps is "real", is not this, indeed, the only fruit, albeit a fruit of the shadow, that we need?

.

All objects exist and survive solely through the reconstitutive power of imagination and memory. But with each reconstitution of the object we journey further into a world of procumbent percepts. Its objects, because reconstituted by memory and imagination, are buried so deeply within what we see, hear, touch, taste and smell, that we really do not see, hear, touch, taste and smell them at all, so much as, through a dark filter, infer them. If it were not for the continuous affirmations of our memory and imagination, such objects, and such a world, would disappear.

.

In the twilight of each moment—each point-instant—history disappears. Within the incessant flow of events it salutes a continuity of perishings. Here, in this precise moment, where there is no relation between succeeding moments, the world withers on its stem. You are nothing but the rhythm of these energies which seek to pattern and draw you together again and again, across innumerable horizons and through a plurality of times. You return—not entirely unwillingly—from the derelict order of a past which you have been unable to dissolve. Scavenger of occluded waters, you who put your foot into this tremulous flow, have realised, too late, that there is no before and no after. Forger of ideologies, feel the warmth seep from them now. "Tamer" of the flow! On the far bank countless shadows form, and re-form. One, as you can just make out, a blizzard whitening the cockade of his hat, is bent too low to see where he goes. What super-imposition of thought can hold back these who, within the desiderata of empires and ontologies, break continuously upon the edge of a moment that is gone: and, yet, a moment which cannot expunge completely, in its going, every trace of itself?

.

On the first day of the tenth month do not forget to inscribe on our winter clothes (how the cold strikes to the bone here) the correct designation—person, family, generation—before you take them to the outer gate and send them, by fire, to us here. Stove of amianthus fetched from the Western Hills. Proclamation of the calendar. Peddlers with it in boxes on their backs singing like crickets. Chestnuts roasted amongst small black pebbles. Kumiss and sugar cooked during the night. A pure whiteness, like crunching on snow, while the mealy redpoll picks the lock. No more moving water on the Lake of Ten Temples, the city moat, the Second Sluice—marooned and drinking wildly in the middle of ice, until almost unconscious. Do not forget, too, the steamed offering of gruel, with the figure of a lion carved from red dates, to Door, Kitchen Stove, Main Gate, Well and Impluvium. Will you receive your share of spotted red deer after the putting away of seals? Scribes, in the front of shops, writing "Spring couplets" extolling the pine and cypress, the epidendrum. Before twilight the hanging of ancestral pictures and the lighting of incense—garoo, sandal and sapon wood—to greet in the dark (how the cold strikes to the bone here) descending spirits. Afterwards to lie down, the whole household, and to sleep with clothes on together until dawn. And then to wake to the jingle of silver in the money shops being exchanged for red notes.

# LXXXVIII

No smell of pancit or bibingka over broad fens. In clean and orderly avenues winding their way beneath suburban trees no haphazard creation of accommodation, shacks of tin and wood, on pavements. No criminal syndicates cruising streets in Telephone Company look-alike vans demanding entry to effect "repairs". No disconnection of telephone lines at the Department of Labour for failure for years to pay its bill. No private accounts at the Bureau of Internal Revenue into which tax payers' payments are diverted ... Fingers patiently restore deep azure to a faded Iberian sky. Bent over a low wall, that has absorbed years of moisture from tropical air, they tease from pigments of a fresco soluble surface salts that have effloresced into a white escutcheon. Later when on the darkened varnish that covers the impasto of a muted Mediterranean sea her forehead sweats she raises her head and thinks, again, of clean well ordered streets surrounding the cathedral. Of the town she would so dearly love to paint where the objects retain, all year round, their clarity of outline.

.

Dreaming of voyages of exploration and discovery, of overland expeditions, outfitting a battalion they went marching off into the interior. The house of the local lawmakers stands in its grounds of amethyst gardens, ringed with a cordon of barbed wire. Its intricate cornices drip as power lines spark and flare above monsoon wind and rain wracked tree tops. Ships are patrolling the harbour mouth preventing anyone from leaving—or returning. O the pinnate fronds of the palm tree beneath which the innocent tourist once lingered. In the countryside people are celebrating in yet another fiesta while on the outskirts of the capital it is rumoured armed and disgruntled elements of a persecuted sect are gathering. The telephone cable linking the police headquarters to the main exchange has been stolen and, reportedly, sold in a night market. Boxes of guidebooks composed in a pidgin few foreigners, now, can understand wait on the quays to be loaded onto a boat. No one can say where they are going.

.

# CONGRESS OF TEACHER/EDUCATORS FOR NATIONALISM AND DEMOCRACY

## Death Comes amid the Sugar Cane

Whereas some quarters in academe have aligned with the discourse of capital in their celebration of democratic space and the decentering of class politics, farm workers in Hacienda Lusitra, owned by the influential comprador Cofuangco clan, were massacred last November 16, 2004, by military troops and the Cofuangco's other loyal agents. The farm workers were gassed, hosed and then brutally gunned down with an assortment of guns including 60-caliber machine guns while they were upholding their democratic rights.

Long mired in destitute poverty brought about by feudal relations, the farm workers of Hacienda Lusitra resisted the Cofuangco's renewed scheme to evade land reform. The workers launched a strike to resist the stock distribution option (SDO) peddled by the Hacienda in lieu of genuine land reform. The Hacienda Lusitra case exemplifies the failure of land reform under the administration of regimes beholden to the interests of the few and powerful. The Cofuangcos, with an ex-president and powerful politicians within their ranks, indeed belong to the few and powerful in a nation of exploited workers and peasants ...

The neo-liberal agenda that structures our political and economic policies is the modality of one superpower's imperialism mobilizing the ruling classes of the neo-colonies to protect imperialist interests: the perpetuation of a backward agrarian economy controlled by the landlord-comprador bourgeoisie such as the Cofuangcos, the maintenance of a corrupt government by the same ruling elite, the violoation of workers' rights and repression of the people on a grand scale (contractualization of labor, union busting, low wages, retrenchment and murder in its extreme form).

How dare the President, Loria Apagalam-Oyo, assuage the public by blabbering on the benefits of the free market when it is the very thing that kills and maims thousands upon thousands of farmers, workers, government employees, professionals and the youth! This we are certain: the farm workers who chose to remain silent suffer continued exploitation while those who courageously fight have been maimed by bullets. We have no reason to keep the president and her cohorts in power especially after this bloodshed.

The alignment of academe with the global capitalist order has more than ever been challenged: that this is no ideal democracy where dialogue between conflicting classes happen, that this massacre is an instance of the class struggle which has long been effaced from the vocabulary of intellectuals, that bullets speak in this part of the world.

Justice for the martyrs of Hacienda Lusitra! No to militarization!
Condemn the repression of workers' rights!
Oust Loria Apagalam-Oyo!
Struggle for genuine agrarian reform!

NOVEMBER 18, 2004.

.

Five days a week a long queue snakes through the embassy's bougainvillea covered compound, each person clutching an interview card, out onto the pavement and around the block. Sweating food and drinks vendors hover beside it like flies. Nearby, the park where the country's national hero was executed by an occupying foreign power fills with coach loads of tourists. Adjacent to it in a hotel facing the bay the president of the nation sits naked upon the edge of a bed, his legs wide open, praying. The wind sweeps down the palm-lined road carrying odours of puto and sampaguito. In the heat the lengthening shadow of desire moves. Across the road, in the Galeria de los Conquistadores, Philippe Alonzo is looking at a painting of light.

# LXXXIX

With the frequency of the attacks of emphysema, and their threat to his health, growing weekly, Andrie Carpuscii, being no longer a young man and possessing a weak heart, had decided to take a holiday in the country of his birth which he had not visited for many years. His doctor had prescribed it for its dryness of air and all year round sunshine. On the voyage back he paced the deck each day, much to the amusement of other passengers, humming and whistling, his head alive with the sound of bird melodies. It amazed him to think how, generation after generation, a species carried its song within it. One could, in some cases, hear its motifs in the frozen precincts of a city and, simultaneously, in a sweltering jungle at the other end of the earth. The sea heaved and rolled its enormous mass each day beside him and in it, too, he began to hear the sounds of the land he was leaving and its music. Unlike the music of that land for which he was heading it laid no value whatsoever upon harmony and its development. Rather, its focus was on the shifting and altering shapes of rhythm; and it had as its aim, rather than the development of a harmonious edifice of sound, the creation of a meditative inner space. In short it was, he reflected, intent not on moving forward in a series of formally calibrated steps, of going somewhere, but on being somewhere; being within the condition of a dominant Emotion in which the rhythm was free to move forwards and backwards at will, exploring both its highways and its byways. While his head was full of such thoughts the ship docked at the port of Caraphiae. Disembarking he made his way by carriage up the coast to the small village in which he had decided to stay. After some months his condition, aided by the sea voyage, had begun to improve. But then, whilst out climbing a steep cliff one day to hear more clearly the song of a bird he had not heard for many years, he took a fall and fractured a small bone in his foot. Whilst only a minor injury the relative immobility it imposed upon him threw him into depression. Because of this he took up his old habit of smoking which only brought on his attacks of emphysema again. Though not as bad or frequent as before they plunged him further into depression. Some nights he lay awake only to listen to the sea pounding on the shore a short distance away. It was during this time that he began to dream of being with his family when he was a small child. For nights he dreamed of nothing else. Was such a state, he wondered, a counterpoise to all those years he had spent wandering. Such early years, he thought, emerge almost like a still point in the eddies and swirls of a life. Emerge not so much as a sanctuary for the exhausted mind but as a confirmation that the end of all journeying is to arrive at where it began. "The day ends. The end begins." The idea of stillness began to dominate his mind. And that distant country which he had over a year ago departed from, and its music, once more drew him. He pictured himself travelling down its wide rivers shaded by over-arching jungle, through its mangroves and high upland forests of pine, listening. Reduced, now, to a hobble and short, again, of breath he longed to be there. Longed, also, to listen to its music. Surrounded as he now was by that of his own culture he began to feel a profound dissatisfaction with it. Indeed he began to wonder whether in its insistence on an ordered harmonic progression it was less like a form of adventure than a staying at home. Perhaps it does not, he thought, ever leave home. For in its attempt to transcend time, by dominating and imposing an order upon it, it always fails to reach that sense of being attained only through giving oneself up to time, where, as at the centre of a storm, we encounter the stillness and silence around which the debris of all our thought-constructions flows. These are sustained, he knew, by an indefatigable will to dominate. A will he had whilst abroad frequently observed etched deeply into the looks of his fellow countrymen. "Do the natives sing?" he had once heard one of them exclaim; for he'd arrived late to lunch at Government House one day because of the beauty of the wayside song of a woman planting rice that he'd stopped to listen to. Would they, he further wondered, have understood if he had said to them that the aim of all music, as he'd come to believe, was not the creation of a perfect arrangement of sound … His hands suddenly slid from the arms of the chair in which he sat and his breath took hold of and shook what seemed to him the fragile frame of his entire body. A fragrance like that of the blossoms of the neem tree seemed to enter the room. Looking at the floor, his head having fallen upon his chest, he saw that the white thread he'd been given before he'd embarked by his friend Unsworth, and which he'd been told not to take off, had broken and been wrenched from his wrist. It lay there.